THE CONVERT

Books by Margaret Culkin Banning

A HANDMAID OF THE LORD

PRESSURE

THE WOMEN OF THE FAMILY

MIXED MARRIAGE

MONEY OF HER OWN

PRELUDE TO LOVE

PATH OF TRUE LOVE

THE THIRD SON

THE FIRST WOMAN

THE IRON WILL

LETTERS TO SUSAN

THE CASE FOR CHASTITY

YOU HAVEN'T CHANGED

TOO YOUNG TO MARRY

OUT IN SOCIETY

ENOUGH TO LIVE ON

A WEEK IN NEW YORK

SALUD! A SOUTH AMERICAN JOURNAL

LETTERS FROM ENGLAND

CONDUCT YOURSELF ACCORDINGLY

THE CLEVER SISTER

GIVE US OUR YEARS

FALLEN AWAY

THE DOWRY

THE CONVERT

 *The* CONVERT

by Margaret Culkin Banning

78904

Harper & Brothers
Publishers, New York

Library of Congress catalog card number: 57-8199

To

Ramona Herdman with gratitude for years of help
and friendship. And once more to Carl Brandt, who,
even in times of greatest stress, holds his literary
dependents and their work in the depths of his mind.

The physical setting of this novel will be identifiable to my neighbors and should prove once more that I love the region. The compulsions of the story are, I hope, equally real. But there is no character in the book who lives, or has lived anywhere except in the imagination of the author.

BOOK ONE

1

Tʜᴇ plane no longer seemed to be making any headway but only fighting to hold its own against the frontal attack of wind and rain. A passenger strained against his seat belt to open the vent above his head but the furious gust that whistled through it forced him to close it again. It was impossible to read, for the pilot shifted the transport from level to level often and abruptly, and the gale made it tremble.

The odds were on safety. This was a routine flight from Chicago to the north, and when it had been cleared for departure a few hours ago the weather it would meet must have been known to those who were dispatching planes. Most of the passengers were cradling that thought in their minds now. They sat quietly enough, but no one could help being conscious of the storm, except one man who had drunk himself into apathy before leaving Midway. It was the kind of hour when thoughts of life insurance, and of love, and of the accidents which have happened to other people rumbled in the minds of the travelers.

Mark Worthing was hoping that Olive would not try to meet him at the airport if the weather was bad at home. It meant a six-mile drive from the city and that highway could be dangerous. But he knew his hope was futile. She would be there. He embraced the thought that he would be with her tonight, rested on it. I get worse and worse, he told himself happily. I want to be with her all the time.

The plane dipped again and the woman beside him said under her breath, "Holy Mother of God!" Through his half-shut eyes Mark saw her making the sign of the cross, touching her veil, her massed breasts, and the animal heads on her ugly little shoulder furs. She was very frightened. And she's trying to protect herself with signs and incantations, thought Mark, she's one of those. He was reminded of an immediate problem. He said to himself, I wonder if I should talk to Alan, unless the whole thing has blown over since I've been away. I'd hate to do it. But I think he'll make a bad mistake if he marries that Catholic girl. She may be attractive and all that, but it would never work. What did they tell me her name was? Rose Mary, that's it—Rose Mary Carroll. It's a sentimental name. She's Irish, I suppose. How would Alan feel when she went around making signs to keep the elements in hand? Alan has a very good mind.

The woman's lips were moving. She was older than Mark, and, except for the courtesy of finding the lost end of her seat belt as they took off, he had paid no attention to her. The word was full of such middle-aged women, peeking hopefully into the mirrors of their compacts, pretending to read, hoping for conversation. Mark had been sure that, if he said two sentences to this one, she would talk for the whole five hours of the flight. So he had given her no opening. She's having a tough trip, he thought uncomfortably. Nobody around to talk to and she's obviously scared out of her wits.

The plane quivered, tipped slightly. A pillow fell from the coat rack above, and Mark's seatmate drew back tautly as if this were the beginning of the end. He broke his silence. He could not let helplessness suffer.

"We seem to be running into a little weather," he said.

"I suppose it's really quite safe," she said questioningly, trying hard to meet his composure.

"Oh, yes. They always know what's ahead."

"But it is so terribly wild out! And that lightning—it does seem so close—does lightning ever strike airplanes?"

You bet it does, thought Mark, and remembered one time over the Pacific during the war.

"I wouldn't worry about that," he said, "not any more than you would on the ground."

She turned her head. She had a soft-skinned face on which the flesh was no longer smoothly fitted to the bones, and big shallow

[4]

gray eyes. An old prettiness, almost worn out, still clung to her.

"I was just thinking that maybe it's a sin of presumption," she said, "this flying through the sky—as if we were angels."

She hadn't looked like a woman who would make wisecracks. No, she seemed to be in earnest. She was very tense.

"We know more than angels ever did about flying," he said. "There are planes taking off every second. We've probably taken the sky away from the angels by this time. The way we took the land from the Indians."

He was smiling as he spoke, trying to make her take it easy. But she drew a frightened breath.

"Oh, you mustn't talk like that," she protested. "Not now—not in the middle of this terrible thunderstorm!"

"You think the angels might resent it and gang up on us?"

She put a nervous hand on his sleeve. "Please don't," she begged. With her other hand she crossed herself again and began to murmur a chant not quite audibly. Mark could hear repetitions, "Jesus . . . heart and soul . . . Jesus . . ."

Poor thing! thought Mark. She's primitive. He did not interrupt her praying, and as she withdrew her hand from his arm he tipped his seat back a notch and closed his eyes again, reverting from the woman's absurdity to the risk of his brother wanting to marry a girl with such notions. Not that there aren't a great many fine Roman Catholics, very good citizens some of them, as I'll tell Alan. I do business with plenty of them all the time. It's not that I have any prejudice against anyone's religion. I would have to make that clear to him. But Catholics are very clannish. He might think he could steer clear of the girl's religion, but those priests get their hooks in wherever they can. I suppose Alan knows that he would be expected to sign papers about bringing his children up Catholics. They make all sorts of excessive demands. They want their own schools and pretty soon they'll want government money to support them. The country will never stand for that. But it's a powerful lobby.

While he considered his approach to Alan and whether it was sensible to make one, the plane ceased to jerk and tremble. It was

[5]

steady again. They must have flown through the storm. Mark glanced at his watch. They should land in about fifteen minutes. He straightened up with anticipation and noticed that the woman in the seat by the window was staring through the little pane. She turned with a look of elation.

"The stars are actually out! It's like a miracle!"

"You can go through those squalls pretty fast at this speed," said Mark.

"I'm sure that St. Christopher looked after us tonight."

"Do you give him all the credit?" asked Mark with amusement. "None to the pilot?"

She had opened her purse again and was stroking her cheeks with powder, gazing in the mirror in the cover of the case as if the reflection were interesting. Then she put it back and continued to dig around in the contents of the bag, searching for something else. Mark didn't watch the details. The nervous, now fussy stranger only made him think of how different his wife was, his own girl.

He thought of Olive as a girl. He called her that. Mark did not want her to be a finished woman, not yet. There were delights they had not found in spite of all they had, and there would be many new backgrounds for their love. Olive was always fresh, always surprising, though they had been married for almost eight years. Love was always new to her and always better. She could be as tempting as a virgin or companionably erotic, and what she gave him was created for him and in no way related to the experience of her first marriage. That seemed to have left no mark on her and would have been unbelievable except for the two children.

"I beg your pardon," he said, for the woman beside him was saying something again.

"Do you travel a great deal?" she asked.

"When I must. It sometimes seems that way," said Mark rather crisply. He didn't want to answer personal questions or identify himself by name.

"You were so kind to try to make me feel better during that storm. With your joking and all. It's always so much better to have someone to talk to when you're nervous. And I thought—if you don't mind, and if you do travel quite a bit, I'd like for you to have this."

She was holding something out to him. He saw a small, silvery medal, but did not touch it.

"Oh, thank you very much. But I wouldn't want you to deprive yourself."

"But I'm not. I can get another. And I don't take many trips. Goodness only knows when I'll be on a plane again, and I'm not sure that I ever want to! It's a St. Christopher medal. This one's been blessed."

Mark said, with the warm courtesy that charmed people, "It's very kind of you. But I'm afraid I wouldn't have use for it. I'm not a Catholic."

"That doesn't make any difference. It's a good thing for anyone to have."

She spoke with an urgency that seemed ridiculous to Mark and yet was rather touching. This will be a story to tell Olive, thought Mark. I'll tell her a beautiful blonde gave it to me. I don't want that junk—I don't want to hurt the woman's feelings—

"Thank you, but—"

The plane was banking. The woman leaned from her seat and quickly pressed the medal into Mark's hand in an almost motherly way. He wanted to return it, but wanted even more not to prolong the argument. The stewardess was bringing his coat. Mark thrust the image of St. Christopher into the pocket with his loose change. He'd get rid of it later.

Olive Worthing watched the plane free itself from a ruffle of clouds in the half-cleared sky and grow bigger as it circled above the airport. She thought, there is something wonderful in having the man you love come down from the sky. It's always incredible, it makes you feel like part of a myth, with the gods descending to you. For love—maybe they really did. For Leda and me. I'll have to tell Mark that.

What a relief it always is when the plane touches the runway. When I'm flying with Mark, I never have any sense of danger, but waiting is something else. I couldn't get to him—that would be the

[7]

unbearable thing. I hate separation more and more.

He'll be glad to get home. Tired to death too. I must try to keep Pamela off his trail tonight. She's sure to call up and want to talk about that business of Alan's. What can anyone do if Alan is determined to marry the girl? He certainly isn't going to be influenced by his mother or Pamela or Lucy—they know that. He might listen to Mark. Mark's worried about it. He's so protective where Alan is concerned, feels he has to take the place of his father, though he's not much more than ten years older than Alan. Alan ought to know his own mind in a thing like this. He's twenty-eight. I must make Mark feel, if Pamela does call up, that it will keep until tomorrow.

All the Worthings dump their problems on Mark. I suppose it's natural because he's the oldest male in the family. And they've always been close in spite of being such terrific individualists. They've accepted me now. I think they're glad Mark married me, though at the time they must have thought he could do better than marry a girl with no money and two children on her hands. He couldn't possibly have done better. That's one thing Mark and I know. I understand him better than any of his family ever did. They all think he's wonderful, handsome, successful, a credit to them, the very best model the Worthing family ever turned out. But I love him most because he doesn't feel that way about himself. Because he's never quite satisfied even when he's happy. That's why he's different from most men. He's not continually thinking about what he has, what he can get. There's a stretch in his mind— I've felt it so often when we're alone, when we're together alone. Now I know why I'm alive, what life is for, he'll say. To me. I must make it always better, always enough, always enough to live for. Even when we're older, even if we don't have children.

Tonight I'll have to tell him that I was wrong and that there's no baby in the making after all. If that is going to happen, it would have happened by this time almost certainly. Eight years. Funny the doctors don't know why. We're both normal and healthy and I've had two children so I'm not barren. That's the lucky thing. If Mark and I never have any children of our own, we have Tim and

Jenny, and by this time they belong to him almost as much as they do to me. He's the only father they've ever known. Strange how things work out. It seemed so dreadful at the time to be deserted—and yet if it hadn't happened I wouldn't have been able to give Mark either the children or myself.

There they come out of the plane. Certainly those men don't look much like descending gods at close range. That one must have been on a binge. Surely Mark is on the plane—he would have let me know—ah, there he is—he always lets everyone else go first.

Mark saw her, a bareheaded young woman in a tan cashmere coat, so slim and plainly dressed that she seemed taller than she was, the pale yellow hair drawn back to a knot that gave her head a sculptured look. It used to fall loose almost to her shoulders. Mark liked it better this way, decided that again in this sight of her. He felt the comfort and pleasure of being back as he stepped from the plane—the familiarity, the sense of ownership, and also belonging. This was his own neck of the woods, where he had been born, where the money came from, where his name got attention and respect, where he knew not only the city but the whole region like the palm of his hand. He was already figuring on taking side roads that would get them home quickest. It was a mosaic with Olive's rejoiced face in the middle of it.

Mark was recognized by people waiting at the barrier to meet incoming passengers, though he did not know them or even see them as he hurried to his wife. A druggist who had come to meet his daughter, a young fellow who worked in the Worthing Mining Laboratory, a car dealer, and an undertaker all knew Mark by sight. They would mention later that Mr. Worthing had come in on the 7:45 flight from Chicago and that his wife was there to meet him.

A girl in a red coat with a scarf tied over her head came running out from the waiting rooms, as if she had just arrived and feared she was late to meet the plane. She saw Mark, stopped, and quickly changed her direction. But he did not notice her except as a passing figure. The girl's eyes searched the line of disembarked passengers, and then she went with open arms toward the woman with animal heads bobbing on her scanty furs, the one who had been Mark's seat mate.

"Was it a good trip?" asked Olive.

"A little rough after we left Minneapolis. I was afraid it might be snowing here."

"We had a flurry this afternoon but it melted."

"How are you, darling?"

"Fine. We all are."

"Tim get over his cold?"

"Yes—he was horrible when he was shut in. He's back in school, thank heaven."

"Anything else new?"

"No," she said, putting it off.

"Mother all right?"

"I'm sure she is. There was a big write-up about her in the Sunday paper. With a very good picture of her. It was some award she was getting. I should know—but I forgot the organization—"

"It doesn't matter. She gets those by the dozen. How are the rest of the family?"

"Pam dropped in this afternoon, looking particularly chic. Lucy's still in Arizona. I haven't seen Alan."

"He hasn't been around at all?"

"No reason why he should be. He's busy. Are you very tired?"

"I could use some sleep—in the right company."

"Did the business go well?"

"I think it was a useful trip. Of course, with some of those people you have to begin before the beginning. They can't think in terms of taconite. They've been used to the idea of rich ore too long. We're going to have a meeting out here and show them the works. Where are you parked?"

"Right in front."

"I'll get my bags and meet you in the car. . . . Olive, are you glad I'm back?"

"Glad? All the word can hold. It's bursting at the seams."

He pressed her arm to his side, paused for a second to feel her near him. "My lovely girl."

[10]

They were observed.

"That's the man I sat next to in the plane," the woman with the furs told the girl in the red coat, "such a nice man."

"It was?" asked the girl. "How funny!"

"Why, do you know him?"

The girl laughed. "No, but I know a lot about him. His brother is a friend of mine. Wait till the crowd thins out—then I'll get your suitcase, Aunt Kate."

Mark put his luggage on the back seat and took the wheel.

"I don't like your driving out here alone. You should have sent Chris."

"He's getting pretty old, Mark. And he likes to go home at five o'clock. Besides, I wanted to come."

"It's a bad time of day for driving. There are all sorts of crazy people on the roads these days."

"Go on, treat me like a delicate flower. I love it! But remember with the part of your mind that makes sense that I banged around for four years by myself."

"You don't have to any more."

"Mark, there isn't any baby."

He put his hand on her knee. "Don't be too disappointed."

"Are you?"

"Of course not. If it had happened, it would have been fine. But I'd probably have been jealous. I want my wife to myself. And I like her shape the way it is too."

"I was thinking while I was waiting for you that anyway we have two children now. They're so excited that you're coming home tonight. Did you remember to bring them anything?"

"I didn't have much time. But I picked up a couple of three-way flashlights in the airport."

"Those will be wonderful. You haven't had any dinner, have you?"

"They don't serve it on that flight."

"I didn't think they did. I took one of your precious pheasants out of the freezer and it's in a casserole with mushrooms. It's Elsa's

[11]

day off and she hates to change. I told the sitter she could leave as soon as I got back. She's giving Tim and Jenny their supper. We're going to have a private banquet—with a bird and a bottle. At least with a couple of Martinis."

"You're treating your husband like a king."

"Who has a better right? And you certainly looked like a king compared to the other men who got off that plane. Before it landed I was thinking of how people used to believe that gods descended from the sky when they felt amorous—how they believed that the sky was full of gods—"

"And angels—do you know that there are people who still believe it is full of angels? Honestly. There was a woman sitting next to me on the plane—let me tell you about her—"

2

Pamela brooks decided at about half-past eight that it would be better to go over to the Worthings' house instead of telephoning her brother. There were things she didn't like to say over the telephone. Someone might pick up the extension in the kitchen. She felt that she must tell Mark this astonishing rumor that she had heard and impress on him that he must talk to Alan right away. She had said that to Olive this afternoon, but Olive didn't seem to realize how important it was.

Of course, it isn't her family, thought Pamela. As long as Olive has Mark, that's all she cares about. Olive can be so indifferent. She remembered again that her sister-in-law wouldn't join the Junior League when Pamela had fixed it all up for her after she had married Mark.

"It takes so much time," Olive had said, "and I'm twenty-six, too old to run around doing good deeds with those girls."

"But you have a daughter," Pamela said, "and it will be much easier to get her into the League when the time comes if her mother has been a member."

"Jenny can paddle her own canoe," said Olive, "in that particular stream."

Olive was like that. But, as Pamela often said, speaking for the Worthings, they all adored Olive. Because she had made Mark so happy.

Also she had not diminished the distinction of the family. The point could be made, and was made, that one of Olive's great-grandfathers had been a governor of Massachusetts. The Warren Hadleys, from St. Paul, at whose summer place on the Brule River Olive had been staying when she met Mark, thought the world of Olive, and social recognition in the Middle West could go no higher. Olive herself was a cause for family pride in ways that it was hard to put a finger on, but which showed in the clothes she selected, the way she wore them, in the parties she gave, and in the fact that she was a welcome addition to almost any group. The men liked her. And the women didn't resent it.

Pamela, who had been president of her class at both Westover and Vassar, thought Olive was very intelligent, but said that it was a pity that she had not gone to college. If she had, her mind would have been better organized. Pamela had taken art as her own central subject of study, and it had helped enormously when it came to planning and building her house. She was proud of this spacious, completely contemporary house which she was leaving now. It was exactly right for her, her friends said, and Pamela believed that too. It was admired, as Pamela was, because it was modern without being fantastic or going too far.

Like all the Worthings, Pamela was handsomely made. She had long since outgrown the campus look, but a little of its independence had permanently branded her manner. Her alertness suggested the leadership for which she was well known. The urge to mix in "causes," which was so strong in her mother had come down to Pamela in muted form. The elder Mrs. Worthing had always been a clubwoman. Pamela didn't go to club meetings. She agreed with the smart magazines that they were subjects for caricature. But she drove with energy through the selected interests on her own calendar. Each was carefully screened for usefulness and for the right kind of backing.

She swung the small foreign car—which was one of her conversation pieces this year—away from Lake Park—which with its widely spaced houses could hardly be called a neighborhood—and spun along the boulevards toward the house which had been Mark Worthing's mistake, even if he and Olive still didn't admit it.

It was thirty years old. It was too big. Olive had only one regular house servant, old Chris, for odd jobs, and sitters by the hour. The house had been built in the days that took more service for granted. It was dated.

One reason why Mark had bought the house, as Pamela well knew, was that Henry Holden had needed to sell it. Holden had been an old family friend, and his fortunes when they had been good had tied in with the Worthing interests. His father and Mark's grandfather had started out together, acquiring ore lands in the boom days of 1889. The difference was that Cyrus Worthing took title to more iron mines, and to some with the richest deposits. Also he formed a company to operate a few of them himself and leased others to the great corporations. Holden was not so shrewd. He leased all his properties and lived high, wherever he pleased, until, during the Second World War, the rich ore was exhausted and his leases not renewed. Comparative poverty crept up and surprised Henry Holden as he was growing old. His wife had died and his children were scattered. He was stuck with his large house. And Mark had married Olive and was looking for a place to live.

Pamela knew all about that. But Olive shouldn't have saddled them with an old house, she thought. They could have built out near us. Of course, she's done things to this place. As she drove around the curve of bricked driveway, Pamela tried to figure just what it was that Olive had done.

It was still a three-story brick house spread comfortably on a couple of city lots. Its impression was of privacy and capacity. The shining brass doorknobs and plates respected the traditions of Old and New England, but it did not look like a copy or a memory. It looked all right where it was and as if it would last a long while yet.

Of course it was a very well-built house, thought Pamela, aware of something about it that was praiseworthy, though her architect would have wanted no part of it.

She tried the door and found it unlatched, so she went in without knocking. In the hall, which was such a terrific waster of space, she paused, listening for voices. No sound of children—they must be in bed. No one in the big room on the left, and the white-paneled doors of the dining room were closed. Pamela felt slightly intrusive. As a member of the family it would have been ridiculous to ring the bell when the door was unlocked—and it wasn't safe to leave it unlocked when nobody was in the front of the house. In her mother's house or in Lucy's, she would have called out instantly. Olive and Mark had been married for years, but they sometimes acted like honeymooners. And he was just home.

Then she heard Mark's laugh and realized they must be in the kitchen. She found them there, Mark sipping a Martini and Olive pulling a casserole out of the oven.

"Hi," said Pamela, "can I come in?"

Olive turned. If there was any lack of welcome in her mind, it didn't show. And Mark flung an arm over his sister's shoulders and said he was glad to see her.

"I just stopped in for a minute."

"Stay and have a piece of one of Mark's pheasants."

"No, I've had dinner long ago."

"You can have a nip of gin anyway," said Mark. "Where's Brad?"

"I left him looking at a prize fight. He's the one, you remember, who had no use for television. Now he's almost an addict."

"That's what often happens when you get over a prejudice. I suppose a prejudice is a secret yearning," said Olive. "Bigots yearn for religion. Wanderers want the homes they run away from. Maybe."

"Here you are, Pam."

"Thanks. It's very good. Olive, you should have a waist-high oven. It's so much easier than doing that stooping."

"It's good exercise. How do you think the boss looks?"

"I never saw him looking better."

"I'm reviving," said Mark. "How are the rest of the family?"

"All right," said Pamela, "except—that's why I came over—"

"Look," Olive said, "you two go in the study and talk while I finish up here. I have to make the salad."

"I'll help you," Mark offered.

"No, go along with Pam. She wants to talk to you."

"I really do, Mark."

"Come on, then," he said reluctantly. "Don't be long, darling."

He led the way to the room given over to books. This is the only thing I miss in our house, thought Pamela irrelevantly. Here in this room it was obvious what Olive had done. For it had been a conventional library, paneled in dark oak and walled with unused books. Pamela could remember the red Turkish carpet that had been on the floor when this house belonged to the Holdens.

The walls had been lightened, and book shelves sacrificed for windows. Nothing seemed out of reach or use. There were books everywhere, not only along the walls, but on small tables by the sofas, which were deep and crushed from sitting. They were covered with a subtle green velvety stuff. There were two desks. On Mark's, a picture of Olive was half-hidden by the accumulated mail which waited his attention here. A book of modern photographs lay open on Olive's desk. When Mark touched the light switch, an illuminated globe began to glow, as well as the lamps, and the scuffed red bedroom slippers of one of the children lay forgotten on the amber-colored rug beside the globe. An unframed lithograph of a gaunt woman peeling apples was propped on the mantel.

"This is a very nice room," conceded Pamela.

"It's where we live," said Mark with satisfaction.

"I'm really apologetic about breaking in on you tonight. Your first night home. But I thought I should. I thought you'd want to know what's going on."

"Something wrong, Pam?"

"Alan—and that Carroll girl. It's really serious."

He had guessed that would be the subject for discussion. Mark frowned at his thoughts, not at his sister. He said, "Alan's old enough to take care of his own business."

"I know. But can't you talk to him? He'd listen to you."

Though he had been considering a talk with Alan, now that Pamela pressed him, Mark resisted.

"He has to make his own choice of a wife. It may not suit you, Pam. It may be a disappointment—she's not one of your set, I know—"

"Oh, Mark, it isn't that! Don't talk as if I were a snob. It's what she's doing to him. Already."

"What do you mean?"

"She's got Alan going to a Catholic class!"

"A class?"

"A class where the priests tell them what they have to do. Imagine Alan!"

"What are you talking about? I know he wants to marry this girl, but he isn't going to become a Roman Catholic!"

"You wait—I think that's what she's trying to do. The way I happened to hear about it was this. You know who the Blakes are—"

He said yes, picturing Timothy Blake with his curly prematurely white hair and shrewd blue eyes. Thinking instantaneously of the Blake Construction Company and several million dollars.

"I've never known that family," said Pamela, "but Anna Blake used to be on a committee with me in the League—we always take in some Catholics—and she came beaming up to me at a meeting the other day, getting very cozy like a conspirator or informer or something, and said wasn't it nice about my brother. I looked perfectly blank, and she went on about Alan and this Rose Mary Carroll going to these classes together, and so was her brother and the girl he is going to marry—you can imagine how I felt. They're sort of premarital things. The priests run them."

"What's the idea?"

"Well, you know how Catholics are about marriage and how they fight birth control and want these pathetic creatures to have fourteen or fifteen children whether they can take care of them or not. A tremendous number of Catholic women come to our planned-parenthood clinics in spite of what the priests say—that's common knowledge."

"Stay on the point, Pam."

"I am. That's what Alan is falling for."

"Are these things you call classes obligatory? For anyone marrying a Roman Catholic?"

"I don't know. Susan Staples married a Catholic, and she was a very good friend of mine. I never heard of her having to do anything like that. But she married a Baltimore man. It was a very good, very old family."

Olive opened the door.

"We shouldn't let this beautiful bird dry up," she said lightly. "Come on, join us, Pam."

"No, I have to get back home, thanks ever so much. I have to get a letter off to Dick tonight."

"How is my Dick?" asked Olive.

She said it affectionately. Dick was Pamela's oldest son, who had come home from his last year at Exeter with an enthusiasm for nothing but modern poetry. His mother and father had found him difficult, but Dick had discovered that Olive understood what was on his mind. He had almost lived at this house that summer, a year ago.

Pamela said, "He seems to have come down to earth, thank heavens!"

"A fallen angel?" Olive teased her.

"Well, at least he begins to make some sense. Brad said he would, when he got to Yale. I must go along. I feel horrible, Olive, about barging in like this on Mark's first night home, but I didn't want to say too much on the telephone—my beloved Annie is a very devout Catholic. Never misses her Mass on Sunday. She loves to listen in too when I'm on the phone. But she's the best cook we ever had and I couldn't live without her."

Olive laughed. "This gets more and more complicated."

"You can laugh," said Pamela. "I'm pretty broad-minded too, but

[18]

when it's your own brother and his whole life—that's another thing about it, Mark—Catholics are so dreadful about divorce! Otherwise it wouldn't matter half so much."

"It does no good to get all worked up about it, Pam," said Mark.

"I'm not. But you will talk to Alan?"

"I'll think about it," he answered in half-promise.

The break in the evening could not be completely mended. When Pamela had gone, Mark was no longer a husband thinking of no one but his wife, with other cares put away until morning. He tried to regain his earlier mood, but Olive could feel the difference. They sat at the little side table in the dining room where they usually ate when Olive cooked a meal—"What is the sense in having a dining room if you don't use it?" Olive questioned. She had put two candles in slim silver sticks on it, and their supper made a fine still-life picture—the bottle of Rhine wine, the legs of the pheasant, the green and red grapes festooned in a rare china bowl.

They pretended for a little while that nothing was wrong, that Pamela hadn't brought in trouble. Mark talked of the place where he had shot the bird, on an old fire trail near the Brule River—not far, he reminded Olive, from the place where they had seen the she-bear and her cubs last summer.

"I wish it weren't so long until spring," said Olive.

"We'll have to go down now and then this winter after the snow comes, and have a look at the river."

"Let's surely do it . . . it's always good for us. . . . Mark, don't worry any more about Alan tonight."

"I'm not worrying. But if Pamela has got it straight, isn't that the damnedest thing?"

"What?"

"That indoctrination business. It's right in line with other things that are beginning to appear on the surface. The Roman Catholic Church is working every minute to extend its control. I was reading in something the other day about the value of its holdings, real estate and buildings and so forth. It's astounding."

"There are so many Catholics. I suppose they're generous."

"That's all right. That's their racket, as far as the money goes. But what gets me is the attempt to control the lives of people—control their thinking. I've been watching this parochial school business. Quite impersonally. It doesn't affect me at all. Just as a matter of interest. It looks to me like segregation in its worst form. In colored schools, at least the kids are taught the same things as the white kids are. But in parochial schools that's not so, and that's why they exist. They teach a brand of religion, not freedom of religion—but that one is right and the other's wrong. They catch them when they're young and make bigots of them. And now they're beginning to insist on their own brand of marriage. In a Protestant country. You know what was eating Pam, don't you?"

"She told me this afternoon."

"I can't understand what's got into the boy."

"Mark, he's in love."

"Maybe he is, but he doesn't have to go overboard like this. He doesn't have to have a priest tell him how to marry a girl."

"That's not what they tell them."

"How do you know?"

"I know a little about those marriage-preparation classes. We had a sitter last year—remember a girl called Kathleen?"

"I can't tell them apart."

"She had very curly red hair."

"Oh, that one—she didn't last long."

"She got married. But when she was doing baby-sitting, before that, she went regularly to one of those classes. She explained to me that she never could come to us on Tuesday or Thursday nights because of that. I asked her about them, because I was curious, and she thought they were wonderful. She said that they made her think. That was certainly a step in the right direction for Kathleen."

"I can't make myself believe that Alan would get mixed up in a setup for baby sitters!"

"It's not just for them. It's for any couples who are going to be

[20]

married—Catholics, and I suppose people who are going to marry Catholics. Actually I thought it was a good idea from what Kathleen told me."

"You don't mean that. How would you like to have some priest tell you how many children you had to have?"

"I'd settle for all I could get! I wish that a priest or anyone else would tell me how to have just one."

"It must be my fault."

"The doctor said it wasn't," Olive answered, sorry at once that she had brought that up again. She went on quickly, "Kathleen said that what they do is give a kind of course of lectures. Not just by priests. They have bankers to talk on how to make budgets and how to keep out of debt—experts in different fields—I should think it could be a good thing for a lot of people who don't know what they're getting into when they marry."

"Alan is a graduate engineer," said Mark. "He'll be a vice-president of the company before too long. He's twenty-eight years old. He's beyond that sort of thing."

"But it won't hurt him. If he really is doing anything of the sort, it's only to please his girl. You might have done the same thing."

"No," said Mark, "I never would."

Olive regarded him thoughtfully. He met her eyes and smiled.

"Not even for you, darling."

"I guess that's right," said Olive. "I don't believe you would. But that's because with you reason has to come first. You couldn't even seem to ignore what you really believe. But that's you, not Alan."

"That girl must have him right where she wants him. I suppose she went after him tooth and nail."

"She doesn't seem like that sort. Not at all aggressive."

"You've seen her?"

"So have you."

"Never."

"Oh, yes, you must have. You just didn't know who she was. She works in the Medical Records at St. Barnabas Hospital. When you've been there for hospital board meetings, you must have noticed her. You have to go through that office. Very lovely looking. Irish type, dewy, sort of innocent and pliant, at least on the surface."

He thought, said, "There's one pretty girl—"

"You've seen her all right."

"I wouldn't know her if I saw her again. I can only think of how beautiful my wife is."

Their eyes met in desire.

"You're not going to bother with these dishes, are you?"

"I suppose I should. But I'm not."

"Let's go on up."

3

THE Worthing Building had occupied the same site since 1887. The city had only the rating of a village then, but it had vast ambitions. It had fought its way back from complete bankruptcy after the panic of 1873, and its rough, untidy port already was handling more grain than was being shipped out of Chicago. It had a grand opera house and a new hotel, where the bill of fare advertised a possible dinner of eight courses including roast and boiled. It had zoned a red-light district down by the bay, and weathered a strike of sawmill workers, which increased wages to a dollar and seventy-five cents for a normal twelve-hour working day.

The family name had been made important by Theron Worthing, and he had it carved on the front of a squat little business block made of local stone. He made his first money in timber, but at his roll-top desk in his own office building, at the mahogany bar in the hotel next door, and as he bargained for new acreages of land covered with scrub pine or bullied Indians out of their scrip, he was always thinking of minerals. When the first rich iron ore began to be shipped from the region, Theron was already in on the ground floor of that great development.

Twenty years later a narrow brick building with an elevator replaced the first one, and that structure lasted so well that only six years ago the newest Worthing Building had opened its gliding glass doors to the public. Mark's father had planned the modern structure, and he expected to enjoy it for a good many years. But to everyone's amazement as well as his own, he died before he was sixty—before the building was quite finished. Its completion and the management of the family's fortunes had put heavy, premature responsibility on Mark.

He had only turned thirty-two when his father died and had not been long married. Although he had been taken into the Worthing-Ingalls Company two years before, with the vague title of assistant to the vice-president, Mark had not been convinced at the time that he wanted to make mining operations his life work. But after his father's death he had little choice. The family eggs were almost all in that one basket.

In order to get the value out of the estate, it had to be held together. Leases of family mineral lands must be renewed to advantage when they expired, and in other mines to which Worthing-Ingalls held title and also operated, work either had to be continued or contracts canceled at a great loss.

There were the widow's interest, Pamela's interest, Lucy's interest (and her husband was no help, nice fellow though he was), all to be conserved. Alan's future was at stake too. He was not through with college, and since he was studying mining engineering, it was important to hold a place in the company for him and let him grow up to it. Also there were all the people who worked for Worthing-Ingalls to be considered, many of whom held their breath for fear of losing employment and security after Philip Worthing's heart gave out so unexpectedly.

Around the city the comment had been at first that the boy—that was how the older businessmen spoke of Mark—was too young to hold things together. But if he couldn't, there was no one else to do it. Ingalls was only a name that represented a large amount of Eastern money which had been put into Worthing operations almost at their beginning. A third generation of the heirs of old Bill Ingalls still were living on their mining royalties, but they were

[23]

absentee owners and never contributed more to the management of the company than signatures as requested.

Mark did have Harry Tuttle to count on. Tuttle was the vice-president to whom Mark had been more or less apprenticed, and he was rated as being probably the most experienced mining engineer on the Iron Ranges. Mark could also rely on the Hubbard law firm, which was very expert in dealing with mining leases and legal problems, and closely tied to Worthing-Ingalls after many years of generous retaining fees. And as Harry Tuttle pointed out to Mark in their first thorough conversation after the funeral, Worthing-Ingalls was lucky on two other counts.

The first one was that the rich ore in the two largest Worthing mines was not yet exhausted, though the bottom of the barrel had been scraped in adjoining mines held in fee by larger corporations. This was due more to shrewdness than luck, but Harry Tuttle was not a man to brag. The other advantage was that Philip Worthing had stubbornly held on to a great tract of property in the mining region which had been considered nearly worthless. Such iron ore as was known to exist there was embedded in taconite rock. It was low-grade ore and would cost too much to mine. Philip Worthing had always believed that a way would be worked out to process the lean ore in the rock, and he had stood back of many a discouraging experiment. He had lived long enough to know that not only had it been proved possible, but that mining the lean ore would usher in a second big era of mining in the region, comparable perhaps to the period in which his father had grown rich.

"It's no time to sell," Harry Tuttle advised Mark, "and while we're getting in on the taconite game, there's rich ore enough left to pay the bills."

"You'll have to take over, Harry," said Mark. "I don't know enough."

"I'm too old," said Tuttle, "I might go any time the way your father did. You know more than you think you do, boy. You've been around here for nearly ten years, and besides you grew up with the ore business. It's in your blood. Hell, what's there to know except to find the stuff and get it out of the ground cheap enough, and get it moving? It's got to be your show, Mark. You can kick me upstairs if you want to. For the looks of the thing."

So they had reorganized, and Harry Tuttle now was president of the company, with headquarters in the square office at the end of the corridor on the tenth floor, which had been planned for the use of Philip Worthing. Mark became the vice-president in charge of production and also a director, of course. Clifton Wells took over transportation, for the head of that division was retiring, and although there were other promotions and fill-ins, the rest of the organization was not greatly changed.

Mark's major disadvantage worked also in his favor. The very men who said he was too young knew that, because of his age, he would have plenty of time to establish himself. He could make long-range plans and carry them out. That made for financial credit. There was a feeling for young men in the air. Men of forty or less were taking over important jobs. Larry Sheldon, who had been sent up from Chicago to take over the presidency of the Merchants National Bank in that same year, was only forty-two. The governor of the state was not even that old, and he had won the last election against a veteran politician. The man whom Big Steel was building up to take over their operations before too long was in the forty bracket. The president of the university looked, at a little distance, like one of the students. After he had been in the saddle of his own company for a year, Mark Worthing didn't feel out of place. By that time he had lost his first unsureness.

But no one, even the older men, considered him cocky. Perhaps his generosity in taking over the Holden house and paying well for it had made the older generation feel that Mark was a young man who recognized obligations to it. His feet were on the ground; that was the verdict.

On the morning after his return he was early at the Worthing Building. The glow from his banked emotions, the energy of happiness, was the base of the good humor and efficiency with which he met the piled-up work. Effie Dwight, his secretary, was there earlier than he was. She had worked for his father, and

Mark had flattered her permanently by saying that Harry Tuttle couldn't have Effie, that he himself had to have her or he wouldn't dare take over.

Effie was not quite old enough to be Mark's mother. Her hair was a furious red, for she dyed it herself, but its color did not destroy her basic look of primness. It was always carefully over-curled and netted and she wore a minimum of powder. Her lipstick seemed only to accent the firmness and decency of her mouth. It was bright but never curved. Underneath the tortoise-shell trimming on top of her glasses was a pair of clear, pale blue eyes that were never abstracted by a hangover of alcohol or love. She was thin, ungraceful, healthy, and solvent on her own earnings. Everyone in the organization liked Effie, though the girls who did filing and typing had a variety of disrespectful names for her.

Mark looked over the letters which she had sorted out for his personal attention, and told her what to say in answer to most of them.

"That's all for now, Effie," he said. "I'll be busy with Mr. Tuttle this morning. I have some things to go over with him. So keep everyone off my trail, will you?"

"Yes, Mr. Worthing."

"And I'm going to have lunch with my brother."

"You have a luncheon meeting with the Hospital Committee this noon at 12:15, Mr. Worthing, in Room B at the Chamber of Commerce. Mr. Haynes called up yesterday to be sure that you'd be in town. The meeting was the one you wanted them to put off until you got back, you remember."

"I'd forgotten about it. Well, I guess I'll have to be there. Will you call Alan—catch up with him somewhere—and tell him I'm stuck for lunch? Ask him to drop in at the office this afternoon if he has time, to say hello."

"Yes, Mr. Worthing."

"There was something else I wanted you to attend to. Oh, yes —Mrs. Worthing had a little trouble with her car. A smashed fender—someone backed into her. She says it wasn't her fault."

"Mrs. Worthing is a very good driver."

"You women all hang together when it comes to driving. I've forgotten what is deductible on that policy."

"Twenty-five dollars."

"All right, call the insurance company and tell them to have an adjuster look at the damage. And you'd better call Mrs. Worthing and make sure she'll be home."

"Yes, I'll do that. And may I have your hotel bills and flight tickets for the income-tax files?"

"They'll be in my brief case."

"Thank you, Mr. Worthing."

"It feels good to be back, Effie."

"We're all glad to have you back, Mr. Worthing."

Olive was glad too, thought Mark. She had proved it. That little crack of Effie's about Olive's being a good driver tickled Mark. She really wasn't. On a straightaway Olive was steady and fine, but she never had learned how to back a car. She did it just like a woman, and half the time was badly parked, with part of the car sticking out in the street. No wonder somebody backed into her. That was why he had put the twenty-five-dollar deductible clause in the policy for her car, though he carried a hundred on his own. He had a pleasant sense of taking care of Olive, his dear and very feminine wife, as he went up to Harry Tuttle's office.

Harry asked how Olive was, and Mark said she was fine.

"I caught a glimpse of her at a cocktail party that the Whittiers gave last week. She was looking very lovely."

"Yes, she told me they gave quite a party."

Last night Olive had told him. Lying in the curve of his shoulder. She had said, "I hate going to parties without you, Mark. I feel so conspicuous and so inconspicuous. I feel half-dressed. It was one of those enormous pay-your-debts parties, an ocean of a party. I drifted around, trying not to drown."

Harry Tuttle was a lanky, completely bald man, who was never seen in clothes that looked new or well pressed. His manner was slow, almost lazy, but Mark knew that the engineer-president's mind was always in perfect working condition.

Tuttle said, "Well, how did it go? From your telegrams and

what you said on the long-distance, you seemed to get along all right."

"The Crane-Eliot crowd didn't think they'd have to put up so much money."

"They've got plenty of money."

"I had a long meeting with their directors. And later I had a talk with Eben Crane himself. He took me out to his house in Westchester. He's quite a character, isn't he?"

"He's a very pious man, you know," said Tuttle. "Very high up in church circles. Gives a lot of money to good works, I forget what sect. But that doesn't keep him from being very shrewd in financial transactions. He didn't make his money out of prayer! Did you convince him and the rest of his crowd that they wouldn't lose money in taconite?"

"I certainly tried. I went over the figures with them, showed them that revised sheet that gives the breakdown of the total cost before we get into production and the estimate of earnings in the first ten years. They had plenty of questions."

"What worried them?"

"Well, they wondered why we didn't wait and see how the two other companies that are in the field now come out before we get in too deep. I think I talked them out of that. I told them that we ought to get in at the start, before they repeal the protective tax laws and while there still are open markets. I suggested that they come out here as a group before things freeze up completely and see what progress has been made already. And then make another trip, maybe in midsummer next year, when we should be about ready for production. They lapped that up."

"Did Eben Crane go along too?"

"In the end he did. He had a notion that it might have been better to confine ourselves to a small experiment station or pilot plants to test methods, the way Big Steel is doing. I tried to make him see that we can't afford to experiment as that corporation can, that we have to give our stockholders something to show for their money just as quickly as possible. I quoted you on that. Mr. Crane has a very high regard for you, Harry."

Harry Tuttle grunted in disparagement of praise of himself. He said, "Crane wouldn't pull out. He couldn't stand not to be in on this. He knows it's a good place for venture capital, and he always likes a venture."

"That's the way he struck me. All of them were cordial enough, they just wanted to be reassured that their money was safe. I encouraged them to keep in close touch, that's why I built up the inspection trips."

"Right. It keeps them from worrying, makes them feel their fingers are in the pie."

"One thing Mr. Crane likes is not having too many companies involved in our operation. He told me that he thinks that always tends to in-fighting."

"We don't need anyone except Crane-Eliot. If they'll put up the money we asked them for. Our banks here will do the rest."

"I may be wrong, but I think everything is in good shape."

"You did a job."

"I just said my piece. I told them about the new village that is developing around the plant and harbor on the lake shore. Mr. Crane was very interested in that."

"He likes that sort of thing. As I said, he's a philanthropist."

"They questioned the layout of the power plant. They might have something there," said Mark. "Have you got the plans handy? I'll show you—"

Later they called in the head of the accounting department, and they were still talking to him when the noon whistles shrilled.

"Twelve o'clock," said Tuttle, checking his watch. "How about some lunch?"

"I'm sorry. I have to go to a meeting I can't duck this noon."

"Okay. See you later."

Private dining rooms A, B, and C filled up quickly at the Chamber of Commerce. These were the rooms where committees met to discuss civic projects, to plan the raising of a half-million dollars for good works, to decide whether an orphanage should be reroofed, a furnace put in a home for delinquents, or ten Boy Scouts sent to Europe for the summer. In the larger dining rooms there usually were luncheons going on at which a congressman or a local educator would make a speech. A, B, and C were smaller rooms, and the tables were set up with no pretense of style or luxury. The tablecloths were cotton, the china was heavy. But a vast amount of money was allotted over them, and those who made the allotments were well used to coming often to these rooms at noon, where a mimeographed report and a piece of pie were usually at each place when the men and women sat down.

Mark's committee was meeting in B, and since he was its chairman, he went to the end of the table where the secretary of the meeting was already eating broiled trout. There was always broiled trout, and usually breaded veal or meat pie, and cabbage salad. Two of the millionaires at the table were eating crackers broken into bowls of milk.

The waitress said, "We have trout and casserole of beef and chicken pie, Mr. Worthing."

"I'll try the casserole. And coffee, please."

"When did you get back, Mark?"

"Just last night."

"How's the weather down East?"

"Big rains."

The talk was as commonplace as the food. The men and one woman around the table were not here for either reason. The one woman was Miss Jackson, the head nurse at St. Barnabas Hospital. There was Isaac Elting, head of the Jewish hospital board, beautifully tailored, immaculately rich, but with the weary eyes of the Jew who never forgot the sufferings of his race; Lou Sinnott from the bank; Edgar Roff, the best man in town when it came to raising money; Theodore Jones, who could give away a million and never miss it; the superintendent of the county hospital, who was needed to answer any questions; and someone whom Mark didn't know, a priest. He watched Mark as he came in and made his way to the head of the table, and finally Mark's eyes reached him. Mark paused a second. Edgar Roff, who was sitting by the priest, leaned forward.

"We have a new member of our committee, Mark. I want you to meet Father Kenedy. He's taking Joe Nolan's place, representing the Corpus Christi Hospital."

The priest rose to take Mark's hand. He was as tall as Mark, with deepset eyes and a high forehead. His black hair was lightly sprinkled with gray, perhaps prematurely. He was very much at ease as he said he was glad to meet Mr. Worthing.

"We're happy to have you with us, Father. I hope there's nothing wrong with Joe."

"I don't think so. He seems very busy, and the Bishop thought that I might be of service to your committee."

"Good," said Mark.

Fine-looking fellow, he said to himself. First time they've sent a priest. The Catholics usually work through Joe Nolan. It doesn't matter at all, if this fellow has power to act. And I suppose the Bishop wouldn't have sent him if he didn't.

Mark had fallen into some civic responsibilities as inevitably as he had into the mining business when his father died. He hadn't wanted to take on the chairmanship of the board of St. Barnabas Hospital, but there was no one else available who seemed to be the right person. And Olive had encouraged him.

She had said, "If you're going to do anything for the town, isn't the hospital work the best? There's no hokum about that. And, after all, your father was interested in St. Barnabas—it's a family thing. I'd like to help."

Olive did help. She was at the hospital in a yellow smock three mornings a week, doing odd jobs for the nurses, writing letters for the patients, taking up the slack, Mark said. He never saw her there, for his board met in the afternoon or evening. But they often discussed the problems, particularly the one which was the reason why this committee had come into being.

All the hospitals in the city needed money. "Then why," Mark said (or maybe Olive had said it first), "can't we put on a joint drive and raise a large enough sum so that we can allocate enough to each hospital, and save a lot of time and energy? The people who always give the money in the end would prefer it that way if they have sense."

It was practical, but there were dozens of problems. Mark looked over the agenda now. The Committee on Allocations—that was Sinnot's job—the Committee on Solicitations—what a lot of words, he thought. You have to remind yourself that it's a matter of getting actual beds and medical treatment. Roff was heading that one up. Isaac would work with him to get the Jews to give. Would this priest be the one to tap the Catholics?

Theodore Jones was droning on about what the government ought to do to remain solvent, suggesting impossibilities with which no one took issue, because it was useless to try to make any impression on the prejudices of Mr. Jones. They were set in the cement of great personal wealth. Mark tried the beef casserole, found that it had been a mistake to order it, ate half of the wedge of custard pie, and told Al Haynes, secretary of the meeting, that they might as well get down to business for some people might have to leave early.

"While you are finishing your lunch—don't let me hurry anyone —we may as well get some of our routine business out of the way," Mark said. "I want to thank you all for being here and for changing the date of this meeting so I might attend personally. All our hospitals seem to be represented here today, and that's fine co-operation. I don't know, Father Kenedy, since this is your first meeting, whether you have been already briefed on the purposes of this committee."

"I've had some conversations with the Bishop and Mr. Nolan," answered the priest, "but I'm sure that I have a good deal to learn."

His voice was temperate and modest, yet confident. He sounds like a well-bred fellow, thought Mark. There aren't many of those priests who fit in the way this one seems to be able to do.

"It's a very simple project," said Mark, "undertaken because at least three of our local hospitals intended to make capital drives within the next two years. Some of us believed that it would be far better to make one drive for an inclusive sum of money to be allocated to all the hospitals according to their needs. We hope that we can cut down the effort involved, and hope too that we can raise a lot more money than we could otherwise."

"Many people would rather give five or ten thousand in a lump than split it up," said Roff. "It's one simple tax deduction, and the contribution can be spread over five years. We had a good editorial on it last week."

"Somebody must have planted that."

They all smiled in collusion.

"I want to see that piece," said Mark. "Send it over to me, will you?" He went on, addressing himself still to the priest, who was giving him close attention, "Another good result ought to be to get the people of this town thinking in terms of general hospital needs instead of their own pet institutions."

"Perhaps so," said Father Kenedy.

Mark turned to Roff. "Let's have the report of our Committee on Solicitations. That's you, Ed. How's it coming?"

"You know what it gets down to," answered Roff. "We just take the usual list of big givers, shuffle the names up, and go after them again. There's been some question as to whether we should make a general canvass. I'd like the opinion of this committee on that."

"Sure we should," said Ted Jones. "Everybody uses the hospitals. So everyone should be given a chance to come across."

"It's a lot of hard work, organizing a house-to-house campaign. For a small amount of money."

"But it's the best possible advertising."

"Surely we should make a public appeal," said Isaac Elting gently, but with emphasis.

"That appears to be the consensus of this group," said Mark, looking around the table for contradiction and receiving none, "though I agree with you, Bill, that it is slim pickings for the amount of effort that goes into it. But it puts the thing on a broader base. And you never know—somebody who gives ten dollars and gets interested might be able to shell out ten thousand a few years from now if we should have to pass the hat again."

"Someone suggested that the women's groups already working for the hospitals might help out in the campaign," said Roff. "How about that, Miss Jackson?"

"We have a women's auxiliary at St. Barnabas, of course," said the nurse. "I don't know how they would feel about house-to-house soliciting."

"A lot of women enjoy that sort of thing," said Alfred Brooks. His wife, as they all knew, was bedridden.

Mark said, "Why don't we ask the management of each hospital to provide us with a certain number of its own supporters who would be willing to help in the campaign?"

"That's the best idea. Put it up to the hospitals. This is their show."

The priest spoke. Heads turned toward him in curiosity and shrewd eyes sized up this newcomer as he asked, "Concerning the solicitation of the general public, will an individual who makes a subscription be free to designate the particular hospital who will get his money?"

"No. That would defeat the purpose of the whole thing," said Mark. "There are always a few people who want to do that, but I shouldn't think it could be allowed."

"We used to let Community Fund subscribers do that," said Mr. Sinnot. "There are, as Mark says, usually some givers who have an ax out for some agency—they don't want to help the Y.M.C.A. —or else—pardon me, Father, but I'm sure you know this as well as I do—they sometimes have a prejudice against Catholic institutions. So we let them indicate on their pledge cards where they wanted their money to go. But of course it was so much eyewash. Even if they marked their subscriptions, there were ways in which the budget committee could straighten things out. It was just a sop to a few bigots, and we discontinued the practice after a year or two."

"I see your point," said the priest, "and sympathize with it. But in this campaign for hospital funds a problem may present itself if the subscribers cannot indicate how they want their money assigned and be very sure that their wishes are carried out."

"Just what is the problem, Father Kenedy?" asked Mark.

"We have a women's auxiliary in our Catholic hospital," said Father Kenedy. "I have little doubt that its members would be willing to help in this work if it would not mean doing violence to their consciences."

"Raising money for the sick surely wouldn't do that."

The priest went on, "A Catholic woman—or man—would not be willing, nor permitted, to solicit funds for the use of any hospital in which human life is not respected."

"Respected?" repeated Mark.

The nurse was watching the priest with an expression of controlled hostility. In the short ensuing silence, everyone around the table seemed to be mentally backing away from an idea which had been dropped in their midst. Then Isaac Elting said in his wise, wearied way, "You have in mind, sir, I suppose, the planned-parenthood clinic at City Hospital."

"I think it best to make one thing clear," said Father Kenedy. "The Church cannot sanction, aid, or seem to encourage any practices which are contrary to the law of God."

The name of God created a slight embarrassment. It was out of key with these practical plans for raising money. It was the wrong time of day for theology; it was out of place over these half-eaten pieces of custard pie. When God came into meetings in these rooms, it was only during the saying of grace before a meal, if that was done. Then He went out, and the business of the meeting proceeded.

During the next minute or two, each person left response to the priest to someone else. The waitress was collecting the money for each lunch, and her murmured thanks for tips was oddly audible. The lighting of several cigarettes made a use for the interval.

Mark needed no more than those few minutes to realize that this was why the priest had come today, and why Joe Nolan had been relieved of his place on the committee. Probably by his own choice. Joe would have been very reluctant, probably unwilling, to bring up this matter among his friends. It would have embarrassed him.

Who had made that remark about Joe Nolan that he began to be penitent when he began to enjoy sex? That came into Mark's

[35]

mind. And it was a joke among the men at the Town Club, to which Joe Nolan belonged and in which he always seemed an outsider, that sex was always catching up with Joe. He would always get drunk at the hardwaremen's conventions and then he would want the girls around. He always had a new off-color story in his mind, and he would come out with it and then redden up with shame. He'd be the last man in the world who would want to sit in at a meeting with these other men and argue about a birth-control clinic. He had ducked it and the Bishop had sent this priest to carry the ball.

Were they really going to make an issue of this?

The waitress was gone now and the door closed. He must say something now.

"I'm sure that we all respect your principles, Father Kenedy," said Mark, "but what we are trying to do is to pool the interests of the local hospitals. If we let one subscriber say, 'I want my thousand dollars to go to Corpus Christi,' and someone else say, 'I'll give fifty if I can be sure it's spent at City Hospital,' we might as well have separate campaigns. Which is just what we are trying to get away from."

"We approve of a joint campaign," said the priest, "but if it is impossible to designate the recipient of subscriptions, and that should put the Church in a position of impossible toleration, we would have no choice but to withdraw from this project."

Withdraw the Catholic hospital from the pool—there wasn't a person at the table who didn't realize the seriousness of that threat. Corpus Christi was the largest and oldest hospital in the city. For years certain doctors, including Protestants and Jews, had preferred it to any other for surgery. Many people who were not Catholics had a personal loyalty to it because their babies had been born there or because of an affection for one of the nuns who supervised the work there. Aside from wrecking the plan for co-operation, any announcement that Corpus Christi had pulled out would tear the town wide open, and over the most painful of arguments. For the reason would leak out, of course.

"We would greatly regret the necessity of withdrawing," said the priest.

He sounded as if he meant that. There was no harshness in his voice, no dictatorial sound. But nothing could have been more final.

Ed Roff said thoughtfully, "This clinic is the single obstacle to your going along with us, Father?"

"It is the only thing I am aware of that violates the principle I have mentioned."

"Are you aware, Father Kenedy, that many members of your faith are clients at the City Hospital planned-parenthood clinic?" asked Miss Jackson in a dry, clipped voice.

So Pamela had told Mark yesterday. He remembered that now. He supposed it was quite true, but he wished the nurse hadn't thrown the fat into the fire like that. Yet Mark was curious to know what the answer of the priest would be.

"That fact, even if true, Miss Jackson, would in no way alter the position of the Church," said Father Kenedy.

Mark was thinking, what it gets down to is an offer. The price they mean to ask for their co-operation is the closing of that clinic. It's blackmail. It's out of the question. It's cleverly timed, for they've let us go this far with plans and publicity, and now they come up with this.

City Hospital wouldn't do it. But City is worse off financially than any of the other hospitals, thought Mark. This campaign is its big hope. That endowment it has, made years ago "for the sick and worthy poor," can't be stretched to keep up with present costs. Part of the building will be condemned if they don't get the money for a reconstruction job. Lou Sinnot from the Midland Bank knows all about that. He told me. He's a trustee of City Hospital. Mark glanced at the banker, who was studying the texture of the cotton tablecloth.

The thing was fantastic. Everyone practiced birth control these days. They were getting ready to put preventives in food. There wasn't a man at this table except the priest himself who didn't believe it was a good thing. Back of all these poker faces every man was undoubtedly thinking of his own habit, his necessity, his good reason—it's different with Olive and me because we want a child—

[37]

"Are we, as a volunteer committee, in any position to suggest to City Hospital that it alter its services to the public?" asked Theodore Jones, looking coldly at the Catholic cleric. Another prejudice was frozen in his eyes.

Quickly Mark intercepted any answer.

"Gentlemen, this discussion is getting rather far afield. Going back to the coverage of the campaign, I think we agree that it should be city-wide. The matter of who will do the actual soliciting can now be referred back to Mr. Roff's subcommittee and any problems thrashed out without taking the time of the full committee. If I can be of any use, Ed, I'll be glad to consult with your committee. Father Kenedy, may I ask you to serve on that committee in Mr. Nolan's place?"

His eyes met those of the priest, conceding nothing but requesting that the argument be narrowed.

"Now I know," Mark went on, "that some of you are pressed for time. While we still have a quorum, there are several matters that must be settled today. The first is the dates of our campaign."

4

THE family look had been relaxed in Alan Worthing. Both his parents had been marked by an air of authority and had passed it on to the rest of their children. It was written all over Pamela. Lucy, even when she was her most amorous self, could not help taking full responsibility—as her husband, Gregory Searles, often told her with amusement.

Mark too had something of the Worthing manner. It had been forced on him, been necessary since his father had died, although he managed to wear it without the slightest arrogance. But in Alan the family look was not evident at all. Even his complexion was different from the others. He was the only fair one. He was buoyant, apparently careless. His relatives loved him the more because they could not be quite like that. But they often worried about him. Alan was the least predictable member of the family. Agreeably he had baffled all the efforts of his mother and Pamela to organize his personal life or weed out his friends.

He came into Mark's office late in the afternoon. "Am I snarling up traffic, Effie?" he asked her. "Is your employer as busy as you pretend he is?"

"Well, he hasn't had a minute all day," she said, "but I know he wanted to see you, Alan. He's talking long distance right now but he'll be soon through."

Effie never called Mark by his first name now that she was his secretary, but with Alan anything else would have been silly. He would have laughed her out of it if she had tried to be formal with him. Ever since he was a small boy, her extraordinary red hair had been part of Alan's background.

"You're looking younger than ever, Effie. Why don't you grow up?"

"Oh, you—" she said fondly.

Alan sat down on the edge of her desk.

"Effie, you know me better than anyone. Do you think—now please don't be perfectly frank with me—do you think I'd make a good husband?"

She looked at him sharply. She had heard what was going on.

"You'd soon find that's no laughing matter," Effie said.

"So they all say," agreed Alan. "I guess it must be a grim business, this mating. You're a smart girl to have nothing to do with it."

Effie picked up the interoffice telephone and said with dignity, "Your brother is here, Mr. Worthing."

"Good—tell him to come right in."

She had a glimpse of their meeting before the door closed. The two tall young men were glad to see each other. They began with the usual words. But they did not look commonplace. Effie regarded them with pride. They belonged to her in a way. Nice that they are so close, she said to herself. He'll straighten him out, she thought, identifying the pronouns in her mind. I don't believe that Alan's in earnest about the Carroll girl. She's a pretty thing,

[39]

but she's not nearly good enough for Alan. He could have any-body. She's a Roman too, and the Worthings have always been Episcopalians. Mrs. Worthing gives a thousand a year to the Procathedral. Effie smiled deprecatingly. The bit of badinage with Alan had been stimulating. I'd be a fool to let it go white, thought Effie of her hair.

Alan asked Mark about his trip and got an outline of it. Mark did not go into the business in detail as he had with Harry Tuttle. For Alan was not important enough in the organization to be a full consultant. At present he was one of the engineers employed on the construction of the new taconite processing plant thirty miles distant, on the lake shore. There were several layers of bosses between Mark and Alan.

"How's the work on the lake shore coming, Al?"

"We're knee deep in mud after these last rains. But it's beginning to take shape. We should be under cover before the snow comes."

"We've got to be. Some of the big shots are coming out to look the job over before long. I'd like to have you meet Eben Crane. It's an experience."

"You don't have to drag me in," said Alan. "I'm not in that league."

"It would be a good thing for you to know some of our backers. You have a piece of money in this deal—we all have. And everybody in the family may feel a little pinched before the new plant goes into production. We'll have to dig up our share of the costs. But it will pay off in the end."

"Won't we get the usual cut in December? Royalties on the mines that are operating now?"

"Yes, but we might want to plow some of them back into the new works. Are you short of money?"

"I'm going to need something to get married on. I guess that runs into money."

Mark was glad that Alan himself had brought up the subject. But now that he had spoken of marrying in that take-it-for-granted way, it seemed awkward to plunge into objections or arguments.

"Planning on that soon?"

"When my girl says the word. Now that you're back, I want you to meet Rose Mary."

"This is the same girl?"

"Identical. This is the real thing, Mark."

"You want to be sure of that. Marriage is something you can't fool around with."

"Effie just told me it was no laughing matter."

"Effie has a good head under that forest fire. Of course, this is something that a man has to decide for himself. But you want a good life, Al. The chances for that depend a whole lot on the kind of marriage you make. I'm not preaching to you—I happen to know it's a fact. You ought to look at this from every angle."

"It looks the same from all the angles," said Alan. "This is it."

"Have you made definite plans?"

"Mine are definite. Rose Mary won't let me crowd her, or we'd be married now."

"What do you mean? That she isn't sure she wants you?"

"That's all right—she's sure of that," said Alan. His voice was more tender, more mature than Mark had ever heard it. "But she's a Catholic. She wants me to get the low-down on how they feel about marriage in her Church. And that takes a little time. They like to brief you."

"Yes, I heard she was a Catholic."

"Pam's been after you, I suppose. She's been giving Mother an earful too. I'm pretty sore at Pam—she's turning out to be a nasty bigot. She tried to tell me that I was making a mistake. She doesn't even know Rose Mary—Pam's only gripe is that she is a Catholic."

"Pam's very fond of you."

"She takes a hell of a way to show it," said Alan, dismissing that.

"But doesn't it complicate things for you yourself—I mean, your girl's being a Roman Catholic?"

"I like Rose Mary's being a Catholic. I don't object to it in the least."

"How does she feel about your not being one?"

"She knows I never could be. I've told her that."

Mark felt definite relief. He said, "It's looking pretty far ahead, but how about your family if you have one? Won't she want any children you might have to be brought up as Catholics?"

"You have to agree to that," said Alan, "beforehand. They feel pretty strongly about that. You have to sign an agreement."

"That's what I've been told. It's your own business, Alan, but don't you feel that sort of mortgages the future?"

"I don't see why. It's a good religion. If it makes my kids as sweet and as honest as Rose Mary, it's all right with me."

"But don't you think they ought to have a right to a choice? There would be a lot of your blood in them—and there isn't any Catholic tradition in our family on either side. All I mean is that maybe your children wouldn't want to be Catholics. Why sew the whole thing up for them in advance?"

Alan forgot one cigarette and lighted another. His long, vigorous body was restless. Mark didn't press the point, but the question was there, between them. Something had to be done with it.

Alan said, "Well, I didn't like that part of it too much myself. Not at first. But Rose Mary didn't make the rules, poor girl. She just has them handed to her. You see, Catholics take marriage very seriously."

"So do a lot of other people. So do I, for that matter. So does Olive."

"Not in the same way."

"What do you mean?" asked Mark, as if he were interested, not arguing.

"I mean that the Catholics have worked out a system. They give a regular course on marriage, sort of a lecture series. For people who are in love, who intend to be married. The idea is to go over the things that might come up, tell you what to expect, the problems—you know the sort of thing—"

"There were sex lectures at college—pretty stupid—"

"These aren't like that. It's the Catholic point of view."

"You're not a Catholic. You don't have to be briefed on that. I can hardly figure you—"

"I didn't have to," said Alan, defensively now. "I thought it might be a good idea. Rose Mary thought so too. She's not much on explaining, and she wanted me to get some things straight. I've only been to a couple of talks so far, but they struck me as pretty sensible. Of course, they lay it on the line about divorce. They're dead against divorces."

"What if it happens to be necessary?"

"They leave an out on that. They admit that a couple may have to separate if a man or a woman turns out to be a complete heel. What they draw the line at is marrying again. And they could be right. If a person can't make a success of his marriage, he's probably a menace. Why turn him loose?"

Mark said abruptly, "You don't know what you're talking about." And Alan remembered that Olive had divorced her first husband.

Quickly and with apology, Alan said, "Of course, there are cases in which it's entirely justified—"

"Never mind that now," said Mark. "We're talking about you. You haven't been married yet. All I wonder is if you're trying to swallow a lot of stuff you don't believe in and if it won't make trouble for you later."

Alan stood up as if he wanted to be on his feet for what he had to say. He wandered from his chair to the window. Came back. He made no motion toward leaving the office. Mark sat at the desk realizing that Alan had come here for reassurance, for backing. He needed help. He was alone in this thing. Always before I've been able to come across, thought Mark.

Alan began over again. "Suppose you fell in love with a girl, and she happened to be a Catholic. You wouldn't let that make any difference to you, would you?"

"I couldn't prevent its making a difference," answered Mark.

"Well, maybe. But what I mean is that if you wanted to marry a Catholic, you would."

Mark said slowly, "I don't believe I'd want to."

Hostility flashed over Alan's face. "Well, that puts you right in Pam's corner."

"No, you're all wrong," said Mark. "I know Pamela as well as you do. As far as she's concerned, it's being on the wrong side of the street socially to be a Catholic. It's stepping out of line, mixing

[43]

breeds. I don't give a damn about any of that. When you choose a wife, you choose the woman you want, and hope to God she'll have you and that you can make her happy. It's nobody's business where you find her."

"That's what I say!"

"But you asked me what I'd do if I wanted to marry a Catholic, and I said I wouldn't want to. Now let me finish and get it straight. What I mean is that I wouldn't want to marry any woman, any girl, who had all those controls over her that you've been telling about. I want a woman who can exercise her free will in our life together, who wouldn't want us to follow a pattern that any priest laid down for what we were going to do or not going to do, or laid down the law if we didn't want to live together. And what's more I certainly wouldn't agree to turning over my children to any dogma. Or to signing their minds away."

"You don't do that," protested Alan.

"Then what is the deal?"

"You only agree to let your children be exposed to the Catholic religion—it's a formality, a protection against bigots who might not want a woman to practice her religion or tell her children about it, that's all—"

"You don't really believe that, do you? Look, Al, this is a very powerful institution you've come up against. I've reason to know. I'm having a run-in with it right now that might interest you. We've been served notice that the Catholic hospital will withdraw from the general campaign for funds we're putting on, unless City Hospital closes down a miserable little birth-control clinic they've set up to tell women how to keep from having children they can't support. It's in a poor district and those women can't go to expensive doctors. But the Catholics don't believe in birth control. So if this place doesn't shut up shop, they won't go along with the campaign."

"Then let them get out," said Alan.

"That's no way for you to talk. This girl you're going to marry wouldn't be allowed to collect money for the hospitals if there was a birth-control clinic in any one of them."

"Rose Mary works at St. Barnabas. That's a Protestant hospital."

"I know. But you ask her what her point of view on birth control is, and if she doesn't have to do what the priest tells her to do about having children. You know how they work it. They get it out of the women in the confessionals. Do you want some priest to hear all about your private life?"

"You're exaggerating that."

"Maybe. But this Father Kenedy has me over a barrel. If they pull out, the campaign ends in a religious row. And they won't even discuss the matter. They aren't open to reason. As you just said, they lay it on the line."

"You're free to do as you please."

"So were you," said Mark, "and they've already got you going to a class somewhere to be told how to live with the girl you want to marry. You're not getting advice. You're getting directives. Your Rose Mary knows that. Of course, she may not take it too seriously. I guess a lot of Catholics break their own rules."

"Rose Mary doesn't," said Alan quickly, as if he couldn't let that pass.

They had reached a limit in disagreement, and became silent, gathering control.

Finally Mark began to sum it up in slow-paced words. "If you really want to go through with this marriage, Al, all right. Nobody can stop you. And nobody's going to try. I've known what you had in mind, but unless you brought it up yourself, I wouldn't have said some of these things. You asked for it."

"I wanted to talk to you. That's why I came around."

"I wish I could go along, that I could be more encouraging. But you wouldn't want me to put on an act, to fake anything."

"No, of course not."

"All I hope is that, for God's sake, you'll look squarely at what you're getting into. Don't kid yourself. I wouldn't pretend to that girl that I was agreeing to anything unless I meant to follow through. It isn't fair to her. If you can take what seems to me would be a good deal of interference with your personal life, go ahead. Just know what you're doing and what you're taking on."

"You make it sound a lot more unreasonable than they do."

"They're masters of seeming reasonable. Don't think for a minute that I underestimate the Catholic Church. The people who run it know every trick in the bag. They're closely organized, and strong and rich and powerful. But like that Father Kenedy who threw a monkey wrench into our hospital drive, they don't give an inch. You take it or leave it."

The face and manner of the priest was curiously clear in Mark's mind. He hadn't hesitated to say his piece, to put his cards on the table. Obeying orders, of course, but there was more than that. The fellow had been thoroughly indoctrinated.

Mark said, "Alan, the trouble is that if you marry a Catholic girl—one who plays the rules, you'll have a wife who isn't able to think for herself. Or go along with your thinking."

"Rose Mary thinks for herself. You needn't worry about that."

"But you said just a minute ago that she had to accept the rules that were handed out to her."

"In a way," said Alan uneasily, "but she has a mind of her own, all right. You have to know her to understand what she's like."

"I haven't any doubt that she's a lovely girl. Olive tells me she's a beauty. Olive thinks—and so do I—that it's fine for you to get married. That you should. We aren't against this, Al. We're afraid of it for you, that's all."

"Is Olive afraid of it too? Does she feel the way you do about Catholics?"

"I haven't any quarrel with Catholics. It's not that, at all. As for Olive, she doesn't get worked up like Pam. But she wants the best— the right—thing for you. She doesn't want you to make a mistake."

"Why should it be a mistake?"

Mark said, "Maybe it wouldn't be. But I've told you how I feel."

"I've never heard you talk against Catholics before."

"I'm not talking against them now. You've got me wrong. I'm saying that they won't come halfway. You have to go all the way. It seems to me you're doing it already, going to their marriage school or whatever it is."

"I did that because I wanted to. I wanted to get their point of view. I'm not narrow-minded," said Alan.

"Okay," said Mark. "Well, you'll have to work it out for yourself."

"I think so," Alan said. "Well, I guess I'll go along."

Mark stood up. He didn't offer his hand. It wasn't that kind of a farewell. But he had a helpless, lonely feeling reflected from the loneliness with which Alan was pursuing this girl. All by himself, going into strange territory, probably being let down, changing from the kind of person he was—it wasn't normal for Alan to let a priest give him orders. He would have made fun of anyone else who did what he was doing.

"Good luck, Al—"

"Thanks," said Alan, but his voice was hostile.

In the outer office Effie looked up to say good-by and to take a little kidding. But there was none. Alan looked grim. Effie stared after him. They've had an argument, she said to herself. They've had trouble. Maybe over that girl.

Why hadn't he done a better job with Alan? Mark was dressing to go out to dinner. He could hear Olive stirring in the adjoining room as she got ready, and the high voice of the child who was with her. Mark hadn't told her of his talk with his brother. There hadn't been any chance after he got home tonight, for Tim and Jenny were around.

"Can I come in?" asked Tim.

"Sure, come on in, fellow."

Tim was still Timothy Grant, and Mark wanted to change his last name. He wasn't hurrying the adoption because it would mean explanations that the child might worry about. Tim was taken care of as far as inheritance went, so the other matter wasn't urgent, though it must be settled before he went away to camp or school. He was a thin, strong little boy with a sensitive face and a manner which he tried to make rough and burly, especially with Mark.

"Do you know who's going to win the Series, Mark?"

"I know what I think."

"Aren't you sure?"

"I'll bet on the Yankees."

"That's good. Because I'm for the Dodgers."

"Going to put some money on them?"

"Sure," said Tim.

"Well, you dig up a dime and take one of mine from that bunch of silver on the bed and give both of them to your mother to hold until after the last game."

"Okay," said Tim. He went over to the bed, on which Mark had emptied the contents of his change pocket when he took off his business clothes. Coins, keys, his lighter—

"Here's a dime," said Tim. "What's this, Mark?"

"What's what?" Mark turned and saw the object Tim was holding up. "Oh, that's a medal."

"What's a medal?"

"It's a thing people carry."

"Who's the picture on it—the old man with the stick and the baby?"

"I believe he's called St. Christopher."

"What does he do?"

Mark found a black tie. "I don't know that he does much of anything."

"What's he supposed to be doing?"

Mark looked at the medal. "He's carrying the child. The child is Jesus."

"Is it a locket?"

"No, not exactly. People carry it because they think it makes them safe from accidents. In cars and boats and planes and things."

"How could it?"

"It's beyond me, Tim."

"Where did you get it?"

"A lady gave it to me."

"To keep you safe?"

"I guess that was her idea."

"I know what it is—it's for luck, like a four-leaf clover. I know a boy at school has a horseshoe for luck. Can I have it, Mark?"

"What for?"

"I'd like a lucky thing—"

The woman had said in that devout voice, "It's been blessed." Let the child have it.

Mark turned. "No," he said, "you see, it isn't just a lucky piece, Tim. Some people believe—well, they believe that, if they carry that, it is a kind of prayer—you don't want to throw it around. Here, I'd better take it. You go dig up that other dime."

5

ALAN still lived in his mother's house. He still slept in the one of the two "boys' rooms" on the third floor, which had been his place for as long as he could remember. Now he could have occupied Mark's room, which was bigger, or one of his sisters' former bedrooms on the second floor, if he had wanted to make the change. His mother had suggested that. But Alan said he was all right where he was. The India-print bedspread that didn't soil easily, the cherry chest-on-chest and highboy, the pictures of a storm at sea on one wall and a fox hunt on the other were familiar things among which he had lived during all his school vacations. They didn't mean very much to him, but nothing else in the house meant more.

Nowadays Mrs. Worthing often said that the house was much too big for her. But it was hard to imagine her in any other setting. She herself could not imagine it. Other well-to-do widows usually went to live in apartments a year or two after the estates were settled. They paired up and went on cruises. But Mrs. Worthing did not fit into that kind of leisured life. Even husbandless, she had not long seemed bereft or at any loss as to what to do with her time. She had too many interests.

She had always had a firm impersonal life along with being a wife and mother. Part of her desires and energies had never been given over to her family, nor melded with her responsibility for her home. From her early twenties, when woman's suffrage had seemed to her to be even more necessary to a good life than a husband, she had been a follower and leader of causes. She had upheld organizations fighting sweatshops and child labor, worked for peace, sold bonds in wartime, and, with complete conviction, had spent a year helping to get prohibition repealed. Her name was still on dozens of letterheads as a sponsor, adviser, or director. At almost every banquet for charity in her city, she was at the speakers' table. She often "opened her house" for meeting, and four dozen small gilt folding chairs were stacked in a corner of the laundry when not in use. The house had been opened so often to strangers that intimacy seemed to have gone out of the big, orderly rooms.

Her four children had grown up among her causes and good works, and they had never been neglected. Mildred Worthing was a very conscientious mother and was active in parental organizations, especially at the national level. When it was necessary for her to attend a convention or distant conference while the children were small, the household ran like clockwork in her absence. The items on lists she left behind ticked off—cod-liver oil for Lucy, Pamela's music lesson on Thursday, roast lamb on Friday and croquettes made from the leftovers on Saturday. The Worthing children were used to seeing their mother's pictures in the newspapers. Often there was a cluster of orchids on her shoulder, and a governor, a senator, or a visiting lecturer would be smiling at her with admiration. They knew she was wonderful. "Your wonderful mother," people said to them. They believed it, without excitement or delight.

Philip Worthing did not go along with his wife's projects. He never made a speech in public. He wouldn't listen to one if he could get out of it. He was cheerfully cynical about his wife's activities. "Mildred is off somewhere, picking goats' feathers," he would say teasingly. He made no fight for the principles of repeal of prohibition, but he had a trustworthy bootlegger and plenty of liquor in his house and in his personal lockers at various clubs until the law was changed.

His life was as full as that of his wife. A good part was taken up in making the money he had inherited increase, and much of the rest of his time was spent at his clubs. He was good at games. His golf score was low and he played a master hand of both bridge and poker. The money he won from his friends always delighted him.

There was no friction between him and his wife. Nor any apparent intimacy. Their children never heard them quarrel or came upon them in an embrace. They talked things over—Mildred Worthing was careful never to detract from her husband's authority in the family—and backed up each other's decisions. Perhaps they got along too well to create a warm and spicy home life. If there had been passion between them in the beginning, it had dwindled or been sublimated by the time Alan was old enough to take notice. When Lucy learned about sex, as she did when she was very young, she told Pam she was sure they were all adopted children. Her mother and father wouldn't have done it. Mark was the only one who could remember that his parents used to share a room, but that was before the house was done over and the old-fashioned conservatory and sleeping porch made into a new wing.

Her husband's sudden death bewildered Mildred Worthing more than anything that had ever happened to her. There was sorrow as well as pity that he was cut off so abruptly from the things he liked to do, and also an upsurge of memories of youth. She bore these things as ably as she did everything else. It was the interruption of plans and habits, the feeling that she should reschedule her life, the question as to what her duty would be now that confused her. It was too late for the children to absorb her into their lives. They knew that and urged her to keep her house. Mark broke down the figures of her income and showed her that the rent of a good apartment would be as much as the fixed charges on the big place.

"Stay where you are for the present," he advised her. And the years were drifting along with no defined end to the "present." Sometimes Mrs. Worthing said it would be different after Alan married. Or if she could not get household help. But Carrie had worked for the Worthings for thirty-two years and was still in the kitchen. Carrie's husband was houseman, when one was needed. What would Carrie and her husband do if I moved, Mrs. Worthing asked.

The big house was still "opened" occasionally when a meeting needed or deserved its hospitality. When he came home this after-noon after his talk with Mark, Alan saw that some group had been there. The people were gone, but the chairs from the laundry were still ranged in rows in the big living room, and in the dining room there was a lace cloth on the table. A silver urn for coffee and a silver tea service faced each other at opposite ends of the table, and Alan could imagine the affable, flattered ladies who had acted as hostesses. He went to the sideboard and took out a decanter. He needed a drink. As he was pouring it, some sight—perhaps the lace cloth—or some smell—perhaps the sweet, staling smell of frosted teacakes—reminded him of the time he had run away from this house when it was full of strange women.

They must have scared him or made him feel that he was crowded out. He was ten years old, he remembered, and was supposed to be up in his room. Instead he sneaked out of the house and went through the alleys to the back street where the Horne family lived. Bill Horne was one of his friends. He had a dog that slept at the foot of his bed. Mrs. Horne did her own cooking and she was always scolding the boys and giving them things to eat. It was a house to which Alan liked to go. He remembered that and also that he had stayed for supper. Then he must have cooked up some story or other, for Mrs. Horne said he could spend the night and sleep with Bill and the dog. In the meantime, the police had been notified, for Alan's mother thought he had been kidnaped. It wasn't until there was a house-to-house check in the neighborhood that he was found. His mother wanted him to explain and he couldn't explain. Mrs. Horne didn't welcome him after that, and before long he went away to school.

Alan heard his mother coming with the quick firm step that always knew where it was going. He saw her in the doorway, still looking like the beautiful Gibson-type girl she had been forty years before. Her eyes were happy with worthy achievement.

"Had a party?"

"I told you the Foreign Policy Study Class was meeting here today, dear."

"Yes, I guess you did. I forgot."

[52]

"We had such a good speaker and very interesting discussion afterward. Of course, the British will have to give up Cyprus eventually. We're going to have a very simple dinner, for Carrie had her hands full this afternoon. But it's one of your favorites—chicken Charleston."

"Don't bother about any dinner for me. I just came home to change. I'm going right out."

"Before dinner?"

"Yes, I've a date."

His mother restrained the question which he knew was in her mind. Instead she asked, "Did you see Mark today?"

"Yes, I stopped in at his office."

"I was talking to Olive on the phone and she said he was back. I so wanted Olive to come this afternoon. She would have been very much interested in this talk."

Alan doubted that. For years his mother had been trying to get her own children to meetings, with no success. Now she's working on poor Olive, thought Alan amusedly.

"But she couldn't come, she had something else to do. Olive is such a dear girl."

"She's quite something," said Alan.

"And she's been so good for Mark. They're so congenial."

Alan could tell where this was leading. He moved toward the staircase.

"Alan, dear," said his mother pleasantly, "when you have time, I want to have a little talk with you."

Alan knew those little talks. The theory back of them was that a child must be made to understand. Not coerced, but talked to reasonably. About trying to spend the night at the Hornes'. About the girl he was going to marry.

"Fine. But right now I have to be on my way."

She was expertly not asking him where he was going. Not interfering so deliberately that it was interference. It ought to be funny—usually it struck Alan that way. But tonight it made him edgy. All he wanted now was to get away before any little talk broke over him. He went to his room, changed quickly, and ran down the stairs again. No chance of escape. Not unless he went out the back door. His mother was standing by the long table in the hall, gathering up pamphlets that had been put there for the Foreign Policy group.

"Will you be late?"

"Probably not."

"It doesn't matter. I was just wondering whether to lock up."

"You'd better do that. I have my key."

"All right, dear. Alan—just a minute—I don't want to keep you but there is something I feel I should say—"

He waited for it, but he didn't meet her seriousness. He looked a nonchalant young man in a hurry.

"I'm sure you know, dear, that nobody could be more broad-minded than I am. I've always worked against intolerance—I've been a director for years of our branch of the Christians and Jews."

"You're a wonderful woman," he said lightly.

"Darling, I'm not boasting about it. I only mentioned that because it shows that I have nothing against any religion. I believe that everyone must serve God in his own way. That's why we put up all those billboards—you know, GO TO THE CHURCH OF YOUR CHOICE NEXT SUNDAY. All religions are good—the point is to make our Christian faith so strong that in the end it will defeat Communism. That was brought out so well this afternoon."

"Sure, but—"

"Just one minute, dear. About the Roman Catholics. I haven't one iota of prejudice, and I've always insisted that Catholics should be represented on any board I've had anything to do with."

"Why not?"

"The only thing is that they don't co-operate. Actually they're not allowed to. I hate to say this, but there is something not quite American about their point of view. In a way it is understandable because they regard the Pope in Rome as their dictator. And he tells them they must believe such extraordinary things! Like last year when there was all that publicity about Christ's Mother rising up to heaven. Fully clothed! So preposterous—of course, there are a great many ignorant people in the Catholic Church—but I

[54]

understand that even the intelligent ones have to believe anything the Pope tells them—"

"Look, Mother, I haven't time to discuss theology right now."

"I know. I'm not going to detain you. But, my dear boy, don't rush into anything. I do wish that before you get involved in a situation that might be very difficult you would have a little talk with Dr. Powell."

"Powell?"

"Our Episcopal rector. He's the new one, still quite young and very good with young people."

Alan gave a gasp of laughter. "I'm past the Boy Scout age, Mother. Look, you stop worrying about the Pope bossing me around. You worry about Cyprus. I can take care of myself. Good night."

She made a gesture but he ignored it and went off. He didn't want to kiss her. He had been taught to kiss his mother good night, but it had often been a false caress. He had kissed her because he had to. Tonight he balked. He swung his car into the highway, eager to put distance between himself and his home. Why didn't his family mind their own business? As Mark had said, it was completely up to him—nobody could stop him—and nobody was going to keep him from marrying Rose Mary.

But Mark had tried, just the same. He had come right out with it, said that he himself wouldn't marry a Catholic. Because Catholics couldn't think for themselves, because Mark believed he would have to share his wife with a priest in some way—where do they get ideas like that—they'll be crazy about Rose Mary when they get to know her. If they aren't, that's their loss. She can think for herself, all right. I ought to know, Alan said to himself. You can go just so far with Rose Mary and no further. If she believes a thing is wrong—why, of course, she decides for herself whether it is wrong or not. What if she does go along with her religion? She's a sweet—she's passionate too—little saint, saving herself for me. She's my girl, the kind of wife I want. We'll have a good life together.

He looked sophisticated, this fair, well-kept, slim young man. He had chosen the manner that best would protect the loneliness in him, that would keep the deep desire for a simple, warm, and loving life well hidden. No one could mock it if nobody knew it existed. No one could discuss it, and Alan disliked discussions.

Still, he had hoped this afternoon that he could really open up to Mark. He had counted on Mark and Olive. Mark was always clear on things. What a guy he is, thought Alan, and the disappointment of their talk today hit him with full force again. Alan didn't even admit to himself how great his admiration was for his brother. After their father died, Mark had treated Alan like a man and a friend instead of like a college boy. And Mark had steered him right. The operating end of the mining business is where I belong, thought Alan, and Mark said so from the start. This afternoon was the first time that I've ever known him to be way off the beam.

I didn't get a chance to tell Mark what I mean to do, that I want to buy or rent one of the little houses near the taconite plant and live close to the job. Rose Mary will like that. She wants a home to look after and her man, and that's all she wants. Cyprus can go to hell for all she cares. She works now only because she doesn't want to sponge on her family.

We can get along by ourselves, if they all feel this way about Rose Mary. I certainly wouldn't want to put her up against any of that talk of Mother's about what the Virgin, as Rose Mary calls her, wore when she went up to heaven. Of course, I can see how that kind of fairy story would affect a literal-minded woman like Mother. And as for Pam, what's really eating her is that Rose Mary isn't Junior League. Pam's been trying to sell me down the river to her crowd for years. She was all smiles when I was dating Dot Langhorne. That's her gripe. Mark said so too.

With him it's different. Mark has a wrong slant on Catholics. He talked as if he were almost afraid of them. He doesn't think I know what I'm doing. I should have told him that he's worrying the way I did when he married Olive. Before I met Olive, I thought Mark was making a mess of his whole life by taking on a widow with two children. I thought somebody ought to stop it. It's the same kind of thing.

The similarity Alan discovered pleased him. He felt better now

[56]

as he drove on, taking short cuts from the district where his mother lived to higher streets along the bluff above the lake on which the city was laid out. Cottages, little frame houses, gas stations, and grocery centers lined the two-lane streets, where the pavement showed breakages and holes because the people who lived along the streets did not want to pay the assessments to mend them. A year ago North Hillside had been a part of the city that Alan hardly knew was there. Now it led to his love. He knew the Mobilgas sign four blocks away from her house, the bride's cake in the bakery-lunch, and the big, yellow brick church that crowded the second block.

Passing the church he thought, I hope she'll skip that business tonight. I'm not much in the mood for it.

The Carroll house was one that a man with a steady job in a railroad ticket office could pay for in time and one that his wife could be proud of. It looked weather-tight and respectable. A row of African violets in pots, all white and all blooming, stood on the sill of the picture window which dated the construction of the house no further back than twenty years. Behind the violets was a lamp with a white shade, and behind that people were moving about. Alan parked by the curb and waited in the car for a minute, hoping that Rose Mary would be watching for him and come out. That would save him from having to repeat conversation that had become rather typed and monotonous—with her father, her mother, her young brother, Bart, and any of the married sisters and brothers who didn't live there but often dropped in.

He saw Bart stare out the window and turn away, probably to yell to Rose Mary that the car was there. But the door did not open, so she wasn't ready. Alan couldn't sit there as if he were reluctant to go in. He pulled himself from behind the wheel. It didn't matter, he would soon have Rose Mary to himself. And the Carrolls were all right. He liked them. They were still surprised at having him around, surprised that he could sit down and play a game of rummy with Mr. Carroll. Alan knew that they had thought it wouldn't last, that they didn't think he was serious about Rose Mary. They had been polite but standoffish, at first. But they changed when Rose

[57]

Mary said one night that they were going to the marriage-preparation class at the church. She said it shyly, with shining eyes, and she had never looked lovelier.

"Well, well," said Joe Carroll, "well, that's a fine thing. Those classes are a great thing. I was reading in *The Register* that they have them all over the country now. Pity there wasn't any in our day, Mamma." He winked. "I might have had a better wife."

"Pity for you," said Mrs. Carroll. "There was plenty you could have learned and still is."

Rose Mary was the flower of the Carroll flock. They all seemed to feel that, including the indistinguishable brothers and sisters. Rose Mary had been sent to a nearby Catholic college for girls, and as a boarding student. It had been a major expense for the Carrolls, involving sacrifices, but they were paid back in pride. For she had been the flower of the flock in college too, and her honors and popularity reflected glory on her family. She had a talent for dramatics, and pictures of her in various costumes competed in beauty on the walls of the living room. She laughed when her mother showed them off and said that ever so many people thought that Rose Mary should have gone to Hollywood.

"Oh, Mother, don't be silly—"

She hadn't tried to go to Hollywood. The nuns at her college gave special training in work on hospital and clinical records, and when Rose Mary graduated she found a job at once.

The records which she compiled at St. Barnabas Hospital included Alan Worthing's. He had been brought in for an emergency appendectomy, which gave trouble at the start, and it was two weeks before he was fully recovered. The feeling between him and Rose Mary had flamed up against the background of hospital corridors. When he went home he had her telephone number, and it went on from there.

"Good evening, sir," said Alan.

"Glad to see you, Alan," said Joe Carroll.

"How are you tonight, Mrs. Carroll?"

"Just fine. I want you to meet my sister. She just flew up from Chicago on the airplane. Kate, this is Rose Mary's friend."

"This is the young man I've been hearing so much about," said the middle-aged woman with sly interest. "This is a real pleasure. Rose Mary is a great favorite of mine, always was since she was just a little thing, all big blue eyes. I hear you're going to the Cana class. That's lovely."

The way she spoke was suddenly and strangely irritating to Alan. He felt that something was being taken for granted which he hadn't conceded.

"I hope I'm taking her out to dinner anyway," he said.

"Rose Mary, you'd better get a move on," called her mother. "The Cana class begins at eight, doesn't it? And you know how mad it makes Father when people trail in late. He'd call you down in front of everybody if he felt like it."

"Coming," answered Rose Mary.

She had the beauty that cannot be explained by its immediate source, that is scattered among women at random, but rarely. It was out of place in the small, ordinary room. The soft freshness of her skin, the pliancy of her body, the molding of her lips, the black-lashed violet eyes haunted Alan when he was not with her, and always surprised him when he saw her again. She was completely feminine, but not with guile. Her deference to the male in Alan was natural, unconscious.

"I'm sorry to keep you waiting. I just got home ten minutes ago."

"I haven't been waiting but a minute. All set?"

He felt awkward for some reason. He hardly ever felt that way in any company. Tonight he wanted to get Rose Mary out of here. Her mother, her father, and especially that aunt were standing there, all gloating over this deal—and that was all right, except that he was going to those lectures just to please Rose Mary. As he tucked Rose Mary into the car, he knew the family was watching, back of the white violets and the pedestal lamp, and he drove away quickly.

"Shall we go to the Flame?"

"I love it there. But they take so long to serve you. And we don't dare to have more than one drink if we're going to the class."

"Then let's not go to the class."

[59]

"Oh, we have to."

"Why do we?"

"You know—it's a course. Each talk in on a different subject, and he said that you wouldn't get the good out of it unless you heard them all. And you paid for the whole course."

"That doesn't matter. I'll take the loss. Let's skip it tonight, my sweet. I want you to myself."

"It's only an hour and a half."

"Let's settle it later," said Alan. "You know something?"

"What?"

"I'm in love—"

She would only take one cocktail at the restaurant. And when she looked at her watch an hour later and wished the waiter would hurry with the coffee, Alan tried again.

"We don't want to go way back to hear that talk tonight. It's raining anyway. Take your time and finish your lobster. How about a movie?"

"Not tonight. Honestly, Alan, we shouldn't miss it."

"You know all you need to know about marriage. You will. I'll teach you."

She looked at him with a shy devotion that made him tremble. She said, "Come on, please. Let's go—"

6

TONIGHT a different priest was conducting the marriage-preparation class, and Alan didn't like his looks. He didn't like being stuck up in the front row either. The bleak, efficient lights of the church's clubroom exposed thirty or more young men and women, most of them strangers to Alan. He had seen a couple of the men around town. He and Rose Mary had taken seats at the back of the room when they arrived, but the priest had requested them to move forward, and obediently Rose Mary had led the way.

Father Carter was plump and suave. His kindliness struck Alan as very professional. He looks like a eunuch, thought Alan. Probably he gets quite a kick out of talking about sex. This is certainly raw stuff he's dishing out. The first talk on the history of marriage had been all right, and the one last week on the way Catholics felt about divorce had made some good points, even if naturally you couldn't go along with it all the way. And that other priest was a nice old fellow. But tonight—if I'd known that we were going to have to sit and listen to this sort of thing for an hour, Rose Mary couldn't have dragged me here.

Having children was all right. But from the way this fellow laid it down, there was nothing else to being married. If he could have his way, the country couldn't feed the surplus population. He'd been pounding away on preventives and birth control for the whole talk, trying to throw a scare into these people. What was that story Mark had told him—the Catholics brought pressure on the hospitals to close up some birth-control clinic, that was it. You couldn't blame Mark for being sore.

The priest said solemnly, "So you must never forget that the frustration of the natural purpose of the act of generation is immoral. Any use of matrimony whatsoever in the exercise of which the act is deprived, by human interference, of its natural power to procreate life is an offense against the law of God."

The young man wearing large yellow shoes, who sat beside Alan, shifted his feet uncomfortably. Rose Mary was motionless, a beautiful statue of listening. Alan himself was embarrassed, both for her and because he had to sit there like a dope and pretend to swallow this whole. People had different problems. They had to work out these things for themselves. Decide for themselves—Mark had said that Catholics couldn't, never did—

"My dear young people, tonight I have emphasized and repeated the law of the Church, so that you will fully understand the conditions under which you may contract and live in accordance with the sacrament of marriage. I can only say to you further that if you are not willing to accept these conditions, do not marry. You are free to live in chastity and in single blessedness. But—do not marry and come to me later to say, 'Father, I am exhausted by bearing children. We think our family is big enough. We cannot afford another child.' I can make no exceptions for you. There are no exceptions to God's law. And never dare to come to me and whisper in the confessional, 'Father, I have committed murder!' "

He stopped dramatically, tasted the grave hush he had created in the room, then broke it. He said, dropping the threat from his voice, "That concludes the formal part of our program for tonight. Stand up and stretch for a minute, and then we will open the meeting for discussion."

Chairs scraped and Alan said in a low voice to Rose Mary, "Let's get out."

"We can't," she murmured.

"Why not?"

"It's so conspicuous. They'd think we didn't like it."

"They'd think right—"

"Please, Alan, sh—"

The priest resumed. "Now have any questions arisen in the minds of any of you?"

A young man with the manner of a high school debater stood up promptly.

"How large a family does the Church require you to have?"

Everyone laughed, the girls rather wildly.

The priest smiled with tolerance. "Catholics are not required to have large families. The only thing the Church insists on is that they must not exercise the marriage act in a sinful manner."

A girl spoke rather pertly, "But, Father, don't some people sin and get absolution anyway?"

Father Carter became stern. "Yes, people sin. It is always possible to consign your soul to hell. Wives and husbands come to my confessional every week. What they tell me are inviolable secrets. But to obtain absolution you know what they must do. They must make good confessions, holding back no sins. They must do penance and they must resolve to amend their lives. There must be sincere contrition. Otherwise they commit sacrilege, and God help those who do! But, my dear child, do not concern yourself with the sins of others. Your only task is to save your own soul."

[62]

Alan was thinking with distaste, it was this confession business that Mark was objecting to. But Rose Mary would never talk to a priest about us. She's too shy, too decent.

The questions grew fewer, scattered, stopped. They were out of the place at last, to Alan's enormous relief. It was raining heavily and they ran to the shelter of his car.

"What do you say to finding a band and doing a little dancing?" he suggested. He wanted to get back to normal, to overlay the last hour and a half.

"There's no good place open. It's Monday."

"That's right, it is Monday."

"And it's a horrid night out. We'd better go back to the house."

Alan didn't want to do that. Her family might close in on them. But where could they go? Not to his mother's home. She would make a project of being broadminded. He would have liked to take her out to meet Mark and Olive—that was a nice house and he wished Rose Mary could see it, but if Mark felt that way about his marriage—impatiently Alan wanted a place of his own, any kind of a place so long as it was his and nobody could interfere with them there. He drove a short distance, stopped the car in shadows and pulled Rose Mary close. The rain beat on the windows of the car, hammered on the canvas top. She gave him what she could. It wasn't enough.

"No, Alan, don't—"

"It's all right, sweet. We're going to be married—"

"But we aren't married yet—"

He allowed her gentle, distressed resistance to master him, let her go. She smoothed and ordered herself, and he pulled out a cigarette.

"This is no good," he said. "What are we waiting for? We haven't any place to go. And all this fooling around and letting everyone mix into our business gets me down."

"You don't seem like yourself tonight, Alan."

"Sorry. It's not your fault. It's all this interference. It's the damned advice. Everybody with his ten cents' worth. We can handle our own lives."

[63]

"You mean the class tonight?"

"Not just that. But that certainly was grim. That oily old bird—"

She had a bubble of a laugh, soft, involuntary. Alan loved her laugh. Sometimes he imagined how it would be to hear it—in the dark—after—

She laughed now as she said, "I don't like Father Carter as much as the other priests. Sometimes I think he missed his calling. He should have been an actor, he's so dramatic."

"A bad actor."

"But he's really very popular. They just crowd his confessional. There'll be long lines of people waiting for him when hardly anyone is going to the other priests."

"You wouldn't confess to him!"

"I go to him sometimes," she said indifferently. "But don't worry, someone told me that the next talk in the course is going to be given by Father Kenedy. You'll like him. He's just back from Rome. He's very intellectual."

"You'll never get me to another one of those affairs."

"Why, Alan, last time you said you liked it!"

"That was before they began to pull this kind of stuff. Honest to God, I've heard plenty of raw talk in my life, but that pretty nearly topped anything I've ever heard. In mixed company."

"What do you mean?"

"You heard him. According to him you have to have a baby every year or else."

She gave a soft sigh. "That's it—I would hate to be like that all the time."

"You won't be."

"Of course, lots of Catholics have small families. I mean it's just the way it happens. And there's—you know what he said about rhythm, that's not forbidden. It isn't that I don't love children— I do, but—"

"Don't worry. We'll figure it out when the time comes."

"I know it's the law—and, of course, they're right."

"Who's right?"

"I mean that the Church is."

[64]

"The Church may be right in its own field," said Alan, "but there are places where it doesn't belong. Some things men and women have to settle for themselves."

"Alan, let's not talk about it any more tonight. I'm not much good in an argument. But it will all be clear, I'm sure, before we finish the course—"

"The course is finished, as far as I'm concerned."

"You don't mean that."

"I sure do. God, didn't I feel a fool—"

"But, Alan—"

"Look, my sweet, I don't object to your religion. I know it means a lot to you and I want you to have it—"

"It's not a pet," she said. "You talk as if it's a pet or a hobby. Alan, religion's behind everything. You have to know what's right and what's wrong. Especially in the big things like getting married and dying. And if we go to the marriage course, you won't have to take nearly so many instructions."

"Instructions?"

"You know. When a girl marries a non-Catholic, there have to be instructions before you can do it."

"I've had plenty. I'll figure it out from here in."

"You can't. It isn't allowed. They wouldn't let us marry."

"I can run my own life."

"Of course. But nobody can break the laws of the Church."

"I can—I'm not a Catholic."

"But I can't. Oh, Alan, I do pray so hard for us. I love you so much!"

He reached toward her but couldn't reach what was troubling her. He fell into silence, trying to think it out. Then he said gently, "Rose Mary, let me ask you something, and don't take it wrong, will you?"

"Of course not."

"We're going to be married. We both want children, so that's no problem. But maybe the time may come when we don't want another. And when we're living together—I'll want you—"

He stumbled and she helped him.

[65]

"Go on—"

"What I'm trying to say is that, not being a Catholic, I don't have to do what your Church says is right or wrong. But you wouldn't go running to any priest and tell him what goes on between us, you wouldn't do that—"

"Not if it was right—"

"But maybe he wouldn't think it was right and I would?"

"If it's a sin you have to confess it, Alan."

"But you decide for yourself what's a sin—"

"You don't exactly decide for yourself—of course, you examine your conscience, you have to do that every time you go to confession—but you know what the sins are. They teach you those. They're all in the prayer book."

Alan said, "I guess Mark knew more about it than I did."

"Your brother Mark? I suppose he doesn't want you to marry a Catholic."

"Oh, the hell with that," said Alan. "It doesn't matter what anyone wants as long as you and I are sure."

"Did you talk to him about me?"

"I told him we were going to be married."

"When?"

"I had a talk with him this afternoon."

"That's why you feel this way tonight?"

"I feel fine tonight." He laughed to prove it.

"Did your brother tell you not to marry me?"

"Of course not! It wouldn't have made any difference if he had. I'm my own boss. But Mark isn't like that. No—what he said was that he thinks I should be married."

"But not to me."

"Mark will fall in love with you himself when he gets to know you."

She said, as if the reassurances didn't touch her, "Is it because of my family? Because we aren't important the way your family is? But you knew that—"

"Your family's grand," said Alan. "And don't get that idea about Mark. He's no snob, even if there were anything to be snobbish about, and there isn't."

"Then it's because I'm a Catholic."

"What is?"

"You're different tonight. I felt it. You didn't want to go to our class. Maybe I shouldn't have made you. You're different because you've talked to your brother. I know how much his opinion means to you. It sticks out all over you all the time. He's against me."

"You're wrong, Rose Mary. He said he'd heard only good things about you, that you were a beauty. He was just worrying the way an older brother does—he was a little afraid—"

"Afraid of what?"

"Well, it's just ignorance. He doesn't know many Catholics. He had an idea that there might be a children problem, about their education, I mean. He was afraid that we might not be able to decide things for ourselves. In the back of his mind, he may have had some idea that I was going over to your Church. I set him straight on that."

"He'd hate that, of course."

"Don't get the idea that Mark is a bigot," said Alan, "he's anything but that. But Mark is the sort of person who has to work things out for himself. The only thing that worries him about you and me seems to be—darling, are you crying?"

"Not much. Let's go home, Alan. I want to go home. I don't want to talk about religion any more—"

"Poor, sweet girl—my girl—I knew it would upset you to listen to that stuff tonight—that's why I wanted to get out of there—"

"But, Alan, we'll have to finish it! Or you'll have to go talk to the priest—"

"I'm not going to talk to your priest and I'm not going to talk to our rector," said Alan.

She did not ask him to come in, and he was glad she didn't. Much as he hated to leave her, it was better tonight. He drove away, thinking grimly that it would be all right when they were married, when he had her to himself, when she knew what it was all about.

The street lamp lit the row of white violets. Above, Rose Mary pulled down her window shade, began to undress. Then fear and love struggled for her so fiercely that she fell on her knees beside the bed, beating the counterpane.

"Oh, Mother of God, who has never refused anyone who had recourse to Thee, please grant him grace—let him become a Catholic in spite of his family—don't let it make any difference—make him go on with the class—"

7

ED ROFF said to Mark, "I didn't call any committee meeting on this business, Mark, because I thought that hashing it over wouldn't get anywhere, and I was afraid that the newspaper boys might get hold of it and then the fat would be in the fire for sure. I just moseyed around and talked to a few people who'd keep their mouths shut."

"How did you come out?"

"It's going to work out all right, I think," said Roff. "As a matter of fact, City Hospital will be glad in a way to get rid of that little clinic that's making the trouble. Not that they like to be pushed around any more than the rest of us. But the clinic didn't bring in any money. If they can use that space for another ward for county patients, they'll be able to get more money out of the county commissioners."

"What about the people running the clinic?"

"Well, they were pretty sore, of course. You can't blame them. They don't think that any one sect has a right to dictate in a general drive for funds. But they're going to be taken care of. Some of their backers were so hot under the collar that they've put up the money to lease another place, where the birth-control outfit can be on its own. I understand it's going to be close to Medical Center, handy for the doctors, a better setup. My guess is that Ike Elting came across with a big piece of money for it. If he did, he won't miss it, and he won't cut his other subscriptions either. Ike's a very good citizen."

Mark was frowning. He said, "It gets under my skin to have them put that over on us."

"I feel the same way. But what can you do? If we split with the Catholics in this campaign, it would tear the town wide open."

"Did you talk to that priest?"

"Not after the first time. You couldn't get anywhere with him. He has to do what he's told. I thought you should be the one to take it up with him now, tell him it's all ironed out. And I hope you bear down hard on him about getting his people to go out and bring in the money."

"They'd better deliver," said Mark grimly. "I'll get in touch with him. His name is Kenedy, isn't it?"

"That's right. He's a new man here. I think he's kind of a trouble shooter for the Bishop, from what they told me. You can probably locate him at the chancery office."

"I'll write him a letter," said Mark.

Roff said dubiously, "I don't know—one thing—I wouldn't make any record of this deal if I were you. I wouldn't put anything in writing that might set a precedent. Know what I mean? All we're going to admit is that this birth-control clinic is moving because it has found a better location, one it likes better than the one at City Hospital. So there isn't any problem."

"I see. That probably is the best way to handle it. I'll make sure that there's nothing in the minutes of the last meeting about it either. Just the statement that there was a discussion of the best method of soliciting funds."

"That's the idea."

"I'll ask that priest to come to see me. He won't get much out of me. Thanks, Ed. You did a real job on this."

"Well, I guess everybody's going to be happy," said Roff.

But Mark was not happy about it. When Effie, at his instruction, got Father James Kenedy on the telephone, Mark made no effort to keep the chill out of his own voice.

"This is Mark Worthing talking. In regard to the campaign for the consolidated hospital fund. Are you still representing Corpus Christi Hospital, or would it be better for me to talk to Mr. Nolan?"

The quiet answer had authority. "If it is possible for me to be of any service to the fund, I'll be glad to substitute for Mr. Nolan. I know he's a very busy man."

"Then at your earliest convenience will you come to see me?"

"Certainly. At almost any time that would be agreeable to you. This afternoon?"

"I'm sorry. I have a directors' meeting."

"Then could you give me a few minutes this evening?" asked the priest.

Mark had meant to have the meeting in his office. But tomorrow he was driving up to the taconite location. Let the priest come around to the house tonight. They were having dinner at home. Mark thought, I'd like to have Olive see this fellow anyhow.

"This evening would suit me very well. Could·you come to my house?"

"I'll be glad to, Mr. Worthing. At what time?"

"Shall we say about eight-thirty?"

Olive said, "I've never had a priest come to any house where I lived. What's the protocol?"

"I don't know, any more than you do. But we don't have to make any fuss over him. Treat him like anyone else. Take his hat and ask him to sit down. Begin with the weather."

"I'm not going to be around. This is your show."

"I'd really like you to size up this priest."

"Well, I'll stay for a few minutes to be polite and then leave you and him to have your talk or battle or whatever it is. I wish it didn't disturb you so much, Mark. It's going to work out all right."

"We took a beating. I'd like to tell Kenedy just what I think of this blackmailing stunt he pulled."

Olive said, "Of course, he won't look at it like that. He will think he's done his duty. But doesn't it seem strange that a church which keeps all its officials—what's the word I want—keeps them celibate, should think that they are competent or understanding enough to interfere with the most intimate things between men and women, like having children. They never have to wonder—or wait another week to see—or worry about having to move out of the

[70]

apartment if it happens, or pay the doctor's bill. They don't know what it is to be disappointed—that doesn't happen in their lives. What I mean is that the priests and the monks and the nuns don't mix personally in this lovely—suffering—terribly uncertain business—they can't possibly get close to it—and yet they dictate to other people about it. Don't they really know what the problems are of those people who go to birth-control clinics? How dreadfully embarrassing it must be? Why do they want people to be born against the will of their parents?"

"Maybe because it means more money in the collection box."

"Not from the poor!"

"They get something out of them," said Mark cynically. "The Catholic Church has always gone in for quantity, not quality."

"I don't think it's for money, Mark."

"Oh, probably not," admitted Mark. "I said that because the whole thing gets my goat." He added after a minute, "To be fair about it, I suppose they have a conviction that life is worthwhile no matter how it has to be lived. It's an old church. They can take the long view. Maybe, philosophically, they have a case."

"But children who aren't wanted," said Olive, incompletely, pityingly.

"What I can't understand," said Mark, "is why Catholics do as they're told. Or pretend to. Is it because they're scared or because they believe it? It's the compulsion that interests me. It must be terrific."

"It's very hard even to imagine it, I should think, unless you are one of them."

"That's what I tried to make Alan realize."

"You did?"

"I told him that the priests would have influence, a big hold over this girl that he wants to marry. She can't go along with him— you know what I mean—if they lay down the law, say it's wrong. And he says she takes her religion very seriously. Poor Al, he's really up against something."

"Darling, if Alan wants her, there's nothing to be done about it. You mustn't spoil it for him."

"I haven't done anything to spoil it."

"I hope not. But from what you've told me, you were pretty outspoken."

"All I wanted him to do—and I told him so—was to look at the thing from every angle."

"But he didn't come to you for that. Pamela had hurt him—I'm sure of that. And your mother wouldn't be much help, though she adores him. People should be congratulated on being in love—they need to feel that they've accomplished something wonderful—and they have—and that everyone is happy because they are—"

"I told Alan we'd both like to see him married. But when he asked me how I'd personally feel about marrying a Catholic, I had to give him an honest answer. I couldn't do anything else."

"How could you know how you'd feel about marrying a Catholic unless you were in love with one!"

Mark laughed and said, "Well, don't worry. I didn't make a dent in him."

"You don't know." Olive gave a little shiver, and said, "Alan's lonely—he's never been loved enough." She crossed the room, kissed her husband, and said, "You weren't either, until I got hold of you. I'm going upstairs and bed down the children. Better light a fire in the study. Show your priest how cheerful a sinful Protestant home can be!"

When she came downstairs half an hour later, Father Kenedy had arrived. As Olive met him for the first time—always afterward it was the same—she was conscious of a serenity, detachment, and confidence that seemed strange in so young a man. She could tell that his attitude was not put on for the occasion. It was not a cover-up for shyness or uncertainty. This is the way he is, thought Olive, realizing in the same instant that he was an unusual person, thinking that few people whom she had ever met had given her a like impression. Was there in fact anyone else? Assertiveness, cocksureness—they were common enough. So were the vanity of a bigoted point of view and self-satisfaction. From what Mark had told her of the priest's insistence, she had been prepared to find any or perhaps all of these attitudes in him. They were not there. She felt something impersonal in Father Kenedy that chilled her.

She had thought that she would not like this priest. But she had meant to be tolerant and as pleasant as a hostess should be. She liked him less than she had expected. She did not know why. Instantly he put her on guard. He antagonized her. Not because he did not meet her as a man usually did, with the observation of beauty and gallantry of sex. She felt that in the greeting of almost any stranger, of men old enough to be her father, of men who deeply loved their wives, of the man who came to fix the furnace. The priest offered her none of that basic, often unconscious admiration.

Olive felt the lack, but she was not vain enough to resent it. What she did not like was an indifference which he brought into her house, as if the charm of the home and the warm human relations within it were not important. A dirty basement room, a castle, herself or some other woman as Mark's wife—it wouldn't make any difference to him, thought Olive as, after all, she did begin with the weather. His sights are on something else. She felt as if she were an interruption. Of course, his business was with Mark.

She glanced from Father Kenedy to her husband. Mark was regarding the priest with interest, as if he were trying to make him out. Suddenly Olive wanted Mark to get this over with. This was not the kind of person who belonged in this house. She felt absurdly as if an enemy were under their roof. He'd never understand us or the way we feel and live, she thought. He comes from a different world.

He was younger than his graying hair. He doesn't take good care of himself, thought Olive. He was tall, bony, in cheap clerical-cut black clothes, knobby-toed shoes. His heavy eyebrows drew straight lines under the forehead of a thinker. His complexion was white, and Olive thought curiously that confessionals were probably dark as cellars. His hands were pallid too. An ascetic mouth and strange eyes. Not cold eyes—there was a kind of radiance—but they were not warmed by the interests of most men.

How much more handsome Mark is, thought Olive. How much more human. He wants me to stay, but I won't. He'll get rid of the priest more quickly if I don't make this into a social visit.

She left the room and Mark offered his caller a cigar. He had a notion that all priests smoked cigars. Father Kenedy refused. He had his own cigarettes and lit one.

"I appreciate your coming in tonight," said Mark. "I wanted to make sure there was no misunderstanding about the campaign for the hospitals. I've had a talk with Mr. Roff. He fully explored the situation and he didn't see any reason for calling his committee together to discuss it further at this time. He told me that there was no cause for concern about that matter which seemed to be worrying you. The little clinic which was mentioned has found a new and fortunately a better location for its work."

"Is the new location disassociated from any of the hospitals which are connected with the fund drive?" asked Father Kenedy.

"That is correct."

"I am very glad to hear it. I am grateful. It would have been unfortunate if our Catholic hospital and our people could not have shared in this fine project."

"I should think it would have been too bad for any hospital to be left out," said Mark coldly. "Mr. Roff is counting on you to get him some good solicitors."

"I'll surely do my best. And I hope you'll express my gratitude to Mr. Roff for his good offices."

I'm not fooling him for a minute, thought Mark. He said, "There's no particular reason for gratitude. The matter has been arranged to the satisfaction of everyone. I am glad to say that the clinic will continue in business. Personally, I would have objected if it was forced to shut up shop."

"I can't go along with you on that. We realize, of course, that you think we were not co-operative."

"Other words occurred to me," said Mark dryly.

"Such as blackmail," said Father Kenedy, smiling.

"You take the word out of my mouth."

"I wish I could prevent it from poisoning your thoughts in regard to Catholic doctrine, Mr. Worthing."

Mark said, "I may as well be frank. I can't understand your point of view. These people that you had your ax out for, Father Kenedy, are only trying to help poor creatures who can't take decent care of the children they might bring into the world. It seems to me a good service."

"There's no doubt that the advocates of birth prevention often have the good intention of alleviating human misery and want."

"If you admit that, why do you fight them?"

"We cannot allow Catholics to support action which is declared to be wrong by Holy Mother Church."

"I think it was brought out the other day that Catholics support the action anyhow—there's no doubt that some of them go to clinics like that."

"The law may not be accepted by people who are nominally Catholics. And there are always those who fall into error. But any Catholic who practices his religion must obey the law," answered the priest quietly.

"When did your Church make that law?" asked Mark. "In the Middle Ages? Standards of living were different then."

"The Church did not make the laws regarding the obligations of married persons. They are derived from the natural law, which is nothing else than the law of God."

"Other sects interpret the law of God differently."

"That does not alter truth," said the priest.

The words aroused a curious stir in Mark's mind. Truth, he thought. That's how they hold the people. The priests make Catholics believe that they know the truth, that everyone else is a liar or off the beam. He looked at the priest, clothed in certainty, and for an instant felt a kind of envy. Then he wiped that out with his own good sense.

He said, "Well, Father, your law makes it tough for the lower-income brackets."

"Not so tough as loss of faith would be."

We're going around in circles, thought Mark. But he wanted to dig some more out of this fellow while he had him here.

He said, "Of course, Father Kenedy, nobody can help admiring the organization of the Catholic Church. It's amazing how it holds together, jumps over national lines and all that. But I should think it would be self-defeating."

"In what way?"

"It leaves you with people on your hands who have no wills of their own. I don't like to use the word *slaves*—but after all, Catholics do seem to the outside observer to be moral slaves. The Catholic is deprived of free will. He has to take what you put in the package."

"On the contrary," said Father Kenedy, "the will plays a prominent part in the act of faith. It is the will which directs the mind to God. May I stay on a few minutes? May I explain a little further?"

"I very much wish you would," said Mark. "Can I get you a little drink?"

"Thank you. A light bourbon and soda would be fine."

Mark mixed it and brought the glasses back with a feeling of something like adventure. He'd never had an opportunity to talk with one of these priests before. This was a chance to find out just what their angle was. The fire blazed lazily. He was going to enjoy this argument.

Waiting upstairs, glancing again at the clock, Olive wondered why the priest hadn't left. It couldn't have taken as long as this for Mark to explain the situation about the birth-control clinic. Maybe Father Kenedy had brought up some new obstruction. Poor Mark —the thing made him so furious, and it would make him feel even worse about Alan and the Carroll girl. If those two were deeply enough in love, the religion might be an irritant once in a while, but it wouldn't be a real problem. Olive went downstairs again, paused outside the open door of the study to get the drift of what had been going on for nearly an hour. Mark was saying something.

"But no matter how you try to cover it up, faith is intellectual submission."

"Oh, no," said the priest, "faith is the highest and most completely free act of which the intellect is capable."

I'd better break this up, Olive decided. Those two could never agree on anything.

She felt the impasse as she entered, but it wasn't uncomfortable or contentious as she had feared. The men looked poised and interested. Mark seemed more relaxed than he had been at dinner.

"I hope I'm not interrupting," said Olive. "Please go on."

Mark laughed. "I'm afraid we've come to a dead end, darling."

"Oh, I hope not," said Father Kenedy.

"Perhaps we can talk again sometime," said Mark, to his wife's surprise.

"It would be a pleasure." The priest got up, refused to have his drink freshened.

"There is one other thing I'd like to speak about, Mr. Worthing," he said. "Perhaps I'm in a poor position to ask a favor, but it's not for myself."

"Go right ahead with it."

"I drove up the other day to the location of the new little village by the taconite plant you're building. That's going to be a very pleasant place to live, with the great lake in full sight."

"We hope they'll like it there."

"I understand that the houses are for rent or sale but that the store building and the schoolhouse are owned by your company."

"We had to underwrite those. But we're not in the real estate business."

"What I wanted to ask was whether a room in the little schoolhouse might be made available for church services. It's a long drive to the city for those who must go to Mass on Sunday."

"I don't know how many of them there would be."

"Always more than you imagine," said the priest with confidence.

"The school isn't equipped for church services."

"We would take care of all that, and I can promise that there would be no damage to the building. We would be glad to pay some rental for the privilege."

"I don't think that would be necessary. If the arrangement is possible. I'd have to think it over and talk to my directors."

"Of course. It would be quite temporary, I hope. Those who live there permanently would soon undoubtedly want to build a little chapel that could be properly consecrated."

"You expect to have priests move in out there?" asked Mark, suddenly resistant.

"More likely it would be run as a mission," said Father Kenedy.

[77]

Olive said, to divert Mark, "That was a mission at Chippewa Lake, you know."

He said with surprise, "How do you know so much about it?"

"I used to drive the cook in every Sunday," said Olive, "that summer when I had the Hadley lodge, you remember."

Mark said, "That summer—yes, I remember."

8

OLIVE felt that she had known nothing about marriage until she became Mark Worthing's wife. The piecemeal, untrustworthy relationship she had endured with Tony Grant for five years had been a series of bad bargains, in each of which she had paid out all she had at the time and got nothing worth having in return. When finally he deserted her, he left her convinced that she was not beautiful enough, rich enough, or sexual enough to hold a man's desire.

"Why did you want to marry me in the first place?" she asked Tony when it was obvious that he did not want to go on with it. As if she thought that if she could get at the original reason she could try again to build on it. She hung on past humiliation, past the sharp point where cynicism began, past the time when she saw Tony Grant as he was always going to be.

When she met him first, he was living in a dreamed-up future and it was that future he offered her. He was still in uniform, still getting government pay and privileges, and able to promise anything to anybody, for delivery after he was separated from the Navy. Possibly he himself didn't know why he married Olive. When she pressed him for an answer, he said first one thing and then another. Of course she was beautiful. One other thing was certain. He thought there was more money back of her than there turned out to be.

He was a ruthless and expensive young man, who had no intention of ever living on mean streets or buying savings bonds. The houses of his rich friends suited him, and he paid his way by being good at gentlemanly sports. From the start, Olive failed him in several ways. Her only rich uncle did not endow her marriage, somehow having got the notion that her husband could and would look after her needs. Olive did not do her part in weaving together a succession of invitations so that they could stay luxuriously with "people they knew" for a good part of the time. Nor was she clever about avoiding pregnancies or doing something to check them soon enough.

Olive was an orphan. She had a little money of her own, tied up in a trust fund that couldn't be tampered with or altered. She spread the income from that over the edges of their bills. Tony, out of uniform, tested various occupations. None of them stuck to him or he to them. For a few months he was on a television circuit doing sports reporting. Briefly he was in a brokerage office. And he had windfalls. He would win a steeplechase event which offered a big money prize. He was lucky at cards and in Calcutta pools. But his real talent lay in exploiting social connections. He would get the use of a guesthouse on some estate. He would drive a Cadillac or Jaguar north or south, as a favor to some friend.

The important things to Olive, in her life with him, soon became the small income from the trust fund, comfort and safety for first one baby and then two, and cocktails, which could make things matter less for a few hours. Nothing else was sure, neither lodging nor fidelity. She tried desperately not to overhear the things that were said about them, in pity for her, in contempt for Tony, in question as to how long their marriage would last.

It lasted until Tony met the right girl. She had a couple of million dollars, a stable of good horses, and a ruthless resolution to do what she wanted that exactly matched his own. To speed up the thing, Tony had to walk out on Olive, and he did. To prove how right he had been, there was his picture in the current *Town and Country* magazine—a laughing, handsome member of a group at a very fashionable resort in Virginia. Olive had come upon it in the dentist's office and stared for a minute at a picture of a stranger that sickened her.

After the divorce she had the children to look after. She got her decree in Nevada, because after she realized that Tony had gone for good and why, haste in wiping out every claim to him seemed a matter of decency, almost of cleanliness, to Olive. The six weeks in Reno had no personality. She did everything that had to be done, saw lawyers, signed papers, took the children to a park to play, read rented books instead of sleeping. When it was over, she decided to go to Minneapolis for the thin reasons that her mother had come from there, that someone had told her there was a remarkable nursery near the university where women who had part-time jobs could safely leave their children, and because she and Tony had never been together in that city.

She had cousins in Minneapolis, but she was determined not to be a burden to them. Olive was searching for an honest base. Only a few people knew how badly off she was, for though one of Tony's windfalls had helped pay for the divorce, she couldn't take alimony for it would have to come from Tony's new wife. She was even more poor in spirit. But it didn't show. Her natural elegance kept her from looking poor even in old or cheap clothes, and she never told anyone that the worst thing Tony Grant had done to her was to destroy her faith in herself.

She was in that secret state of shock when her cousin Maud Hadley offered her the use of the family lodge on the Brule River in Wisconsin for the summer. Olive refused with gratitude. She wanted to do no more sponging, though the alternative would be living in a couple of hot rooms near the nursery.

Mrs. Hadley insisted. She had warm memories of Olive's mother, and the plight of the girl troubled her. She said that it was really true that Olive would be doing her a favor by taking over the place. The lodge would deteriorate if it was not aired or opened. She and her husband did not want to rent it or offer it to careless people. They were going to be in Europe for the three summer months, and what to do with their country place was a problem.

Olive had visited there once or twice when she was a young girl. She remembered the clear river, the enormous pines—thought she remembered a remoteness and peace that she hadn't needed then.

"But isn't there a colony of gay people along the river?" she asked. "I'm not any good socially right now."

Maud Hadley said, "You don't have to see a living soul unless you want to. That's one of the Brule traditions. It's the reason we all adore it. People leave each other alone—unless you invite them to come around and if you're invited, you can go or not as you please. Your nearest neighbors would be the Worthings from Lakehead. Did you ever know them?"

"No."

"Well, they won't bother you. You can't even see their place from our dock. And they always bring their own friends. I know it would be good for the children, and it certainly will take a load off my mind to know that you are looking after the place. And the right kind of job is much more apt to open up for you in the fall than now."

Such kindness was irresistible.

To Olive the loneliness of the next weeks was delicious. The Hadley lodge was a rambling, old shingled house that had always been used generously and affectionately. It felt and looked that way. Things that had been left there could and did grow old without fear of being discarded. A rainbow trout, mounted and hung on one wall of the living room, had been proving someone's good luck for more than thirty years. The bad painting of a bend of the river would always stay there, uncriticized. On the tables were books that had been enjoyed—Little Women, War and Peace, Trader Vic's Recipes, How to Make Trout Flies. A book that no one had ever read, The Basis of the Capitalistic System, lay in its fading jacket, with pages uncut but respected.

The coverlets on the beds were handwoven and beautiful, the comforters filled with down. A rug in one bedroom had been chewed some years before by a squirrel, before he was discovered in his housebreaking. There was plenty of china, some of it rare, but few perfect dozens of cups and plates. The bathtub which the children used was of enameled tin. It was still all right inside, although there were one or two marks that couldn't be scrubbed away. There were great, shabby chairs, a hard old-fashioned settle, as well as the big, burrowing couches, and much silvery wicker in all sorts of useful and ridiculous shapes. A willow workbasket was lined in faded green. Fireplaces faced in stone were ready for use in the living and dining rooms, and there were neat woodpiles outside the back doors. For some reason, a map of southern Asia had been tacked in the corridor near the row of pegs on which several fishing poles were laid horizontally.

Whoever had built the house had known that the river would always be the real host. The long porches never let it out of their sight. The sound of the hastening stream was constant in the bedrooms at night when the windows were open, as they almost always were. Olive lay awake at first to listen, but after a few nights she trusted it to go on while she slept.

She had been in beautiful settings before. In her life with Tony, she had become used to the filtered swimming pools and the bright beaches where wealth was exercised. She had seen racecourses almost as well groomed as the horses that won on them. She had been a guest in houses that had been restored to an over-perfected past, or projected into a future that didn't yet exist. She had been lonely before too, in beautiful places.

But this loneliness was as different as the beauty was different. She did not feel deserted here nor as if she were intruding. For company Olive had the growing, mysteriously changing children, and even the baby in her crib seemed to listen to the river. Olive also had her isolation broken by the sight of fishermen wading the river, casting skillfully and patiently, and sometimes lifting the lid of the baskets slung on their shoulders to drop a trout inside. That was pleasant companionship.

She talked to almost no adult except Agnes Dupray, the middle-aged woman who lived on one of the scanty farms nearby and was hired by the Hadleys to clean and cook.

"We have to pay Agnes anyway—she'd starve without the money she earns in the summer—and if we once let her go, somebody else

[82]

on the river would hire her and we'd never get her back, for help
is so scarce," Mrs. Hadley had explained to Olive. "Let her do all
she can for you. There's only one problem about Agnes. She always
thinks she has to go to church on Sunday; she's a Catholic. She
hasn't any car, and when we aren't there, I suppose she thumbs
a ride into Lake Chippewa Sunday mornings. There's a little
church there. When she's working for us, Warren or I usually
drive her in. There's an old station wagon there. It doesn't look
like much, but it still runs and it goes with the place. I don't know
how you'd be able to take Agnes to church because of the children
—just tell her so—"

"I can manage it easily," said Olive. "If I can't leave the children
I'll take them along. Tim will go quite mad over a station wagon."

"You need it to go to town for the groceries. There aren't any
deliveries."

Mark Worthing had first seen Olive in the Co-op store at a cross-
roads town three miles from the lodges along the river. He had
come in to get some cigarettes and rubber tape, and his sister,
Lucy Searles, had asked him to bring back six quarts of strawberries
if they were any good. The two Searles were spending a couple of
weeks at the Worthing lodge, and Mark had come down for
Saturday and Sunday to fish.

Olive was considering buying one quart of strawberries. She
was wearing faded blue shorts, red tennis shoes and a blue-striped
cotton blouse. Her hair fell to her shoulders in denial of the boyish
clothes, and an Alice-in-Wonderland celluloid band held it across
the top of her sun-tanned head. She was holding Tim's hand and
swinging it back and forth to amuse him, as she tried to decide
whether twenty-nine cents for a quart of strawberries was an
unjustified extravagance.

They looked so country, so fresh-picked. They would be sweet.
It was a long time since she had felt so tempted by any food, and
it made her feel young and foolish. This morning as she had
rattled along in the old station wagon, she had rejoiced because
two months more of this kind of life lay ahead. To be happy seemed
possible again. Happiness was natural to Olive—perhaps Tony

[83]

Grant had married her for the thing he had destroyed—and this morning she had felt it come back, like a kind of physical strength. Two more months—she would be strong enough for anything by that time.

The laugh in her voice was at herself as she said, "Do you think we should have a box of beautiful strawberries, Tim?"

"They do look good, don't they?" said Mark.

She looked up. The hand stopped swinging. He saw that this was no Alice in Wonderland, no girl with her little brother. This was a woman who wanted to be left alone.

"Yes, very," she said in cold politeness and would have gone away quickly without the strawberries if Tim hadn't yelled that he wanted them.

Mark wondered a minute and forgot her. But that afternoon, when he was one of the quiet men in waist-high waders and old slouch hats fishing the stream, he passed the dock of the Hadley place and saw Olive again. She was in a bathing suit, guarding the little boy as he paddled around in the water, and there must have been a baby in the clothesbasket on the dock, for every now and then she leaned over the basket and spoke with love to something. She had a beautiful body, but it was the sound of her voice that made Mark say to himself that some man was certainly lucky.

But strangers beware, he thought, remembering the way her look had frozen in the grocery as he had spoken to her. He didn't repeat that mistake now. Half-turned away, he took out his fly box and stood there for a few minutes, changing the fly on his line. She paid no attention to him.

"Many people on the river?" he asked Lucy when they were having drinks before dinner.

"Greg says that he thinks every camp must be open."

"I thought I saw signs of life at the Hadley lodge as I passed it."

"Oh, yes, you know who's there, don't you?"

"I saw some kids."

"You didn't see the mother?"

"I wouldn't know her if I saw her." Mark was always careful

with Lucy in mention of any girl. Her mind ran to that sort of thing instinctively.

"Blonde," said Lucy, "quite handsome. I saw her in the village. I've never met her, but of course I know about her."

"What's there to know?"

"She's some relation to the Hadleys, a cousin or niece. They're in Europe and let her have the place. She's just been divorced—you know who it was—from that Tony Grant who married the Middlecoff girl. Middlecoff Drugs. His picture was in *Town and Country* this month. Where is that copy?"

"Don't look for it on my account," said Mark. "Is this girl staying there alone?"

"I guess so. I'd ask her over for you, but I don't believe she wants to know people. She's been here for weeks and I haven't seen her at anyone's place."

"Isn't that the best idea around here?"

"Well, up to a point. But you'd think she'd be awfully dreary."

She didn't look dreary until I spoke to her, thought Mark.

"You know who she was, Mark."

"Don't keep accusing me of knowing things, Lucy. I'm not to blame."

"Her mother was a Wayne from Minneapolis."

"I've heard the name. I think they were in the lumber business."

"It used to be a prominent family. I'm sure Papa would have known them. I forget who told me, but it was someone who would know. We were talking about this girl the other day, the one at the Hadleys' who's just been divorced—"

"Or maybe doing the divorcing—"

"Well, whichever—he seems to have come out better than she has. Anyway she's had a terrible life. It seems that her father killed himself back in the depression—"

She wouldn't have been more than a baby then, thought Mark. He said, "That would be a bad start."

"Then something happened to the mother; apparently she died, and this girl was brought up by some uncle or other—all this was in the East, it seems to me it was near Philadelphia. She's just now

[85]

turned up out here—probably because of the Hadleys' giving her this place for the summer. She looks quite attractive—maybe I'll ask her over for cocktails."

"I'd leave her alone," said Mark. "She probably knows what she wants."

Olive had worked out a routine so that she could take Agnes to eight o'clock Mass on Sunday morning. Pierre Dupray, Agnes's husband, stayed at the lodge with the children for those two hours. He was a half-breed Indian, and Tim thought he was wonderful. He whittled things for Tim, whistles and little boats, while Jenny took her morning nap. That was better than to take the children along and have them swelter in the summer heat while Agnes was at her devotions.

Agnes loved to go to church. To her it was evidence of being respectable and of having a share in parish social life. Besides, she had to go.

"If you miss a Sunday, they can tell by your envelope," she told Olive.

"Envelope?"

"With your dollar. You always have to write your name on the envelope. They send you one for every week and for the special collections, and if you miss, Father says you have to bring it the next time."

The service was supposed to be over at nine, but on the first Sunday it was much later when the congregation poured out, and Agnes was full of apologies.

"I thought he'd never begin Mass! I'm sorry to keep you waiting like this, but there wasn't anything I could do about it. There was such a terrible lot of people waiting to be heard—"

"Heard?"

"To go to confession—he hears them before Mass because he has to come all the way from Superior. This is a mission church; the priest doesn't live here. And now with so many people living in cabins on the lakes all around here and coming to the eight o'clock, there's a lot of confessions."

"Do people who are on holidays have to go to church?"

"Oh, they have to, if there's a church within a reasonable distance. It's nice for the church, for in the summer the money comes in from all the strangers. And there's still a big debt for the furnace, and now Father wants a new organ—the old one's got a funny whistle in it—you never can tell when it's coming. But two collections—it used to be that a dollar a Sunday was the most anyone gave, and now they want two, though plenty of people don't put in more than a nickel when the box comes around the second time."

"Put this in for me the second time," said Olive, "and say a prayer for me, Agnes."

"Why, I sure will, Mrs. Grant. Thank you!"

Olive was in no position to be lavish with dollar bills, but she felt that she should make some recognition of the service going on in this shabby little church set in a plot of weedy grass at the edge of the village street. She parked her car under a maple tree that offered the only shade near by, and watched the people stream in, time-conscious and hurrying.

There were women wearing slacks, with scarves tied over their heads, who would be the "summer people" who came from the cabins on the lakes. Children slicked up, but in blue jeans. Dressy little girls with bonnets that matched their purses, obviously wearing their Easter clothes. The older women in hats must be villagers. A young man came, carrying a baby who was certainly about to cry, and his wife pulled on white nylon gloves as she followed. They didn't have anyone to leave the baby with, thought Olive, but they came anyway. They must think that they have to.

She felt out of place. She would have felt the same on the edge of a picnic ground watching a crowd with which she wouldn't naturally mingle, or in a store where she wouldn't find anything she wanted to buy. She felt somehow apologetic for being different from these people, and she hoped she wasn't conspicuous. In the glove compartment she found a reprint of a detective story and tried to interest herself in the crime.

On the next Sunday it was very hot. Another car had parked

under the maple tree, and the old wooden station wagon when not in motion became hot as an oven. Olive had forgotten to bring anything to read. She chased a bee out of the car. She thought idly, that man in the grocery who spoke about the strawberries must be one of the colony on the river. The last thing I want to do is to meet any of those people. I have to figure things out, make a fresh start, make plans. I have two months—not quite two months—more.

The door of the church was open and tempting. Maybe it's cool in there, thought Olive. Churches are always cool. I could slip in the back, no one would notice me. You have to wear something over your head in a Catholic church. It doesn't matter what it is. At the big Catholic weddings a band of flowers is enough. In Europe you see people with handkerchiefs on their heads in the cathedral. Kleenex won't do, and I don't have a handkerchief. Maybe there's a scarf in the glove compartment.

There was a soft, old red-silk one at the very back, under a dusty book of instructions. She shook it out and folded and knotted it over her head, glanced in the rearview mirror, and left the car, going lightly up the sidewalk to the church door.

It wasn't cool. It was stifling. And crowded. But a man at the back was indicating that there was a seat over there. She couldn't turn around and go out without being insulting. She slipped into the vacant place. It wasn't pleasant. The nearest window was only open half an inch, and the little church smelled of its unopened weekdays, of the big hot man in a sport shirt darkened by sweat, who stood up to let her get into the pew.

Nothing was going on up in front. Two half-burned candles were lighted on the altar, but no one was there. Olive heard a broken whisper behind her and realized that she was sitting very near the confessional. They do it like that, she thought. I don't understand how they can.

Another whisper, this one smooth like a blessing; then a girl went up the side aisle. She must have been in there, thought Olive. I wonder what she told him. A minute later, a cassocked priest, mopping his forehead, strode down the aisle and disappeared behind curtains near the altar. When he reappeared he was carrying a covered thing which he put on the altar, and the rites began. Kneeling, standing, a quick mutter of Latin—a baby began to cry painfully. Everybody seemed to know just what they should do and when. Now they all sat down again and the priest came to the edge of the chancel and began to speak in English.

It was hardly a sermon. He seemed a determined, not very friendly young man. He said that he knew the Mass did not begin on time, but that an immortal soul was more important than a waiting breakfast, and that he would hear every confession no matter how long it took. He gave the hours of the services and said that the second collection would be for the seminaries which educated priests, that there was a shortage of priests and must be more. He said he would read them a letter from the Bishop, which in graver and more dignified language said the same thing. The priest finally said that he wanted to talk to the local men's committee at the end of the service, that the furnace must be paid for, and the church painted, that a new altar cloth and vestments were needed.

Then he resumed the service, and when people began to stand up and move, Olive did the same, until she realized that the others were going up to the altar and she was moving toward the door. Most of the congregation seemed to be in motion. She was going against the tide, but it was not far to the door and she slipped out, feeling now that even the heat was fresh.

What do they get out of it, she asked herself, pausing on the sidewalk to untie the red scarf. An open car, smart and expensive, rushed by on the highway. Mark, coming back from the airport where he had met some guests of Lucy's, saw Olive again, and this time she recognized him, for he turned his head to look at her with curiosity. He said to himself, so she's a Catholic girl. I thought Catholics didn't go in for divorces.

Often in the summer afternoons there were thunderstorms. They came like fits of temper in the overheated hours. Thunder would mutter resentfully, lightning petulantly strike at the clouds, and finally the sky would burst into a rain of weeping, until it had cooled off. Then it would quickly clear and seem to pretend that it hadn't had a tantrum, thought Olive in amused fancy. To Timmy she made the storms seem like displays of fireworks. They sat on the deep-eaved porches and enjoyed them.

But it was different on one Sunday afternoon in July. Agnes had gone home after lunch and was not coming back until tomorrow. Olive and Timmy were hunting for blueberries in the woods close to the cottage, where she could hear the baby if she woke and cried. She became conscious of a darkening sky and didn't like the way it looked. It was purple, blackening and heavy. This was going to be a bad storm.

"It's a funny time to get night," said Timmy.

"It's going to storm," said Olive. "Come on, run back with me. We'll sit on the porch and watch the fuss."

The darkness became almost sinister. We'll stay inside, decided Olive, picking up a few cushions that might get wet on the porch if the rain should be a driving one. She turned on a couple of lamps and was busy with the baby when she heard a roar of wind and a moan among the pines, as if the trees knew what was coming. Looking out again, she saw the small trees bending, trying to escape, the big ones proudly resisting. She went out and brought in all the books and magazines from the porches.

The thunder barked sharply, and the almost-black sky was cut with jagged lightning. Nothing can happen, thought Olive. Then the lights went out, and as the rain came in so wild and driven a way that it was like an attack, the wind began to destroy. There was a crack, a curious soft smash, and Olive realized that a tree had fallen somewhere near. She hoped it wasn't a big one, and then another fell, and another. Through the windows that were almost dark, she saw toppling, struggling shapes.

"Turn on the light," begged Timmy.

"The light's broken, Tim. We'll light some candles. Come, we'll do it together." She held his hand and kept the baby in her arms as she hunted for candles. If anything should happen to the roof, she must protect them with her body. Now the tempest was mad

[90]

outside, and destruction seemed completely loosed. I shouldn't have brought the children to this place, thought Olive—all my life I've done everything wrong—I mustn't let Timmy know I'm frightened.

"Isn't it exciting, Timmy? This is like the pioneer days with only candles. The Indians used to have to stay outdoors in storms like this." Oh God, please spare us!

A tree hit the roof. She could hear bricks fall from the chimney. A few came down the aperture and smashed on the hearth. Timmy moved toward them, and Olive cried out, "No, Timmy, stay here!"

Incredibly, the door opened, and a man, streaming with rain, turned to force it shut with his shoulder.

"Hello," he said. "How are you coming over here?"

"I don't know—the trees are falling all around!"

"Yes, a lot of them have gone down. How do you like the storm, young man?" asked Mark Worthing, without sounding panicked.

"It's worse than the Indians were out in," said Timmy proudly.

"You bet. That's the spirit," said Mark. He looked at Tim's mother. The candlelight showed courage over fear in her bearing and utter welcome in her eyes.

"Don't worry," he said, "I think we got the tail of a tornado, but these things don't last. The worst is over now."

"It's so good of you to come—"

"I just wanted to be sure you were all right over here. I'm Mark Worthing. I'm a neighbor of yours. At least, I'm visiting my sister on this quiet Sunday. There are some scared people over at our house."

"I'm Olive Grant," she said. "But it was so dangerous to come through the woods with all those trees falling!"

"I know my way around here pretty well," said Mark. "See, it's definitely getting lighter now. Do you feel all right?"

"I'm fine now. It was just not knowing what to do—that there wasn't anything I could do—and being alone with the children—"

"I'm afraid you think we've not been very sociable."

"I'm the one."

"But you know we're here—somebody is—if you want anything. We are friends of the Hadleys, of course."

"They let me have the place for the summer."

"And you like it?"

"It's been heaven—until this afternoon."

"You looked as if you were enjoying yourself."

"Did I? When?"

"When I saw you in the co-op. And when I've been fishing I've seen you on the dock with this young fellow. I saw you coming out of your church in Lake Chippewa last week. That's better than the rest of us do on Sunday."

"I was there under false pretenses. I can't claim it as my church. I'd driven over the woman who works for me, and went in to get out of the heat. Don't give me any credit for piety."

He laughed. He didn't know why, but he was glad to hear that it wasn't her church.

The light was almost natural now. They went out on the veranda, where the wicker chairs were strewn and tipped over, and viewed the tragedy of broken Norway pines that should have lived nobly for another half-century.

She said, "It's dreadful to see them like that!"

"It will mean a big clean-up job up and down the river. I never knew anything like this to happen here before."

"What should I do?" asked Olive. "The Hadleys are in Europe."

"Oh, we'll all get together on this," Mark told her. "We'll have to get a crew in here."

In spite of the damage, he was feeling cheerful. Since he had opened the door, he had known that his instinct was right. When the storm broke and he thought of her alone, he had to come. This girl and her children needed protection. He couldn't leave her without it.

9

I<small>T WAS</small> the morning after the conversation at his house with
Father Kenedy, and Mark Worthing was on his way to inspect
the progress of the taconite-processing plant which his company was
developing on the north shore of Lake Superior. The location of it
was seventy miles from the city, but at the speed Mark drove, it
would take him less than an hour and a half to get there. The day
was clear and the weather cool. It was good hunting weather. Mark
thought of that with pleasure, wondering if he would have a chance
to get a gun out over the week end. He went over the list of things
that he meant to go over on the location today. And then his
mind went back to what had been said the night before, as if it
had not quite finished with that talk. He found himself rearguing
the matter of faith.

It's adding insult to injury, he said to himself. That's what I
should have told him. They set up this terrific body of dogma,
they force acceptance of it by using all sorts of mystic threats and
preposterous promises, and then they cap it all by insisting that
the whole thing is voluntary. What I object to most is the hypocrisy.

I can see the way they work. That priest is all ready now with a
plan for infiltrating even this little new village of ours, which is
hardly built yet. First they get their foot in the door by having
services in the school. Then they'll put on pressure to build a
church. Then pressure for a Catholic school, the public one won't
be good enough, of course. But they can't dominate us that far.
I'd like to tell them to keep out of our bailiwick altogether. I
couldn't do that, of course. That would make us as bad as they are.
If people want to be Catholics or Methodist or Buddhists, that's
up to them.

Where the Catholic Church is smart is in not yielding an inch.
If it did, its hold would slip. People like discipline up to a point.
They want to feel that something doesn't shift around, doesn't

change. Even if they cheat, they want the consistent thing to be there. It gives them something to come back to, something to lean on. As I told Kenedy last night, it's the dependence that I can't take, the mental slavery. That's what it is.

What I said to Alan won't have any effect. Olive is wrong about that. She needn't worry. The boy's in love. He wants that particular girl. He's got her on his mind. And whether she's cross-eyed or whether she's Catholic doesn't matter, no one else will do. Well, anyway, I've said my piece. I told him that I wouldn't let myself in for any marriage that a priest could interfere with on the side. I'll never say another word to him about it. Alan's old enough to make his own decisions. I hate to see him hamper himself in any way, that's all. He's doing well—better than he knows—in the mining business. He's a natural for it. He has more of his father and his grandfather in him than I have. By a long shot. Too bad that he wasn't old enough to take over. He's basically better suited to the job than I am.

If Alan had headed up the company instead of me, I wonder what I would have done? Now that I'm in this groove, I like it all right. But the thing is that it takes all your time. You never have time to figure out what it's all about, what you're here for. That doesn't bother me the way it used to before I married Olive. Living with her is reason enough for living.

He came in sight of the first of the taconite processing plants, and instantly that great undertaking took his mind off himself. On his right, close by, Lake Superior stretched to the far horizon, sapphire blue this morning. On his left, seventy miles to the northeast, was the region where, over the ages, iron had accumulated in the rocks. For three generations the Worthing family had been committed to the project of getting the ore out of the ground, peeling it off the hills, transporting it to the lake shore, and shipping it to the steel mills by way of the chain of great lakes which began with Lake Superior. It had been a dream, a gamble, a battle with nature, a business deal. It was personal adventure, mathematical calculation, and big industry. From those ancient rocks seventy miles away had come the successive Worthing office buildings, and money for their luxuries and good works, for mink coats and distant Negro colleges, for servants' wages and community funds, for fabulous taxes which made social security possible for old people in Florida and Maine, for Lucy's husband, for substantial houses, beautiful silverware and a mausoleum in the cemetery in Duluth. The mine-pocked face of northern Minnesota was as familiar to the male Worthings as that of any member of the family. They knew the date of almost every scar.

When Theron Worthing had begun to buy mining properties, the engineers he worked with had no interest in taconite. It was known to prospectors as the hardest rock in the world. Though there were streaks of ore in it, there was no way to get them out. Who would bother to try at that time, when the Merritt brothers had just discovered areas where rich ore lay almost on the surface and could be scooped up by steam shovels as easily as clay? There were always a few calamity-howlers who warned that the rich ore deposits would not last forever. But the pits were enormous, and exhaustion of the ore seemed—in the early days of the iron ranges—too far off to worry about. There were big immediate fortunes to be made.

Two world wars worked the mines hard. The second one shortened the life of the greatest mines by twenty-five years. Philip Worthing realized that they would scrape the bottom of the richest mines owned by the family in his sons' lifetimes. He began to study the reports of the constant experiments of taconite that had been going on in the University laboratories for years. They were getting somewhere with the experiments. Every failure created a special problem to be solved, and sooner or later somebody solved it.

Everything but the cost of production began to be feasible. New giant machines succeeded in crushing that rock which was harder than granite. Magnetic separators sorted out the useful ore until at last there was left a powder-fine black muck that was rich in iron. It remained only to make the muck into pellets that would be hard enough not to fly to pieces when the blast furnaces began to convert them into steel. A few years ago this last hurdle had been taken.

It meant renaissance. A possible boom. The thing ahead for

the region now was not the dwindling away of iron ore mining but the beginning of a new phase of mining which could last for a century. A hundred miles of taconite rock awaited processing. There must be new harbors along the lake shore, into which ocean freighters could sail and carry away the ore. There must also be miles of new railroad, over which the rocks from the iron ranges could be brought to the processing plants on the edge of Lake Superior. The companies which were not frozen out by the cost of production began to pour millions upon millions of dollars into new developments.

The Worthing interests had taken their time. Because they had more high-grade ore left than many other companies, they didn't have to hurry. They planned to operate on a smaller scale than some of the big corporations and to profit by watching the experiments of the others. They were the fourth company to dredge a new harbor and build a taconite crushing plant on the lake shore.

Each company had sprouted a little village for its permanent employees. Silver Bay, Taconite Harbor, Rocket, and now Baraga. The last was the village which the Worthing-Ingalls Company had underwritten. The name was inevitable because they were building in Baraga Cove, long ago so named because a missionary priest had made a legendary trip from the place, rowing across the lake in rough weather to make a sick call on the opposite shore.

Silver Bay looked settled and well established. But the contractors were still building in Baraga. The layout of the place was defined. From a rise in the road, Mark could see the embryonic settlement before he got there. The practical little houses were set in circles on a slope, which overlooked the plant across the highway and the lake beyond it.

He turned his car into the unpaved road which led up to the houses, and drove by them for a quick look. They were all right, he thought with satisfaction. This was not at all a bad place for men with families to live. Some houses were already occupied. The store was doing business, that was obvious, and the school too.

Charley Johnson, the contractor, was giving instructions to a man who was painting the outside of a house which was just finished. Mark hailed him as he passed, put his foot on the brake.

"How do we look?" asked Johnson.

"You look fine. I'd like to live there myself."

"This is the one your brother was looking at not long ago. Him and the young lady," grinned the contractor.

"It is?"

"She liked everything about it."

"He's taken the house?"

"He hasn't signed up yet. If you see him, tell him not to wait too long. Though we wouldn't let anyone else have it without giving him first chance."

"Good of you—I'll be seeing you," said Mark, and drove on. He was startled and moved by hearing this. So that was what Alan intended to do, to live up here—it wasn't a bad idea at all. He'd come home to that little place at night—it wasn't very glamorous —what was it Olive had said about Alan? That he was lonely; he'd never been loved enough. If he comes up here with his Catholic girl, I suppose I'll have to let them have their church in the schoolhouse. It will become a family matter, thought Mark ironically. They'll have children, of course. Poor Olive—she was disappointed again. I want to give her a child.

He drove across the highway to the plant, trying now to see it with the critical eyes of the financiers who would come to inspect it before long. The great storage tanks for ore were almost completed; the building where the pellets would be made had a roof on it. The power plant looked all right, but that dredging concern wasn't delivering on its job. He'd have to go after that outfit. Mark stopped at the building which was used as an office. Becker, the superintendent in charge, was waiting for him. The two men soon fitted themselves into Becker's jeep and went around the whole area, Becker explaining, Mark listening and looking.

They were down by the harbor when he saw his brother. Alan was studying a blueprint spread out on a packing case. Mark yelled at him above the noise of the waves, and Alan turned. He was hatless as usual, and Mark had a quick impression that he looked bad. As if he had been drinking too much or sleeping too little. He looked nervous and rather sour, not like his usual blithe self.

"How's everything?" asked Mark.

"Okay," said Alan unsmiling.

"Got a problem there?" asked Becker.

"Yes, sir," said Alan. "I think we can improve on that conveyer system."

"How?" asked Becker, stepping promptly over the side of the jeep and looking at the blueprint.

Becker likes him, thought Mark with pleasure. Alan is doing very well. Maybe it's overwork that makes him look like that. Too much girl. Too much love.

Effie Dwight never let Mark forget any responsibility. When he got back to his office in the city that afternoon, she reminded him that there was a meeting of the directors of St. Barnabas Hospital at four-thirty.

"They'll have to get along without me," said Mark. He wanted to go home early. A longing to be with Olive had come over him on the ride back, as it sometimes did, unexpectedly and with curious force. He would get a sudden feeling that he was wasting time that should be spent with her, that they'd never get this time back. It was like an instinctive sense of danger.

"They need you for a quorum. That's what they said on the phone," Effie told him. "It's the budget meeting."

"Oh, hell," grumbled Mark. But it was compelling. He would have to go, and once in the hospital board room, he gave the work before him full attention. He even lingered when the meeting was finished to talk to the manager of St. Barnabas about the campaign for money which was in the offing, so it was nearly six o'clock when he came out of the inner room and walked through the office where the records were kept. There had been no one at the desk in the corner when he went in, but now a girl was sitting there. He remembered instantly that Olive had said this girl was the one Alan was in love with, and gave her a quick glance. She met it directly, almost as if she had been waiting for him

[98]

to look at her. He gave a little impersonal nod, but suddenly, swiftly, she left her desk and came toward him.

"Mr. Worthing, may I speak to you for a minute?"

"Why, yes—of course."

"I'm Rose Mary Carroll," she said, as if that were the whole thing, all the explanation that was needed. As she faced him closely, chin lifted, eyes wide, Mark thought he had never seen a more perfect face. It didn't stir or excite him as Olive's thin face could, but it was impossible not to admire it, to rather wonder at it.

"I'm glad to meet you," said Mark civilly. "I've heard my brother Alan speak of you."

"Yes," she said, "Alan." She was very serious and determined, and yet speaking the name seemed to leave her breathless. "You see—Alan and I were going to be married."

"He told me that was the plan," said Mark. His voice wasn't cordial. What did this girl want of him? Trying to charm him? To put herself over?

"Mr. Worthing, you must think it's very queer, my stopping you like this. But I knew you were in there at the meeting, and I hoped maybe there would be a chance."

"You mean you were waiting for me?"

"I wanted so terribly to speak to you. About us."

"Alan and yourself? That's entirely his business. His and yours, of course."

"I know I could make him happy, Mr. Worthing. I could have."

Mark said stiffly, "I would hope so."

"Please," she said, "don't be against it! Please don't make Alan feel the way he does!"

"I'm not making Alan feel any way—"

"Oh, yes—you are. Since that day that he told you about us, he's not been the same at all. At first I didn't realize what had happened, but I know now that was what made the difference. Before that—well, before that, he wasn't so—so critical of everything. But since then he is. It gets worse all the time, the more we talk about it. He doesn't want to do the things we have to do.

If you would just tell him that you think it will work out all right —give us that much of a break. If you'd try not to feel the way you do about me—"

"About you?"

"About my being a Catholic."

He stared at her, frowning now.

She said, "With us, marriage has to be a Sacrament."

"Many people take marriage seriously. Not only in the Catholic Church."

"It was what you said about thinking for yourself," she said, sounding rather desperate. "Alan keeps coming back to that. I do think for myself. But the Church has laws about marriage. For everybody. For centuries it's had them. One person can't go against them."

"I wouldn't argue that. But I might point out that Alan doesn't have to accept those rules. He's not a Catholic."

"No, but he has to agree to some of them. He can't—oh, this is so hard to say—he can't thwart me."

Strange word, thought Mark—probably the right one too.

"I have to obey," she said, "or stop being a Catholic."

He was conscious that the forces bearing down on this girl were terrific. He thought, that's what I warned Alan about.

He said, "I think you're worrying unnecessarily. From what Alan said to me, he seems quite willing to have you practice your religion, and even to go along with you to some extent."

"He was in the first place."

"He said he was even attending some classes studying marriage in your church—"

Rose Mary said, "He won't go any more. Not since the day you talked to him. That was the night it began. Now everything seems to be so difficult—he doesn't want to take instructions, and you have to when you marry a Catholic, because you have to make certain promises—"

"Look, these are matters you must discuss with him—"

"Oh, we have, and the more we talk about it the worse it gets—"

"But I can't mix in your quarrels—"

"You're the only one he'd listen to. And it wasn't a quarrel, not until you started it. He told me what you said, that you'd never marry a Catholic. Oh, he was sorry he'd told me, but we were arguing and it came out. You made him feel—demeaned. He didn't when we first knew each other. Now he says it's all right for me to go to church but he hates the idea of confession—he thinks that's demeaning—he won't talk to the priests—I don't know what to do—"

Mark remembered how tired Alan had looked this morning. Now he knew why.

"It's a little rough on him too, you know."

"Don't I know! That's what makes it so—suffering."

"I can understand that it's difficult. But you knew that Alan didn't share your faith, that he wasn't and never would be a Roman Catholic."

"You can pray for grace," she said, and there was a lyric, mystic sound in her voice.

"You mean you would hope to convert him?"

"Why, of course. I wouldn't ever insist on it—you have to have faith before you can be a Catholic. But I could pray for it. I'd have to."

"I see," said Mark. "May I ask just one question?"

"Of course."

"You don't go fifty-fifty on this? I mean, you don't leave the door open to the idea that you might become a Protestant?"

"I couldn't—"

"Couldn't, or wouldn't?"

"I couldn't. For me it would be mortal sin."

This was familiar. This was the way that priest had been about the birth-control clinic. No yielding, no coming halfway. There she stood, looking like Joan of Arc, wanting him to take her side.

"I haven't any right to ask you. But it's Alan's happiness I'm thinking of, more even than my own. You probably don't believe that. There's no reason why you should. But I'd do anything for Alan."

[101]

Mark's disbelieving smile was the answer to that. She flared up quickly.

"Except break the law. I can see why you have so much influence on Alan. You're stronger than he is."

"I'm older."

"You know what you believe, and you say it and stay by it, no matter what it does to other people. But Alan's confused. He respects your judgment more than anyone's. He's afraid to go against it."

Her eyes misted with love and pity, and, as she felt the tears, she changed from angry emotion to a convent-parlor politeness.

"I shouldn't have stopped you and taken up your time. I beg your pardon, Mr. Worthing. It was pretty inexcusable."

"It was all right. If there was any way in which I thought I could help, but—"

"But there's none. I can see that. You can't help what you believe. Goodbye."

Mark said to Olive, "And that girl looked at me as if she thought I was the antichrist!"

"It's probably the way the poor thing feels about you."

"But obviously I was dead right. Alan's the sucker. He said to me that of course he'd never be a Catholic, that he'd told her so. Why, she'll have him in the fold within a year."

"I doubt that."

"She's a very strong personality. They've built this thing up in her—religion I mean. And she is beautiful. She and Alan will be quite a couple."

"Maybe she won't marry him now."

"Look," said Mark, "you can fight all you like about religion, but when it gets down to a man wanting a woman who wants him —the way that girl obviously does want Alan—well, you know what's going to win out, don't you? Not any religious prejudice."

"I hope not. I'm rather frightened for Alan. He must be very much in love if he was trying to go along with her as far as he did. Classes and discipline aren't up his street. And she's evidently desperate to waylay you and talk like that. Feeling as she must that you're against her—knowing that you dislike her religion—"

"I don't dislike her religion," said Mark. "She has no reason to think that."

His tone was almost contentious. It so surprised Olive that she turned to see if he was serious. She said, "I mean she knows you don't believe in it."

"I couldn't believe in it. I couldn't accept the Catholic obligation to believe. Faith, or whatever they call it."

He was sitting, hunched in thought, on the ottoman in front of a chair which usually made him comfortable. They were in their bedroom. Olive was ready for bed when she would toss off the cloud of blue fabric which drifted unfastened about her. Mark was still half-dressed, as he had been when he began to talk about this again.

He said, "I wonder why it is so impossible for people like us. Maybe we've lost a kind of simplicity—aren't primitive enough. Kenedy says that the natural law is God's law. They get around some things that way. You see, that means that they accept the idea of God, and that God created natural instincts."

"You can do that without belonging to the Catholic Church," said Olive. "I believe in God. And creation too up to a point."

"But they make a business of it," said Mark.

Her glance was puzzled, but he did not notice that. He said again in meditative admiration, "You should have seen that girl this afternoon. Fighting to get Alan, but not giving an inch. Telling me right to my face that she hoped to convert him."

"She's lovely looking," said Olive.

"Isn't she? And she wants me to interfere, to tell Alan that it would work out all right—"

"Are you going to do that?"

"I certainly am not. It's none of my business. It's completely up to Alan."

"Yes, it should be, of course. Unless—"

"Unless what—what were you going to say?"

"Unless you did make Alan feel different about the religious end of it, after he talked to you."

"If he feels different, it's because he's come to his senses after seeing more of their tactics. Hearing more of what Catholics think and what he'd be up against. There wouldn't be any sense in my talking to him again. I haven't changed my mind. In fact, I feel more strongly than before, after listening to this girl. If Alan marries her, he will have to make all the concessions—"

"About religion."

"Yes, of course. I can see that she's very attractive. And she says that she loves him—"

"Did she talk about love?"

"Love? It was about Alan."

Olive said, "It makes me feel queer. It makes me jealous."

Mark laughed aloud. "You've never been jealous of me in your life."

"I was just now. When you said I should have seen her this afternoon. You said that as if you were looking at her again, admiring her in spite of not agreeing with her. As if you were seeing her in this room. I know how beautiful she is. I really did have the strangest feeling—wanting to get her out of here. This is our room. Out of your mind, I mean—"

"You're taking me for a ride. You know what bothers me. It's the effect on Alan's life."

Olive did not move, and Mark, suddenly disturbed, went to put his arms about her.

She shivered close to him. "It's the effect on you that I worry about," she murmured.

"Why, darling, what's got into you?"

"I know it's silly. I ought to be ashamed of myself. And I am." Olive made herself laugh. She drew away from his arms tenderly, righted the long slope of her body. The blue fabric trembled about her. She looked enchanting after the little outburst of possessiveness.

She said, "And I couldn't be more sorry for anyone than I am for Rose Mary Carroll. I can remember what it's like to be afraid that the man you love will never marry you—"

"You! Do you remember how many times you turned me down?"

"Only because I was afraid of everything. Most afraid that I'd not be enough—not be everything you wanted and needed. Sometimes even now I'm afraid that I won't be able to satisfy you forever—"

"Foolish girl—my lovely girl—I'm the one to worry about keeping you happy—"

10

Mark had asked Olive to marry him four times. The first one had been inevitably toward the end of that summer season when he first met her. He had realized after only a few weeks that his life was turning in a new direction, and that his thoughts were constantly following this shy young woman whose elusiveness instead of discouraging him, seemed to build up a new confidence in himself.

During the cleanup after the storm, it had been easy and natural to make occasions to see her. Broken trees had to be treated by experts, or cut down and hauled away; roofs and chimneys needed repairs; and Mark sent the local workmen who did such jobs to Olive at the Hadley place and then came over himself to see how they were getting along with their work. Even before she heard it from Maud Hadley, Mark told Olive that the cost of putting the lodge and its grounds back in good shape was covered by insurance against wind damage. That, he could see, took a weight off her mind.

"Anyway, it's not up to you. You weren't responsible for the worst windstorm we've had down here in years," said Mark.

"I was living here," said Olive, "and you're always supposed to leave a place in as good condition as you found it when you took over. I've lived in so many rented places that I know it's expected, and this is even worse because—because, you see, I'm the Hadley's guest, even if they aren't here. You really think there is insurance?"

"Of course," Mark told her, thinking that if the Hadleys didn't carry it, he must figure out some way so that this girl—who probably had very little money to go on (he had seen signs of her frugality before, and heard money worry in her voice just now) —would not be stuck for any extra expense.

The repair work to be done made a base for their conversations. Mark built on it. Often he would stay on at the Hadley lodge after his errand was done, talking about the history of the river, its storms and its habits. Mark knew all the exaggerated tales of battles here between the Chippewa and Sioux Indians, and with these he quickly made Tim his friend and follower. He described the early camps on the river, when all supplies had to be brought by canoes to the rough docks, and only lanterns and kerosene lamps broke the black dusk of the virgin forests along its banks. He told Olive about men who had made great fortunes and could afford to live anywhere in the world, but hankered for the river and the pine woods and came there from choice. They bought the land until some of them owned very large estates. Then they built lodges suitable for such holdings.

"They used to say of one old fellow that he always went out every day and bought a few more acres so he would have an appetite for his supper," said Mark, "but nobody could ever keep the river for himself. It's a navigable stream, you know; anyone can fish it. There was a whole lot of money spent on some of these camps— the old-timers always call them camps no matter what's been put into them, and it's never been a place to show off. Fishing and cards and drinking and bird-shooting, that's what the old boys came here for in the first place. It's still pretty much the same. Basically. Even if the drinking now is at cocktail parties, not out of the bottle."

"I'd come just to listen to the river," said Olive.

"You do like it, don't you?"

"I couldn't tell you how much."

"You either do or you don't," said Mark. "My father always liked to come down here for week ends with some of his special friends—they always opened the trout season in May and closed it with another bang on Labor Day. But Mother has never cared for it. She says there's so little to do. It always seemed a waste of time to her. Of course, she has a lot of civic interests, that sort of thing. . . . My brother Alan isn't keen about it either, but he's always liked to sail on the big lake in summer—this seems pretty tame to him, I guess. Not enough excitement for Alan. My father didn't leave our place to any one of us specifically in his will, so it belongs to the estate. I wouldn't want to sell it. The way we work it out is that the girls—I mean my sisters, Pamela and Lucy —each take over for a month or two in the summer. Pam doesn't get the same kick out of it that Lucy and her husband do. He's a painter, an artist—not much good at turning out masterpieces, but an awfully nice fellow. You'd like Gregory."

"Do you come at special times, yourself?" asked Olive.

"I come down for week ends—the original camp has been made into kind of a guesthouse, and I always have some gear there. Once in a while I come down by myself after it gets too cold for the girls and the water is turned off."

Mark told her such things about his family and himself almost from the start. As if he felt that Olive should know about him, should see the picture of his environment. But after the debris from the storm had been cleaned up and the repairs were completed, it was not so easy for him to see Olive Grant. She gave him no help or encouragement.

"Of course I asked Olive Grant for cocktails on Saturday," said Pamela when Mark questioned her about that. "I invited almost everyone in the whole colony. I couldn't leave her out when she's next door. But she sent over a note by Agnes and said she couldn't leave her children. I don't see why Agnes couldn't stay with them for a couple of hours. Anyway, I have another girl for you this week end. I asked Dot Langhorne to come down. She's always fun and very pictorial, though I don't think you'd want her for keeps."

"Don't count on me for that picture book," said Mark. "I'm going to get some fishing."

Pamela and Lucy were always "asking a girl for him," here and in the city. But Mark treated girls, said Lucy, as if they were land mines. He always seemed afraid they would explode, she told him, and that his precious detachment might be blown to bits. He grinned at the shrewd truth of that, but made no effort to change his ways. Girls and women liked him and he had a good time with many of them, but he stopped before a liking could turn into a claim.

"Honestly, Mark, you should have been a monk!" said Pamela, after one of her matchmaking failures with him. "I really worry about you. She has everything—looks, brains and money—"

"Too much of everything," said Mark. "I couldn't handle all of it."

He was no innocent. He had read a great deal about sex and love, and he had been in the war. There were experiences in his own book which he didn't regret, but he didn't talk about them. They had been transient and he knew he was the one to blame, if there was any fault. He had never yet been possessed by a desire that seemed stronger than his judgment. And he did not worry about that. Not that he felt monkish or had any intention of being a permanent bachelor. He expected to meet a girl someday—vaguely he thought of her as very young, innocent, having beautiful legs, and not a liar. When he had a little more time to give to it, he would fill out the picture, and he and this girl would make a good thing of it.

When he met Olive Grant, everything became different. She was a divorced woman, with two small children, a woman who had recently belonged to another man. That should have made him uninterested in her, for Mark usually kept away from girls who had sex histories and emotional troubles. Instead, almost immediately Olive seemed completely right for him. She was just as he wanted her to be, children and all. To find that he was capable of being so irresistibly attracted at first astonished and then excited him. He began to have hopes, plans, and determinations which he couldn't control. Not being able to manage them added to his certainty. It was fast. It was single—no one else but Olive would do.

He had to use his wits to make occasions to see her. She shied away from any of the informal social life along the river, like Pamela's cocktail party. After that day when he had come to her through the storm, she was always friendly and still grateful. But she never asked him to come to see her. He had to persuade her to give him her company, and he spent a great deal of time in his office during the week figuring out new persuasions. She loved the river, fortunately, and he used that to tempt her. "Haven't you been to the fish hatchery? You must come. Bring some stale bread along and we'll feed them." . . . "Have you seen the rapids by the Harris place?" . . . or "Tim, do you and your mother want to see a covey of partridges?"

They were, in the local phrase, "on the river" when he first tried to tell her what had happened to him. To go "on the river" did not mean to paddle around your own dock, Mark told Olive. It meant spending a whole day canoeing from its headwaters toward the lake, into which it finally plunged. Olive had not done that, and, beginning to argue for it two weeks before the time, Mark made her promise to come with him one Saturday in late August. It was too long a trip for Tim, he explained, but Mark made up for that by giving the boy a bow and a quiver of arrows. Agnes, who loved both the baby and the river, urged, "You ought to go, Mrs. Grant. You ought to go on the river once while you're here. You don't have to worry about the baby one bit."

It was a day of varying motion and moods and lights. Of swinging through the curling, foaming rapids, keeping the canoe from losing its course or overturning by using the pole and paddle skillfully. Mark, who was expert, told Olive what to do, and avoiding the rocks and shallows was a series of laughing triumphs. Sometimes the canoe would drift into a part of the river which was completely calm and as wide as a lake, and Mark would tell Olive to sit back, do nothing. They slid into shadowed coves. Fish jumped, and once a deer showed on the opposite bank and they held an exquisite silence and motionlessness for several minutes until she bounded away. They talked. Not only of the river. It soon led to themselves, though Olive began impersonally.

"Where does the name of the river come from?" she asked, trailing a hand in it.

"It was named for Etienne Brule," said Mark, "and he was quite a fellow. Nothing seems to have fazed him at all. He and another man with him, called Grenoble, are supposed to have been the first white men to dip a paddle into Lake Superior. He came along here, looking for a trade route, more than three hundred years ago, went to the mouth of the river, and the story is that he got as far as Isle Royale on the other side of the lake. That's not far from the new taconite plant that we're developing. Getting across the lake was something in those days. This was all wild, unexplored country."

"How did he happen to come?"

"He was an interpreter," Mark said. "The French sent him over to live among the Indians, learn their languages and their ways and how to deal with them, I suppose. Then he reported back. They found out about the copper on this side of the lake from the Indians. The early explorers were always looking for minerals, of course. They hunted for gold. They didn't know about the iron ore, which turned out to be the best bet of all for this region. That came much later. But it was still pretty rough around here when my grandfather came out prospecting."

"Did he find iron ore?"

"He found a piece of it," said Mark. "That's what our family has been working on since then. And living on. My father and grandfather were both in the mining industry."

"And you are too?"

"Yes. By sort of an accident."

"An accident?"

"I had to take over," said Mark. "My father died. There wasn't anyone else."

"Didn't you want to do mining?"

He laughed, rested his paddle on his knees, and they drifted. Mark said, "I don't really do any mining. Maybe I'd be better off if I did run a steam shovel or if I were an engineer on the job, like my brother Alan. I'm in the business end. Counting costs, scaring up the money for new developments and expansion. Of course I have to understand the processes, but my work's mostly on paper."

"Would you rather do something else?"

He thought, nobody has asked me that in years. Not straight out. Not since I was a kid taking aptitude tests. How sweet, how natural this is. Why didn't it happen before? I should have had her with me a long time ago.

He said, "Oh, I don't know. I used to have a lot of ideas. Everyone has, I suppose. Other fields always look greener than the family business."

"What was the one that looked greenest to you?"

He thought back. He couldn't find old ambitions in firm enough shape to express, to offer her. Yet he wanted to tell her that once there had been something else in his mind.

"It was never very definite," said Mark. "I just used to think I'd like to find the answer to a lot of things. I always liked history. And it probably sounds pretty silly at this stage, for a business man, but I did fairly well in philosophy. I had an idea I might do some postgraduate work at one time. But the war broke out the year I got out of college, and that settled that."

"And when the war was over you didn't want to go back?"

Mark could remember his father saying, "But what would it fit you for, that sort of library work? I haven't any objection to anything you want to do with your life, but I think it's up to you to find out where your money comes from. You don't have to stay with the company unless you like it, and nobody will want you unless you fit in. But you should give it a try. You're only a boy—you have lots of time."

Mark told Olive again, "I didn't have anything very definite in mind. And my father thought I should learn something about the mining industry. I hadn't been with the company very long before he died."

"And then they needed you."

"They thought so. It's worked out pretty well."

It will be better, he thought. I know what I want now. I know what I've been waiting for.

Early in the afternoon they came to the picnic place that Mark had been planning on for lunch. An old piece of weathered dock, which had long since lost the lodge it belonged to by fire, stretched out almost unseen in a bed of rushes. Mark tied the canoe to it, and when she took his hand as she stepped out, he felt the rush of his senses at their solitude and nearness. But, he told himself, not yet. He showed her the old mossy logs that were like benches, and the stone stove where he was going to cook the corned-beef hash that was the classic food on river picnics.

While he started the fire, Olive found a garden of blue forget-me-nots on the edge of a tiny lagoon made by trees that had fallen long ago.

"You look like an enchanted child," said Mark.

"I am enchanted. I don't believe this place is true!"

"Thank you for coming with me, Olive."

She met his eyes, turned from his glance and said, "You must let me help," in a very practical and useful tone.

He did not press her. They ate the browned hash and the hard-boiled eggs that Agnes had put in the basket, and drank the beer which had been kept cool in the fish box in the canoe.

"I never liked beer before," she said.

"You never had it here."

"I'll probably never like it again."

"Until next time you're on the river."

"There won't be any next time."

"Of course there will."

"The Hadleys won't be going to Europe next summer."

"That doesn't mean you won't be here."

"I've taken too much from them already."

"I wasn't thinking of the Hadleys."

She was very still, and he felt, as he had when they watched the deer, that flight was imminent if he frightened her.

"Olive, will you marry me?"

"Oh, please—"

"I have to say it. You know I must. I love you, Olive. I've come to love you very much. I feel as if I had been waiting for you, watching for you all my life. Don't you think you could be happy with me?"

"Please don't spoil this lovely day, Mark!"

"It doesn't spoil it—it's what this day is for—"

"No, I was wrong to come. I knew it. I knew—"

"Of course you knew—"

"It couldn't be. It's impossible. I'm very—very grateful. But let's not mention it again."

"Why is it impossible?"

"I'm not good at marriage," she said, in the first hard, cold tones he had ever heard in her voice. "I'll never try it again. Let's pick up our things and go now. I must get back before it's too late."

He moved toward her. She did not stir. But what he saw in her eyes stopped him. She didn't want him to touch her. She was frightened, deeply unhappy.

"Don't look like that, Olive. . . . Don't take it that way."

"I shouldn't have come," she said again.

He felt guilty, almost cruel. The enchanted child, the gay girl who had so enjoyed her beer, had gone. This was now the almost hostile young woman whom he had seen first in the grocery store. No—it wasn't hostility—more as if she were afraid or shocked—

"Of course we'll go if you want to," he said gently.

The river was not so brilliant as it had been in the morning. Long before it set, the sun was hidden by the great pines along its banks. Mark and Olive talked little and of obvious things. As they went through more rapids she did exactly what she was told to do, but the fun of sharing precarious moments was gone. Mark thought of what he would say before they parted. But when they came to the Hadley dock, Tim was waiting with shouts of welcome, Olive hurried in to see the baby, and Mark had no chance to tell her that he would certainly ask her again to marry him.

She made that difficult, guarding herself in an unexpected way. When he tried to see her on the Sunday after their day on the river, he could not find her at home. She had taken the children and gone off somewhere in the old station wagon. He went over to the Hadley

[113]

lodge twice to find it deserted, and in the evening he had to drive back to the city in a baffled mood. When he came down to the river on the next week end, he was determined to penetrate her isolation, but she defeated him by changing her habits and never being alone. There was a spate of parties in those days before the season was over, and before the lodges along the river closed for the winter. Mark had anticipated that and imagined it would mean that he would find Olive alone. Instead, she went to the parties. She even gave one.

Lucy, who was in residence at the Worthing place for this last fortnight, said to Mark at breakfast one morning, "Greg and I are going over the Hadley lodge for cocktails this afternoon. Will you come along? I think she'd love it if you did."

"The Hadley lodge?"

"Yes, Olive Grant asked all of us to come over. She's evidently broken out of her shell."

She was beautiful out of her shell. When he saw her as a hostess in this borrowed house, Mark realized how much experience in social life she must have had. This was not the repressed girl who kept to herself, nor his sweet companion. This was a young woman who was skilled in the art of meeting strangers, making them enjoy themselves. He watched her listen gracefully to men repeating themselves, and admire other women enough to make them feel very well received.

But she did not let him stay longer than the others. Her good-by to Mark was as impersonal and final as it was to Gregory Searles.

"I think Olive Grant is terribly attractive," said Lucy, looking in a mirror in the Worthing living room. "Don't you, Greg?"

"It could be a good description," said Greg.

"What do you mean? Don't you think she's rather beautiful?"

"I'm in no doubt about that."

Lucy's hand caressed her hair. "Poor thing," she said. "Of course, she is looking around for another husband."

Mark got up abruptly and left the room.

"What's the matter with Mark?" asked Lucy. "He seemed so impatient and bored this afternoon."

"Thwarted," corrected Greg.

"What's thwarting him?"

Gregory said, "Your brother gave me the impression of being in love with Mrs. Grant."

"In love with her! Don't be silly. She has two children! Can you imagine Mark falling in love with a woman with two children?" exclaimed Lucy incredulously.

Mark had asked Olive how long she would be there, and she had been indefinite. It depended on the weather, on when the kindergarten opened, she said, but she gave him no dates. He began to live in fear that she would be gone before he had a chance to see her alone. He got through Monday in the city, but on Tuesday noon he told Effie that he would not be back in the office that day and to cancel a couple of business appointments.

"I have to go out of town," he said, and before she could pin him down as to where he was going, he was out of hearing.

Long afterward Olive said, "Do you remember the color of that day in September when you came down to see me at the river? It was all brown and green, matching oak leaves and pine needles of that brown you never see in anything dyed—it comes from having been green and alive. And the ground pine and the little berry plants were all through the woods, and the red squirrels were throwing down acorns at us."

"And you were wearing your yellow sweater."

"I still have it."

"I was afraid you'd shut the door in my face that day."

"I couldn't have—I was so glad to see you."

"You sent me away a pretty discouraged fellow just the same."

"It seemed so impossible then—"

That was what she had tried to explain as they walked through the almost-stripped woods on trails that were soft with pine needles.

"You mustn't mind my coming, Olive. I have to talk to you. These last times I've seen you—at these parties—with all these people—"

"I hated myself. Putting on an act."

[115]

"You were lovely, but not the girl I took on the river. Not the girl I hope will marry me."

"You mustn't hope that. I told you it was impossible."

"But you must give me reasons, Olive. You're free to marry, aren't you?"

"Legally. But I have two small children."

"They aren't the reason. Why, I love those kids because they're yours, Olive. And Tim's a friend of mine."

"Tim thinks you're the greatest man that ever walked the earth."

"It's not because of the children."

"No. All right, I'll tell you. It's me. I've nothing to offer. I'm not the type. I've tried marriage. I failed. Don't you see?"

"You didn't fail. You happened to marry someone who wasn't good enough. Not right for you. From what I hear of Grant, he's just a playboy."

"He's no good. I know. But neither am I."

"You mustn't say a thing like that. You're a beautiful—"

"I know I'm pretty. That's what fools you. And it's so heavenly here, and—oh, don't you see that it's all a kind of wide-awake dream? But in other places, where things are real, it would be different."

"Listen," said Mark, "do you like me?"

She said reluctantly, as if she must tell the truth, "Yes."

"And I love you. I thought this kind of love was a fairy story until I met you, Olive. I always thought I'd marry someday, but I didn't particularly want to. Now I think of nothing else. I want to live with you—"

Olive shivered. She said almost under her breath, "I'd disappoint you. I won't do that. Please, Mark, don't ask me any more."

He found out from Maud Hadley where Olive was living in Minneapolis. Olive had given him no address.

"I don't know exactly where I will be," she said, on that day when they walked in the brown and green woods. "And anyway it's better not, Mark. You'll get over this when you don't see me around so much. It will just seem a foolish idea you had—if you think of it at all."

[116]

He thought of almost nothing else for the next ten days. He went over every word exchanged between them, trying to understand her refusal. For it had been refusal, not coquetry—that he knew. But he did not mean to accept it.

Lucy told Pamela what Gregory had said about Mark's being in love. Pam didn't believe it until Mark seemed so strange and anti-social that she asked him outright, "It isn't true that you are interested in that girl who divorced Tony Grant, is it?"

Mark said almost savagely, "I don't know what you call interested. I'm trying to get her to marry me."

So they all knew in the family and worried about it. None of them thought it a proper match for Mark, and though nobody said that to him in so many words, they tried to divert him—"asking girls for him," suggesting that he could marry anybody, and should take his time about it.

But at the moment he knew that wasn't true. He couldn't marry anybody because Olive would not agree, and taking more time frightened him because she might marry someone else. Perhaps she really didn't like him—in some way found him repulsive to her. Nonetheless, he called up Mrs. Hadley and found out where Olive was living.

"Oh, Mark," said Maud Hadley, "she's such a lovely thing."

"Thank you very much for giving me her address," said Mark.

Olive was renting two rooms and a kitchenette in an old house not far from Tim's nursery school. She slept in the sitting room and the children shared the bedroom. There were a few distinctive things in the flat, small enough to have been carried in a suitcase here and there, but it was makeshift and shabby. When he went to see her this time, Mark discovered another quality in her which he loved at once, her indifference to possessions.

She caught his glance of concern and said, "We're very comfortable."

"I should think Maud Hadley could—"

"She could but I wouldn't let her," said Olive. "She's done too much for me. I've a very little money of my own and I can manage this. Later on, when Jenny's older, I can get some sort of job. The trouble is that I was never trained to do anything. But there will

[117]

be something I can do—look after children, work in a store—"

"You should let your friends help," said Mark. "Olive, you told me not to come, but—"

"It's all right. But don't pity me. Because this is what I want for my children, how I want it to be. I want them to be real persons and so they must have a home that is their own, no matter if it's poor and shabby. That's what is wrong with me. I've never known what I am because I've always been a guest. A transient. Even when I was married, it was like that. And long before—"

So Mark came to know her better, sitting in an old Morris chair, the only one big enough for him in the room, the only armchair. The baby was asleep in the bedroom. Olive's hair was drawn back from her beautiful features, but there was a loose wisp of gold which fell over her ear, and she pushed it back now and again as she told him what her life had been like. The sleeves of her white blouse were rolled up and she wore no stockings. Her legs were still summer-tanned.

Olive told him about her uncle's house in Philadelphia where she usually had gone for holidays from school. She had been sent to boarding school when she was very young.

"There was nothing else they could do with me. And the schools and camps were very good. I liked to go. But—"

It came out that she had been too young to suffer when her father killed himself, and there was a long period when her mother was in hospitals and sanitariums before she died. Those relationships were very dim.

"And everyone protected me," said Olive. "I always had a special attention that other children didn't get. I could tell when people looked at me that they were thinking, 'Poor little thing.' And then sometimes they'd say I was pretty, and I didn't know whether that was good or bad to be. I remember worrying about it. And about the way mothers looked at me—as if they knew secrets about me—not only when I was small, but much later on when I began to visit around. By that time, I knew it was pity, of course. I don't like pity. I never did. I was very ungrateful, I suppose. But I didn't show it. I was polite. I was a good guest. I was very neat. I knew I'd better be."

"Figuring it out all alone. I'm not pitying you! I'm admiring you."

"No, I wasn't alone very much. That was one of the things people were careful about. I can remember being terrified when I used to have to go to children's parties in Philadelphia, so I would know children my own age. But I got over that. I was what they call 'popular.' Which means you get asked to places. I had friends and I lived along with their lives—they had debutante parties and I got on the Bachelor's Cotillion List. And after a while—not long—the girls I knew were marrying boys in uniform, so I did that too."

She paused, didn't look at Mark. She said, "My uncle gave me my wedding, paid for it all, my trousseau, the decorations in the church, the wedding cake in white boxes—he liked it so much that he soon got married again himself. Tony had thought I was a rich girl. I should have made that clear—that it was just that I'd had things done for me—"

"And never enough," said Mark.

"Too much. I'm just trying to tell you! I'm trying to make you understand why I'm what I am. I'm an imitation, Mark. There's nothing to me."

"You don't understand yourself."

"But I do. I've lived among things that didn't belong to me until I'm a parasite."

"If you will marry me, everything I ever will have will belong to you, Olive."

"And what would you get out of it?"

"Oh, Olive—"

"I'd let you down," she said quickly, "I know. I've lived around too much to be a real person. This hole in the wall is the first place where I've really belonged, unless you count a bedroom in Reno. And I'd much rather be here than in guest rooms with linen sheets and embroidered towels. I want my children to have their own place, no matter what it is. I can't marry you for what you'd give me and the children, just because it would be so good."

"I want you for what you'd give me. For what I need," said Mark. "I want you to fill my hollow life—"

She shuddered and said, "Don't."

Tim came running in from school, and Olive kept him with her like a shield until Mark was gone.

He came again, as soon as he could get away from his work, flying down to Minneapolis one afternoon.

He said, "I came to beg for an evening."

She looked at him hesitantly.

"You're tired," she said.

"It's been a tough week. Full of problems I want to forget for a few hours. Can't you find someone to stay with the children and go to dinner with me?"

"Yes," Olive said in her straightforward way, "if you want that."

She meant it to be only that, as he knew. He had planned to take her to a private club in which he had a membership and where he thought they could be quiet. But tonight the club was overflowing with people after some enormous wedding reception, so they taxied around looking for a hotel or restaurant which was not crowded. Every place was nearly full. Finally, after substantial tipping, Mark was given a table in a noisy gilded dining room on the edge of a dance floor. The orchestra was so close that it was difficult to talk. He ordered cocktails and dinner, and they were almost silent as the waiter came and went.

"Do you want to dance?"

She smiled and shook her head.

"I don't want to push you around in that jam," said Mark. "I'm sorry this is turning out to be so grim."

"It's not grim."

"Not for me, because I'm with you. I can see you at least."

She gave a queer little nod of agreement.

"My God, Olive, I need you so much. There's nothing in life worth anything unless I'm with you."

She closed her eyes for a second, and when she opened them he saw the shine of tears.

"I shouldn't make you miserable—"

"I'm not miserable—"

She saw the weariness in his face, felt the ache of responsibility and the irresistible desire not to let him go again, to try, to yield—

"Olive, I love you. Won't you marry me?"

The orchestra blared. If she spoke in answer, he could not hear the words. But he felt her hand stretched to touch his in promise.

Two months later Mark woke from a drift of sleep after love. He saw that Olive had not gone to sleep. She was standing at a window, looking down at one of the unfamiliar streets through which their wedding journey was taking them.

"Anything wrong, my darling?"

"No, everything's right," said Olive. She came to him and knelt for a minute beside their bed. "Mark, I feel as if for the first time in my life I know who I am. Why I am."

As Mark reminded her, all of that doubt and struggle came back to Olive's mind. But it was vague and almost unbelievable now.

11

ONLY two weeks later it happened. Thanksgiving would cut into the calendar before long, and Mark was hoping that there would not be a heavy snowfall before the Crane-Eliot people came out for their promised inspection trip next week. The elder Mrs. Worthing had been in Chicago to support one more effort for peace in the world, and when she came back one morning Alan's absence from the house was only natural. She assumed that he was at work.

"So I thought nothing of it," she repeated to Pamela, again going over what she had excitedly told her daughter on the telephone. "I thought he would probably be home for dinner—although lately he has been out so much—" She paused and said in a puzzled way, "I was so sure that he was devoting himself to that other girl, the little Catholic one. But when I was speaking to Carrie about what to have for dinner, she asked when Alan would be back from his trip. I didn't know what trip, but of course I assumed that Mark had sent him somewhere on business. Then an hour afterward this telegram arrived."

Pamela had come over to her mother's house immediately. She was still holding the message, and looked down at it again.

> *Dot Langhorne and I were married last night are en route Antigua staying friends there will inform address later affection from both Alan.*

Pamela said, "Of course he took Dot out for a while pretty consistently. It's a silly way to do it but quite like Dot. She adores to dramatize herself, fancies herself as unconventional. And she would know she's not the type for a big wedding. She's a little old for that. She's been around too much."

"They could have had a small wedding. For the family. It would have given them something to remember."

"Maybe she hurried it up because she was afraid he'd get away," said Pam. "Well, anyway Dot's somebody we know. That's something to be thankful for. Though I never believed Alan was serious about that Carroll girl. I didn't think that would come to anything."

Her tone was slightly defensive, as if there were blame somewhere and she would accept none of it.

Mrs. Worthing said uneasily, "I hope it was nothing I said to Alan. I mean, I hope I didn't say too much."

"Too much?"

"I had a little talk with Alan," explained Mrs. Worthing. "I wasn't trying to influence him. I only wanted him to think it out. Of course, Alan knows that I'm completely broadminded, that no one could be more tolerant—"

"He could have had anybody," said Pamela.

"I hope he's married a lovely girl. I know the family, of course, but I haven't seen Dorothy since she was a little thing. She used to come to Alan's birthday parties."

"She came to Lucy's parties. She's at least a couple of years older than Alan. And she's certainly been to a lot of parties since! I'll bet the Langhornes are breathing a sigh of relief to get Dot off their hands."

[122]

"What do you mean? Isn't she a nice girl?"

"I don't know about her being nice—she's exciting," said Pam. "And Alan won't have to worry about money. I never thought she was exactly pretty but she has quantities of style."

"All I said to Alan, when I talked to him, was to give it serious thought."

"Mark probably talked to him too. Does Olive know about this?"

"I called their house after I talked to you. But she was out. Do you suppose they'll want to live here, Alan and Dorothy? There's plenty of room."

Pamela shook her head with certainty about that. "No, she'll want something stylized. Something out of this world."

"I don't know what I'll do with this big house now that Alan is married. I suppose I should get rid of it."

"Don't be in a hurry. You need it. You're always opening it up for things."

"Yes, I have the D.A.R. here next week," said Mrs. Worthing, brightening up at the responsibility, "and, of course, I want to entertain for the young people when they come back from their honeymoon."

Lucy Searles took the news of the marriage into her husband's studio. She loved to have an excuse to interrupt him, and he was rarely working hard enough to have that matter. In a city where all males were expected to go to work on weekdays unless they were ill, aged, or mentally unfit, Gregory Searles had made himself the popular exception. No one expected him to earn a living. There were those who laughed at him, and others who said that maybe he had the right idea. Everyone of their acquaintance knew that he lived on Lucy's money and that her fortune had been one of the reasons he had selected her in the first place.

She knew that too. But she knew that it wasn't the only reason. There had been plenty of passion in their bargain, and it had never worn thin or disappointed her. She lived for Gregory. She wanted no children in their way or sharing. She wanted to be free to do the things he wanted to do. Sometimes they would go to

[123]

Greece or Mexico or Spain. Never to a cold country. Gregory was fond of the colors of the Southwest, of the sound of the Brule River, and they wintered and summered according to his moods, which were never impatient or demanding, but invariably satisfied.

He was not an unsocial or bad-mannered artist, and he had an irony and vocabulary which added flavor to dinner parties; so they had many invitations and gave some care to entertaining. They lived in a little house on the edge of the lake, small enough so that they could "lock up and go" when they felt like it. It had a studio which had been once used by a far better artist than Gregory, one splendid bedroom, and another for emergencies. Since Gregory regarded cooking as an art, Lucy had become an excellent cook. He had painted amusing murals on the kitchen walls.

Pamela was always the more intelligent and more beautiful of the Worthing daughters. But Lucy brimmed over with sex, with desires that seemed to have been omitted or transmuted in her mother and father but proved that some ancestor had been a boisterous character. She had been that way since her adolescence. The worst day of her early girlhood had been the one when her mother had embarrassed her by making a talk in public on sex education. Lucy had sobbed herself to sleep, sure that such a talk would drive the boys away.

She loved this studio. It did not matter to Lucy that the pictures did not sell, even if Gregory finished them—and often he did not. She knew how good they were. There was a water-color sketch of her on one wall—it was the back of her naked body. Wonderful day when he had been working on that, wonderful when he had stopped working. She often posed for him even now. Her secret pride was that he said she was the best model he ever had used.

He was a little bald, a little plump, with lazy brown eyes and delicate long-fingered hands. She came in, stood behind him, said, "I like that ever so much—what do you think has happened?"

"Since breakfast?"

"No. Last night. Alan is married."

"Good. I think he'll do all right with his pious little girl. That church teaches its women to be tractable."

"He didn't marry that girl. He married Dot Langhorne."

Greg looked to see if she were joking.

"He did. Mother had a telegram and she says Mark had one too. He married Dot and they're on their way now to Antigua."

"Well, I'll be damned," said Gregory.

"Everyone is simply speechless. None of us had any idea that he was in love with Dot."

"Is he?"

"He must be. He'd better be."

"Better indeed," said Greg, changing the color of a shadow on the canvas before him.

Lucy sat cross-legged on the low divan, where she could see his face, and lit a cigarette.

"What do you really think about it?" she asked almost pleadingly.

"I think Pamela will rejoice that her clan is saved from the papists. Let them remain in their ghetto."

"I've known Dot all my life," said Lucy. "In a way she's one of my oldest friends. She has lots of good qualities. It's just that I remember some things about her at school—she's a year younger than I am, a little older than Alan—not that it matters. But I mean that she seems quite a lot older. Do you understand?"

"I follow you easily."

"She's very decorative, don't you think so?"

Gregory's murmur might have been yes or no.

"Of course, it would have been a mistake for him to marry that Irish Catholic girl—"

Like Pamela, she seemed to be aware of fault, of disappointment, and was denying it.

"Why?" asked Greg. "The Irish have the oldest known culture in Europe, and the Catholic Church is the repository of much of the greatest art in the world."

"You don't marry cultures or repositories," said Lucy. "When you marry into a parish in North Hillside."

Effie Dwight had opened the telegram from Alan before Mark came in. It was addressed to him at the Worthing Building, and she always prepared the mail for his attention, sorting out the tares.

She slit open the yellow envelope and noted the signature. A long breath of amazement escaped her as the typed and pasted words were photographed indelibly on her mind.

> *Can a two-week vacation for me be arranged married Dot Langhorne yesterday am on way to Antigua think my job can be handled by Andrewson during absence will omit summer vacation as necessary to make up time regards Alan.*

The girl's name stood out in Effie's mind. It was familiar to anyone who understood the commerce of the city. When a traveler approached, it was one of the first things to be seen—the Langhorne name painted bold and large on grain elevators. That girl! thought Effie, recalling what she knew about her—a white roadster, an incident in the Black Bear Café. Of course, I knew there was nothing to the talk about Alan and the Carroll girl, but it must be hard on her. Alan shouldn't have put ideas in her head. And maybe he would have been better off at that. Effie read the telegram again to be sure it was true and took the mail in to Mark's desk, the telegram spread open on the top.

He came in cheerfully, and she thought, of course he knew about this, it must have been brewing. But he left the door of the inner office open and she heard the violence of an oath. Maybe it had come as a surprise. She waited for orders, but after a minute Mark closed his door. She could hear the vague sound of his voice. He must be talking on the private line, probably calling his wife.

Olive said, "Oh, no, Mark—I don't believe it's true! A telegram? It's somebody's idea of a joke."

"No—it comes from Miami."

"You say—Dot Langhorne!"

"That's what he wired."

"Mark, he wouldn't do that."

"He has a right to get married," said Mark, "to anyone who'll have him."

"But that other girl—"

"I suppose something must have happened. She said they were fighting."

"Alan's not cruel—"

"He may have wanted to cut it off completely."

"But, Mark, after what she told you that day in the hospital, that they were so much in love—"

"That's what she thought."

"I don't like this, Mark."

"It doesn't matter whether we like it or not," said Mark in a hard voice. "Nobody consulted us."

"She did—that girl—"

"I couldn't mix in it. You know that. You didn't expect me to, did you?"

"No—" doubtfully.

He asked angrily, "What did you want me to do? Take Alan by the hand and lead him to her marriage classes and priests?"

"Oh, Mark, don't take it like that."

"Well, I called you because I thought you'd like to know. But don't worry about it. He's old enough to know his own business."

"Yes."

"You might get in touch with Mother."

"There's a message here that she called up while I was at the market."

"Then she's probably heard. If she hasn't, will you break the news? I have a big day—I haven't time to listen to a lot of talk."

"I'll go out and see her. And, Mark—"

"Yes—yes, dear—"

"Come home as early as you can."

On the beach at Antigua, the two lay resting after a swim, she on her yellow mattress, he on the white sand. No one came near to disturb them, for it was taken for granted that in these first days they would have no time for anything but love, nor any interest except in discovering each other and contemplating the discovery with wonder and delight.

Alan thought of the girl beside him. Who wasn't girlish, as he knew now. He told himself, I'm grateful to her for everything. I should be. Now I'll be able to get down to earth, put my mind on something. It was the best way all around. Dot had the right idea. She certainly puts her man first. She knows what it's all about.

He did not harbor the thought of what the gentle teaching of innocence might have been. As it flitted across his mind, he brushed it off. He lay as if relaxed, but he was still tight with determination, as he had been for the past week. He thought, maybe it's not two people who matter so much but what they make out of it. The joined thing. I'm committed now. I have to do a job. She and I begin from here. And no questions asked.

His wife pulled herself up to a sitting position and drew up her knees, displaying the supple action of her body. She was a lean girl, enameled and polished, with eyes so narrow that they seemed to be always half-smiling. It was a face capable of secrets.

"You're such a beautiful man. I wanted another look."

"I have a beautiful wife, anyway." Say it, believe it.

"Anyway, I think I'll be good for you."

"I'm sure of it."

"What did you wire your brother?"

"I just said we'd done it and asked for two weeks off."

"I wonder how he'll feel about your marrying me."

"It will suit him right down to the ground," said Alan, but suddenly his voice had a sharper edge.

"He's your boss?"

"Of course. He's president of the company. Not my immediate boss, but I thought this had better come through him."

"Do you have to work for that company?"

"There's no law about it. It's where the money in our family comes from. As it happens, I just naturally like my job."

"I'm vague about what it is."

"Well, you know I'm a construction engineer. I'll have to take you up to the location and show you the works. For the next five years we'll be getting this taconite plant into operation—that's the first thing—and then working it over so that we can cut costs and compete as favorably as possible with the other companies that are doing the same thing. It's not going to be too easy either. But it's fun to get your teeth into something with so many possibilities.

When I get back, I'm going to dig right into my end of the job."

"Don't forget me, will you?"

"Not likely. I'll come home to you."

"Where will we live? I don't want to go to your mother's house. When I used to go to parties there, I always was terrified about spilling things. Your mother is wonderful, but—"

"I know," he agreed. That question of where they would live had struck a memory. He had to dispose of that before he answered. Grasp the nettle.

He said slowly, "It might be a good idea to live up on the location."

"Location?"

"There's a nice little town going up at Baraga right across from our plant."

"One of those development things?"

"That's right."

"Oh, you're kidding—"

He was quiet.

She said, "You know one place that might be all right?"

"What?"

"The new Mirador apartment building. There are some big ones on the top floor. They're stunning. Very exciting—"

"No place for a young engineer. Not on what I make."

"Oh," she said, and lay back again on the mattress.

Mrs. Carroll said to her daughter, "Aunt Kate and I will be back in an hour."

Rose Mary said in an impenetrable way, "All right, Mother."

"You don't want to come with us?"

"No."

The two women walked down the street carrying a little of her pain with them. It made her mother sigh sharply.

She said, "I'm hardly fit in my mind to enter the church and begin the novena, the way I feel about that fellow. The way he treated her! I'd just like to give him a piece of my mind!"

Kate said, "My heart aches for her. Never so much as mention-

[129]

ing a word about it. It gave me a terrible shock when I saw that in the paper tonight. But she must have known about it beforehand. He hasn't been around lately."

"Not for more than a week. It must have been ten days or more ago that he brought her back to the house one night, and they were out in front in his car for a long time. It made me nervous, but I never had to worry about Rose Mary. Then after I heard her come up the steps and close the front door, he drove away like a bat out of hell. I could hear his car squeak like a crazy thing as he turned the corner."

"Was it the matter of religion, do you think?"

"He was going with her to the Cana class. I think more likely it was his family made the trouble. His mother is one of those great clubwomen, always gadding about the country. I don't know how she managed to bring up her children. Not too well, from the looks of this."

"The brother was on the plane with me when I came down. I didn't know who it was at the time. Rose Mary told me later, after I pointed him out in the airport. He seemed a friendly man."

"It's different when it comes to marriage," said Mrs. Carroll sharply. "Then you're not good enough for them."

"Rose Mary is good enough for anybody. For royalty."

"To treat her like that!"

"Maybe it's her own choice, May. And maybe it's all for the best. A mixed marriage is a dangerous thing. She'll find a fine Catholic boy—"

"She's never been a girl to run around. She was set on this one."

"I'm making this novena for her," said Rose Mary's aunt. "For her special intention."

Her mother said, over a little sob, "That's what I'm doing too."

Rose Mary put away the dishes. There was a stain on a piece of pink shelf paper in the cupboard and she got some fresh water and rubbed it away. She slowly straightened the rows of glassware, putting the tallest goblets back where they belonged. The kitchen was in perfect order, but it was not yet nine o'clock. She went into the living room, where Bart was yawning over a schoolbook and her father watching television in a disinterested manner.

He looked up. "Want a game of rummy?"

"No, thanks, not tonight, I've some things to do," she said in the impenetrable way. She went upstairs to the clean, dainty, commonplace bedroom which was her refuge and cage. To be on the safe side, she locked the door against the intrusion of her mother or aunt. Then she took the newspaper clipping out of her purse to read it again. She had torn it out of a newspaper bought in the hospital. She had been watching for this ever since she had his letter a week ago, since she had known it was hopeless and had refused to believe what she knew. For there could always be a miracle.

Mr. and Mrs. Clinton Langhorne announce the recent marriage in Miami Beach of their daughter, Dorothy Wayhill, and Mr. Alan Peter Worthing. After a brief wedding trip to Antigua, Mr. and Mrs. Worthing will be at home in Duluth. Mrs. Worthing was graduated from Forest Hill Academy and is a member of the Junior League. Mr. Worthing is a graduate of Andover Academy and Harvard University. He is the son of the late Mr. Philip Worthing and Mrs. Worthing, nationally well known for her civic and philanthropic activities.

Antigua—how do you pronounce that? Is it in the Caribbean? What is it like there right now this minute? He never spoke of that place to me.

Rose Mary thought, it's his brother that I hate. If it hadn't been for him—I could see the prejudice sticking out of him when I talked to him that day. "Alan doesn't have to accept those rules," he said. He must be very well satisfied tonight. Alan will never have to now.

She took out Alan's letter again. She carried that with her.

". . . so it gets down to this. You say we can't be married unless I take these instructions. Maybe I could do it with my tongue in my cheek, but that's no way for us to live. That priest—the Father Kenedy you wanted me to talk to—laid it on the line. He said that I'm unduly resistant, that I'm not in the proper frame of mind to make a success of a mixed marriage, as he kept calling it. I'm mixed all right. I didn't want to go to him in the first place. I had a hunch that it would only make things worse and it did. Why couldn't we have worked this out between us? I don't think a marriage can work unless a man and woman put each other first, unless they don't let anything else interfere. It doesn't seem to me that you want me as much as you want other things . . . you were the one who called it off, you told me not to come around unless I was ready to do what the priest said. . . . I guess I'm not a good liar and that seemed to be indicated. . . . I think you should know that I am probably going to marry someone else. A girl I used to play around with before I met you. It sounds corny to say that it won't be the same thing that it might have been with us, but I'll say it for once. . . . I . . .

She had finished it again. It became more dreadful every time she read it. She walked across the room, and looked at a statue of the Blessed Virgin set on a shelf between the looped white window curtains. Not reverently, but bitterly.

She whispered, "Remember that never was it known that anyone who fled to Thy protection, implored Thy help, or sought Thy intercession was left unaided. . . . You left me unaided!"

She took the image down from the shelf and shoved it in a bureau drawer behind a pile of underwear. She started to write a letter, tore it up, undressed slowly, went across the hall to take a bath, tried to read, tried to sleep.

About three o'clock Rose Mary got out of her bed, took the statue out of the bureau drawer and put it back on the shelf.

BOOK TWO

12

THE four financiers from the East had been more than impressed
by their inspection of the taconite processing plant at Baraga. All
of them were men who spent their working time in city offices, and
the sight of this actual conquest of nature and the feeling of having
a hand in it was a stimulating experience. They were familiar with
this job from paper study of the prospects, reports, and accountings.
But here they touched it physically, and it was enough to stir any
man's imagination and secret pride, if it was part of his affairs.

Before them was the great lake, which was being made sub-
servient to their purposes and profits. They saw for themselves how
vast and how dangerous it looked on this November day, ridden
with cold white crests of foam. They studied the conformation of
the harbor, asked questions about the great stone breakwater which
had been built—in part with their money—incredibly far out into
the lake to form one arm of the shelter for ships.

Mark explained the wave motion, how high the waves could be
expected to rise, ten feet once a year, fifteen feet once in ten years.
As he spoke, he recalled that it was Alan who first had given him
those scientific averages. Too bad Alan wasn't back on the job yet.
He would be a good guide for these visitors and his enthusiasm
would show off the project. A sense of having something to make
up to Alan grumbled in Mark's mind.

He took his backers to the growing structure of the mill which
would soon pulverize the once indomitable rock to flour fineness, and
pointed out the place where magnetic separators would attract the
ore and reject waste products. It was all rough, crude and muddy
now, but the smooth order of the process that was planned began

to be apparent to the visitors. They stood in the rutted clay access roads, looking at the railroad layout. They turned up the collars of their city coats against the rough breath of the lake. They looked odd under the metal hats that Mark made them all wear for safety. And they felt adventurous and powerful.

They were men who were well used to luxurious living. Howard Eliot spent several months of every year on his yacht. But they took a homely interest in the four- and six-room houses in the new village and went through one of them.

"All very shipshape," said Howard Eliot.

"All anyone could want," said Eben Crane. "In a place like this there should be a fine community spirit. Young men and their families. Ideal."

Would Alan live here now, wondered Mark. Would he remember taking that other girl around to choose a home?

The inspection party lunched in the commissary where most of the men on the job ate, but they had a special table set in the room where pinball machines lined the walls. Mark had consulted Olive about the lunch. "Should I bring up some steaks from the Club, do you think?" And Olive had said, "I wouldn't. It would spoil the picture. Let them have the usual hamburgers and pork chops and apple pie." So Mark did.

Over the food they tackled the biggest problem.

"It's a terrific job," said Eliot. "I hand it to you, boy. I hope we haven't bitten off more than we can chew."

"I don't think so," said Mark. "It's taken a lot of money but every other combination on the lake shore has spent more."

"You think we can make a profit?"

"We can if we get a tax break," said Mark. "At the minute we have one. The high-grade ores have been taxed without any mercy. But the state wants to get this taconite production underway. They know that if that doesn't happen we'll have ghost towns all through this area, and what can they tax then? We didn't have much trouble in getting through a law which declares the mining of taconite to be in the public interest. That gave us rights of eminent domain, so we've been able to condemn property and get our roads and railroad sites where we want them without being held up for outrageous prices. When we get into production, we'll have to keep playing up the public-interest idea. Make it clear that if we can't mine at a profit, we can't go on, and it will be the state that will suffer."

"Can you control the legislature on taxes?"

"We have some good friends down there. But it's not so easy as it used to be."

"In the old days," said Harry Tuttle, "we used to be able to boss the mining towns. We usually had a fellow close to us who ran the political end for us, somebody who would be in cahoots with the local priest."

"Why the priest?" asked Eben Crane.

"Well, we employed a lot of foreigners in the mines," said Tuttle, "and they were just beginning to vote. They didn't like even then to vote the way the superintendent did. But usually they'd do what the priest told them to do. Fear of hell and damnation. And if he wanted a new church or to put a steeple on an old one, he knew which side his bread was buttered on."

"Sounds reasonable," said Eliot. "You'll know what to do when someone comes asking you for a steeple on the church, Mark."

"I didn't see any church," said Eben Crane.

Mark said, "There isn't any. The Catholic priest wants me to let them hold services on Sunday in the schoolhouse."

"But you couldn't do a thing like that," said Eben Crane, "unless you let all denominations use it."

"Nobody else has asked for it so far," said Mark. He recalled that Eben Crane was a crank on religion.

Crane persisted, "What did you do? Tell the priest he certainly couldn't use the school for his Masses?"

"I haven't given him any answer."

"Why don't you tell him he can use it for nondenominational community services? Open to all?"

"I don't think he'd be interested in that," said Mark drily.

"Then turn him down."

"The trouble is that some of the people living here would have to go a long way to get to a Catholic church. And the weather can be bad."

"That's their choice."

"With them it's an obligation. They can't take it or leave it," said Mark.

Harry Tuttle said, "One thing is in our favor. The Speaker of the House is pretty clear-headed on the matter of mining taxes."

The conversation shifted to costs.

In the late afternoon Mark and Harry Tuttle took the inspection party to the airport and jovially loaded it on Mr. Crane's private plane. Watching it take off, they appraised the day.

"It came off pretty well, don't you think so?" asked Mark.

"It was a very good job. Now that they can visualize the whole thing, we'll have them right back of us."

"Was Mr. Crane satisfied that we weren't throwing away money?"

"Apparently. He was enthusiastic—for him." Tuttle chuckled, "There seemed to be just one thing that bothered him. He came up to me after lunch and wanted to know if you were a Roman Catholic."

"If *I* was!"

"Yes—I saw his hackles go up at the idea of the priest using the schoolhouse. He thought you were for it and that you must be a fisheater."

"It's none of his business, a matter like that. That's for us to decide."

"I know," said Tuttle, "but he's a funny guy. I straightened him out about you."

"The old bigot," said Mark. "He's not giving any orders around here."

He said good night to Harry Tuttle and went home, making his way through the darkening evening to the circle of light and warmth that was his own, that Olive created for him. Mark loved to open his door, to call out, "Hello!"—and the word always brought some answer of welcome, perhaps the run of the children, Olive's "I'm upstairs, darling." Or it might be stillness, for she was in the kitchen helping the untrained maid, or changing her dress, and the children might be absorbed in a game on the library floor. Whatever the routine of the evening was, there was a place waiting for him.

He saw a memorandum on the telephone stand in the nook by the stairs—that was where messages for him were always left. This was in the maid's awkward writing, "Mr. Worthing—your father called. Please call DA 4-2116."

That crazy girl—my father. Mark carried it upstairs, found Olive, kissed her and said, "They got off all right on schedule. That guided tour's over."

"Weren't they delighted?"

"They don't overdo it, but Harry and I think they were pretty well satisfied."

Olive had met them the night before at dinner. She said, "That Mr. Crane is quite a character."

"A tough nut to crack."

"All through dinner he explained to me just what was wrong with the world. He believes in revivals and evangelists, did you know that?"

"I know—look, Olive, what's this message—my father—what does she mean?"

Olive said, "Fantastic! Oh, I know—it was probably that priest, don't you think? He'd call himself "Father," and she'd just take it for granted that he was a worldly one."

"That's probably just what it is."

"Are you still arguing about the birth-control clinic with the priest?"

"No, he wants a place in Baraga to hold church services. He wants favors on his own terms, that lad."

"You couldn't very well refuse that."

"Why couldn't I?"

"Not if people wanted to go to church—and it's so near Christmas," said Olive. "Oh, I must show you what I found for us to give your mother. It's an engagement calendar that practically speaks."

"What do you want for Christmas?"

"What I have," said Olive.

13

Effie Dwight was unaccustomed to receiving priests in the Worthing offices. There used to be an elderly, fat one from the mining towns who called once in a while on the late Mr. Worthing —always, as Effie knew, to ask for a donation. Philip Worthing used to joke about the "holy Father begging from the damned." She was aware that these men expected a special deference, and she tried to balance a proper amount of respect on a manner which would show that she was a practicing Protestant who needed to bow down to no priest.

"I am Father Kenedy. I have an appointment with Mr. Worthing for five o'clock," said this youngish man.

"He's not in his office at the moment, sir. But I expect him back before he goes home."

"I'll wait a bit," said the priest. He sat down in a chair on the far side of the office and immediately took a small black prayer book out of his pocket. Quietly he read. To Effie he seemed very much out of place.

Mark had the same impression as he came in. He had been forced to leave a conference to keep this appointment and wished he had not made it. But Father Kenedy had said on the telephone last night that he would like to talk over a matter of business with Mark. Mark himself had thought this would be a good opportunity to make it clear that, if he granted any favor, it must not be taken as a precedent.

Now that he saw him again, the priest seemed a very familiar figure. There was the same look of not being woman-tended, the same big shoes, the same extraordinary aura of confidence.

"Sorry to keep you waiting."

"Not at all. It is very good of you to give me a little time."

"Come right in. Effie, you needn't wait. I shall be leaving after I've talked with Father Kenedy. Good night."

He closed the door of his private office, offered the priest a comfortable leather-covered chair, and took his usual place behind the long shining steel desk. As they lighted cigarettes, Mark had a curious feeling that he had been waiting for this encounter, that something needed to be finished off. A favorite picture of Olive lay on the edge of his blotter. It was a cheap little one, taken in a booth in a railway station when they were on their wedding trip. He had always liked it, wouldn't throw it away. Mark thought, she said I should give in to the priest, because of Christmas. Just like her. Generous as the day is long.

"Well, Father Kenedy, I suppose you want to know if you can use the little school at Baraga for your services?"

"If you've come to any decision."

"I think it can be arranged as a temporary thing."

"That's very kind of you, Mr. Worthing."

"Do you have any idea of how many people of your faith live up there?"

"Yes, I've canvassed the situation pretty carefully. The whole community will include about seventy to eighty families, I was told. Thirty-two of those have some Catholic connections. I don't mean to say they are all good Catholics, but if they are not, this may give them a chance to rejoin their faith. There probably also are some farmers and fishermen in the vicinity who have fallen away for lack of a convenient church. We might serve them as well."

"The trouble is that yours is only one of the religions who might want the same privilege," said Mark. "That objection was made when the matter came up."

The priest said nothing in answer.

"But I suppose you don't think that going to church matters much to those who aren't Roman Catholics," said Mark, with a grin.

"For Catholics, it is a necessity. A Catholic is required to hear Mass at certain intervals."

"No matter what?"

"The Church is never unreasonable. It makes exceptions. But this arrangement will be a blessing to a number of good people. And I assure you that it will be temporary. The Bishop feels that in

[141]

the near future—perhaps even next spring—we could build a chapel in Baraga which would take care of the needs of that village and also of those in nearby towns where there is no church. That is another thing I wanted to talk to you about. The diocese would like to purchase sufficient land for this purpose, and your company owns most of the property in that area. We'd like to buy a piece."

"How big a piece?"

"Perhaps a few acres."

"You won't need that for a chapel!"

"We have to consider the future. There may be a tremendous development along the north shore."

"It's going to grow, all right."

"We would have to begin in a small way. But plan for expansion at the right time. In connection with any church, we always must think of providing room for a school."

"A Catholic school, you mean?"

"A parochial school."

Mark said, "I don't particularly like the idea of that."

He could feel that his reaction made no difference at all.

"We aren't planning that this will be an old-fashioned company town," Mark went on. "The people who live there aren't going to be subject to any kind of pressure from us because they're employed by our corporation."

"You'll have a better community spirit that way."

"Yes—so I'd personally not want to see religious factions destroying a good little town."

"That should never happen."

"It will happen if you start this parochial school thing. I don't want to be rude, Father Kenedy, but I think your insistence on separate schools for your people is one of the most dangerous things in this country. I wish you'd tell me why public schools, supported by the taxpayers, aren't good enough for all American kids. They can get their religion on the side in their own way."

The priest said, "A Catholic's religion cannot be on the side. It's not a supplemental thing. Religion must permeate a Catholic's whole life, all he thinks, all he does."

[142]

"We get that preached in our Protestant churches too," said Mark, "that you can't be a Christian just on Sunday."

"With a Catholic," said the priest, "religion must be the central fact for existence. It is the reason for his life, the seed from which his actions grow. A Catholic needs a Catholic education—"

"Does he need to have history slanted in favor of the Church and science made to fit its dogmas?"

"The Church has been the deepest student of history. It has no quarrel with science."

Mark said, "That's hard to believe. For example, artificial insemination is a scientific discovery. I saw in the paper just the other day that the Pope had come out with a blast against it. Catholics were told they couldn't go along with that scientific advance."

"And so good Catholics will not."

"But that's not thinking for yourself. That's being told."

The priest said, "You see, Mr. Worthing, a Catholic does not walk alone. He is part of a great corporate body of belief and practice and worship."

"I'm glad to hear you admit that," said Mark, "for that is just about what I told my brother when he talked to me about the possibility of marrying a Catholic girl. I said that he would find the priest would be part of his family."

"I see that Alan has married elsewhere."

Mark's face was startled. "You know my brother?"

"I had some conversation with him at the time you mention."

"I didn't know that."

"It was a little irregular," said Father Kenedy, "but there seemed to be some antagonism between him and the priest in Rose Mary's parish, who would normally have instructed him. She wanted him to talk to me. So he did. He quoted some of the things you had said."

"I didn't interfere. I told Alan it was his business."

"You probably influenced him more than you knew. And perhaps for good. I was disturbed about the possibility of that marriage. I know Rose Mary Carroll. She is a devout girl."

"Alan was going right along with her."

"He was trying to please her. He was willing to accept her faith if he had to—to tolerate but not to share it—in fact, he was very resistant to it. I'm inclined to think—no doubt you agree—that the outcome has been fortunate."

"So you found Alan resistant—"

"I'm not criticizing him for that. There was nothing hypocritical about him at all. He's a splendid young fellow in many ways. But he seemed to me, if I may say so, inflexibly bigoted in regard to Church doctrine. He had none of the spirit of intellectual inquiry you yourself have."

"I have? I'm afraid, Father Kenedy, that you have me wrong."

"I don't believe so."

"Any inquiries I have made have been only for the sake of proving myself right."

The priest smiled. Mark had an extraordinary sense of friendship, offered but not pressing or demanding.

"I'm impressed by the power of your institution. Who wouldn't be? But I'm sorry to say I have no friendliness for it."

"Some of the greatest services to the Church have come from those who have begun by being inimical to it. At least, you are interested in the truth. With your brother it was desire for the girl, and compromise in order to fulfill the desire. They wouldn't have been happy."

"I hope you're right about that," said Mark.

The priest stood up. He spoke as if his mind were not on what he was saying. "I'm afraid I'm taking too much of your time. Once more, I'm grateful for your generosity in the matter of the use of the school. We can discuss the matter of a church site at your convenience."

"I'll take it up with the proper people. There's no hurry about that, is there?"

"No." The priest hesitated, but not in awkwardness. He was thinking something over. Then he gave the thought to Mark. He asked, "Why don't you look into Catholic theology? You'd find it interesting even if it does strengthen your present position."

"I have very little time."

"You should find time to complete your philosophy, Mark. Every man has that right."

He used Mark's first name simply and naturally, as if the time had come for that. He used it without personal intimacy, as a teacher might.

"I suppose so," said Mark. "I suppose that's true."

"Let me send you a couple of books," said Father Kenedy.

14

WHEN she saw them come in, Olive had the same sensation that she had when she first met Alan with his wife. To her it was like sensing an odor that was familiar and reminiscent. It was an odor blended of primitive desires and social sophistication, of private clashes and devotion in public, of alcohol and sex that was slightly rotten. The girl wore a starkly white dress, simple and high as a baby's bib in front and naked in back to her polished bronze middle. Alan, handsome as a young god tonight, was behind her, smiling mischievously, as if he had put something over on everyone and was enjoying the sensation. It's not right, thought Olive; he's almost defying us all; he's not softened or deeply stirred. It's false romance. He's had her—he has her—it's fun and exciting. He's not tender enough. It's not what he expected, just as beginning to live with Tony was such a shock, not what I expected. Or wanted. I had almost forgotten about that. For some reason, seeing those two here tonight brings it back so clearly.

And as she stayed a little aloof from the rest of the guests, waiting for Mark to join her, Olive remembered an odd mixture of events and places and moods—the shouts of laughter from a swimming pool beneath a bedroom where she was lying in despair. Tony's laughter—the horror was that he could laugh in spite of what he had just said to her. She remembered how it felt to put a good face on misery and try to keep it from slipping off. She remembered that there had been a polo game while Tim was being

[145]

born and she was nearly dying, and how Tony had come to the hospital a day later, smiling, charming the nurses, making them believe that he cared. Olive glanced again at the honor guests.

This was Pamela's party for Alan and his bride, an affair of cocktails and supper which proved, as the architect had promised, that Pamela could entertain fifty people without having her house crowded. Pamela had held it down to fifty-three tonight. It was Christmas week, and so she had used a Christmas motif in her decorations; but there was no commonplaceness of tinsel or Santa Claus. A tall spruce tree, sprayed with white paint and trimmed only with pale pink carnations, was moving slowly and musically on a turntable in the glassed-in patio. Faceless plastic angels presided over the buffet table in the dining area.

The Worthing family was doing what was proper under the circumstances. Mrs. Worthing had given a family dinner party last week for the bridal couple, using her classic menu—turtle soup, breast of guinea hen, and marron soufflé. But it had been a rather labored affair. Mrs. Worthing tried with conscientious kindness to welcome Alan's wife as her new daughter, but it was a role into which Dot did not fit. That was obvious to all of them.

Olive had felt as if she were attending a banquet given to promote some good cause and that speeches would be inevitable. She was sure that Dot, although she was as polite as a little girl at a birthday party who had been told to mind her manners, would ridicule this affair when she got away from it. Perhaps not to Alan just yet, but to her gay friends. Yet Olive had never liked her mother-in-law better than as she watched Mrs. Worthing attempt to make this collection of individuals into what the experts said a family should be.

She's so good—she's so clumsy in human relations, thought Olive.

Alan had made several rounds of Martinis, so it was difficult to keep the conversation steady or in line at the dinner table. But Mrs. Worthing tried her best to guide it. She said, when the champagne was poured, "I think we should have a little toast to

[146]

our bride and groom. Mark, will you propose it?"

Mark got it over quickly. "Here's to you both. The best of luck!"

"Have you and Alan found a place to live yet, Dot?" Pamela asked.

Dot said with a docile look, "The Mirador Apartments. Alan adores the penthouse ones."

"Oh, I do, do I?" asked Alan.

"Darling, of course it's a mess now, how could anyone help loathing it? I mean that you saw the possibilities, and when it's done the way we want it—"

The odor of pretense had drifted to Olive.

Lucy and her husband had done their share by entertaining the bride and groom at one of their Sunday-night suppers, which had won a good deal of local renown. They always hired a colored butler to mix drinks and serve at their parties, but Lucy and Gregory did the epicurean cooking themselves. The *pièce de résistance* for this supper was a mystery based on veal. Lucy was stirring in sour cream and wine at the proper intervals when Olive came out to the kitchen—painted with bright, cynical murals— to see if she could help.

Lucy looked up, saw who it was, and asked, "Is it going all right, do you think?"

"Everybody seems to be having a wonderful time."

"I felt I had to do something for them," said Lucy, "but doesn't it seem difficult? I suppose it's because it's so queer to think that she is Alan's wife."

"Does it seem that way to you?"

Lucy said, "Yes, sort of weird. As if he'd married the cover of *Vogue!* Dot's frightfully decorative—but for Alan—what do you think of it, Olive? I mean really?"

"Well, I'm glad Alan's going to have a home of his own."

"Yes, that. And she has wonderful taste. But—she's older—"

"Only a couple of years, isn't it? And she can look like a child."

"I know. She always could. Always will. She'll see to that. But if anyone had told me that she'd turn up as Alan's wife—now if it had been Mark—"

"It wouldn't have been Mark."

"I mean before he met you. Because Dot has been around so much. She was very popular, you know, used to be."

"How did it happen that she didn't marry before now?"

"I think she was having too good a time. And her sights were pretty high. But you know how it is sometimes, even with a girl who's had a lot of attention and is attractive to men. If she doesn't concentrate on anyone, all the men of her own age get married, and all of a sudden she's just an old story in a way. Of course, people always ask Dot when they have an extra man—"

"You're speaking of the past," said Olive.

"Well, I still find it hard to believe. I thought Alan would want someone who was fresh—I don't mean bold—"

"I know what you mean."

"Greg said something creepy about her. I suppose I shouldn't repeat it." But she went on before Olive could stop her, "I was saying that Dot was sexy and he said no, not our way. He said, 'She practices sex.' You know, like a lawyer or a doctor practices. Doesn't that sound awful?"

"Yes," said Olive. "I hope Greg's wrong—completely wrong."

"He hardly ever is—well, here she is in the family, and maybe it will work out perfectly. As you say, it was time Alan moved out of Mother's house, and he's so kindhearted that he never would have up and done it unless he had married. Dot will have a beautiful setup, that's for sure. He'll have a place to entertain, and Alan loves people. And—well, he would have found the lace-curtain Irish Catholic crowd pretty hard to chum up with."

"Not if he loved that girl," said Olive. "It wouldn't have mattered."

Lucy put the cover back on her French copper kettle, saying with certainty, "Ten minutes more will do it." Then she said uncertainly, "I wish I knew what really did happen. With that other girl. If his marrying Dot was sort of a rebound."

"I'm afraid that's none of our business, Lucy."

"No. He was always very closemouthed about her. But Alan is such a dear. I so want him to be happy. The way Greg and I are.

And look how Mark has simply blossomed since you two have been married."

"Give Alan time. He'll blossom in his own way," said Olive, not quite believing what she was saying.

Tonight, in Pamela's house, Olive again felt doubt. There was something artificial, contrived, about the gaiety surrounding Alan and his wife. Also she had been unable to forget what she knew of that talk between Mark and Rose Mary Carroll at the hospital. It haunted her because she could imagine the desperation of the girl in accosting Mark and begging for his help. Alan must have been very much in earnest or he would not have begun to go to those marriage classes. He must have given Rose Mary every hope, a genuine belief, that he would marry her. The thought of the shock that Alan's sudden marriage must have been to the Carroll girl had given Olive many a sickening twinge of pity. Had Alan given her any warning?

But, no matter what, it wasn't fair to blame Mark for the outcome, as he said that girl had done when she talked to him. Perhaps he had influenced Alan, but Alan had asked for it. Mark had only given his honest opinion. He had told Alan how he himself felt about Catholicism, that was all. She thought, Mark always bends over backward to be honest. And Alan is a grown man, old enough to think for himself.

There's not the slightest reason for Mark to feel guilty about any of this, thought Olive. But he's not happy about it. He's worried. I must make him believe that Alan's marriage will come out all right. It will have much more chance if we all believe that. Mark should stop thinking about that other girl, and stop wondering if there's something in the Catholic point of view. That's why he reads those books that Father Kenedy wished on him, though he doesn't agree with a word in them. They just make him more prejudiced.

Alan came up to interrupt her thoughts.

"How are you tonight, Alan?"

"Everything is under control so far."

"Your bride is looking very beautiful."

"I told her so a couple of times. She insisted on it. Where's Mark?"

"Coming. He dropped me here and went on an errand. He wanted to return some books he's been reading to the person who lent them to him."

"So the old man's learned to read."

"And how! He's been poring over theology lately. He has a standing quarrel with a priest named Father Kenedy."

As she said that, Olive knew she had blundered. Alan's expression changed from one of casual enjoyment to surprise and hostility. Olive had been talking naturally, as she always did with Alan, telling him facts that didn't seem important. But she saw that she had torn something wide open. She should not have mentioned anything that had to do with Catholicism.

"Mark quarreling with Kenedy?" Alan asked incredulously.

"Oh, I'm exaggerating—they had an argument, that's all. And the priest sent him these books, trying to prove his point, I suppose, but they certainly didn't have that effect on Mark."

"Argument about what? I didn't know that Mark knew Kenedy. What were they arguing about?" persisted Alan.

Olive realized that Alan thought he had been the subject of the argument. His face was bitter. She must destroy that idea.

"It was a hospital matter, connected with the big drive Mark's heading up. That's how the priest happened to come to the house."

"He came to your house?"

"It was easier for Mark, that was why."

"Well, I'll be damned," said Alan. "So that priest is trying to get his hooks even into Mark. You say he's been sending him books on religion? And Mark sat down and read them?"

Olive said, "You know Mark. He always wants to get to the bottom of things. He's curious about what makes people tick. The hold the Catholic Church has on people interests him, rather appalls him as a matter of fact. He wants to find out how they do it. He thinks it's almost sinister."

"I know he does," said Alan, "and he could be right. But there's

[150]

no use arguing with that closed corporation. He won't make a dent on them. He won't get anywhere."

His wife came over to Alan, her smile lifted for everyone to see.

"Hello, Olive, isn't this party heaven? What's the matter, darling? You look so glum. This party's for us, didn't you know?"

"Sure, I know."

"Then look as if you were enjoying it, my bridegroom!"

Alan's glance at his wife chilled Olive. For a second she thought that he was going to say something insulting, tell Dot to go away, to leave him and his mood alone. Then he slipped into the nonchalance that was his habitual cover.

"Happy days," he said. "I need a refill. What can I get for you, Olive?"

"A Martini, please," she said. She had meant to wait until Mark came, but a drink at once might help this sickening pity, this apprehension, to fade away.

Mark was quite late in arriving. He seemed in excellent spirits as he made his way through the crowd of guests to his wife. Olive did not ask him what had delayed him. He always told her.

"That fellow is really something," he said, sounding stimulated.

"Your friend Father Kenedy?"

"Yes, he happened to be there, so I went into his place for a few minutes."

It must have been nearly an hour, but Olive did not mention that.

"He wanted to get my reaction to those books."

"I hope you were more polite in choice of your words than you were when you were telling me what you thought of groveling penance and such."

"He can take it. I went right to the mat. I told him—"

"Better get yourself a cocktail, Mark. We're going to eat in a few minutes, Pam says. Tell me about that later, when we get home."

Pamela's eldest son, Dick, had also just drifted in, as if he didn't want to be here, giving the stereotyped courtesy of a bored college man to his elders. He broke through that when he saw Olive.

"It's good to see you, Dick. How are you?"

"They've all been telling me I've grown," he said sarcastically.

"And that you look more like your father every day," Olive said, conspiring with him.

"I think parties like this stink," said Dick. "What's the use of them? Mother's been busy as a bird dog all day doing nothing. For what?"

"For your uncle Alan and his wife."

"He pulled a fast one, didn't he? Did he have to marry her? Was it the old shotgun?"

"Dick, don't talk that way."

He laughed. "All right, don't tell me, I'm too young. Say, Olive, did you ever read Eliot's *Cocktail Party?*"

"Of course."

"All those frustrated people are here tonight."

"And plenty more."

"It's so futile and confused."

"You won't think so in a few years."

"Yes, I will."

"Well, maybe. You've always been a boy to walk by yourself."

"I'm always going to."

"That's hard when you have to earn a living, Dick."

"Can be done though. You know," said Dick, his intolerant eyes surveying the company, "what I'm thinking of doing, Olive?"

"I'd like to know."

"I think I may be a monk. Decide to lead a contemplative life."

"Oh, no!"

"It shocks you because you don't understand. I know a couple of Catholic fellows at college. They have a terrific philosophy."

"I know it's terrific. But give that idea time, Dick. Don't rush into anything. And don't spring it on yor mother during the holidays. Come over and see me. I'd love to have a chance to talk it over with you."

"I'd like to come. I really want to talk to you, Olive."

Later it was Gregory Searles who floated to her on the currents of the party. Like the college boy, he came to rest beside her and began to free his thoughts.

"Let me hide behind your lovely skirts, Olive."

"You can. Lucky it's a good full skirt. Aren't you having a good time?"

"I'm exhausted by these past two weeks. It would have been so much better if the Worthings had been willing to admit they made a mistake."

"Greg, if you mean what I think you mean, it shouldn't be said."

"You're taking on the family coloration, Olive."

"I'm certainly not following you."

"You're refusing to follow. After all, you and I are in a very special position in regard to the Worthing conscience. We're married to it. Brad Brooks is married to it too, but he's not a sensitive person."

"The Worthing conscience?" she repeated.

"Poor things," said Greg, "what a spot they're in. They are all aware of injustice having been done and that they helped it along. From Mamma Worthing to Alan himself. That's why this is so unhappy an occasion. It was less unhappy at our house on Sunday night because the veal was so good."

"Greg, I love you but you're crazy." And Olive said against her will, "You mean injustice to that girl Alan didn't marry?"

"Of course. They probably aren't much to blame. But it's their nature to feel responsible. The Worthing conscience is a terrible cross. It's kept Mamma Worthing on the run for years doing good works, and Pam trying to prove that the best people are the best, and Lucy working at believing I'm a genius because her conscience wouldn't allow her to be married to a loafer. I suppose it even pursued old Philip in his games and trades."

"And Mark?"

"You know best about that. Mark follows his conscience in being the young patriarch in the family and in the town. He's lucky," said Gregory admiringly, "and happy because his conscience can have nothing against his delightful wife."

"Thank you, let's hope so. Oh, Greg, they're good people. You know that as well as I do. They're dear people!"

[153]

"Of course, they're good people. That's why they are slightly pitiful."

"I don't know what you mean, if anything."

"They're pitiful because they can't cast their burdens. The Worthings don't believe in fairies. Or in God."

"Of course, they do—in God."

"Not in the kind of God I was brought up to believe in. He took the responsibility."

"What religion was that?"

"I'm a renegade Catholic."

"I never knew that."

"I don't advertise it. I'm very apt to forget it myself. But not completely. If I were dying, no doubt I'd ask Lucy to send for a priest. And how it would bewilder her!"

"You would?"

"I expect so. I'm a lazy, lustful fellow. I've broken all the rules and have no present intention of being any more obedient than I am. But I'd probably sneak back to the fold *in extremis,* I know it's there. Now the Worthings have no fold. Some of them help to support the Episcopal Church, but they get none of the comforts of the supernatural. I don't think they get their money's worth. It would have been good for the Worthings if Alan had married that other girl and brought a little mysticism—and absolutism—into the family. The need for those things is likely to crop out in time, and they're quite unable to cope with it."

Olive did not mention that Dick Brooks had just told her that he wanted to be a monk. She thought, this is foolish talk, but there's a little truth in what Greg is saying.

"Alan," said Gregory, rounding off his theory, "was probably unconsciously seeking for the mysticism which he found in the Catholic girl. It was one of the things that attracted him."

"Then why did he marry someone so completely different?"

"Oh, revenge, lust—to deny openly what he really wanted— why do you think he did?"

"I don't know. But perhaps he felt outcast," said Olive slowly. "Maybe he thought the other girl cared more for her religion than she did for him. His pride was hurt. And he saw that Dot didn't have what she wanted either. She may have told him that she was lonely, felt a failure—"

"So he thought they were birds of a feather."

"That wouldn't be the reason. Alan needed to make someone happy. It was all built up in him. Waiting. I only hope this comes out all right."

"So do I, very definitely. Now that Alan has burned his bridges so completely. He can never have the other girl now, even if this ends in a smash."

"I wonder—"

"Well, of course, the Catholic girl might have married a Protestant—with the Church holding its nose—but she couldn't marry a divorced man."

"I hadn't thought of that," said Olive. "How hopeless for her!"

"This is really a melancholy occasion," said Gregory cheerfully, "how little laughter means!"

"Except in children."

"That's true. Before they've learned to use laughter as a cover-up for other feelings. Those are charming kids of yours, Olive."

"They're happy children."

"The little girl—Jenny—has the face of a rejoicing cherub. I must do a sketch of her someday."

Olive drew the rosebud comforter up close to Jenny's neck and remembered Greg's description. The round but delicate little face seemed to be rejoicing even in sleep. She opened the adjoining door to be sure that Tim was all right. He was a thin, relaxed bundle under tumbled bedclothes. Christmas presents, so greatly coveted last week, were scattered in both rooms, and the children were now in some deep, happy consciousness which had no need of such artificial aids.

She stood in the doorway between the rooms, loving the children, thinking gravely of the necessity for making them strong and directing them toward happiness. The encounter with Alan to-night, the flashes of dissatisfaction she had seen in him, made her sad, and it was sadness that she must not share with Mark. She was sorry for the boy Dick, whom his mother would never understand, groping for something he did not see around him—trying last year to find it in obscure poetry, believing now that he wanted a life of religious contemplation. Alan needed love, she thought. He was never close to his mother—she's too impersonal, her affection was too diffused, spread too thin. This girl he married is provocative, passionate—she doesn't seem loving. Perhaps children will make it up to him, poor Alan.

In their own room she said to Mark, "The children are sleeping it off. They've been greedy little pagans all this week. We must give them fewer things."

"Good idea."

"Because I don't want them to think of Christmas as a time for loot. Of course, I've read them the Bethlehem story, and they adored fixing the crèche by the tree; but what the day means hasn't penetrated very deep with either of them."

"They're pretty young."

"Yes, but it's when they're young that things should take hold. What's that old saying, 'Give me a child until he is seven—' "

"That's what the Jesuits say. I think it's the Jesuits. Maybe they've got something there."

"I certainly wouldn't want to give any child of mine to Jesuits until he was seven."

"I should hope not."

"I want my children to think of God as a friend. Not as a judge. I don't want them ever to believe in hell. That's really what makes me shudder at the Catholic Church. When I read Dante I was fascinated because it is such a horror story. In magnificent words. But think of circles of hell, and everything worked out and ready for the torture. Isn't it a fantastic idea? Golden streets and golden slippers may be silly but they're gay. I'm not prejudiced against the Catholic Church as much as you are—I love its music and some of its customs. But it teaches fear. That I don't like. It's so wrong for children."

"Not only fear—suffering is its central idea."

[156]

"I know—crucifixes—and a good man in agony on them. Imagine telling little children that's what happens if you're good," said Olive, "giving them the feeling that cruelty is basic, injustice basic!"

Mark was sitting on a bench with curved arms that stood beside the fireplace. He often sat there to watch his wife.

"They believe in unhappiness," he said, as she paused. "I wish you'd heard him tonight."

Olive knew he was not speaking of anyone at Pamela's party.

"That's almost the way he put it, in that dogmatic, cocksure way of his. He said, 'Catholicism is the religion of the crucifix. Suffering has tremendous importance and can be put to supreme use.' And then he said," Mark added, giving the words incredulity, " 'In learning to suffer, you can reach peace and finally joy.' "

"That may be all right for incurable invalids," said Olive. "It might give them a lift. But it's not for normal people."

"But just think of it," said Mark, in the same meditative way. "Think of their being able to instill that grim philosophy into the minds of the ignorant, the stupid, the selfish. And they do. That's what gets me. Millions of people want it, ask for it, stay by it. Why? I tell you, Olive, that priest is the most convinced man I've ever met in my whole life. My God, if I had half as much confidence in being right, I could do anything!"

15

THERE had always been three types of men who dreamed and planned about what could be accomplished in the region surrounding the immense, cold, unmastered upper lake of the great inland chain. It had been known as *le lac supérieur* to the French explorers and map makers, but its name was mistranslated as the years went on. The English name of Superior finally stuck, perhaps because of the fitness to its size and beauty. Always the three—the trader, the missionary, and the engineer—had been tempted and inspired by the end of the watercourse and the opportunities to which it gave access. To buy and sell fish, furs, virgin timber, and to deal in land fabulously rich in iron on the north side of the lake, and with fortunes in copper to be made on the southern shore. To capture the souls of savages and to serve the spiritual needs of pioneers. To invent the whaleback and the long, slim ore boats and to devise new machinery that could break into the treasures of the earth in grandiose and unexpected ways.

It was still that way. The plans and dreams went on.

In his New York office, the millionaire trader, Eben Crane, was talking of the region to Howard Eliot. The two men had not seen each other since they had parted at Idlewild on their return from the inspection trip to the taconite development. Eliot had been fishing in Florida and had come back with a sportsman's color. The pallor and gauntness of Crane seemed more suited to the gray winter sky outside the high windows.

Below the lights were coming on to show the rhythmic and colorful ballet of Park Avenue, at the start of its late afternoon scene. Between Crane and Eliot lay a blueprint, a letter signed by Mark Worthing, and a small block of mahogany on which was mounted a piece of black ore. The mahogany was inscribed with the compliments of the management of a manganese mine in South America—to Mr. Eben Crane.

He turned the inscription for Eliot to read.

"That's all I ever got out of those people," he said. "The beauty of this taconite is that it's not foreign ore. We won't have any of those complications. Take that ore in Venezuela where Big Steel and Bethlehem have been pouring in their money for years. The natives have to use American money and know-how at this stage. But one of these days they may rise up on their hind legs, put on a revolution, and expropriate American holdings. They did it in Mexico with silver. The Brazilian government is squeezing the life out of our mining operations down there." He fingered the mahogany block and said, "I got out of this just in time."

I'll bet you did, thought Howard Eliot. Mr. Crane had asked him for a meeting, and Eliot had come here because that left him in control of getting away. There were some papers to sign, a matter or two to agree upon. That was done, and he wanted to leave now, but the older man was droning on.

With his carefully bred lack of exaggeration, Eliot said, "Well, this taconite looks like a pretty good thing."

"It's safe in the middle of our own country," said Crane, "and there's a hundred miles of it. Also we have a way to get it to our markets without crawling on our bellies to some half-baked foreign government."

"Our own government will put the bite on us," said Eliot.

"They'll have to come to their senses in Washington if they don't want to bankrupt the country," growled Crane. It was a stock remark. The next one was not. He said, "If that operation out there is managed right, plenty of profit will stick to our fingers."

"They seemed to have it pretty well in hand."

"Harry Tuttle's a good man. And if Phil Worthing were alive and running the show, we wouldn't have to worry. He had this all sized up before he died, of course. He was the first one to come to me about taconite. Phil Worthing always knew where he was going, how he was going to play it. Always agreeable. But he never gave away a trick."

"Mark Worthing seems to have a lot on the ball too."

"I hope so," said the older man.

"Didn't he impress you that way when we were out there?"

"Yes and no. He's able, all right," said Mr. Crane judicially. "But I felt a certain lack of leadership. I can always sense leadership in a man."

Eliot felt as unresponsive as he looked. He disliked words like leadership. It suggested good works, community singing, exposed feeling. But he didn't want to argue with Crane. He said something about Mark Worthing being a nice fellow.

"But a little unsure," said Crane, "not firmly decisive. Take that matter about using the school in the company village for Roman Catholic services."

"Not a very important thing."

"A straw in the wind perhaps," said Crane sententiously. "He should have turned down such a proposition instantly. The American flag flies—should fly—over every public school in the land. Our schoolhouses can never be used for rites imported from foreign countries!"

The old bigot's letting loose, thought Eliot. So that was what got under his skin. He knew that this kind of feeling existed but he always ignored it. It was why there would never be a Catholic President. He thought of his delightful, sophisticated friend Catherine Ridell, who had married an Italian count with the full Catholic ritual. Very beautiful and elegant, it was, when it was done right. Eliot had once told Catherine that if he ever joined any religion it would be the Catholic, that the other sects only held town meetings. If I said that to Crane, thought Eliot, I suppose he'd have a stroke on the spot. He rather enjoyed the idea.

Crane leaned over to tap the letter with Mark's signature which he had just showed to Eliot. It was an informal progress report.

"I told him I would be interested in knowing how he disposed of that matter. He doesn't refer to it, however."

"It probably came to nothing."

"Worthing isn't a Catholic himself, I know. I asked Henry Tuttle. I don't know about Mrs. Worthing."

"Not likely. She's a cousin of the Warren Hadleys from St. Paul. And she was married before, to Tony Grant."

"A charming lady. I enjoyed visiting with her very much. I know who the Hadleys are, of course. I don't place Grant."

"He's something of a playboy," said Eliot. "When I was out there on our inspection trip, I didn't know she had been his wife. But someone spoke of it the other day."

"So he's her second husband," said Crane. "She seemed very young for that. Was Mark Worthing married before too?"

Eliot found the financier's curiosity rather offensive. It wasn't as if Crane would ever know these people socially. He said that he didn't know, and that he must run along.

"Before you go," said Eben Crane, raising a delaying hand, "I want to speak to you about another investment."

"I'm not interested—at the moment I'm too poor. Have too many irons in the fire now."

"You'll be interested in this," said Crane. "It's the soundest proposition I know and will pay extraordinary dividends. I'm asking a small group of forward-looking men to help me underwrite a summer conference of young people out in Michigan. You made a contribution last year."

"Did I? Then I suppose I'm hooked again. That's the way it goes."

"You're not being hooked," said Crane. "This is an opportunity, Howard. Think of it that way. You're projecting yourself into the future of America. The conference trains carefully selected young men for Christian leadership. Not for the ministry, you understand, though some do go into the pulpit. But the purpose of the conference is to give these lads a belief that religion must permeate not only private living but business and public life. It gives them both faith and know-how to use it, so that when they take their places in the American democracy—"

No doubt he had said this often, and was quoting from one of his own money-raising speeches or letters. But his face changed as he spoke. The shrewdness vanished, overcast with the fervor and devotion of a missionary.

Funny guy, thought Howard, and interrupted, "All right, put me down for what I gave last year."

"No, I want you to double or triple it, Howard. We shall have a bigger attendance this year. You must realize that in time these young men may be the saving force of our nation!"

"Well, I'll see what I can dig up," said Howard Eliot reluctantly.

The missionaries planned too. In the dining room of the episcopal mansion of the diocese, Bishop La Fresne listened to what the young priest at his dinner table was saying. He noticed that Father Kenedy had ignored his dessert and let his coffee become tastelessly cool.

"Better finish your coffee, Father," he said.

Father Kenedy obediently lifted the cup, dipped a spoon once into the thick chocolate pudding before him and forgot it again.

"The especially commanding site," he said, "overlooks the harbor

[161]

which they are making at Baraga. It's back of the village, and as the land rises sharply there, it's above the town. A church in that location would be seen by anyone traveling east or west—"

"We might outdo Mont-Saint-Michel," said the Bishop with dry humor.

Father Kenedy looked as if that were possible.

He said, "There's a natural magnificence in the area. It well deserves a church."

"Will there be enough parishioners to support one?"

"It should give many people a reason for settling there. And there must be people living farther up the shore, and back on those little farms, who have had some Catholic upbringing and have fallen away from their religion for lack of a church nearby."

"The buses run into Two Harbors on Sunday," said the Bishop.

"Of course, I'm not excusing such people, Bishop. But I'd like to get them back."

The Bishop enjoyed the company of this young priest. Too many of the younger clergy were shy, or a little apt to bootlick, or seemed to conceal criticism of their superiors under well-behaved silences. This one was not tiresomely docile and yet he never presumed. He had come back from Rome a learned man, a theologian, but he had not lost humility.

"Well, at the moment we can't think in terms of building a church up there," said the Bishop. "Certainly not until the reconstruction of the cathedral is completely financed. But it seems a good time to buy some land, if it's cheap enough. It will probably never be any cheaper than it is right now, and it can always be resold if it seems advisable. Mr. Worthing didn't give you any notion of what the price of a few acres might be? As I told you before, if we should go into this thing, we must be sure to get enough land for a school."

"Mark Worthing didn't like the idea of a parochial school in the new town, Bishop."

"Ah—one of those, is he?"

"He was quite frank about it. He said the usual thing, that he was afraid it would split the community up into religious factions."

"Couldn't you convince him that it doesn't take a parish school to do that?" asked the Bishop with his long-tolerant smile.

"I haven't convinced him of anything," said Father Kenedy.

"I wouldn't be too disappointed. His prejudices naturally would run deep."

"Why would they, Bishop?"

"It's a moneyed family," said the Bishop easily. "They've been here a long while and always on top socially and financially. Caste enters in. The first Catholics who came here were largely foreigners from the working classes. And the Worthings have never had any Catholic affiliations."

"Mark seems an unanchored man. Unsatisfied."

The Bishop's ragged eyebrows went up.

"You surprise me, Father. He's extremely well regarded. It's an orderly family as well as prosperous. The father was extremely worldly. But the old lady—his mother—is often cited for her secular good works. This young man has been very generous with his time—his money too, I suppose—in such things as this hospital project, which has put our own Corpus Christi on a sound footing. I hope you conveyed my compliments and thanks to him for letting us use the school up there for Mass on Sunday."

"As warmly as I could, Bishop."

"I thought the school authorities would balk."

"The mining company owns the school building, so they couldn't balk."

"Oh, that's it. If they convey the building to the regular school system, we'll be tossed out of there. While we can, we must make the most of it, try to build up a skeleton parish that will be self-reliant. But I'm interested in what you just said, Father. You found young Mark Worthing an unsatisfied man?"

"He has no frame of reference," said the priest. "I think he knows it, perhaps not altogether consciously."

"I see what you mean."

"His rather sharp criticism of the Church in my conversations with him sounded as if he were protesting too much."

Bishop La Fresne said, "Don't tell me that you think Mr.

[163]

Worthing is a convert in the making."

"No, I wouldn't go that far, Bishop. Certainly not under present circumstances."

Bishop La Fresne eyed the young priest.

He said, "He has been a good friend. That's what we need. Zealousness can sometimes defeat itself, Father."

"Yes, Bishop," answered the priest.

The Bishop saw that there was no use in pressing the matter of the scarcely tasted chocolate pudding and cold coffee. He pushed back his chair, and Father Kenedy was instantly on his feet, joining in the blessing after meals.

And the engineers were working. Though winter had gripped the whole region now, making it a constant struggle to keep living normal, they went on with their new projects. The great ports at the head of the lakes were idle. Shipping was over until spring came again, and the ore boats lay side by side on the sheltered side of the harbor. The city had a look of having slipped back to primitive conditions when the sight of the sky was lost in whirling, stinging snow, through which the snowplows and buses lurched and lumbered.

But winter in the city was gentle in comparison with its attack on the new little towns on the north shore of the lake. There the one-story houses barely topped the snow drifts. The roads between them were white tunnels with frozen sides. On the lake savage waves ripped and tore in fury at the ice which was trying to cover and quiet them, and sent sheets of it rattling against the sea wall.

"Anyway, we're on schedule," said Mark Worthing with great satisfaction. He had driven up that day to the location of the taconite plant, in spite of a gathering storm. The final work was being done on the inside of the building where the iron pellets were to be manufactured, and some decisions had to be made at once or time might be wasted. Mark had gone over them carefully with the general superintendent.

"We're doing all right so far," said Becker. "When spring comes

[164]

and they can slap down the rest of the railroad up to the mines, it shouldn't take too long to get into production."

"Is the breakwater holding all right?"

"There are a few weak places. Alan has a crew down there now, fixing them up."

"That's a tough job in this weather."

"It has to be done or it gets worse. They keep at it. They work in the open for a while and then get in a shelter with a fire and warm up. We give them a hot lunch down there—a thermos job. They couldn't eat better on a cross-country airplane. Say, that kid brother of yours certainly has a lot of steam in him."

"I thought so."

"He's going to go places in the mining business. Give him a few years and he'll be superintendent. If he doesn't kill himself in the meantime."

"What do you mean, kill himself?"

"That driving back and forth from town every day is a tough assignment. And he has to be on the job as early as the others."

"It took me more than two hours to get here today," said Mark.

"Alan would do better to live out here. He told me once that was what he was going to do when he got married, but I guess he changed his mind. He's making a mistake. The boys who live out here have it fine, especially the married ones," said Becker.

When he was going to marry a different girl, Alan planned to live in the new village, Mark remembered. They had looked at a house, he and the Carroll girl. But he made his own choice. Nobody could make it for him. He went off half-cocked. Mark buttoned up his rough coat again and went down to see how Alan was doing on the job.

It was a hard and hazardous one. The men were bolstering the break in the wall by moving rocks from a stock pile—dark, icy rocks that were so large they were difficult to handle even in fair weather, even with the big trucks and tools they worked with.

"You've almost got it—lower and a little to the left—" Mark heard his brother shout before he saw him silhouetted on the shore. Alan looked vigorous and strong against that background of rocks and waves. I wonder if that girl appreciates what she's got, thought Mark. I wonder what the boy has to go home to.

"Good work, Alan."

"It's a temporary patch. But it should hold—we're pretty sure it will."

Close up, Mark saw that Alan's face was weathered and hardened to its bones. But he was pleased with this job. He looked cheerful.

"You don't want to kill yourself on this job," said Mark.

"Oh, hell, no."

"Why don't you stay out here during this kind of weather? Save yourself that drive to town every day?"

"I'm a married man," said Alan.

"Couldn't you both move out here for a month or two? One of the houses might still be available—Johnson would do what he could for you—"

Alan said abruptly, "It's okay the way it is. Everything's under control."

Mark could go no further in urging it. There had always been considerable reserve between him and his brother. It was partly due to the difference in their ages, and partly because each of them would never let his deep attachment to the other show, lest it seem sentimental or be embarrassing. Lately, since Alan had his own wife and home, the reserve had deepened.

Mark asked, "How is Dot?"

"Fine. Busy taking the apartment to pieces and putting it together again."

Mark was suddenly reminded of their father. Alan resembled him, and at the moment he sounded like Philip Worthing, detached, slightly mocking, complaisant. Mark remembered how his father used to say of his wife, "She's off somewhere, picking goats' feathers." Queer that Alan's comment should bring that to mind. Funny that the same tolerant contempt was directed at noble causes and esthetic decorating. Or maybe at the women themselves, Mark thought, with one of those quick, secret perceptions which never interrupted the work he had in hand. He thought, my

[166]

father let Mother go her way, led his own kind of life—has Alan begun to do the same thing? It's all wrong if it's like that—Alan deserves better—he should have what Olive and I do—but that's a rare thing, I suppose.

Alan was saying, as if he enjoyed the prospect, "We've got one more place to fix up on the breakwater, Mr. Becker—we'll get it done today. Then she can rip."

When it was done, the winter twilight had settled in. Alan took his car from the shed where it had been all day. The morning snow had frozen on his windshield and rear window, and he scraped it off and coaxed the engine into starting. As he drove up from the plant to the main highway, he could see, in spite of the high snow drifts, lights in the houses in the raw village. Lights in front of the doors twinkling for the men who were not yet home from work and for the children who had been sent to the store for groceries. It was dark and he was alone—on the job all day Alan had looked confident and almost relaxed, doing his strenuous work, but the faint light from the dashboard now showed tension in his face.

He made the trip to the city more quickly than most men could or would, beating the risks of collision or of sliding into a ditch or of foundering in the heaped snow on the sides of the narrowed highway. Finally he ran the car into the stall that he rented at the rear of the Mirador Apartments. The day was over, he'd got something done, and here he was again. He wondered what there would be to eat upstairs. Dot certainly wasn't much of a cook— he'd never thought that would matter. But it did, just like in the comics. He wondered how she would be feeling. This was the day that the doctor had told her to call him.

Ten floors up. They had one of two penthouses on the top of the building, far more room than they needed. Alan had never been one to hoard money or worry about it, but this outlay galled him. It wasn't going to bankrupt them, and a girl had the right to choose the place to live—she was the one who was there most of the time. But Alan never told anyone on the job where he lived or how. He would have felt a show-off or a fool. They all knew how much he earned a week—what he was worth at this stage.

There was a second when he paused outside the door. Alan tried to put on his old look of meeting the world without worry or too great seriousness. It didn't quite cover the tension. Nor quite conceal his satisfaction in twisting a key in the lock of his own home. For there was someone within who would be expecting him. Whatever it was like tonight, whether trouble was waiting or not, this was his own, anyhow. A hope, a wish to be tender rose again.

"Hi, Dot!"

She answered from the direction of the bedroom—"Hi—I was just about to go out and buy a St. Bernard dog and send him after you with a bottle. I thought you must be under a snowdrift."

"No dog would get far tonight."

He took off his jacket and cap and stowed them in the coat closet by the door, where they seemed unsuitable against a merry wallpaper with cartoons of famous people scattered over it. In the foyer there were only two pieces of Chinese porcelain and an old letter rack on a heritage table. Nothing else. Nothing in the apartment was cluttered. In the big room which Dot had been able to create by having a partition removed, Alan had no quarrel with her deft taste and choice—the elegance which allowed ease and comfort, the suggestion of use. He saw no sign of food in the dining area at the end. That made him hungrier.

Dot lifted her face. She was wearing a soft red dress and looked good to the touch. She was enameling her fingernails.

"I really thought you'd never come," she said.

"I'm no later than usual."

"It feels as if you were—look out, the polish isn't dry. I broke one off, getting out those damned ice cubes."

"Are we having ice cubes for dinner?"

"I thought you might like to go out."

"Oh, no—cars are stuck all over town."

"All right, I don't care. There must be plenty of food in the refrigerator. There's some of that roast turkey, quite a lot. They didn't nearly eat all of it the other night. I'll find something."

[168]

The caterer's turkey. He knew it well.

"That's a good girl. How did you come out?"

She pretended for a minute. "Come out?"

"Didn't you call the doctor? I thought this was the day he'd know."

"Oh, the rabbit test. It was a very nice rabbit. He said it was negative."

Alan felt a secret, slight slump within himself. He said, "Well, that's off your mind."

"Off our mutual minds. You didn't want it either."

"I didn't want you to be let in for something you didn't want."

"It would have been so difficult, that's all. Right now. We haven't the room."

"We're not exactly crowded."

"Darling, it's not floor space. It's arrangements. They won't have babies in this building. We'd have to move."

"I know."

"It's getting impossible to have children. There are no nurses—only these grisly little baby sitters. And you live in terror that they'll be kidnaped."

"A lot of people seem to go ahead anyway—"

"Look, Alan, if you really want to breed—"

"We've been all over this. I'll go and clean up. And let's have some food."

"Don't you want a drink first?"

"Sure—"

He passed the enormous outsize bed which Dot called Worthing Field, and made himself clean and dry in his perfected dressing room. In ten minutes he was wearing a sport jacket and loafers. Dot's nail polish was not yet firm, as he could tell from the careful way she used her hands, placing glasses and bottles and the ice bucket on a serving table. She had found appetizers too, potato chips and crackers and a tray of small cheeses in jars. Just as last night. He thought, I hope there's some bacon out there.

"Here you are, Dot."

"Thanks."

Now it was beginning to be all right. The potato chips and the cheese took the edge off his hunger, and the drink was good and recommended another. There wasn't any hurry.

"Mark came up to the location today," said Alan.

"What does he do up there?"

"Looks it over. Gives the orders."

"Do you have to take orders from Mark?"

"I take orders from the people who work for the people Mark gives orders to," said Alan. "That's where I come in."

"It's silly. Your father left you just as much."

"Not so much brain power."

"You should never run yourself down. People take you at your own valuation."

"Better than pricing yourself too high."

"I don't think so. You know, I'm not convinced of Mark."

"What do you mean, convinced?"

"Just that. I can't join in the accolade. Everyone in your family thinks he's so perfect. He and Olive and the ideal marriage. Maybe—but she cracked up before. . . . Mark and Olive don't like me."

"Don't be silly."

"I can tell. They're much too conscientious about being nice to me. They should be grateful. From what Pam says, they were terrified that you'd marry that Irish girl. I saved them from that, anyhow."

"Let's drop that once and for all, Dot. For good. Drop it!"

"All right—don't be so savage."

"Sorry. Here—"

"Thanks. Are you very hungry?"

"No, not particularly. Take it easy," said Alan. "There's another dividend here."

"Good. I love being married to you, Alan. This is such fun."

"Great fun."

"Only I wish you were around all day."

"You'd like to be married to a loafer?"

"We wouldn't loaf. We'd go places. This town is a morgue. Do

[170]

you know, I've never stayed here through a winter before?"

"We didn't get back from Antigua until almost Christmas."

"The holidays aren't so bad. It's after Christmas that everyone goes away. There are such divine places. Even if you haven't one of your own."

"That's all right for the old retired boys. They can follow the sun. A young fellow can't do that, Dot."

"You'd be surprised how many of them do. And you could afford it."

"I couldn't afford it."

"I don't see why. You don't even have to buy my clothes."

"It might be better if I did. Maybe that's the trouble."

"What trouble?"

"Just get it straight, Dot. It's not only the money. I like my work. I like the mining business. I can see even now the possibilities of our own organization. Ahead of us, I mean. We can expand. But everything has to be watched, tried out first, all the corners cut—"

"You're wonderful," she said.

The lack of understanding deflated him. He took another drink almost sulkily.

She said, "Of course, you must do it if it's what you want, but I don't see why Mark gets all the credit. And I get lonesome without you."

"You wouldn't live up there."

She made a shudder.

"There are lots of young married people here in town. Not like your smart friends who go to Florida, but they make sense."

"All they talk about is children and how long to cook it."

"What should they be talking about?"

Dot said, "They could keep still. Housewives in three colors bore me to extinction."

"Well, you ought to get interested in something."

"I am."

"What?"

"You," she said, "my man."

[171]

She could be very tempting like this, suddenly simple. He came closer, kissed her deeply.

"You don't want me to be one of those do-gooders, do you?" she asked with a submerged laugh.

"I want you to be happy. Satisfied. That's part of my job now."

"You do all right. Sometimes better than others."

"I feel very competent right now."

"You do?"

About ten o'clock they had another drink. Then Alan, wearing his bathrobe, cooked bacon and eggs. Dot dropped slices of bread in the toaster. They ate at the counter in the very modern kitchen.

She said, "We've still got that turkey. Do you want me to get it out?"

"Never again. I couldn't look it in the face."

"I hate it too. Always there."

"We'll go out tomorrow night and get a couple of good steaks."

"Yes, let's go out somewhere. Alan, everything was all right tonight? You're sure? Nothing to worry about? I mean for rabbits?"

"Not a thing. You're in the clear."

He got up from the counter and went into the big room, where beautiful fabrics hung over the windows. Pushing them back, he looked out at the storm, looked out for quite a while.

"What are you doing?" asked Dot.

"Nothing. I was just wondering if a patch in the breakwater is holding all right."

16

ONCE when Mark went through the record room at St. Barnabas, on his way to a board meeting, there was no one at the desk in the corner. Though he hardly looked in that direction he was conscious of the vacancy. The Carroll girl was probably somewhere else in the building, he told himself. She must still be on that job. Nothing had been said at any meeting about a vacancy or new appointment in that place. But he might not have heard. It might not have been a "board matter." She might have left her job. Because he himself was connected with this hospital and she didn't want to run into him after that impetuous conversation? Could she have had a breakdown or anything like that? He wanted to ask about her but did not, for such a question might attract too much attention. Alan's interest in the girl no doubt had been a matter of hospital gossip.

The next time there were several people standing around the desk. He thought Rose Mary Carroll was there. As he turned he saw a dark-haired girl, but he was not close enough to be sure it was she. And then as he was leaving the hospital on a February night, he met her at the door. She was leaving too, and there was another girl with her. He held the door open for them to pass and said, "Getting cold again. I hope your car will start."

"We don't have that problem," said the other girl. "We go on the bus, if and when it gets here."

"Can't I drive you girls home?"

"Oh, no—that would be too much of a bother, Mr. Worthing."

"Not at all. My car's right here."

Rose Mary spoke. She said in a tight, soft voice, "Thank you, but it isn't necessary."

"I wish you'd let me."

The other girl laughed and said, "We're really getting a break, Rose Mary. Come along. It's wonderful of you, Mr. Worthing. I'm Barbara Simmons from the diet kitchen."

Mark knew that Rose Mary Carroll must be making a choice between going with him and making her resistance conspicuous. He was almost sorry he had suggested the lift. He put the other girl in the car first so that she sat next to him, and Rose Mary was by the door.

"You'll have to direct me," he said.

"I get off first," said Barbara. "It's 1156 Lexington. Is that terribly out of your way?"

"Not a bit."

"I'll get off there too," said Rose Mary.

"But you can't," her friend objected. "Your bus doesn't go on that street."

"That's all right. I can transfer."

"Oh, let me take you the rest of the way," said Mark. "It's no trouble."

He began to talk of the crowded state of the hospital and the diet kitchen. Barbara told funny stories about it. But when she got out of the car with repeated and excited thanks, silence was heavy between the others as they drove on. He asked for her address and Rose Mary gave it.

"It's miles out of your way," she said. "I wish you hadn't insisted. I didn't know what to say."

"I'm sorry if I embarrassed you."

"It doesn't matter. . . . I embarrassed you once. . . . this makes it even."

"I haven't forgotten our conversation."

"It would be kinder if you would. All that is past."

"I suppose it must be."

In the pause he felt both her emotion and her control. Then she said in that soft, melodious voice, "But I would like to know if he is happy. There is no one else I can ask."

It was a hard question. Mark balanced the worth of a lie. He said after a minute, "I don't know."

"Ah—" she sighed, "may he be—"

"You want him to be happy?"

"Surely—of course."

"You're generous. You have every right to hate the lot of us. To wish Alan and the rest of the Worthing family unhappiness."

"We're not taught to hate," she said, "except to hate evil. Alan isn't evil. I'm sure you aren't either. It's just that you were prejudiced."

"I don't think I'm prejudiced."

"Oh, many people are. They're misinformed. They're not to be blamed," said Rose Mary, as if she were repeating a lesson, one she sought to memorize.

Mark said, "My wife—my wife didn't like what happened. She was very unhappy about any pain you may have been caused."

"I see Mrs. Worthing at the hospital sometimes. She is beautiful."

"Yes," said Mark, with love in his voice.

The girl heard it and turned her head toward him, then back to the frosted window. She was not quite so taut. He could sense that. He drove slowly, very safely.

"I was disturbed, too," said Mark. "I wouldn't say this except that you once gave me a certain amount of your confidence. I won't say it again. But if I insisted on driving you tonight, and it was done on impulse—it just happened this way—it was partly because I wanted to tell you that I was sorry, and that my wife was sorry if you were hurt."

"Hurt—"

"But Alan had to make up his own mind."

"You had something to do with his decision."

"I don't believe that's true. I told you that before. I had nothing at all to do with his marriage. He went off and did it. Told none of us beforehand."

"He wanted love," said Rose Mary, with yearning. "He wanted a home."

"I suppose so."

"I should not speak of him now. I should not think of him. He is a married man. But you have been honest with me. And kind. So I'm going to say one thing more. I really blame myself more than anyone. If I had believed the way I should, I would have done differently. I would not have gone to you and asked you to tolerate my religion. I should have made it seem so beatuiful to Alan that he would not want to live without it. I should have convinced him."

"You tried in every way."

"No, I just coaxed him a little. I exposed him to a few little lectures, and when he didn't like them, I asked the priest to argue with him. I was the one who should have made him see the loveliness, the grace, of a Catholic marriage—but I was always afraid of losing him, and in my heart that was worse than anything else. I wasn't strong. That was why Alan yielded, because I wasn't strong enough."

"You're very strong. You wouldn't take him on his terms."

"But I couldn't," said Rose Mary.

We're back where we started, thought Mark. It's inconceivable to her that she might give up her doctrines for a man. She's rationalizing all this—no, sublimating it—it's one way of getting by. The poor kid—she had to ask if he was happy. She's even trying to make herself believe that she's willing to have him happy with another woman.

"It seems a stupid thing to say, but maybe it's all for the best," he said.

She didn't answer. When she spoke, it was of Alan and her voice was tender with his name.

"Alan has a sweet nature," she said. "He has lots of friends, but I don't think many people know him very well."

"I think you're right about that."

"My family—of course, it's natural, they're very fond of me, and Alan was around the house so much that they took things too much for granted—they wish now that I'd never met him at all. I don't feel like that about it. We had lovely times together, lots of them—he's a very gay person, and yet underneath his making fun of this and that, he's not at all silly. Not trivial, is what I mean. He loves his kind of work and he always respects real things—"

She couldn't go on with that.

Mark said, to help her, "He's doing very well on his job."

"Is he? Do—does he live up there on the north shore?"

"No, his wife didn't want to, I think." That may be some comfort to her, Mark thought. At least she hasn't been dispossessed by another woman of that little house she looked over.

"I'm glad you picked me up tonight," she said after another silence. "I was just trembling when I got in the car, and I didn't want Barbara to notice. But I'm not now. It's really helped to say some of these things that get bottled up. You can't tell them to anyone except to—not to anyone."

"I wish I could help. So does my wife, so does Olive. Not because I accept any responsibility for making up Alan's mind—I don't—but because I think we should not have been so careless, let things happen so hastily—maybe it would have ended the same

[176]

way, I don't know. Anyway, if there is anything we can do—"

"There's nothing. Nothing that should be done. Oh, you spoke of my being hurt—it wasn't the obvious things. What hurt was what was forever lost between us. But the rest, the being ashamed because everyone thought a rich man had jilted me—of course, there was a little of that, but you have to offer it up along with the empty evenings—and knowing that somebody else—that's a thing you can't help—"

"Offer it up?"

"Of course, that wouldn't mean anything to you. But it's a thing we Catholics do with pain and trouble. Offer them up to God. As a kind of very little return for His sufferings for us and the world."

"I see," said Mark.

"We're nearly there," she said. "Would you mind stopping at the next corner?"

She didn't want him to stop before her house. He didn't blame her for that. He did what she asked, stopped the car on the corner, where a large, gloomily lit church reared up. A severe flight of steps led up to its entrance.

"Good night," she said. "No, please don't get out. And thank you. I mean that. Will you do another thing, one thing more? Will you please not tell Alan that you saw me or that we talked together?"

"If that's what you want, of course."

"I do."

"All right, I won't mention it."

She smiled, and her beauty struck him again. He thought, Alan kissed that lovely mouth. Poor fellow. Mark drove on. As he turned the next corner he looked back the length of the block to see if she was in sight. He saw that she had climbed the church steps and was going in. Against its brick ugliness she seemed to Mark to be pitiful, a sacrifice. I suppose that's where she goes for a little comfort, he thought. To be sure she was right. To offer it up, as she says. It's so unnatural.

BOOK THREE

17

MRS. PHILIP WORTHING unpinned the purple orchid from the left shoulder of her dress and put it in one of the silver bud vases on the desk in the den. That room had been planned originally for her husband's use at home, and finished with the oak paneling considered suitable and dignified for a masculine background. But he had used it so seldom, and his wife had found it so convenient a keep for the many papers and pamphlets that flowed through the mails to her, that gradually it had become her own office, long before he died.

Philip had given her the pair of silver vases on one of their first wedding anniversaries. He had given her a couple of rare orchids to wear on that occasion too. The fair, handsome, serious-minded girl had taken them off after the guests had gone home because she did not want him to crush them, and he was amorous with champagne. She had put one in each vase and said, "They're perfect for orchids! I'll put them on your desk so you can enjoy them too." And a habit had been established.

Not that Philip Worthing kept on giving her orchids. Or stayed at home to enjoy the sight of the ones she got from other sources. She had worn thousands of them over the years, so many that in a "profile" of her written by a columnist for the local paper, she had been referred to as the orchid-bearing lady of the head of the lakes. Almost always, when she was attending a meeting somewhere else in the country, she would carry a box with one or more orchids back home. She was always appreciative, for, as she said, she realized how much they cost the organization which presented them to her, and she made them last as long as possible.

She took the vase into the pantry to pour a little water into it, unwrapped the foil, and placed the wired stem of the flower where it would be moist. The house was very quiet this afternoon, almost slumped into stillness. It was Thursday, and Carrie's traditional day off. She had, of course, left a tray set out with the proper dishes and silver for her employer's solitary supper. There would be food waiting and ready in the refrigerator—slices of cold lamb or beef and a fruit or vegetable salad, all carefully garnished and covered with waxed paper. There would be no more domestic work for Mrs. Worthing to do than to assemble the food and eat it. Carrie was always home in time to open her bed and lay out her night clothes. Mrs. Worthing had never been expected to do such things for herself. She was always much too busy.

Yet she was tired. The luncheon and subsequent afternoon meeting at the Woman's Club had wearied her today, though she had only to sit at the head table and be introduced to the audience at the proper time.

"And now our beloved past president, as well as the dean of our standing Committee on Youth, Mrs. Philip Worthing—we want her to rise and take a bow at this time."

She had risen, the orchid trembling delicately as she moved, her smile gracious and affectionate. Then, after all the others had finally been introduced, she had listened to the speaker, who had been glancing irritably at his watch during the preliminaries. His subject had been juvenile delinquency, which was one of the club's projects this year because it was such a pressing modern problem. The most important one, the speaker had stated with almost violent emphasis.

Perhaps it was his talk that had tired Mrs. Worthing. She felt rather helpless as she listened to it. Something surely must be done about boys who committed murder with switch-blade knives, who raped little girls of seven, who beat up old men for the excitement of it. But she had felt an unusual remoteness, none of the willingness and eagerness that used to stir in her and make her determined to organize a movement to combat dreadful conditions. As, from her platform vantage, she watched the faces of women with leisure to spend, who were listening to the frank young man (he was good, he was well worth the two-hundred-dollar fee, she admitted), Mrs. Worthing had been oppressed by doubt, not only of the efficacy of the club's Committee on Youth, but of the best way to make life worthwhile.

Always she had been resolved to do that. It was wrong to live to yourself alone. Phil might laugh or take no interest, but she had to do what seemed important and right to her conscience. There was the example to the children to be considered. She wanted them to grow up to be good citizens. And they are, she thought, a little uncertainly. Mark especially, and dear Olive helps him. Alan is more like his father, without a great deal of social responsibility. I hope his wife develops well. She seems rather baffling in her modern way. But at the core, all these young people are sound— she remembered involuntarily a terrible incident which the lecturer had recounted today and left her judgment as to the soundness of youth hanging loose.

I wish the girls, especially Lucy, had more outside interests, Mrs. Worthing said to herself. It's so rewarding. She glanced at the plaques and framed certificates and testimonials that were on the walls beside her desk. Several from various governors, one signed by a President himself. She turned the vase with the orchid so that the drooping petal would not be so conspicuous. It wouldn't last long. It wasn't a beautiful flower, and it depressed her because she couldn't feel pleasure in having it. I'm too tired to keep on making public appearances, thought Mrs. Worthing with sudden secret frankness. I've given the public a great deal of my life. There may not be many years left.

The doctor had not gone so far as to say that when she consulted him the other day. He had said that angina was not so greatly feared a disease as it used to be, and that her case was not severe. One could live with her condition indefinitely, but she should always carry the pills with her and notify him of any fresh attack. She did not have the same kind of heart trouble that killed Philip. Strange that neither of our hearts was very strong, she thought. Of course, Phil overstrained his with all that golf.

There was no necessity for telling the family about it, at least not unless it became serious. It would only alarm them. They might urge her to move into an apartment, and perhaps that would be the sensible thing to do. But not right now. She did not have the energy to face the prospect of disposing of most of the possessions in this house and reorienting her life. Or the children might feel that one of them should come to live with her. She thought, I really wouldn't want Lucy—her husband is rather odd—making all the fuss and ceremony about cooking and recipes. And it wouldn't be fair to Alan, for they've just settled in their own place.

The idea of either Lucy or Dot under this roof with her all the time made Mrs. Worthing uncomfortable. She skirted the thought of what might go on in the bedrooms. Lucy is a dear child, but she has always been like that, she thought. It's because she takes after her father. Mrs. Worthing remembered the shock of finding out that her husband kept a mistress in New York. Until then she had taken it for granted that her own controlled affection satisfied him.

No, she would not bother any of the children about this malaise. Which was all it was. Pamela had that big house, and she entertained a great deal. Mark was carrying so much responsibility. She would rise above this fatigue. When things were difficult, Mrs. Worthing had done that before now. She had traveled so often without a man that she learned to rely on herself in emergencies, as when the Pullman train was wrecked, when she was marooned by floods in Oregon, when the lunatic at the meeting attacked her with a knife. And there was that time when she had been asked to take the presidency of the League for Peace, and then been undercut and defeated by an ambitious and false woman who had no scruples and had almost ruined the organization. Mildred Worthing had come home with a sick heart after that experience and found her children all down with measles. She had never mentioned the affair to anyone, and of course two years later she had been elected president of the League and been able to revive its usefulness.

She thought, this being somewhat exhausted at times seems to have come upon me all at once. I never used to feel like this. I'm probably a little run-down, and I worried today for fear that pain might come on while I was at the head table. The chairman didn't preside well; she talked much too long.

I must go over my will with Frank Hubbard. I wouldn't want to discuss my affairs with one of those younger lawyers, but Frank is an old friend. He is the only one who ever knew about that woman in New York. If it hadn't been for him, I might have let there be an open scandal, considering the way I felt at the time.

My share of Phil's estate will revert to the children. That money of my own would go to them too, as things are. But I've always meant to do something special with that—perhaps establish some sort of fund or memorial. I thought at one time I might give it to the League for Peace for a new building, but that is becoming a very different organization from what it was at first, almost a professional thing. My college has all that money from the Ford Foundation, and I gave the Alumnae Fund two thousand dollars last year. We both did our full share for the church when they built the parish house. It's out of debt. There's St. Barnabas, of course. But a name on a sickroom door or a laboratory—no, I must think it over carefully. I would like that money to fill a real need when I'm gone, to be appreciated. It didn't seem a large amount when I came into it when Papa died, but it's grown. I get very nice dividends since those stock splits were made. It has always been a comfort to me to have money of my own. There were times, when if I hadn't been able to leave Phil and be perfectly independent of him, I could hardly have faced going on living with him.

Only five o'clock. Well, Carrie will be in at nine, and the evening paper will be here soon. I mustn't forget to listen to Ed Murrow tonight at a quarter of eight. I must try to take more interest in television. It is certainly the coming medium. But to sit here alone and look at those contests does seem a waste of time, so inactive—there's no participation.

As you get older, you must expect a certain amount of loneliness. The speaker said today that the basic problem of even these juveniles is a loneliness of spirit and that's why they band together. They have no home ties. My children were never lonely. Never neglected. We always had a fine family spirit. I remember that time when

Alan ran away when he was a little boy, and we found him with a strange family, planning to spend the night. I suppose it's quite possible that if I hadn't talked to him then, hadn't reasoned with him, even Alan might have had a delinquent trend.

She reminded herself, I must see if the newspaper has been delivered. The Senate is debating the foreign-aid bill today and it may have come to a vote. But she did not move. She was limp, as if purpose had run out of her. She sat idly until the doorbell suddenly chimed. Carrie was out, she remembered. She must answer it herself.

"Olive! My dear, how good to see you. Come in!"

"I can't stay long," said Olive, "but I was lonesome for you."

She saw with astonishment tears shining in the stately woman's eyes as she kissed her lightly. Olive was careful to ignore them, talking on easily, giving Mrs. Worthing time for control. The poor thing, Olive said to herself. None of the family realizes that she's getting older, that she needs affection, that good causes can't keep old bones warm. They're all so used to thinking of her as completely self-sufficient.

Though she came from the deep cold outside, her thin cheeks brightened by it, Olive brought warmth into the house. And grace. The little den was not so grim and self-righteous as she tossed off her bright scarf and pulled a chair closer to where her mother-in-law sat. Mrs. Worthing had a second of yearning for something undefined which she herself had never grasped or given. She's such a pretty woman—they are very happy together—was all that came into form in her mind.

"Am I interrupting you in some work?" Olive asked.

"No, I was just sitting here, thinking over a little problem."

"Nothing too bothersome?"

"I was considering the best disposition of some funds," said Mrs. Worthing, to keep the conversation turned from her own health. "How to make a contribution or set up a little foundation—what may seem best."

"I should think that would be a delightful way to spend an afternoon—deciding what to help—and especially being able to do it!"

"I'm sure you do the same."

"I follow Mark's lead. But I'd feel very guilty if I went overboard with his money."

"It's your money too."

Olive smiled. "I still don't believe that's true," she said. "Anyway, Mark does so much for me and the children that I want to keep his ready-made family from exploiting him. It bothers me much more to spend or give away Mark's money than it would if I had any of my own. I know it's silly but I can't help it."

"I know what you mean. I always had a little money of my own. It's a satisfaction."

"Not exactly that—no one could be more generous than Mark. But I'd just like to say for once, 'Look, I'll pay for this, you don't have to earn a cent for it.' Have you been working on this project all day?"

"Oh, no—I was at a meeting at the Woman's Club this noon. I heard such a revealing talk on this juvenile delinquency. Really, Olive, it is hard to believe what those delinquents do!"

"Poor kids," said Olive simply.

"I wonder what we can do about it."

"You did something about it when you brought up Mark and Alan and the girls to be good people—"

"I hadn't thought of it that way."

"I have Tim and Jenny—that's my immediate job as far as delinquency goes."

"You don't have to worry about your children."

"Not now," said Olive with a sigh of sheer happiness. "Not now, for they have Mark to steer them."

"How is Mark? Working hard as usual?"

"Oh, much too hard!"

"He should have a holiday."

"I wish he'd take one. But he won't go anywhere just to play. He has some interests in South America, you know; some mines there. We were talking about that the other night. I wish he'd go down there, even if it's on business—he'd get away from things that bother him here—"

She didn't say what the things were. But there was a shadow of concern on her face now. It wasn't like Mark to be so disturbed, getting angry about what was not and never could be his responsibility. The thing was on his nerves—it had been ever since that night when he had come home and told her about taking the Carroll girl home. He kept coming back to it, hashing it over. They had been having such futile talks. They bothered her. She didn't know how to stop them. She'd tried. He would say things like—

"The morbidity is what gets you down. Look at it. Here is a healthy girl—a beautiful girl—maybe she was jilted or maybe she gave Alan the air—but anyway she lost out with her man. The natural, human thing is to get mad about it, hate him, get over him, and begin to look around for another fellow. Instead she goes into a kind of trance. Offering up her disappointment to God, running into churches—

"If it's any comfort to her, why not?"

"But isn't it a morbid, defeatist comfort? You know, I suppose that's the way they pick up all these nuns—women who are disappointed in love."

"Oh, Mark, dear, that's an exploded theory. That kind of life attracts some women. Honestly, you shouldn't let yourself be so prejudiced."

"I'm not prejudiced. I give that Church credit for tremendous accomplishments. They've got—do you know how many Catholics there are in the world? In the United States alone?"

"No, and I can't seem to care. There are quantities of Methodists too."

"There are more than thirty-one million Catholics in this country. That's a fifth of the entire population."

"Really that many?"

"Those are the statistics. A while ago I happened to read a review of an audit of the Roman Catholic Church that was put out by a very dependable group that examines managements. I sent for a copy because I was curious. It's in the office—I'll bring it home, you might be interested."

"Don't bother—figures bewilder me."

"This isn't just figures. It's an impersonal evaluation of the history and functions and policies. It's very interesting. But that's the figure they give. More than thirty million in the United States, and probably four hundred and sixty-eight million in the world. Think of the coverage. Roughly, it's a fifth of the world. What does that religion tap in the human mind—what kind of hypnotism does it exert?"

"It's not hypnotism. I think it's just that a certain kind of temperament wants that kind of stimulus—or refuge. People who don't have much education or many resources need it more than those who are educated. That accounts for their vast numbers."

"But they aren't all ignorant. They can't be. We know damned well they're not. They can be very smart businessmen. They run a big share of the political campaigns. They handle terrific sums of money, pretty cagily too. And they have their own philosophers— you know, that man Kenedy can throw the book at you. I majored in philosophy—I always liked it—but I'm not one-two-three to him. He's read the works. He can tell you where the Greeks went off the beam, and where Descartes and Kant slipped—according to his own dogma, of course. I wouldn't go along with what he says. But he's a well-educated man."

"Of course, some of them are—there's Graham Greene and Evelyn Waugh—the Catholics get the big ex-Communists too. There must be some sort of thing those people all have in common. Maybe it's a desire to submit, a need to have authority over them—"

"That's exactly the way I dope it out. That's what I told Alan. They don't want to think for themselves so they put themselves in a position where they can't. Of course, Father Kenedy would say that it isn't a desire to submit but an acceptance of submission to truth, to the answer to existence."

"Isn't that just rationalizing?"

"Of course—putting your mind in wraps won't help anyone to find the answer to existence."

"Well, let them think it is if they want to."

"Like the Carroll girl, licking her wounds."

"Mark, don't! Darling, it's not only that you're sorry for that girl, but you still have that preposterous sense that it's your fault she didn't marry Alan."

"No, it's not my fault. He had to make up his own mind."

"It's not your fault and it never was. Even if she is morbid."

"She doesn't think she's morbid."

"This is where we came in. I wish to heaven you'd put that whole unfortunate affair out of your mind."

"I have. But when I see your Father Kenedy again—"

"He's not mine! Don't blame him on me. And for pity's sake, Mark, avoid him because he does get on your nerves. Don't let him pester you with his holy books. Don't argue with him. You can't change his opinions."

"I know that, but it might be good for him to hear a few things."

That was the sort of conversation that had worried Olive and was now casting the shadow on her face in Mrs. Worthing's house. She would have liked to talk to Mrs. Worthing about it, but she was sure that his mother would not be able to tell her how to solve Mark's mood. Mildred Worthing had always been more sympathetic to impersonal than to personal responsibilities. And she was getting old, poor thing. Olive shivered, without showing it. Loneliness always made her shudder. She spoke of the orchid.

"I see you've been getting honors again. There almost always is an orchid on your desk. It must make you feel very prima donna."

"It was very kind of the group," said Mrs. Worthing. "I'm only a past president. But I must say that the meeting—I mean the talk, of course—depressed me a little today."

"Why don't you come and dine with us tonight?"

"No, thank you, Olive, dear. Carrie's left me a tray. And I have so many things to do."

18

As the ship was docking at Buenaventura, Olive woke. She lay in her berth for a few minutes, disentangling the sounds—the rough commands and Spanish chattering on the dock, and the high, sweet, soprano voices of the eight nuns on the deck below, chanting a morning hymn in Latin. Mark had not wakened yet. His state of fatigue had been proved by the way he had slept on the voyage from New York. Olive was very glad that he had been willing in the end to make this journey more than a business trip, and to spend a little time on the west coast of South America before flying across the continent to inspect the ore holdings of his company in Brazil.

Every morning and evening the nuns sang sweetly and with diligence. They belonged to a teaching order and were being sent to Peru, where they would separate from one another. Sister Anastasia had told Olive that they would not be permitted to come back to America, except in case of very serious illness, for at least twelve years. But they were enjoying the voyage and seemed to have no fear of adventure. At Panama they had fluttered off the ship, holding down their wide black robes as they descended the ladder, to visit a lepers' hospital which was managed by some of their own religious community. When their little procession returned, the nuns had seemed more excited than depressed.

"I had never seen a leper before," Sister Brigid said to Olive with an air of achievement.

"But did you want to?"

"I think it may be helpful," said Sister Brigid, "in explaining some of the gospels to the children. How He cleansed the leper. There were so many lepers at that time. I understand it so much better now."

"They are such brave innocents," Olive told Mark. "I adore them. You can't tell me that these nuns were ever disappointed in love. They joined the nunnery to see the world."

Mark had chuckled and said he didn't see how they were going to stand those medieval getups they wore in the South American heat.

"They are cool in spirit," Olive had said.

He was waking now. "The ship's engines have stopped. This must be—"

She looked through one of the portholes and said, "It's a dock. They're unloading freight. A lot of porcelain bathroom things have been smashed and there's a war going on over that. A South American character is staring at me lasciviously. Shall I wink? Would that be good for international relations?"

"Get away from the porthole. They call this the hellhole of South America."

"It will be fun. I'll be out of the shower in just a minute. Oh, Mark, it's been such a wonderful week! I hate to leave the ship, and I can hardly wait to get off and see what happens next!"

On the dock dark-skinned loiterers stared at her, as others did in the office of the captain of the port and in the customs shed. Olive looked rare and valuable in her white linen suit, with no adornment except her wedding ring. Finally she and Mark followed a porter pushing a barrow with their luggage to the Hotel Estaçion, which looked like a tall yellow honeycomb with its recessed open windows. Natives called "hello" and "money pleez" to Mark as they passed.

"See who gets the red carpet," said Mark, with a broad grin.

He was looking across the street, and she followed his glance. The group of nuns in double file had come off the ship and were walking toward the city. They were not disembarking but only sightseeing. As they passed, the natives fell back, plucked off hats if they wore them. One flung out his chest and ostentatiously made the sign of the cross. One sprang forward to move a barrow out of their way. The nuns smiled with dignity, and the one in charge of the party inclined her head slightly to right and left.

"I wonder what will happen to them," said Olive. "We'll never see them again unless we happen to run into them when we fly to Lima. They'll be there before we are."

"Our paths won't cross," said Mark. "What shall we do this morning? They tell me the hotel has a swimming pool, if you want to risk it."

"No—the morning is almost gone and I can swim anywhere, any time. I'd rather see the hellhole. We only have one day here. Let's settle into our room and have some more coffee and then explore."

Their bedroom was on one end of a gallery which was open to the sky. It smelled of mildew and of the uncurtained shower-bath stall, but from the open window they could see the bougainvillaea blazing up defiantly at the sun, and the ocean rolled beyond.

"We must take a picture from this window," said Olive. "Have you a colored one left?"

He brought the camera and focused it on the view, snapped the sight for their memories. "I wish I'd got a picture of that bunch of nuns this morning," said Mark. "Did you see the way the natives reacted to them? I suppose they think those poor women have all sorts of supernatural powers. That's probably one reason they hang on to those costumes."

"They call them habits," said Olive. "Let's go down for that coffee."

By nightfall they knew the pattern of the city, and had the feel of its vitality. The cafés were packed with sweaty men, the streets infested with beggars exhibiting their ailments and their sufferings. They hired a rackety car and drove from the streets lined with shops full of bright cotton goods and cheap kitchenware up on the hill behind the city, where avenues wandered vaguely among the houses.

"This is the red-light district," said Mark.

"How do you know?"

"Don't you see the notices of government inspection on some of the shacks? The captain on the ship was telling me about this."

"I see them now."

"You could spot this district without any notices. Look at the women."

"With flowers in their hair! But there are so many children playing around."

"They don't go in for birth control around here."

"It's queer," said Olive, "that they look so happy and natural. It's a dirty, swarming place, but I don't get the sense of misery. Is that one a prostitute's place?"

"Sure—and we'd better move on. You're collecting a crowd."

"It can't be a prostitute's house! Look at the crucifix right inside the door."

"Hold everything," said Mark. "I want to get a picture of that. I must show that to Father Kenedy when we get back home."

When they reached Quito they dined at the embassy, for word of Mark's connections and enterprises had preceded them. The ambassador plied Mark with questions about the taconite development. Would this mean that North American companies would pull out of Venezuela?

"Oh, no," said Mark, "we need all the ore we can get. War or no war."

He was at his best tonight. We must travel more, thought Olive. It does Mark good to get away from the personal problems at home, the family responsibility. When the new plant gets into operation, and when Alan is a little older and more experienced and can take over some of the load, Mark will be more free to do the things he likes. He might even want to study.

It was a small but brilliant company. There would be, Olive knew, a special reason for the inclusion of each of the guests, and she guessed at the reasons, as one after another was presented to her before dinner, and in brief conversations she identified their interests. The small, alert, flattering man owned silver mines, and so there was a natural link with any North American mining industry. The tall, loose-hung gentleman published a newspaper, no doubt the most important one in Ecuador. Reports and photographers had been sent to meet Mark's plane, but as an added dignity the publisher had been asked to dine with him. The arrogant man—who looked at me as if he were interested in seeing an American product but would never buy one, thought Olive—must certainly be of Spanish descent, and no doubt was one of the small white group in

Ecuador who controlled the mestizos and the Indians who so out-numbered them. The secretary of the legation told her that Señor Perez had oil interests, and from the respect in the secretary's tone they must be very large. Señor Perez was probably always asked to meet guests whom the embassy considered worthy of the intro-duction.

There were several wives, each without a glossy hair out of place. Olive mentally paired them with their husbands, but there was one fascinating-looking woman whose name did not seem to match that of any of the men present. She wore a drifting black chiffon dress and huge topaz earrings which did not glitter, but seemed a little melancholy, like her soft brown eyes. She did not chatter like the other women, but she listened beautifully.

At dinner Olive was shared by the ambassador and Señor Perez. Mr. Norton briefed her on the country, and for some time the Spanish gentleman made no effort to get her attention.

"You stay for a long time in Quito?" he finally asked Olive.

"Only for one more day, and I'm sorry. But my husband has business in Brazil. We fly to Lima from here, then to Rio."

"You get only the view of the bird," he said.

"But birds can get a beautiful view of your city," said Olive, "es-pecially of your golden churches."

He warmed up a little. "You have seen the churches?"

"Only a glimpse from the plane. Tomorrow we mean to visit them."

"La Compania de los Apostolocos is the most golden," he advised her. "I warn that you will be assaulted by the beggars. But you must forgive them. It is their—how do you say?—their hunting ground."

"I won't mind," said Olive. "They have more right to be in the churches than I have."

He said with distaste, "They bring the fleas."

The ambassador leaned toward Olive to tell her, "The family of Señor Perez has been in Ecuador since the sixteenth century."

"As long as that? Your family must have seen tremendous changes," said Olive.

"Changes? Few of importance."

The editor across the table heard that rejoinder. He smiled at Olive and said, "Señor Perez believes that."

"But I am entirely right," said the other languidly. "I am accurate. You speak of change, you think of auto, plane, icebox, telephone, the television. But are they not the very small changes in life? They are convenient, surely—but man eats, sleeps, he loves as always. He must always have the army to defend himself—that does not change. His Church does never change—" Now he spoke directly to Olive, "In my house there is a chapel, veritable date of 1542. The Mass has not changed since the first day the priest said it there, the language is the very same. No, I do not think my family in four hundred years has seen big changes. The Indians have always had the fleas."

"Fleas can be exterminated today," said Olive.

"I doubt. They will come back. It is the little penance of the poor."

When the women left the men to their final wines, they went back to the long drawing room where the air was scented by lilies within and without the windows. After coffee and liqueurs were served, the women scattered. The one in black chiffon did not leave to paint or powder. She chose a white sofa and watched Olive, somehow without staring.

Mrs. Norton said, "I must show you my modern primitive."

She took Olive to an adjoining room where a painting of a Madonna was hanging on a plaster wall under a portrait light, and Olive exclaimed with admiration.

"It must be a very early one," said the ambassador's wife. "Tom saw it in the window of what we'd call a junk shop, guessed it was good, and bought it. We had it cleaned."

"What a beautiful thing to own!"

"I know where I'll hang it at home," said Mrs. Norton, "if we ever get there. . . . Tom is enjoying your husband so much. I would have liked to have a larger party for you but we had so little notice in advance."

"A larger party would completely bewilder me," said Olive. "I'm trying to get people straight. Señora Mendoza is fascinating. Her husband isn't here, is he?"

"She's a widow. They say her husband was too old to be her father," Mrs. Norton said. "I asked her because of Señor Perez."

Olive caught the overtone. Though she didn't ask more, Mrs. Norton went on—"Poor Rosalina—those two have been in love for years, and they can't marry because, of course, he couldn't get a divorce."

"Does he want one?"

"He must—his wife is a horror—oh, a huge, fat neurotic—she never goes anywhere and they say she has fits. I ask Rosalina when I have Perez—everyone does, except a few very hidebound old families."

"She's very beautiful—what a spot to be in! Why can't he get a divorce if his wife is like that?"

"It's quite impossible. His brother is a bishop. It's a very old family. Spanish descent."

"But he's not a priest—"

"My dear, this is a Catholic country! A divorce would put him out of the Church. And even if he did break over, Rosalina is very devout. She wouldn't marry a divorced man. She wouldn't be able to, down here. No one would perform the ceremony."

"Then—"

"That's it, I suppose. Of course, I'm not a Catholic, but I've lived down here five years, and I know how they feel about some things. Sin may be overlooked—not apostasy."

"You seem very close to these people."

"No, I'm not close. It's just the position, the Embassy, that gives me a kind of access to them. But there's no real intimacy possible. That's why I'll be glad when our time is up. Perhaps if I were a Catholic, it would be different. But there's always that barrier. Like the glass in the Steuben showroom windows on Fifth Avenue. You know—it's almost invisible, but it keeps you out, keeps you from touching anything. In the United States Catholics are not like they are here."

"You think so?"

[197]

"I mean that at home Catholicism is just one religion. It has a lot of competition. But here being a Catholic is a way of life. They all belong to the same Church in this country, no matter what they do. They have to be married and buried in it or be outcasts."

"I think that's true of Catholics everywhere."

"Perhaps it is, but there seems more freedom at home. Here the control over the natives is something. Have you heard the bells? I suppose not—you arrived too late. Tomorrow they'll wake you before dawn. We must go back to the others. I hear the men coming. It's been a pleasure to have a little talk."

In the drawing room Señor Perez already stood behind the white sofa, his face immobile.

"That was quite a party," said Mark, opening the door of their bedroom. They had been sent back to the hotel in the embassy car and could not discuss the evening freely while the chauffeur was able to listen. "Did you have a good time?"

"I was fascinated by everything. The dinner. The talk. Especially by that Rosalina Mendoza."

"You know about her?"

"Yes, Mrs. Norton told me."

"They have a great respect for the letter of the Church law, haven't they?"

Olive said, "It's not only cruel. It's false."

She undressed and lay looking up at the painted ceiling. In the center of it a goddess languished on a pink cloud.

"Will she keep you awake?" asked Olive.

"You will, darling—"

"I suppose it's the strangeness around us. I've never felt so close, Mark—"

The bells began at four in the morning. Not merrily, but clamoring. For obedience, thought Olive, vaguely roused. She heard feet running in the street below. They have to go to church, she thought. They're afraid not to. She did not stir for fear of waking Mark, whose arm still circled her. But this morning, after wine and love, Mark was beyond the hearing of any church bells.

A little Indian girl, carrying her brother on her back, was waiting outside the golden church when Olive came out. He was a large baby and her little hump was narrow. She moved toward Olive to beg and dropped him. He lay on the pavement and howled. The rain fell on the ragged scabby children, and on the broad-brimmed hat of the priest who passed without glancing at the little beggars.

Olive stood on the steps of the church, fitting the picture together, the gleaming gold of the altars and the niches, the maimed boy crawling on the floor, the old women with black shawls over their heads, who were all bent in the same weary pious angle at the *prie-dieu,* and the blind horror of a man who had caught up with her in the vestibule. She picked up the crying child and was holding him as Mark, who had stopped to give some money to the padre who guided them through the church, came out. He watched her soothe the baby's frightened gasps and gave him back to the little girl very carefully. He thought, there is no one like her.

"He's too heavy for you," said Olive to the older child.

The small girl only held out a greedy hand, and Olive looked for coins. She had none left.

"Mark, give me some money—"

"It only makes them worse," he said, reaching into his pocket.

"I know, but I must close that hand of hers," said Olive, and put the money he gave her into the thin, clutching fingers.

She and Mark got into their waiting cab.

"Do you want to see the other churches?" he asked.

"I don't think so. Not unless you want to. I've had enough of the glory of golden altars and the misery of human beings for one day."

"The padre tells me that the poor people are very proud of these churches."

"Why don't they sell some of that stuff and put the money into a few clinics?"

"They don't think the way we do."

"That's obvious—"

"They have another dimension," said Mark thoughtfully, "all of them—up and down the line. That Perez last night. Those old hags on their knees in there. What I mean is that they figure they have to take it as it comes—poverty, fleas, syphilis—"

"Not marrying the people they want to marry," said Olive.

"That too—but they believe that if they play the rules they'll come out all right—you know, it all ties in with what Father Kenedy was telling me that time about the Catholic attitude toward personal happiness."

Olive said, "Of course, there are people everywhere who can be deluded into thinking they're going to walk on golden streets after they're dead, and the dream keeps them going. Enduring. The Negroes in the South used to be that way—'Oh, dem golden slippers!' And these golden churches!"

Mark said, "Those poor kids got on your nerves, didn't they? You're tired. And you should be, after last night. I think that a long planter's punch is indicated about now."

"I think so too. This is the part of the trip that ought to be a complete rest for you, Mark. Let's not worry about things we can't help. If the Catholic Church has a stranglehold on these people, there's nothing we can do about it. It's been going on for centuries."

"It certainly hits you in the face down here," said Mark.

When it hit them in the face in Lima, Olive did not talk about it. But she heard. She saw. She wondered if Mark noticed the same things and if they worried him. This should be a vacation. Nothing must spoil it. Mark was so happy when he was at peace with himself, when he wasn't trying to fight other people's battles. He does too much of that at home, thought Olive. When we go back, perhaps he should resign from the board of St. Barnabas. It takes so much of his free time, and he has little enough. And—this she felt rather than thought—then he wouldn't run into that Carroll girl.

In Lima she saw contrasts in living that shocked her. They seemed so barefaced, so irresponsible.

"Your mother would find plenty of worthy projects down here," she said to Mark.

"Wouldn't she just!"

They stayed at the country club, which had been made into the most luxurious hotel in Lima. It had enormous cool halls, lounges set about with impressionistic arrangements of amazing flowers and an outdoor dining room in the midst of the gardens where the flowers bloomed. The native chauffeur provided for them, who was one of the many tributes to Mark's industrial stature—"I had no idea you were such a big shot!" Olive would exclaim—drove them around the city, pointing out the palaces of the millionaires and the high stucco walls and hand-wrought gates. That one had cost three million dollars—within this one were forty bedrooms.

"But where do the ordinary people live?" asked Olive.

Manuel drove them through another stuccoed district with less high walls.

"This is more of the same," said Olive. "Poke him, Mark. I'm tired of stucco and millions."

Mark said, "My wife and I would like to see the homes of people who have smaller incomes—less money—you understand what I mean, Manuel?"

"Sí, señor." Manuel drove them to streets where there were no walls and the houses were smaller.

"I give up," said Olive, laughing. "It's a nice ride anyway."

Manuel turned his head. He said, "Señora Worthing wishes to see where the poor live?"

"Yes, we both would," said Mark.

"Manuel will show you."

He knew where to go. The streets grew narrow and crowded, and poverty rose around them. He stopped the car in one street where he was known by name, for they heard it called out as the car passed. In front of a row of houses with broken tiles and peeling plaster, Manuel stopped the car. He spoke in Spanish to a man standing by an open door, and though Mark and Olive could not understand the swift dialect, they knew he was explaining the curious wishes of his passengers. He turned to them.

"Would the Señor and Señora wish to enter?"

"We wouldn't want to disturb anyone," said Mark.

"You will be welcome."

"We asked for it," Mark said to Olive. "Come along, we can't hurt their feelings."

They followed the man and Manuel inside and saw that there was a flat on either side of a passage that was half-flagged and half-dirt. The one into which Manuel bowed them had a roofless kitchen with a rusted stove in one corner and a dark odorous bedroom clotted with people. A man lay on the bed, an old woman was making lace with needles, a baby was nursing, and chickens walked around the broken cement floor. The woman who was nursing the baby put him down, pulled her dress together, and stared at the strangers.

Mark thought again, there's nobody like Olive. It is her smile that settles everything. They know what she is. And with her few words of Spanish and the same manners she used at the embassy, Olive put the room at ease—was anxious about the man on the bed, admired the lace in the old woman's hands, and went with her hostess to see the other room, which was the parlor. It had a table covered with a white cloth, and three straight chairs. The table was not for eating. It held a wreath of artificial flowers and a wedding picture. On one wall was a chromo of Christ with a bleeding heart, and it had been festooned with strips of palm. Near the door a bowl of holy water had been tacked.

"This is for the baby," said Olive, making the gift of money a privilege to herself, and Manuel looked at her with approval. They were going out through the narrow passage when a priest came through the door. He carried a small black bag. The natives went down on their knees, making the sign of the cross. The priest cast an interested look at Mark and Olive, gravely bowed. He asked a question, and at the answer went swiftly into the flat opposite the one which they had just visited.

Manuel said, "There is a man dying. The priest comes with the *Eucaristía.*"

He put his clients back in the car and brushed off the children who clung curiously to its sides. He took his seat and resumed his aristocratic manner.

But now that he knew their strange interests, he showed them slums on the nearby hills where the shacks seemed to have been flung at random and somehow managed to stick. There always would be the same glint from crazy pieces of tin on the roofs, and the same smears of dust and human filth against the plaster walls. Through the open doorways a confusion of rags and pots and pans and people could be seen. Or the natives could be seen washing themselves and their clothes in the thin streams of water in the irrigation ditches.

"That is forbidden by the law," Manuel told them tolerantly.

In the cool of the lounges at the country club, they asked questions of their callers.

"The solution, of course, is education," said the young man who had been sent down by the State Department. "The crying need is for teachers. They must be native to get anywhere—Peruvians or Indians in some districts. No one else would get anywhere. The job is to establish a few good teachers' training schools, they call them *Normalistas*. And we can give them a lot of help, if they'll cooperate."

"I should think they'd want to take all the help they can get," said Mark.

"Some of them want to. There are others who want things to stay as they are. They don't want the Indians to learn too much because they might become difficult, want more wages, and demand decent housing."

"We've outgrown that in the United States long ago," said Mark. "They'll catch up down here."

"But there's another hurdle and that's the Church."

"Where does the Church come in?"

"It is in. It's controlled education down here from the beginning. In the university, which is the oldest in the hemisphere, and in all the secondary schools. They aren't going to welcome an educational system which they don't dominate."

"Aren't there public schools?"

"Some—such as they are. Theoretically, every child must be taught to read and write. The law is on the books. But it doesn't function without schools. The Church has always educated only a limited number."

[203]

Olive didn't want another religious argument. She said, trying to swerve the subject, "Have you a family here, Mr. Dawson?"

"Yes, indeed. Mrs. Dawson was sorry not to be able to come with me, but she hadn't been well. We have three children."

"Do they like living here?"

"Yes. And they're learning Spanish. Fortunately, we got them in a good school. It's run by an order of nuns, though we are not Catholics. Personally I think the Church will go along with us in our plans for a teachers' college, if we have nuns in charge of the women's dormitories."

Again Olive changed the subject.

They began the long flight to Rio before dawn, before the sun had climbed the Andes, and were soon so high that Olive, looking down from the plane window, could not tell which were the millionaires' palaces and which the slums.

"From this height so many things don't matter," she said.

"You're philosophical very early in the morning."

"I'm happy early on this morning."

"Are you, my darling?"

"It's the most wonderful adventure we have had."

The loudspeaker announced, "We are now flying at 20,000 feet."

"And we seem to be almost brushing the mountains," Olive said. "Mark, this is like seeing the world just after it was created. Nothing is inhabited except this tiny, daring plane. Let's never forget that we've seen this together. When I get bothered by silly things, make me remember this. The world—this morning—so far above the clouds."

"The height doesn't bother you?"

"I'd be terrified if you weren't here. Or if you were and I wasn't. No, I feel exalted. Mark—the children would be all right no matter what, wouldn't they?"

"Sure. And you talked to them night before last and can call them again from Rio if you like."

"I seem so remote from them. From everyone but you. It's a very special feeling. . . . Mark, I want Tim to grow up to be brave. Jenny too."

"They will, you'll see to that."

He took her hand and they fell silent, thinking of each other and happy at sharing this extraordinary flight, as if it were a gift that each made to the other. Hours passed.

The loudspeaker announced, "Ahead of you are three mighty mountains. The one in the center is called Misti."

They saw a black symmetrical cone lifting to the sky.

"It is a volcano, still active. The seething mass in the center still sends up—once in a while—plumes of rising smoke. Not today. Misti is cool. But look closely and you will see a small object on the topmost rim of the crater on the west side.

Most of the passengers—a few were familiar with this route—were at the windows.

"What is it?"

"I see something—"

Someone explained in Spanish.

"It's a crucifix," said Mark, forced to believe his eyes.

The loudspeaker explained grandiloquently, "There, above Misti's sheer forbidding sides, and a thousand feet above the molten crater, you can see a small cross."

Mark said, "By God, they took over even there!"

"But who could get there?" exclaimed Olive.

"It wasn't the Salvation Army, you can bet on that!" declared Mark. He sounded excited—almost exultant—and Olive looked at him with surprise. But everything was moving so swiftly that already the moment and the mood were gone. The mountains were dropping slowly, as if their rage or pride were spent, toward a plateau.

Mark lowered his field glasses and reached for a camera.

"Look, Olive—right ahead on the left. I must have a picture of that for the boys on the taconite location. That must be Lake Titicaca—"

The loudspeaker confirmed that it was.

"It's the highest lake in the world," said Mark. "Just about a third of the length of Lake Superior. This is mineral country. Alan ought to see this—"

The loudspeaker interrupted again. "The ancient people who lived here worked with iron. They were familiar with the process of smelting. And they believed that the god who made the universe rose from this lake. They were a cultured people. Their religion included a belief in resurrection after death, with the good to live in ease and the bad to suffer for their sins."

Olive said, "That Señor Perez—the one we met at the embassy in Quito—seems to have been right about there being no great changes for centuries."

Mark did not answer. She felt that he wasn't listening. Yes, he looked preoccupied. With the mineral country? Olive wondered what her husband was thinking about, but she did not ask. The strange tone in his voice as he had seen the cross on the seemingly inaccessible top of the volcano still rang in her mind. He wasn't conscious of the way he had spoken—why does he care so much about these religious things? Why do they bother him? He seems to be fascinated in a way. I hoped that when we got away from home, from his worry about Alan, from that Father Kenedy—I don't think that priest has any influence on Mark. Of course not. How could he have any?

They are as far apart as the poles. But that night when he came to our house, from the time when he made trouble about the birth-control clinic, Father Kenedy has disturbed Mark. He started Mark thinking about religion. There's nothing wrong with that. Why do I mind it then? I do because it worries Mark, makes him unlike himself. Somehow it takes him away from me—I know that priest doesn't think I'm important or necessary to Mark, I could feel that. Olive moved restlessly in her seat, pushed back her hair, reached for a book—she didn't want to think any further, nor uncover anything that might lie deeper in her mind.

"We'll be over the jungles and swamps for a while now," said Mark. "Getting tired, darling?"

"No, I'm fine," she said, welcoming him back.

They lost two hours by traveling eastward, and finally the evening mists began to appear as they flew lower, approaching Rio. The mountains rose above the bay like outstretched fingers, and the lights of the city were diamonds on the fingers. Olive looked down at the great statue of Christ with his arms thrown wide, protectingly.

Her heart formed a prayer, "Don't let Mark be disturbed."

"That's El Corvocado," said Mark, but in a sight-seer's tone. "Just like the postcards, isn't it? I'll get our things collected before we have to fasten our seat belts. We'll be met by somebody here, I suppose. I have a good deal of work to do in Brazil."

She heard the businesslike voice with relief.

They were met as soon as the customs released them, and paged before that. From some mainspring of enterprise, everything had been arranged for their visit in Brazil, and it was no longer a pleasure trip. Mark belonged to a mining project here. Olive spent two days on the beach, and in the shops, and trying to find something to talk about to the wives of Mark's business friends. She was glad when the day came when they were scheduled to go into the interior to see the actual mining operation into which Mark's company had been putting some of its capital. With one of the engineers who was familiar with the job, they flew to Belo-Horizonte, where it would be possible to get a train to the mining location.

There was a wait of four hours, and this delay was to be taken up by a trip to Pamphula. Olive heard them talk of it, but the name meant nothing. It was hot and they sat stickily in the cars which drove through suburbs which were like small models of those around Lima. The trip seemed very futile in spite of the fact that Mrs. Jelliff, the engineer's wife who had come along, insisted that everybody went to Pamphula between plane and train.

"To see this church," she said. "It's simply fabulous! They wouldn't consecrate it, you know."

"Consecrate it?"

"They have to consecrate it before they can say Mass there. It's never been used. I'm not a Catholic, but everybody knows about this place."

"But why didn't they use it?"

"You wait and see what you think," said Mrs. Jelliff. "I'd like to know."

The cars went through a stretch of land that looked like an abandoned real estate offering, and stopped at the end of a lagoon.

"This is the casino," Mrs. Jelliff told Olive. "It was closed after the new government went in. It used to be very gay. After that, of course, they went broke."

The setup of gaiety was still obvious. The aluminum-faced walls and flights of stairs were still handsome. But it was dirty and as commonplace as any other amusement place. Olive looked down the lagoon and was startled.

"Is that the church?"

"That's it. We'll drive down there."

"Could I walk?" asked Olive.

She wanted to be by herself and to approach it slowly. It looked interesting and completely unchurchlike. It was a modern building, built like a Quonset hut. But as Olive came close she saw that the whole back wall was a mosaic which represented the announcement of an angel to a Jewish girl that she was to have a child. The Jewish girl was ugly, sulky, and resentful, the angel a bizarre figure. They stared at each other, and across the lagoon the sun blinked on the windows of the gambling casino.

"But come inside," said Mrs. Jelliff, who was waiting. Mark was there too, and Bill Jelliff, and they all went in together. There were no pews—it was an empty structure, or would have been except that the altarpiece could not have been removed without destroying the front wall. It was painted upon the wall, and its color and terrific force kept them silent for minutes. Christ was not godlike. He was a workman, with oddly corded legs. Figures shrank away or crouched near him as he emerged from his tomb.

"It's supposed to be quite wonderful. The same man did the stations of the cross, and those have been taken to the museum at São Paulo," said Mrs. Jelliff. She spoke aloud. There was no need to hush her voice, and yet it jarred on Olive. Mark, who was beside her, turned abruptly and said, "Let's go. We've seen the thing."

"It cost a fortune," said Mrs. Jelliff, "but the Bishop wouldn't consecrate it. Some artists think it is wonderful. How do you like it?" she asked Olive.

"It's very exciting and interesting. What do you think of it, Mark?"

Mark said, "It's about as cynical a job as I ever saw."

"You believe that they were right in refusing to consecrate it?"

"What else could they do? They couldn't have services in front of a thing like that."

"Why not?"

He said with almost angry impatience, "Isn't it obvious why not? There's nothing religious about it. It's a mockery of what Catholics believe. Surely you see that."

"But Mary actually was a little Jewish girl. And the angel must have scared the wits out of her."

"Let's go," said Mark again.

Mrs. Jelliff was discomfited. She said to Olive as they walked along, "I'm afraid your husband was quite shocked. I didn't realize that you were Catholics."

"We aren't," said Olive.

Mark's outburst astonished her. It seemed as if he were fighting a battle for his enemies. Why couldn't he have said he didn't like modern art? Why defend the Catholic censorship? But she did not argue it with him. She told herself it was just that he was hot and bored with sight-seeing.

Mark did not speak of it again, and at the mining location he was not bored. They spent the night in the substantial, orderly house which had been built for the American managers. It was on a hill, and a breeze blew pleasantly around it, floating the odor of gardenia bushes. In the bedroom closets lights constantly burned to keep clothes free from mildew. Outside a barefoot watchman stood with a gun, but when Olive looked out later she found him asleep. She could not sleep tonight, even when Mark did. She kept thinking of the mosaic and the altar painting, which had been alowed no altar.

Mark said, as he dressed next morning, "Alan would like a year in a place like this."

"You think he would?"

"Yes, and he needs experience. Of course, we can't spare him now."

Olive thought, Dot would never take it.

"You want to see the mine?"

"The mine, and the village. The natives. The works," she said.

"Good girl."

She thought, but we could come to a place like this. I'd like it better than Lima. The children could learn Portuguese. I could take care of Mark. I'd have him all to myself.

They came back to the village after seeing the mine. Mark brought his camera and they went down the road, which was not quite a street, with Bill Jelliff. The villagers peered out from the doors curiously. They knew, of course, that it was the American boss.

"It's much better than what we saw in Lima," said Olive to Mark. "They're not so crowded. And they all have their little rooms where they don't eat, with its white cloth and paper flowers—I wish I'd brought some paper flowers. What is that shed for?"

"That's sort of a little hall," said Bill Jelliff, "nothing much."

"What do they use it for?"

"Church services—funerals—christenings—"

Mark said, "Let's have a look."

"It's probably locked."

"Who's got the key?"

"Oh, I'll get it opened." Jelliff gave a sharp direction in Spanish, and a boy went running and came back with a rusty key.

"It's not much to see," he said, opening the door of the little building.

It was hardly more than a shack. The light struck through cracks and there was a smell of mildew. A rat ran out quickly. In the front there was a board, nailed to a wall, and on it two candles.

Mark looked around, frowning.

"They use this for a church?"

"A priest comes once in a while—when he can."

"They haven't any seats—any pews—"

"They get along."

Mark glanced from floor to ceiling, saw the traces of bats.

"We ought to do something about this, Bill," he said.

"They asked for a church but we didn't want to put up the money."

"You can't ask them to do business here," said Mark. "It isn't right. I mean, they take it seriously. They ought to have a place."

A couple of five-cent rosaries dangled against the wall. He scowled at them.

"Are they buried from here? Is this where they come on Sunday?"

"The priest doesn't come too often because there isn't a decent place, he says."

"Well, make it decent. What will it cost?"

"Well," said Jelliff, "they could build a neat little place here for a couple of thousand dollars. Maybe fifteen hundred, for you don't have any basement or plumbing to pay for."

"Then get it started."

"Company expense?"

Mark considered that. "No. It will come under contributions. I'll underwrite it personally. But get it done." He turned to Olive, "Necessary, isn't it?"

"It's certainly grim as it is."

"It's a disgrace," said Mark. "These natives are all Catholics, and they think God's right here during their Masses—Father Kenedy says that's the basis of what they have to believe. Just look at that piece of board up there—we can't give them any golden church, but we certainly can make this place respectable for its purposes."

Olive thought, it's not the natives that worry him. It seems to be something else. As if he feels it a kind of sacrilege—odd, but he's always been able to realize what other people are thinking. He certainly doesn't believe God can be brought into this hovel by any priest or ceremony. Mark bends over backward to give the Catholic Church its due. It couldn't be that in a strange way he's attracted— no, that's absurd—but why can't he leave it alone?"

"Ready to go?" she asked, for suddenly she wanted to get out of this horrid place.

"All ready, darling."

"I wish you'd spend the night," said Jelliff.

"No, we must get back to Rio," said Mark. "We want a couple of days to see the sights and relax a bit. This will be my last vacation for quite a while."

"Rio's a good place to enjoy yourself," said Jelliff, and turned to a

[211]

boy who had come in, his heels kicking up dust on the floor, sputtering a message in Portuguese.

Jelliff turned to Mark. "He says that they are trying to reach you on the telephone from the States. We'll go back to the house and see if we can get through. He says it's important."

"I wonder what's broken loose," said Mark.

They drove back to the house for the managers of the mine. Jelliff and Mark went to struggle with the telephone. Mrs. Jelliff was scolding a houseboy, and Olive heard that as she stood in the hallway waiting, thinking with fright in her heart that the message might concern Tim or Jenny.

"Olive, where are you?" she heard Mark say before he appeared.

"What was it? Was the call important?"

He said in a tone of utter surprise, "My mother is dead."

19

PAMELA said, "We've requested that no flowers be sent. If people want to do anything, they can send a contribution to the charity fund at St. Barnabas. We put that in the funeral notice that was sent to all the papers."

"You're sure that's what Mother would have wanted?" asked Mark.

"It's the best thing to do. Mother was so prominent that there would be oceans of flowers. It's such a waste. And they all have to be acknowledged. You can send an engraved card of thanks, but it isn't as nice. Some people always send flowers anyway, so there are sure to be some. I think the procathedral is almost more beautiful without them—"

"Oh, skip it, Pam," said Alan. "Do what you want to do."

"I know how you feel," said Pam. "We're all exhausted. It was so completely unexpected! And with Mark away—I just canceled everything, of course, and came right over."

"Do they think it happened in her sleep?"

"No—evidently she got up—but it must have been very quick."

"She shouldn't have been living here alone," said Lucy.

"It was what she wanted. You know that."

"Where she was living wouldn't have made any difference," said Alan. "I talked to the doctor, Mark. He said so. It might have happened anywhere any time. He had told her she had a bad heart."

"She never said a word to anyone. Carrie had no idea."

"What I thought," said Pamela, clinging to definite responsibility as if it were a handrail, "was that the family might send a blanket of flowers. For the casket. All of us. Maybe white roses —they would look lovely against the oak in the chancel—"

Olive said, "it should be orchids." It was the first time that she had spoken in this first family conference, except to say that she was sorry.

"Orchids? At a time like this?"

"They were her special flowers," said Olive.

Alan said, "That's right."

"She told me once," said Olive, "that her husband had sent her the first orchids she ever put in those little vases on her desk."

The others looked at the empty bud vases as if they had never seen them before. None of them had known that.

"Olive is right," said Gregory Searles. "It should be orchids. Perhaps I could take that off your hands, Pam. If you'd like me to talk to the florist and give the order. I could tell him how to do it."

"I wish you would—if everyone agrees—"

So in the Procathedral, whose nave was such a perfect replica of that in one of the finest English churches built since the Reformation, Mrs. Worthing's casket lay under a blanket of mauve orchids. Gregory's directions had been explicit, so that the blossoms were not massed. Each blossom rose separately from delicate greens and had room to display its pale perfection and to tremble in the spring breeze which had been allowed to come through the slightly lifted windows, because the church was so crowded.

It was a magnificent bouquet. Her pride in it comforted Pamela, who was still greatly shocked. But she had begun to feel that what had been said to her so often in the last few days was true. Her mother would never have wanted to live as an invalid. Perhaps this was for the best. And she had never seen a more beautiful blanket of flowers.

Gregory sat beside Lucy, his mind wandering into a conception of a symbolic painting—casket, woman with a Gothic face, living blossoms, dead face—no, that wasn't quite right.

"Never leave me, Greg," whispered Lucy. "I want to go first."

He hushed her with the pressure of his hand, promising her more love.

Alan sat as if he were unaccompanied, although his wife was beside him. His mind was on his mother. He was full of pity because she could no longer go on doing those things she liked to do, and because he felt that she had been cheated at some point along the line. He thought, she made the best of what couldn't have been too good a deal for her. Father never went along with her. They weren't well suited to each other. It happens like that. You have to go on with it, and she did a good job. They didn't fight with each other—I can take a page out of her book. She built up a life of her own. I suppose she meant something to all these people here in the church. I remember how she tried to talk to me that night before everything happened—she just didn't know how to say it—I could have used a little advice then—but we never could get together.

Mark was nearest to the casket. As a lovely orchid waved, he saw his mother as she used to be, very handsome, very much in command, as she would come into the house wearing one of those things on her shoulder. I suppose we never gave her credit for what she tried to do, he thought. A bunch of brats that always let her down. She was a crusader. I suppose she was a brave woman. It can't be too easy for any woman to go out and face the public. But she did what she thought was right and nobody could stop her. She wasn't a religious woman, though she always made us say our prayers. Most of the time they were just recitations, as far as I was concerned. Not always. I used to try sometimes to establish a personal relation with God. Usually because I wanted something.

[214]

I wish I could pray for Mother now and feel that it would do her some good. I wonder if she believed that there is any life after death. She came to this church regularly, where they say they believe it. But the world was her beat, and she certainly did what she could to straighten out some of the kinks in it. I wish Mother could have had more time, not for her meetings, but for peace and to think things out. I should have spent more time with her. But she never seemed to need her family, not the way Olive does.

He listened to the beautiful words of the service. Wonderful prose, he thought. There's great dignity in this church and its rites. When the British broke with the Pope they didn't let the shape of the religion go at once, and the High Church Episcopals never did. Their creed is very close to Catholicism but it doesn't attempt the impossible. It doesn't ask people who go along with it to swallow the belief that bread can be made God, or to worship a wafer. To me this is more of a religion than sects that have less formality, though any religion is pretty much dependent on how hard you work at it.

"The resurrection and the life." If you could believe in resurrection, the rest should be easy. It presupposes all the rest, creation, return to something, and control while you're on earth would be fair enough. But all the proof is against it.

A lot of people bypass proof. Especially the Roman Catholics. Without a bit of evidence, on the say-so of a bunch of Popes and priests who have everything to gain by keeping people hoodwinked, Catholics defend the theory that life on earth is only preparation. It's subtle, it's clever. And it's basic. For if a person can credit that, he can endure anything.

If anything should happen to Olive, I'd want to believe it myself. I'd have to or go crazy. I'd have to believe that I'd catch up with her somewhere. Nothing is going to happen to her, or to either of us for a long while yet. Poor Mother. She spent a lot of time trying to clean up the world, and the way this church is packed today shows that people honored her for it. But I wonder if she wouldn't be better off if she'd spent some of that energy figuring out the answer to her own life. Complete your philosophy, Father

Kenedy said, and that's one time he was dead right. Everyone should. Why don't I settle for this church if I want a religion at all? Maybe I'd be better off without any. Most of the philosophers couldn't take religion. They never established anything. Golden churches—that cross on top of the volcano—Rose Mary Carroll offering up every natural instinct—to what? What does it?

"We brought nothing into this life and we take nothing out of it."

At the very end, Mother was alone. She took nothing with her. Took nothing where? It's strange—I can't believe it's just a blackout.

Beside him, Olive was thinking again of the quick tears that had come into Mrs. Worthing's eyes on that winter day when she had stopped in for a little visit with her mother-in-law. What she needed was love, thought Olive. She wasn't a cold woman. She must have been chilled.

She thought, I wish she could see all her lovely orchids, see all the honor that they are trying to give her.

The lawyer who had come back to the old Worthing house to pay his respects to the family after the grave-side services took Mark aside. He said, "In the matter of your mother's estate, she left a will. The original document is in our vault. I don't remember whether she put a copy in her safety-deposit box or not. But I'll be glad to go over the instrument with the family, to read it to them, at any time."

"We should all get together for that."

"It's the customary way," said Mr. Hubbard, "the best way. Questions sometimes arise which are of mutual interest. Or need legal explanation. I believe that she named you, Alan, and myself as executors."

Mark said, "I suppose that should be done soon."

"Yes, I wouldn't delay probate procedure."

"Alan had to go back to the location after the funeral. They're very busy right now. Let's see—he should be able to make it on

Saturday afternoon. That's a half-day. Would that be possible for you, Mr. Hubbard?"

"I'll make it possible."

"At your office or here?"

"I think it might be more convenient for the girls if I read the will to them here."

"Then let's say four o'clock. Olive—"

She came to him.

"We don't have anything to do on Saturday afternoon, have we? Mr. Hubbard wants to read Mother's will."

"We have no engagements at all," said Olive.

"Then I'll tell Alan and Pam and Lucy to be here at Mother's house at four."

"And Olive will be here, I hope?" Mr. Hubbard asked her.

"Oh, I don't think so," said Olive. "That would be something for the immediate family."

"You should be here too. I may say, without going into detail, that you personally are mentioned in Mrs. Worthing's will."

"How dear of her," said Olive. "But couldn't Mark tell me afterward?"

"No, you should be present," insisted Mr. Hubbard.

Olive tried to beg off later, when she and Mark were alone.

"Frank Hubbard made quite a point of your being there."

"He didn't want me to feel left out. But it's a time for blood kin, not for in-laws."

"He said Mother left you something."

"Whatever it is, I'll love it. I'd like to have something from that house to remember her by."

"Maybe she left you 'The Garden Party' and 'The Music Master.' "

She winced at the thought of the two color engravings in the living room, and then laughed with him. She said defiantly, "All right, if that was what she wanted me to have. I'd hang them in our room too. But what I'd like is one—just one—of those beautiful Dresden plates."

"Anyway, you have to come along," he told her.

[217]

They were all there, even Pamela's husband, Bradley Brooks. He was wearing his usual air of detachment, but this was a matter of property, and he was a businessman. Lucy would not come without Gregory, and he quite obviously disliked this occasion. But when Alan came in with Dot, nobody knew quite what to do with her. She had never been amalgamated into the family—she was too new a member. They didn't expect her to be grieving, but she was unlikely to get anything personally, and that rather embarrassed Pamela, as if there were no present on the Christmas tree for someone who had to be invited to the party.

There were too many of them for the little den, so they sat in the big, stiffly furnished living room, where "The Garden Party" graced the west wall and "The Music Master" gave his eternal lesson on the east one. Mark nudged Olive and indicated that the picture was hers, and she said stubbornly under her breath, "I adore it!"

Carrie, the old housekeeper, knew how Mrs. Worthing liked to have her house look, and her diligence in making the room ready had been spurred by devotion. The cushions on every sofa and chair had been plumped up almost to their original fullness, and the alabaster ash trays were clean and severely empty. When she had been told that this was to be a meeting with the lawyer, Carrie had put the marble-topped table which was always used at meetings in this house at its customary place at one end of the long room. She place a dignified, tapestried armchair behind it. Also she had set up two rows of the folding chairs from the laundry facing the table. The sight of them seemed to appall Alan when he came in, and he dragged them out of line and folded most of them up. He would have moved the table and the armchair, but Mr. Hubbard arrived before he could do so and seemed to take the arrangement for granted, placing his brief case on the marble top and settling with authority into the chair for the presiding officer.

"Mark," he said, "there is a housekeeper, isn't there? You might ask her to come in, if you think well of it."

Mark went to find Carrie, and Mr. Hubbard took a long sealed

[218]

envelope out of his case. They were all silent, and the half-drawn, old-fashioned window shades suddenly made the room too dark, so the sun must have gone under the clouds.

Dot loosened her tiny mink-trimmed cape and found a cigarette. Her costume was dark blue and high style this spring. None of the young women was wearing mourning. Pamela's new tweeds happened to be black and white. Gregory had an abhorrence of mourning clothes, so Lucy shunned them, and Olive would have considered it pretentious to buy or wear them. But she was the only one dressed in black, a wool sheath with white collar and cuffs that Mark had always liked.

Carrie came in. She knew the Worthings as intimately as a servant could, but the occasion made her shy. She came no farther than the inside of the doorway, where she sat on the edge of a chair. She was now white-haired and wore one of a long succession of maroon uniforms. When she had been asked to join the family, she had hurriedly taken off her apron. Alan thought, she looks like a wall after a picture has been taken down. You know that something used to be there in that place.

"I am very glad to see you all," said Mr. Hubbard. "These are sad occasions when we must gather to acquaint ourselves with the instructions and wishes of those who have gone before us. Yet not so melancholy, because it gives us an opportunity of serving—"

"I'll bet he says that every time he reads a will, thought Alan, as the lawyer droned on. Get on with it.

"I have here the written instrument by which Mildred Emmet Worthing made disposition of her estate, to take effect after her death. It was signed in my office in the presence of myself and two witnesses on February 25, 1956. It was then sealed in the presence of the testator, and since that time has been on deposit in the vaults to which only the members of the legal firm of Hubbard, Owens and Grant have access. I took it from those vaults this morning and present it to you now, still sealed. Are there any questions concerning this procedure?"

There were none. He broke the seal, and as he drew out the will Mark was thinking about that February date. It was just after they had left for South America. She had made a previous will. He knew that. She must have wanted to make some change.

He was reading now, with the solemnity proper to words connected with the dead. . . . "Being of sound mind . . ."

The list of bequests came first. Carrie was crying. She had not expected so much. It was generous. Five thousand dollars, the furnishings of her present bedroom, and such other furniture and linen as she might select, subject to Pamela's approval . . . a thousand dollars to a former secretary . . . now jewelry . . . there wasn't a great deal, and her children recognized each piece as it was described . . . the baroque pearls for Pam, the diamond barpin for Lucy, the diamond earrings for Dorothy, my son Alan's wife . . . queer that Olive isn't mentioned with the other girls, thought Mark—not that Olive cares anything for jewelry.

The children were to have their choice of the furnishings of the house, in accordance with age. The rest was to be sold with the house itself and the proceeds divided.

Mother had money of her own too, thought Mark. I told her that she ought to dip into that if the income that she got from Father's estate wasn't large enough for her living expenses. Can she have run through that?

" 'Realizing,' " read Mr. Hubbard, " 'that the holdings in the Worthing-Ingalls Company, from which the income has come to me during my lifetime, will at my death revert and be equally distributed among my beloved children, and feeling that thus they are well provided for, I do bequeath the rest of my estate to my equally beloved daughter-in-law, Olive Worthing.' "

Olive gets the rest of it? That may be quite a lot of money, thought Mark.

There was a tenseness in the room as the lawyer went on. He read the names of the executors and finished.

Quickly Alan went over to where Olive was sitting. He kissed the top of her head.

"I'm so glad," he said. "You meant a lot to her."

"But I don't understand," said Olive. "What is this, Mark?"

"I don't know until I talk to Mr. Hubbard."

Pamela was slower. But she did the right thing. "I'm glad for you, Olive." And Gregory brought Lucy over to repeat that.

Mr. Hubbard said with a smile, "You see now, Olive, why I thought you should be here today."

"Please tell me what this is about," she said. "I heard my name."

"In simple words," said the lawyer, "after these bequests are paid, you inherit the residue of Mrs. Worthing's private fortune."

Mark asked, "How much will it amount to, Mr. Hubbard? Have you any idea?"

"Yes, I made a little inventory. I should say—at present values, about two hundred thousand dollars. That's conservative."

Mark whistled. "I didn't realize it was that much."

"It's an example of how well-invested funds can grow," said the lawyer. "It wasn't a fourth of that when she inherited it; but it was in good stocks, and what with splits and rising values, it has built up. Your mother never spent anything but the income. Of course, she had the income also from the share of your father's estate held in trust for the rest of you."

Olive said, "I wouldn't dream of taking that money, Mr. Hubbard."

"Why not?"

"Because it wouldn't be right."

The others had drawn away but not out of hearing. Mr. Hubbard did not lower his voice.

He said, "I may say that Mrs. Worthing discussed this with me. It was what she wanted to do. At one time she had considered using her private means for some one of the many good works in which she was so interested."

"She told me that," said Olive, "last winter."

"She changed her mind," said the lawyer. "She said—I repeat the substance of her words—that it would serve a more useful purpose in your hands than if it were under the control of an organization."

"But what purpose did she mean?"

"That she did not define. I was under the impression that you thought alike in certain matters."

"Mr. Hubbard, I really can't take money that should go to the Worthing family."

"Look," said Alan. "Listen to what he just said. She never meant to give it to her kids."

Her conversation with Mrs. Worthing on that winter day was coming back to Olive now. She remembered—I said something about not having any money of my own—she couldn't have thought I was suggesting anything—I only said it must be a pleasure to have money to give—she was talking about setting up a fund that day—this must have been done afterward—we talked about her meeting—her orchid—juvenile delinquency—

"It's not right for me to have it," she said, helplessly. "You tell them so, Mark."

"I can't do anything about it," he said. "This was Mother's own idea." He smiled down at her tenderly. "Maybe Mother thought she couldn't trust me to take care of you."

20

DURING the next weeks Mark felt as if a vague miasma had been lifted and no longer oppressed him. He did not think it would return, but if it should he meant not to allow it to linger in the atmosphere of his life. He had far too much to do, too much responsibility upon him to spend any time or thought on beliefs or practices which did not immediately concern him.

Now that it was spring, the private railroad that would be the property of the Worthing-Ingalls Company was being built from the harbor at Baraga to the taconite mines beyond the hills. The whole project was smoothing out and taking on a more permanent look. Most of the construction gangs who had been living in aluminum trailer camps last summer were gone, their part of the job completed, and the barracks which had been built for unmarried workers was neatly painted. In the new village there were ragged plots of bright green grass around some doorsteps, and plenty of gay dandelions.

The details of management were innumerable. They were financial and operative for Mark. They were both small and large, and at any size might be very important. They involved tricky matters of policy. The railroad must be used only for certain purposes. It must never be made a common carrier for workmen, even if that was convenient, for that would lay the company wide open to interstate regulations that it wanted to avoid. And always there was the political situation to watch, for future profits in taconite processing would waver like the needle on a compass with the amount of taxes levied by the state and federal governments. The public had to be informed so that it might influence political thought. For that, it was necessary to co-operate with other mining companies to buy radio and television time to present arguments. What was a fair share for Worthing-Ingalls to contribute to public relations of this kind? Mark was always the one who had to decide such questions.

One day in his office, as he was looking for a report on iron-ore production in Canada which Effie had piled up with other pamphlets, he came upon the one he had sent for months before, *The Management of the Roman Catholic Church*. He was about to toss it into the wastebasket, then changed his mind. There was some good data in that booklet, and it had not been prepared by Catholics, so it was probably unbiased and accurate. He remembered that a list of the problems of the Catholic Church had been listed, and he wanted to look that over again. When he had time. Of course, thought Mark, any organized body as large as that must fairly crawl with difficulties, due to personnel alone. He said to himself, some day I'd like to study the whole setup. But not now. It bothered Olive to have him talk about that religion. Olive didn't like argument. Perhaps he himself had come at the sect from the wrong end, because of that business concerning Alan.

But everything was working out. Alan seemed adjusted. At least there was no sign of any domestic trouble. Dot might not be quite the ideal wife for Alan, but she was smart in her own way.

If there were children, that would soften her up. Mark thought, poor Olive—my dear Olive—still disappointed. She loves Tim and Jenny, but they aren't enough to satisfy her. She wants another child too, that would be hers and mine. Would there by any use in seeing a specialist about sterility? There must be very good men in that field in New York. It can't be done now. There's no time.

If for an hour Mark was free from the constant consultation and need for decision, if he was not waiting for a long distance call from New York or Cleveland or putting one through, Effie was sure to come in with more papers to be signed. As she did now. The trust that had been established for his mother was being distributed among himself and his sisters and brother, and many transfers had to be legalized. He looked these papers over. Olive would have to sign this one personally.

She had accepted the fact of her legacy with reservations.

"I won't argue about it any more, Mark," she said. "If you think I should, I'll take the money. But I'll be sort of a guardian for it, that's all. I'll keep it until something comes along that your mother would like to have it used for."

"You mean some good cause or other?"

"Not necessarily a cause. It might be a person—people—I don't know. But I think I will know when the time comes."

"You're a good cause yourself. Better get a mink coat," Mark had suggested.

"Here you are, Effie," he said now, "you can mail these back to the Hubbard office. I'll take this one home for Mrs. Worthing's signature and bring it back in the morning. Anything else before I go?"

"Only this crank letter," she said. "I was going to throw it away but I thought that since it evidently comes from somebody living up there in the new village, who might be working for the company, you might want to see it."

She handed him the sheet of letter paper. It was decorated paper, with a bluebird at the top of the page. The handwriting was a woman's and very neat.

Dear Mr. Worthing:

I am taking the liberty of writing to you to say that the people in this community do not like that R. C. ceremonys go on in the school building. If we do not look out the R. C. priest will take over the school. There is one R. C. teacher already for the first three grades which are the formitive ones. Knowing your interest and that you are a Protestant and Christian, wish you would do something about this. There is considerible bad feeling in this community.

Sincerely,
A citizen and mother

"She'll never win a spelling contest," said Mark. "Anyway she lets me out of having to answer her. File it, Effie, under *Freaks*."

"They say it takes a certain type of insanity to write anonymous letters," said Effie.

"It takes a certain amount of viciousness."

It annoyed Mark to think that sort of thing was going on. He could imagine it—a hard-faced woman watching at her window to see who went to the schoolhouse on Sunday, counting the Catholics, setting them apart. She would look at the priest coming along—maybe wearing his robes, perhaps carrying one of those little black bags—she would think he was carrying idols and black-magic apparatus.

When he had occasion to go up to the location a few days later, the sight of the small cluster of houses, with the flag above the schoolhouse, made him remember the letter. The village didn't look as good to him as it usually did. But he told himself that people like that woman were to be found everywhere. There was nothing he could do about it. Certainly an unsigned letter was not going to affect his permission to use the school for those services. He might set a few inquiries in motion, find out if there was any really bad feeling.

He was standing on a temporary trestle, inspecting a conveyer which would carry ore from the railway terminus on one side of the highway to storage bins on the other. From its height he overlooked the village. As he glanced down he saw a tall figure in black clothes and a churchman's hat striding along, and recognized Father Kenedy. And he also saw the boy who picked up a rock, flung it at the priest, and dodged behind a house wall as soon as he had let it fly. It missed Father Kenedy, falling heavily in the path ahead of him. The priest paused, looked down at it. He did not turn his head, and after a minute resumed his walk unhurriedly.

Mark climbed down, very angry. He went to meet the priest. An apology was instinctive, something he must do, as if he were responsible for that hurled rock.

"Good morning, Father Kenedy."

"I'm very glad to see you, Mark. How are you?"

"I'm fine. I saw what happened just now. I'd like to get my hands on the little devil who threw that rock. He went behind a yellow house over there."

"Pay no attention to it."

"But it's outrageous! That was a mean rock. It might have hurt you badly."

The priest grinned boyishly. "A hundred and fifty years ago the savages around here used to make meals off the missionaries. We've come a long way."

"Have you had much trouble like this?"

"Nothing very serious. There are always a few whose misunderstanding goes pretty deep. May I ask if you have heard any complaints?"

"I had one crazy letter. Unsigned."

"I'm sorry if your kindness has only added to your many burdens. All we can do in return is to pray for you, which we do at every service. As soon as possible, if we can get a site, we shall start construction of at least a temporary chapel."

"It seems to me that would be a good idea. You know where you want to build?"

"Could you take a few minutes to let me show you?"

"I'd like to see what you have in mind."

They walked through the village together, and Mark wondered if the woman who wrote the letter was watching and recognized him. He hoped so. He was aware as before of the friendship this priest offered, or something like friendship, which always came through to Mark when he was in Father Kenedy's company.

"May I offer my sympathy in your recent bereavement, Mark?"

"Very kind of you."

"Your mother was well known for her good works. I am sure you are comforted by feeling she has gone to her reward."

"Do you think they will let her into heaven?" asked Mark with a smile.

"I trust our Lord will welcome her."

"But I thought you didn't believe that any Protestant had a chance—if there is anything afterward."

"Surely you don't think that? A man of your intelligence?"

"Yes, I supposed that Catholics consigned everyone who didn't go along with them to hell."

"No—no. Any baptized person, Catholic or not, will be received into heaven, if he or his sins have not rejected salvation."

"But you do insist on baptism? That must leave a lot of people out who have tried to do their best and never heard of being sprinkled with water. It's a big world, Father, with a lot of human beings in it."

"We believe," said the priest. "This is an abstruse subject and I wish I had time to go into it fully—I'm always afraid I may not get another chance at your misconceptions, Mark. But briefly, we believe that, always excepting martyrs and those who die for others, as in war with the right intention, that the sacrament of baptism in reality (by which I mean the use of true and natural water), or in desire, is necessary for salvation."

"I don't quite get that. About desire."

"It's as simple as this. If the opportunity for baptism by water is not possible, the desire of a soul to be with God and to live according to His law may serve as baptism, and wash away original sin."

"So you do it by wishful thinking?"

"By no means. This implicit desire for supernatural grace is no casual wish."

"But you can never tell who is baptized and who isn't."

"The Ultimate Judge is not of this world."

An absurd conversation, it seemed to Mark, to be going on as they walked through a raw little workmen's community in the middle of a busy afternoon. Why did this man always stir him up, make him want to argue? Get down to business now.

"So you'd like to build your church back toward the hill?" he asked, for the priest had not stopped in the middle of the dwellings, and now they were mounting a slope behind them.

"Yes." He went a little farther and turned. He said, "This seemed a fitting place."

Mark stood beside him on a little plateau between the slope of the meadows and the rise of the steeper hills.

"You see what I mean," said Father Kenedy, without elaboration. As if it wasn't necessary.

Mark saw. The view cradled the village as a church that stood there would. It would look down upon the town with dignity and protection. Across the highway was the seemingly endless lake and the place where men would earn and produce. Then they would come back to their homes, and when they needed more than that—

"You'd like to build them a golden church like some of those we saw in South America, Father Kenedy. I can see that."

"I would indeed. The Bishop makes fun of my architectural dreams too," said Father Kenedy, "but the archangels loved heights, as Henry Adams wrote. And a basement with windows would do us for a few years."

"You'll have to do some grading."

"There are some generous workmen here."

"You have it all planned out, I can see that. Well, I won't stand in your way. The sooner you can have services under your own steam and not in the schoolhouse, the better. I'll have to talk to Mr. Tuttle, our vice-president, and our lawyers, but we'll try not to rook you and the Bishop. Come around to my office in town in a few days and we'll see what we can do. What's happening over there, I wonder? There seems to be some excitement."

They could see men running down toward the harbor, but the end of the power plant concealed their destination.

"I hope it's not an accident," said the priest.

"I'd better get over there." Mark ran down to where he had left his car, and headed for the plant.

There was a man lying on the ground when he got to the scene of the excitement. A doctor was kneeling beside him. Alan was standing by, taut and grim. Becker, who was sending the by-standers back to their jobs, came to meet Mark.

"What happened?"

"One of those things," said Becker. "They were moving some of those big boulders that were in the way here. Somebody must have been careless. They had it hoisted to the truck, but a chain broke and this guy was in the way."

"Is it bad?"

Becker said unhappily, "The doctor hasn't said yet."

"I see Alan over there. Is the man one of his crew?"

Becker nodded. "We'll know how he is in a minute. Now the rest of you men get back on your jobs. This isn't a side show and we'll take care of it. Lanehan will be all right."

Now Father Kenedy was there too.

"Can I help?"

"Boys, is Lanehan a Catholic?"

"Yah, Mr. Becker. He is."

"Okay, Father. Then he might like to see you when the doctor gets through."

The doctor said to Becker and Mark, "It's hard to tell. His leg is smashed and the pelvis. I don't know what he may be like internally. There's nothing to do but to take a chance and get him to a city hospital. The one in the nearest town to here isn't good enough. He'll need X-rays that their equipment can't manage, and difficult surgery. But I'll get the ambulance from there—one of the men has already telephoned for that, and it should be here any minute. I'll have to call myself and see which hospital in the city has room for him. They're all crowded."

"Have him taken to St. Barnabas. I'll call them and see that he gets a room," said Mark with authority.

"Fine. And somebody should ride in with him. Just in case. There's no extra attendant with this ambulance. I'd go but I have a confinement case on and can't leave," said the doctor.

"I'd like to go," said Alan.

Becker said, "Okay, Alan. You do that."

The ambulance came rushing down the roadway, its siren whining. The priest was still kneeling beside the injured man, speaking softly to him. The driver pulled out the stretcher and waited for Father Kenedy to finish. The doctor waited. But Alan moved forward.

"We'd better get started," he said. His voice was rough and his glance at the priest was hostile. "Let's cut this stuff."

Father Kenedy looked up. "In a moment, Alan. This is very important."

"It's more important to get him to a hospital—"

Mark laid a restraining hand on his brother's shoulder. "He may not make it to the city, Alan."

"He won't at this rate," muttered Alan bitterly.

The priest made the sign of the cross and rose a minute later. The man was lifted into the ambulance, and Alan climbed in after him. Soberly the knot of men dispersed, the doctor explaining the chances of Lanehan's survival to Mark and the superintendent as they walked to the offices. The priest went alone.

21

LATER in the afternoon, Mark telephoned to Olive and told her not to wait dinner for him. He had not finished his conferences with Becker until well after five o'clock, and it would take more than an hour to get back to the city—where traffic was heavy and slow at this time of day. Then, before coming home, Mark wanted to stop at the hospital and see how the injured man was getting along. He knew that Lanehan had not died on the way there, for Alan had called to report that, but the examinations by specialists had not been completed.

"Don't try to hurry," said Olive. "I'll give the children their supper and wait for you."

"No, you'd better have your own dinner. I might get held up somewhere."

"If you'd rather—you've had a tough day, haven't you? But if that man is still alive, there's every chance for him. The doctors can do such miracles."

It wasn't what Olive said. It was the way she said it that gave Mark the lift he needed at the moment. Instantly she seemed to be with him, sharing even the worries she didn't know about. As Mark left the taconite plant, his next meeting with her, that loved destination, was as always in the back of his mind. In the front of it were several other matters. One was the mounting cost of the new project, which crept up like a tide which always went further than was expected. They might have to approach Crane and Eliot with a request for more money. Would they take Mark's word for it—his personal judgment that this was going to be an even better investment than it had seemed in the beginning?

Also there was disquiet in Mark's mind about Alan. His brother had seemed on edge today. It had shown in his rudeness to the priest, though part of that could be excused because of natural concern about the injury to a man who had been one of his working crew. But Alan had always been good-tempered and well controlled. That sort of angry incivility wasn't like him. Since his break with Rose Mary, Alan must be holding a grudge against the priest, perhaps against all priests.

Father Kenedy handled it well, thought Mark. He was decent about it, but he couldn't let Alan interfere with what he was doing. For that was his job. It might seem like hocus-pocus to Alan, but evidently Lanehan is a Catholic, and having a priest on the spot when you might be passing out for good means a lot to Catholics. During the war I found that out. Catholics believe that you need a priest to take you over the edge into the next world.

They believe there is one, too. You can't convince Catholics that the universe has been pretty well explored by this time and nobody has found any planet set aside for ghosts. Wishful thinking. And most ignorant people want to believe in a heaven that keeps a full set of records and a hell with fire . . . they all aren't ignorant . . . do the educated, intelligent Catholics have their tongues in their cheeks? How can they go along with it? How can they believe that their priests can actually produce God on their altars? How can Father Kenedy himself believe in such an extraordinary theory as transubstantiation? But it was all put down in black and white in one of those books he lent me.

Olive says that being a Catholic is a matter of temperament, of willingness to submit. That's all right up to a point, but where it falls down is that willingness to submit doesn't necessarily match up with religion. I must tell Olive that. In Russia—in Germany under Hitler, when they kicked out the priests and closed the churches—they still couldn't call their souls their own.

Souls their own . . . what was that crack that Father Kenedy made one day in my office? He said that every man had the right to take time to complete his own philosophy. He had something there . . . if it can be done. Suppose I had been the one who was hit with that boulder today. I'm not really organized. I don't know the answer. That's what gets under my skin with Kenedy; he's so sure he knows the answers. All of them. Ask the question and out pops the answer—maybe that there isn't any answer but you have to believe it anyhow.

I think myself that there is more to existence than anybody understands to date. I don't believe that we have sixty or seventy years if we're lucky—the way a dog gets his eight or nine—and then it's all over but the decay. There's something beyond consciousness —it shows under strain—you feel it sometimes when you're in love—maybe at the end it will hit you. Call it soul, call it any-thing, call it a kind of electronic wave in the mind that isn't hooked up to our senses yet. If a man is alive, is it just because his mother and father slept together at a certain time, or is there another reason for his existence? That's what all the old boys used to try to work out. All the philosophers took a shot at that one. Ontology. The categorical imperative. Course 250, Ethics and Moral Philosophy—Professor Pomeroy with the dandruff on his collar. Four points credit.

Father Kenedy would like to make me believe that I haven't got all the packing out of the case, that there's something deeper with my name on it and I ought to dig it out. But the hell with it. I haven't time to spend on that sort of thing. It's for the professors. For the priests.

The woods along the highway were thinning, and here and there the neon signs of a tavern or a clutch of fishing cabins broke the April dusk. Mark began to see the lighted outline of the city, curving along the shore, dropping a necklace of dock lights to float on the lake, whimsically climbing the hills. His heart knew where his own home, housing his love, fitted in the pattern, but he could not take the direct road to it yet. Instead he turned south until he reached the limestone structure that was the hospital named for St. Barnabas. People were coming in and out of its doors, looking cheerful as if an ordeal were over, or somber and with lagging steps as if there were nothing more to be done and nothing to hurry for now. A woman whose child was soon to be born went heavily up the broad steps, leaning on her husband's arm. Mark wondered—will I ever bring Olive here in that condition? And then, as he took the key out of his darkened car, he saw his brother.

Alan and Rose Mary Carroll. They must have come out of the hospital while Mark was parking his car. They were walking along the sidewalk across the street, so slowly and absorbedly that they hardly seemed to be moving.

Mark had no doubt of what he was seeing. They were a man and woman in love. It showed in the bend of Alan's head, in the lifted face of the girl. Never had Mark seen Alan in an attitude of devotion before, nor so tender toward anyone. He held Rose Mary's arm close to his side but without pressing her. They were obviously treasuring even this little walk, these minutes on the street. The value to them of being together was unmistakable.

In the first instant, Mark felt only a wave of pleasure that Alan was having such experience. This was good. This was what Alan needed, to care for somebody like that, some lovely girl. I know how he feels, was Mark's reaction. Then pity swept over the satisfaction and submerged it completely. For this was very complicated. It was a bad mess. Alan was tied to another girl. He couldn't go on with this, not without trouble. Not as things were now. But he was in love with Rose Mary Carroll. A blind man could tell that. He had told Mark the truth months ago, when he was arguing about his intended marriage to her, that this was the real thing. Being married to someone else hadn't destroyed it. Not that impetuous giving himself away, either in anger or stupidity. We've known all along that he shouldn't have married Dot Langhorne, thought Mark. We've been afraid to admit it.

The street light showed the contour of Alan's fair head and the delicacy of the girl's profile. Together they modeled the beauty of youth and desire. Alan was still in work clothes, his shirt open at the throat as it had been when he had climbed into the ambulance with the injured Lanehan. Mark could guess at what had happened. It might have been forseen. In the stress and confusion of the accident Alan had not thought that he might see Rose Mary at the Hospital. There was no plan or device to meet her. But he had come upon her there. And they have had hours together, thought Mark, at least hours of knowing that they were under the same roof. Under the roof where they met each other in the first place, poor kids.

They went past Mark's car, where he sat behind the wheel in darkness, and merged with the shadows farther down the street, beyond the glow of the hospital lights. Where were they going? Where could they go? Alan couldn't go home with her—he was married, and Rose Mary had told Mark that her family felt bitter about Alan. Alan had a wife in the only place that he could call his own. He didn't even have his car tonight, for he had driven here in the ambulance. They'd find a taxi. They might go to some little joint where they could sit and eat together, and starve for each other, thought Mark. Alan will have to tell his wife a string of lies.

Perhaps they'd end up in a hotel tonight. I wouldn't blame them, Mark said to himself. That girl has had a rough deal. It's probably been worse for Alan too than I had any idea of. And if she did go with Alan, what would her priest say to that? They'd drag it out of her, I suppose. Punish her somehow, threaten her with hell. Poor girl, it's not her fault. It's not what she wanted. She wanted to marry Alan on the square, in the open.

Am I to blame for this? Rose Mary said I was. She put it up to me to make Alan think it would work out all right, and I turned her down. I don't know how it would have worked out. Maybe they could have made a go of it. Maybe it would have been better to have Alan marry a Catholic than go sour.

The worst of it is that she believes in the rules they lay down. She wants to be good, poor girl. Some girls might think it was all right—just getting their own back—but not Rose Mary Carroll. The best thing that Alan can do is to leave her alone—he can't make her happy as things are now. Mark was thoroughly depressed as he went into the hospital to inquire about Lanehan.

He found the nurse who was on duty on the case, and she was cheerful and encouraging. Mr. Lanehan was under sedation but doing very well. He had a good chance.

"Your brother left just a little while ago, Mr. Worthing," said the nurse. "He's been at the hospital all afternoon. You just missed him."

I didn't miss him, Mark said to himself.

He went home, never more sensitive to the welcome that was there. It gave him a sense of guilt to see Olive in her soft blue dress, to feel her happiness rise because he was there, to know that he had a right to his love.

She made him a drink and had saved a hot plate of dinner—just in case, she said. He had forgotten dinner, but he wasn't very hungry.

"Was Alan at the hospital too?" asked Olive.

"Not when I was there. He had been."

"Dot called up to find out if he was here. She had been trying to get him at the plant. I told her that there had been an accident but I didn't suggest her calling the hospital. I thought that if Alan was there, he might want to stay."

[235]

"Just as well you didn't put her on his trail." Was Olive realizing that he would meet Rose Mary Carroll at St. Barnabas?

"Dot said that they had a dinner engagement and that he'd probably forgotten it."

"He probably did. He had a lot on his mind."

"Was Alan much upset by the accident?"

"He seemed to be. He was quite ugly with the priest who was praying over this poor guy because he wasn't doing it fast enough."

"You can hardly blame him, if he wanted to get the man to the hospital. Where did the priest come from?"

"It was Father Kenedy."

Again, thought Olive. She asked, "How did he happen to be up there today? It isn't Sunday."

"He was over in the village. He showed me where he wants to build a church. If we'll sell him land enough."

"Do you have to bother with that, Mark? With all the other things you have to do?"

"A kid shied a rock at him," said Mark, as if that somehow connected with what Olive asked. "That was before the accident happened. Before Alan jumped down his throat. Of course, nothing fazes Kenedy. As he said to me, his crowd have been working that territory for a long while. He just brushed Alan off and went on with what he was doing. Extreme unction, I think they call it. They never give up their hold on a person. Alan will find that out."

"What's bothering you that you aren't telling me?"

"Nothing. Well—I saw Alan walking along with the Carroll girl tonight. They were leaving the hospital. I don't think he'll catch up to any dinner party with Dot. Not tonight."

Olive showed no shock. She asked, "Has he been seeing Rose Mary Carroll?"

"I don't know. No—I doubt that."

"He should have happiness," said Olive. "Sometimes, Mark, I don't see how his marriage can last. It's so artificial. You feel it when you're with them."

"He has to make the best of it. He can't have the other one now."

[236]

"That's what Greg Searles told me. Because if he were divorced, Rose Mary wouldn't be free to marry him. But if she really loves Alan—"

"She's too much of a Catholic."

"She's a woman too. Do you remember those two we met in Quito—the woman with the velvet eyes and Señor Perez?"

"This girl wouldn't put up with a situation like that."

"Darling, how can you know?"

"I don't know. But I've talked to her. She's strong. And she believes in her religion. That's where they have the advantage over us."

"Who?"

"Catholics, I mean. Their values are different from other people's. They may not have the men they want or the women they want. But they've got their Church. And when they go without, they can offer it up—as the Carroll girl told me she did."

"You told me that you thought that idea was monstrous!"

"Did I?"

"Yes, you did. You came home storming about it. Your whole point of view seems to be changing."

"I don't think so."

She heard the doubt, the question.

Mark said, "It's just that I'm more sorry for Alan than I am for the girl. At least, she has something to tie to. He has nothing. In our family none of us ever had. I didn't, until I found you."

"Am I enough to tie to?"

"You're all I need in this world, Olive."

22

THE matter of the church site had no priority in Mark's mind, and when Father Kenedy called to ask for an appointment some days later, as Mark had suggested he should do, he felt rather guilty because he had done nothing about it. He fixed a time to see the priest, and took the matter up with Harry Tuttle.

Tuttle grumbled a little. He said that the company was trying to get out of the real estate business, as soon as all the houses in the village were sold to their employees. This would be one more complication.

"And then they'll all be after you, Mark. The Jews will want a site for a synagogue, and every other Protestant denomination will be around asking for company land. And then they come around when they can't raise the money by themselves and want more help—"

"We can cross that bridge when we come to it," said Mark, "but the fact is that I'd like to get these services out of the schoolhouse."

"I don't think it was such a good idea to let them in, in the first place. What do they propose to pay for the land they want?"

"We didn't get that far. That's what I wanted to ask you about. It's not a tract we're ever going to need, as things look now. It's half-wooded and pretty steep—it will have to be graded."

"Are you buying or selling?" chuckled Tuttle.

"I'm selling. But I said we wouldn't rook them. If we are selling the lots that the houses are on at a basis of three hundred dollars for a hundred feet, I thought we might ask two hundred for church purposes."

"Those Catholics are rich as hell," said Tuttle. "They can always pull a poor mouth. But they get all the money they want by bearing down on their own people. I don't care, Mark. It doesn't amount to much except as a precedent that we might choke on later. Do what you think is good policy. I'll back you up, if there's any question about it. And I'd talk to the lawyers before you commit yourself to anything."

The lawyers were very definite. "If you sell for church purposes," said Frank Hubbard, "we want a clause in the deed to state that, if at any time the property is not so used, it will revert to us. That's essential."

"I hadn't thought of that."

"Oh, yes, with any church, but especially the Catholics. They're great property holders, you know, and the management changes to some extent, every time there's a new Bishop. If the land didn't suit them, or if it became valuable, they might sell it for advantage to some business concern. We might have a bottling plant up there, in our way. You have to protect the company from any such possibility. Not that it's likely to happen. How much would you sell them?"

"They want seven acres."

"What do they want all that for? Are they going to build a St. Patrick's Cathedral?"

"They say they may want room for a school in the future."

"There it is," said Mr. Hubbard, "the same old story. The public schools aren't good enough for them."

"I felt pretty much that way myself," said Mark.

"Better tell them so."

"I did, as a matter of fact."

"What did they come back with?"

"I don't remember exactly," said Mark. He tried to recall the substance of one argument he had had with Father Kenedy. All he could remember was they hadn't agreed. "Of course, it strengthens their hold. But I don't think they'd ever get a school up there. It's going to be a small community. We figure it at six or seven hundred people at the outside."

"Why don't you drop the whole thing? Tell them politely that we haven't any property for sale."

Mark thought of Father Kenedy standing there on the hillside above the village. He had a feeling that to refuse now would be close to cheating. Not that he had definitely promised anything. He said, "Well, it's not good business to let these people down, is it? They mean all right. I know that my father always used to come across for churches in the mining towns."

"I know—there are times when it makes for good relations," said Mr. Hubbard. "Just hold them down, Mark. And we'll put that clause in the deed, if there is one, just to be on the safe side."

The impact of both conversations was to make Mark feel that he had committed himself too far. When Father Kenedy came to the Worthing office to keep his appointment, he was met by a businesslike coolness in Mark's manner. Mark said that he had consulted his associates and met with some reluctance and certain stipulations. He outlined first the restriction that the company lawyer had proposed.

Father Kenedy looked thoughtful. "I'm not much of a business-man. Such a clause wouldn't invalidate the deed you'd give us?"

"Not unless you wanted to sell."

"May I talk to the Bishop about this?"

"I think you should."

"I believe he would agree. If no parish developed, the property would have no value for us. And if we abandon a church, it is no longer a consecrated place."

Mark said, "I remember that I saw a church in Brazil that your people refused to consecrate. It was a very modern job."

"You mean the place at Pamphula?"

"That's right."

"I know about that. Tell me, did you blame the Church authori-ties for their decision?"

Mark said, "No—I saw the point."

There was a flash of something close to joy in the priest's eyes. It passed before Mark saw it.

"Did your associates make any other stipulations?" asked Father Kenedy.

"Nothing else that was so definite. To be perfectly frank, none of us is keen about a parochial school up there in the future. If you remember, I wasn't from the start."

"I know that."

"Why don't you let well enough alone, Father? Build yourself a little church and be content with that, the way the rest of us are."

"Are you content?"

"I mean that we go along with the public schools. And the state universities."

"There is an enormous number of private schools in this country."

"Yes, but they're all endowed by people who want to do it. Supported by a group who like a certain locality or tradition."

"Or who believe in a certain sect."

"I suppose there are some like that too. But they don't insist—and with you it's pretty close to compulsion, isn't it?—that everyone who belongs to their religion must go to the school where only that religion is taught."

"I could give you examples of that among non-Catholics."

"But not on the same scale."

"That's true, of course."

"No one could help respecting the enterprise of your church," said Mark. "But doesn't it ever worry you to think of the way you set Catholic children apart from other normal American kids? Do you think it's quite fair to them?"

"Many things on the lips of our critics trouble us. Especially unpatriotic motives that are sometimes attributed to us. And blindness to the necessity of what we try to accomplish."

"Why is it necessary?"

"Because the secular school system is not equipped for the education of Catholics," the priest answered. "With the best intentions in the world it could never give our children what they must have. For to be a Catholic is not a matter of Sunday church attendance, though that is one requisite, of course. You see, Mark, Catholicism is a way of life, a way that is shaped and guarded by the sacraments from the cradle to the grave. To insist on Catholic education for Catholics isn't an attempt to slant history. Nor to thwart science, as you once said to me. It is an effort to give an education which has as its base the belief that this life is a preparation for eternal life. Secular schools do not do that."

"I see," said Mark resistantly.

"I regret that you do not," said the priest with his familiar, friendly smile.

"But I do, up to a point. I see that you deliberately want to set apart the people who hold to your religion. You want to catch them while they're young and make them believe your way is the only way. I've come up against that. But let me tell you something, Father—"

He paused, but he wanted to go on. He wanted to tell this priest about Alan's situation. To ram it down his throat. To get it out of his own system, and put the blame squarely where it belonged.

The priest waited. Mark had the feeling that he often waited like this.

"I've been worried lately about my brother. About Alan. I'll tell you why in strict confidence."

"Of course. I thought that he seemed nervous the other day, at the time of that accident."

"I believe he really cared for that girl who interested you in him at one time. The girl he didn't marry, I mean."

"I'm sorry if that's so."

"I've reason to believe that it is, but I needn't go into that. Well —when those two figured that they might make something of it, I had an unexpected talk with the Carroll girl. I hadn't sought it. But she thought that I might take a hand in the affair—"

"Poor child—"

"But whose fault is it? She didn't make any bones about what she wanted; she wanted to make a convert out of Alan. So I asked her if she was open to conversion herself—as a possibility for herself. She said no, very definitely. Coolly—definitely. She'd been brought up to believe, I suppose, that her way was the only way. And that's what I have against your church, your schools, your kind of education—your system isn't open-minded. Everyone else is wrong. You never are."

"Truth is not."

"And you really believe you have the only truth?"

"We have known it for twenty centuries."

Mark drew an exasperated breath. "You're lucky to be so sure. But my point is that, in this one case, because your church is so inflexible, it may have ruined two lives."

"That is the short view, Mark."

"I'm thinking of this mortal life," said Mark hotly. "The only life that isn't guesswork. As things are—though I haven't even said this to my wife—I think that unless Alan gets a divorce he will be cheated out of what he might have had. And he's not the type that would run out on an obligation unless he can't help himself. He'll carry a scar, in any case."

[242]

"I'm sure of that. Advise him against divorce, Mark."

"I don't know that I would—if he asked me. He has a right to some happiness."

"Would he get happiness? If he were divorced it would not help him with Rose Mary."

"He'd be free to try for her again, anyhow."

"Not for her. She is a good Catholic girl, and the Church doesn't recognize divorce."

"They do sometimes. They make exceptions. I've heard of such cases."

"The Church does not insist that a husband and wife must live together if it is dangerous to safety or health, or if a harmonious home life—at least, one with tolerance—is impossible. But even if they separate, neither partner may remarry while the other lives. A Catholic girl believes that a divorced man is still married to someone else, as long as his first wife is alive."

"No matter whose fault it is?"

"It isn't a question of fault. Marriage is a sacrament. There is no second marriage possible in the sight of God, while the partner of a valid marriage lives."

"Then in your view I wouldn't be married myself!"

The priest looked utterly surprised. Dismay crept over his face.

"You see," said Mark, "it happens that my wife divorced a very bad fellow before she married me."

"I did not know that was your situation."

"Yes, that's the way it was. Now Olive is my dear—I could never tell you what she's meant to me—my beloved wife. But according to what you just said, you wouldn't think so."

"You are not a Catholic," said the priest slowly.

"No. Of course not. But suppose I wanted to become a Catholic? Suppose that someday I got the idea that I wanted to join your Church? What would my position be then? Wouldn't I be married to my own wife?"

"It's possible that some impediment might make her first marriage invalid, that she would have made a good marriage to you only and not to this other man."

[243]

"That's dodging the point. Suppose it was a valid marriage the first time. I think it was. She was married in a Protestant church. She had two children. Our children now."

"Ah," sighed Father Kenedy.

"I just want to make the point," insisted Mark, "that I couldn't join the Catholic Church and have Olive considered my rightful wife."

"I am afraid not."

Mark said, "Not very consistent, is it? You claim that you have the only true religion. You ought to want to save my soul, get me in on salvation, but instead you'd rule me out. Of course, this is a ridiculous argument. I'm not a case in point. But I was only taking myself as an example—"

"You would not be ruled out."

"Wouldn't be? Would you expect a man to join a church which told him he wasn't married to his own wife, and couldn't be because a fellow who ran out on her is still alive! He's married to someone else, by the way, but I suppose that to you that makes no difference either. You'd contend that he's actually not married to anyone else. He's still my wife's rightful husband. That's crazy. I didn't mean to talk like this, but that idea really gets under my skin. Tell me—just what I would be expected to do, if I decided to become a Roman Catholic? Abandon my wife—feel that I had no responsibility, no duty toward her?"

"You have great responsibility for her," said Father Kenedy, "but a man's greatest duty is to save his own soul. That is why he is on earth."

It was the challenge, spoken at last between them. Their glances met, one angered, one grave, each as if he knew this had been bound to come, as if they were gathering strength for a contest. Then Mark laughed on a note of sarcasm, intended to reduce this conversation to absurdity.

"Your rules aren't meant for human beings, Father."

"Definitely for them."

"Well, then they're beyond my comprehension."

"No, you're an intelligent person."

"Not intelligent enough to follow that kind of reasoning. That takes a celibate clergy. I admit your Church has a tremendous hold on its people, and I've tried to figure it out, as a matter of interest. But it's beyond me how you keep your hold, why Catholics all over the world don't revolt against medieval man-made rules—"

"They are not man-made. And thinking man does not revolt against his God."

"Perhaps we'd better drop the subject. My wife says that I've an innate prejudice against Catholicism."

"Not a prejudice, Mark. A yearning for faith, for grace, for the God who made you, and His Church."

The words echoed in Mark's mind. If that was it, if he could find it—

He said, "Let's get down to business, Father. About that land. We'll price it at fifty dollars below the cost of residence property— Mr. Tuttle and I thought that was fair, considering it's for church use. If you'll talk to Bishop La Fresne about the conditions of sale, maybe we can come to terms. I'd like to get the matter settled. The services in the school are having a disturbing influence. Just as I feared."

The priest went away. But he did not go immediately back to the Bishop's residence. He walked for an hour, through the streets where people of Italian descent lived, and then through the French district, where a priest was unremarked as he passed. Once he stopped a street fight; once he picked up some apples which had fallen from a fruit stand and returned them to their place. But he did these things absently, as he strove with his problem, weighing the agony of a temporal situation which he had not known to exist against Mark Worthing's chance of grace and of gaining a faith that would endure. When he finally went back to the episcopal residence, he had submitted his will and intention to the guidance of his God.

23

THERE was a different girl at the record desk at St. Barnabas Hospital. Mark looked again, although he had realized with his first glance that the plump blonde with the great bun of hair was not Rose Mary Carroll. In a very casual way, he questioned the superintendent.

"I see you have a new girl in the office. Where's Miss Carroll? On vacation?"

"No, she's left us for good. And this girl isn't nearly so competent. I don't know whether or not she can handle the work."

"Why did you let the other girl go?"

"We didn't have any choice. She told me that she had decided to give up her job here, and there wasn't any way to argue her out of it. Her mind seemed made up. It wasn't a matter of salary. As a matter of fact, we would have upped that a little to keep her, and I as much as told her so. But she said she was going to Chicago. You know how these girls are. The unmarried ones get restless. They like to move around."

"When did she leave?" asked Mark. He had not been in the hospital for several weeks and had stopped in to sign some requisitions.

"Just a few days ago. I was rather annoyed because she didn't give us more notice. She wouldn't even stay out her month."

It's because of Alan, thought Mark. That thing has come to a head. Is she running away from him or going to him? Are they both planning to bolt?

It was a Saturday afternoon, and business was closing down for the week end. He and Olive had planned to drive down to the country and spend a few hours.

"Let's not even take the children today," she had said, regarding her husband that morning. As he came into the house now, she felt that his mood had changed from anticipation of the little adventure. It was burdened by some worry. He hardly noticed the beauty of the spring day as they drove along. Finally he came out with it.

"The Carroll girl has left her job at the hospital."

"Why?"

"She told them she was leaving town."

"Because of Alan," said Olive.

"I don't know. Maybe she got a better job."

"Maybe," said Olive, sharing his unbelief.

"Could you find out?"

"It's not really our business, Mark."

"No—you're right, of course."

"I can try," Olive said gently.

"I suppose Alan knows."

"I think he'd know," said Olive. "Mark, what could she do but go? One of them had to—to live close to a love you can't reach must be utterly unbearable. And if she cares for Alan, she wouldn't want him to leave his work—she must know he gets some satisfaction out of his job anyway."

"How that girl has been hounded," said Mark moodily.

"What you want to remember is what you said before about her. That she has something to tie to."

"Sure—she'll take it to that church on the corner."

As Rose Mary had feared—was it fear or hope?—his car was parked on the corner where she would have to pass it. Alan had known where she would be on Saturday afternoon. In the happy days he had often waited for her here, until she came out of the church after going to confession. Then it used to be joy to see Alan, not an occasion of sin.

"You must avoid the occasions of sin," the priest had told her only half an hour ago. "Now make a good act of contrition."

"I firmly resolve, with the help of Thy grace, to confess my sins, to do penance, and to amend my life." Had she known, as she prayed, that the car would be waiting? I won't stop. I won't go anywhere with him. I told him not to be here—that he mustn't come. I shall not look at him.

But she did look and saw the hunch of his shoulders. It was

pitiful. It wrung her heart. He looked so tired. How long had he been waiting?

Alan opened the car door.

"I can't, Alan."

"Please," he said, in the voice that wasn't like him.

"I asked you not to come."

"I couldn't help it. Please. Just for half an hour. I want to be with you, that's all. There's nothing wrong about it. I won't even touch you if you don't want me to."

The occasion of sin. I won't be able to go to Communion in the morning, she told herself. But this once I'll go with him. I'll be leaving so soon.

Mrs. Carroll asked, "Where's your sister, Bart?"

"She went off with Alan Worthing."

"You wicked boy—to say a thing like that!"

"It's no lie. I saw her. I was riding my bike down on Third Street. I know that '54 convertible of his. And Rosie was with him.

"You saw nothing of the sort! Get out of my way now."

The boy went out, slamming the door on injustice. Mrs. Carroll and her sister, who was beating up a cake, exchanged a glance of shock and apprehension.

"She'll be all right. She's a good girl," said Rose Mary's aunt.

"I thought she was going to confession."

"And maybe she did."

"But he's a married man!"

"There'll be distance between them soon. I'm going to get her to join the girls' sodality in our parish in Chicago, and make new friends."

"It's good that you're taking her with you. My poor, lovely girl—"

"She'll put all this behind her."

"If I only knew where they were," said Mrs. Carroll, going restlessly to the window, "I'd go after her this minute. And wouldn't I give that wicked fellow a piece of my mind!"

"She's just gone for a little airing."

"I wouldn't dare tell her father."

"No, say nothing at all about it to him."

"Holy Mother of God, take care of her!" muttered Mrs. Carroll.

Alan's wife was angry with waiting.

"You get off at noon on Saturday. Where on earth have you been? It's nearly seven, and we were supposed to go to the Cravens' for cocktails."

"I forgot that. I had some things to do."

"Don't you occasionally remember that you have a wife?"

"Yes, I remember that," said Alan.

"Not with much enthusiasm!"

"Let's not fight," he said. There was no use in fighting. Rose Mary had told him an hour ago that nothing was possible for them even if he could divorce Dot, even if he left her. He had spoiled himself for Rose Mary. He was poison to her now. She wanted him but was afraid to take him. It would be sin, mortal sin, she had said. But she was wrong. The real sin was in his going on with Dot.

"I don't want to fight," said Dot, "but you might make like a husband once in a while."

"I'll try."

"Is it such an effort?"

"There you go——"

"You're not any fun any more," she said provocatively and came close to take his face between her hands, with their long glittering nails. She was about to fix her mouth on his, but he drew away.

"What's the matter? No like?"

"I'm not feeling that way now."

"You never do lately, do you? What's happened to your vigor? You haven't picked up someone else, have you?"

"Cut it, Dot."

"I've been wondering about you—you haven't been seeing your little Irish friend again, have you?"

"I told you to cut it out."

"Those little micks can be dangerous," said Dot. "I know how they work it. Do what they please—run to the priest with it—and then do what they please again——"

She stopped, frightened by the look on his face, the threat in his eyes, the violent hands.

"Don't you touch me!" she cried.

The fury went out of his hands, but they were strong on her shoulders.

"Listen," he said. "You don't deserve to be in the same world with Rose Mary. But you don't need to worry about her competing with you, for what I'm worth. She won't. She never will. And I warn you that if you ever mention her to me again, you've seen the last of me."

24

THE matter of the children's baptism came up with the casual, soft-footed approach that great issues sometimes have. Mark was reading late again, and Olive knew that he was absorbed in one of the erudite books on Catholic theology which Father Kenedy had loaned him. It troubled Olive. With all the work Mark had to do tomorrow, he should be getting his sleep. But Olive hated to assert herself as the caretaker of a man, and so she had turned off her own bed light and lay with her hands locked behind her head, thinking that Mark could only deal with any subject with full attention, with absorption.

Her silence broke down as the clock struck the hour. "Still reading, Mark? Do you know it's one o'clock?"

"Why, darling, are you awake?"

"Not very much awake."

"Does my light bother you?"

"Not a bit."

"I'll finish this in a minute. It's very interesting."

"What are you reading?"

"It's an explanation of the Catholic view on baptism. I never have seen it before. We were talking about it one day and Father Kenedy gave me this book, which explains the whole thing. They are much more broadminded than I realized. Anyone can baptize another person in case of emergency—then there's a thing called baptism of desire. If water isn't available."

"It always seemed a queer rite to me. I had to be godmother to the child of a friend of mine once. She was an Episcopalian like you. And they brought this yelling, simply pathetic baby to church when he wasn't more than a few weeks old. I had to renounce all his sins. Me! I had plenty of my own sins to renounce."

"You were baptized, weren't you, Olive?"

"I must have been—don't you remember?—I had a certificate of it when we were getting our passports."

"That was your birth certificate."

"Oh—well, I have a baptism one too somewhere. I—" she didn't go on because she recalled now that she had needed it when she married Tony in that church where they never went again. The judge who had married her and Mark so quietly on that sunlit day hadn't asked about baptism.

"It's good to have it," said Mark.

"I suppose it's a record. But if Tim and Jenny ever have to prove they were born, they have records in the hospital nowadays."

"Aren't the children baptized?"

"I never bothered. I might have, but it would have meant nothing to Tony, and with the way things were it would have seemed silly."

"Maybe you ought to have it done now."

"I suppose I should. But not tonight. Dearest, it is so late and the radio will be shouting the news of the world before you know it."

"All right—good night, my darling."

She did not give the discussion another thought. But only a few days later Mark brought it up again. He had been having a rough-house with Tim, holding him up in the air by his hands in circus fashion, and Jenny screamed to have the same treat. Olive laughed and then sent the children away because they were getting too excited.

Mark said, "They're a great pair."

"You're wonderful with them, Mark."

"I want them to have all the breaks. By the way, Olive, have you thought any more about having them baptized?"

"I haven't thought anything about it since you mentioned it the other night. It doesn't seem too important at the minute."

"But it is important. It is, if you accept the theory of redemption—"

"What do those infants need to be redeemed from?"

"That's the basis of the Christian religion. You're a Christian."

"Because I believe in Christian principles. Not because I was sprinkled with water."

"That may be a symbol. But it has authority back of it. I don't think you should neglect it altogether, Olive."

She said all right, that she would have it done sometime. A week later Jenny had a feverish cold, and Mark brought the matter up again.

"She'll be all right in the morning," Olive said. "She's scared the life out of me before."

"She'll be fine. But I think you ought to have those two taken care of."

"I don't think she needs a doctor."

"I wasn't thinking of a doctor. I mean that you should have her and Tim baptized. Then you've got it done and you're safe."

"Mark, don't be so horrible! You sound as if you thought they were going to die!"

Mark laughed and put his arm around her. "Those two husks aren't going to die. But don't keep putting that other thing off. We might be away—"

She stared at him. "That's gruesome talk!"

"I'm sorry, dear—I didn't mean it that way at all."

He sounded very contrite, and what had been resistance and almost antagonism for a minute faded from her face.

She said, "If you feel so strongly about this baptism business, I don't mind. I'll talk to Pamela and ask her who does it at the church and when."

"Father Kenedy could tell you," said Mark.

"But I wouldn't go to him, Mark! I wouldn't let them be baptized Catholics!"

"It wouldn't commit you to anything."

"I wouldn't want him mixing in this."

"Pam will make it an occasion for a cocktail party, after the baptisms," said Mark.

"That's not fair. Pamela is very much interested in her own church. That's why she's worried about Dick."

"Does he still want to be a monk?"

"He doesn't know what he wants. Except that he hasn't got it."

"Why don't they leave the boy alone? Maybe he should be a monk or a priest—maybe he has the Indian sign on him."

"Do you call conversion to Catholicism an Indian sign?"

"Oh, you know what I mean."

"I wish I did. Mark . . . Mark, darling, I want to say something to you."

"Say you love me."

"No—please listen. This has been growing in my mind for months. When we were in South America. Maybe even before that. I've thought of it very often lately, and the way you feel about this baptism of the children sort of confirms it. I think the Catholic Church attracts you—interests you—that what you think is prejudice may be just the other thing. You seem to feel that there is something in its doctrines or its ritual that is very important. Maybe you could even go along with it. Please don't stop me—let me finish. Maybe it has something you need, that you've been searching for philosophically. Maybe you've got the Indian sign on you!"

"No, darling—you're way off the beam."

"Don't be so sure. Anyway, I want to say one more thing. If at any time you should want to be a member of the Catholic Church, it's all right with me. If it could give you what you want or what you think you need, go ahead and join it. I'm sorry that I couldn't go along with you because it doesn't appeal to me—I don't understand its approach. It frightens me. But if it is the Church you want for yourself, Mark, don't think I wouldn't be really happy to have you in it. The important thing is to be at peace with yourself. Sometimes during this last year I've felt that you were torn to pieces between a real desire to go along with the Catholics and a feeling that you

[253]

mustn't, because your family—or maybe I—wouldn't understand. Other people don't count when it comes to religious convictions."

Mark said, "Yes. They do."

"No, you shouldn't care what anyone thinks if it's a matter of your own conscience."

Mark kissed the top of her head. "My wonderful girl."

"Tell me honestly. You would like to consider being a Catholic, wouldn't you? You can't seem to leave it alone."

"I never could be one. I never would consider it."

"Don't be so certain. You're naturally rather a mystic—"

"Let's not talk about it."

"But I want to help you if I can."

"Not help me to join the Roman Catholic Church, Olive."

"Yes, I would, if you wanted to."

Mark said, "You don't realize what it would do to us, do you?"

"It wouldn't make me love you any less. You'd still be yourself."

"If I were a Catholic, Olive, we wouldn't be married."

"What do you mean?"

"I mean that we'd be living together but not married. You'd still be married to Tony Grant. That's one reason—among others—why I could never become a Catholic. As a Protestant, I'm married to you. As a Catholic, I wouldn't be."

"You mean you'd want a divorce?"

"No—we just wouldn't be married. As long as Tony Grant lives."

"But we've been married for years!"

"Not according to that Church. We've never had the sacrament of marriage."

"But we didn't have to have it! We were married by the judge. We're not Catholics."

"That's it."

"You mean that's why you couldn't be a Catholic?"

"Well, it's one basic reason why not."

"I had no idea," said Olive. "Of course, I knew they were strict about divorce—so are the Episcopalians for that matter, if you're the one who's in the wrong—but our marriage was years ago, before you ever were at all interested in the Catholic Church—"

"I'm not interested now," he said.

"I should hope not!" she exclaimed in anger. "Of all the silly, utterly unreasonable things I ever heard of! Why, Tony left me! I did the best I could."

"They excuse your not living with him, of course. But it doesn't dissolve the marriage, according to their rules."

"They can have their rules—that marriage was dissolved years ago."

"Of course."

"If that's what their religion is like, so illogical, so unnatural—why, Mark, it's actually horrible! Like being kept in a prison for life for one mistake!"

"Darling, don't get yourself worked up. I'm sorry I said anything about it. But you began that talk about my going over to Catholicism, and I wanted to show you how completely impossible it would be."

"Of course, it's impossible! I don't want you to have anything to do with people who have such ideas. What does Father Kenedy think of me anyway? That I'm your mistress!"

"Olive, of course not. We're not under his discipline."

"Thank the Lord for that!" Olive exclaimed.

The anger and affront faded in Olive's mind after a few hours of her normal living. Trying to dismiss them altogether, she told herself that there were other queer religious cults. The Mormon Church used to let men have bundles of wives, and that went on right in the United States. The Roman Catholics simply went to the other extreme. Mark shouldn't waste any more time on their theories. Perhaps he would be happier if we had closer relations with his own church, thought Olive. Perhaps I should do something about that.

She said easily to Pamela, "Tim and Jenny have never been baptized. Mark thinks they ought to be. So do I, of course."

"Oh, they should be," said Pamela. "Dr. Carroll in our parish is very insistent on that. He says not later than six months—"

"We can't quite catch up with that. Would he do it for us?"

"I know he'd love to. He's such a wonderful man. He's built up our youth groups amazingly."

"I'm going to have Dr. Carroll have a good talk with Dick when he comes home for his next vacation, and get Dick interested in our junior parish."

"Dick is a very unusual boy," said Olive, thinking of the sensitive nature of Pamela's son, his visionary moods, and the difficulty of trying to line him up with a hearty youth group for basketball games at the parish house.

She said, "I think we'd rather have the old rector do the baptisms, Pam. The one who was at your mother's funeral. Mark likes him."

"Mark," said Pamela, her thoughts suddenly deflected. "I heard the most insane remark about him the other day. Somebody said that he was a great friend of this Catholic priest—the one called Kenedy—that—well, this is crazy and don't mention it to Mark, for heaven's sake—but someone had started the rumor that Mark might go over to the Catholic Church. People will say anything, won't they!"

"Don't let that worry you," said Olive.

"Naturally not. I stepped on the gossip but hard. But people say that this priest is one of the hypnotic kind. Like Rasputin. They say he's converted ever so many people. And he did get Mark to let him have some land for a church up on the shore—that's probably what started this rumor."

"Perhaps—"

"You don't think he really has any influence over Mark, do you? I know it seems utterly fantastic, but—"

Olive interrupted with a laugh that she made as light as possible. She said, "Don't worry, Pam. There's room for only one idea in Mark's head this summer. And that's how soon he can get the new taconite plant into production."

"Of course, I knew there was nothing to it," said Pamela, reassured. "Tell me, Olive, who are you going to ask to be godparents for Tim and Jenny?"

"I hadn't thought that far—"

"Of course, I'd love to be godmother to either of them. And we

[256]

will all come back to our house afterward—"

This is what Mark said it would be. This isn't what Mark wanted, thought Olive . . . so they are saying that about Mark and the priest . . .

"Thank you, Pam. We'd love to."

Bishop La Fresne was sitting at his desk, with a list of priests and a small map of his diocese before him. He had been making some new assignments and changes, and would have finished his work before this except that he was spending an unusually long time considering this last one that he had in mind.

He was reluctant to make it. He had enjoyed having this young man with him. He has a vitamin-like quality, thought the Bishop. I shall miss my vitamin. I shall miss his company. He has an excellent mind and is quite a master of theology. Perhaps I should keep him here.

Yet he is attracting undue notice. Though he is personally humble, it disturbs the balance of our little hierarchy here. His conversions have been numerous, unusually so, but he is a handsome as well as a forceful priest. It is difficult for a convert to stand alone, thought the Bishop, difficult to separate motives.

The matter of Mark Worthing presented a problem. For his wife was a good woman and there would be a very serious problem if young Worthing became a convert. The old lady had always done her best in secular ways, been a useful citizen. Possibly Mark Worthing was confusing intellectual companionship and stimulation with true grace. If Father Kenedy were gone, he would soon discover what was true in his case.

Besides, that church at Baraga is going to cost too much for the size of the community, if Father Kenedy is here, thought the Bishop. He is very persuasive, but we must be practical in our building program.

I shall miss him, Bishop La Fresne reminded himself once more. But I must not indulge myself. Father Kenedy may have a future in the Church, with God's grace. He will be the better for not having things come too easily.

[257]

He drew a sheet of paper toward him and began to write firmly:

Reverend and Dear Father Kenedy:

It is our wish and decision that on October first of this year, you proceed to and take over the parish connected with the church of St. John at Meadowville. . . .

25

THE necessity, the sense that this had to be done, took Olive as far as the Bishop's residence, although every step did outrage to her shyness and reserve. It was a big house, and no doubt had once been an elegant one, for even the walls of the barren little room into which she was ushered were covered with faded red damask in the best Victorian manner. A housekeeper had conducted her down a central hall which gave glimpses of larger parlors, and said that she would see if Father Kenedy was in. She said that she thought he was, destroying Olive's last chance of not having to go through with her resolve.

There was a desk and a bookcase with glass doors which made the books behind them darker and remote, a few stiff chairs, and a narrow black-leather settee. On one wall hung a picture of Christ with an exposed pierced and bleeding heart, which made Olive think against her will of a crude valentine. She felt here the same lack of feminine attention and affection that had impressed her when she first saw Father Kenedy. In spite of the housekeeper in her black dress and white apron, this was a celibate place.

She felt out of her element, in the truest sense of the words, as if here in this room she could not breathe, speak, move in any way that was natural to her. She told herself that to have come here was foolish to madness, and was stubbornly glad that here she was, and that she would not run nor be driven away until she had talked to this priest. She had rehearsed what she would say, which was utterly unlike her, but she kept flinging away the beginnings and approaches to the imagined conversation.

And now the priest came, walking so swiftly down the hall that he seemed to be in the room at almost the same time that she heard him coming. As he had looked before—tall, rather uncouth, sure, offering none of the normal pleasure that men feel in meeting a woman. And yet some instinct in Olive felt that he welcomed her.

"How are you, Mrs. Worthing?"

She said she was very well. Then, "I must apologize, first of all, for coming here like this, Father Kenedy. I know it is an intrusion."

"Not in the least an intrusion."

Olive moved her head denyingly. "I have no right to come to you, and I know it. But I wanted to tell you a few things. Things that are very personal, and I didn't know how else to do it."

"You chose the right way, Mrs. Worthing." He smiled and looked younger. "One of the jobs of a priest is to listen. Please don't apologize. If I can be of any help to you, it would be a privilege. Your husband has long ago put me in his debt."

"It's about Mark that I wanted to talk to you. About my husband."

Father Kenedy showed no surprise.

"I've wanted to come for weeks," said Olive. "I think there are things you don't understand. About Mark, I mean."

"Many things, I have no doubt."

"He's very sensitive," she said with effort. "Mark is much more conscientious than most men. He's more—more mental than may appear on the surface. He takes things very seriously."

"That I do know," said the priest. "I admire him greatly for just that reason."

"Yes—but he has been worrying. There are certain regrets and worries in his mind. They began because of your Church, Father Kenedy. I've become convinced of that. Now he can't seem to get rid of them. He—he thinks too much about religion."

"Can anyone think too much about religion?"

"I don't mean that it's too much in one way. But it's affecting his work—his peace of mind—our home life."

"Yes," said the priest, half questioningly, in invitation to her to go on. He made it easier.

"It began," Olive told him, "when his brother wanted to marry

[259]

a girl who was a Catholic. Mark wasn't sympathetic. He didn't think it would be a successful marriage. He told Alan so. Maybe he did influence Alan—I don't know about that, or exactly what happened. But Alan married another girl, and I think that since then Mark has been having—almost torturing himself with a sense of guilt and fear that perhaps he didn't advise Alan in the right way. He keeps wondering if he was fair—if he was right—I know how confused this must sound. But we aren't sure Alan didn't make an impetuous marriage—"

"No, it's not confusing. I knew something of this. You think it began then? Whatever has begun to cause a struggle in your husband's mind?"

Their eyes met. Olive said, "Perhaps not. He was disturbed, of course, by your attitude toward the birth-control clinic. Being forced to give in on a matter which he didn't think was right."

"Or because he subconsciously wondered if it was right?"

"Oh, no, Father Kenedy, he didn't think so. I know. But that gave him a prejudice—"

"A prejudice? Mark seems to me to be more inquiring than prejudiced."

"But, of course, there are things he can't believe—"

"Yes, that is the heart of the struggle. Always."

"What do you mean?"

"Mrs. Worthing—have you ever thought that this disturbance in your husband which so concerns you might go back further? Have a deeper source than either of the circumstances which you mention?"

She said, "He hasn't been like himself since that thing about the hospital drive. That was when it began."

The priest waited.

"Not that Mark hasn't always been thoughtful. He studied philosophy at college. He couldn't go on with what he wanted to do because—but that's long ago—it has nothing to do with this present thing."

"This present thing?"

"I don't like to say this—but the Catholic Church has become

[260]

almost an obsession with him," said Olive. "He doesn't realize that himself. But I do. He can't let it alone."

"You think he should?"

"It's not good for him," she answered, her voice low but intense. "It's changed him. Made him mixed up and unhappy in his mind. And it's all so useless."

"No spiritual interest is useless, Mrs. Worthing. Our faith— many faiths—teach as their first lesson that man is on earth to save his soul."

"Mark will save his soul. It is in no danger." Olive leaned forward, and a ray of sun came through the dusty window and fell happily on her pale gold hair. The priest had once seen a statue of the Virgin in such a pose. She said, "Father Kenedy, I would like to tell you this. I talked to Mark not long ago about this. I told him, and I truly meant it at the time, that if he wanted to join your Church I was not in the least opposed to it. I said that if he would be more peaceful and happy as a Catholic—you see, I had come to believe that what he thinks is antagonism might be the reverse in a curious way."

"I think you were quite right—"

"But Mark told me that he couldn't be a Roman Catholic—could never be—for your church wouldn't accept any man who was married to a divorced woman. You see, I divorced my husband. I had to. Mark said that according to your Church we aren't actually married!"

The priest's face was clouded. "Mrs. Worthing, may I ask you a few questions?"

"If you like—I may not be able to answer them."

"When I heard of your marital status, I was personally disturbed. Will you tell me—are you baptized?"

"Oh, yes—I got a certificate of that when—"

"And your husband?"

"Mark, yes—in the Episcopal Church, of course."

"I mean the man from whom you obtained a legal divorce."

"He had a certificate too," said Olive. "I remember because the minister asked both of us to get them for his records."

"There are a number of things that can invalidate a marriage," said Father Kenedy. "That is why I ask. If, for example, you were coerced into your marriage, if the marriage was not consummated—"

"I have two children," said Olive, her face flushed and yet unembarrassed.

"Then so far as you know yours was a good marriage."

"It was a very bad marriage."

"I am not referring to happiness or those causes which made you seek separation. I am inquiring only for your own sake and that of Mark. You say you are willing to have him become a member of the Catholic Church. If you were not married in such a way that the Church must recognize the marriage as a valid one, your present legal marriage to Mark would present no impediment to his conversion."

"My marriage to Mark is the valid one—the only valid one."

"From what you tell me, it is not in the eyes of the Church."

"I do not belong to your Church! I don't believe as you do. And, of course, Mark would never in the world accept what you say as true!"

"It's very unfortunate."

"It would be all right if you would leave him alone, Father Kenedy."

"I? It is not I—"

"I think it is. That is what made me come here today. I couldn't believe it at first. It started as antagonism, I know. It still is that, in a way. But what you say, what you think, has come to fascinate him, to preoccupy him—I found it out when we went to South America. In those Catholic countries, Mark would carry on a sort of argument with you all the time. It was you he wanted to fight things out with—and here it's the same way. I can tell that you are on his mind—almost constantly—" She broke off and began again, "I don't want you to think that Mark is easy to influence, or weak, or that he takes other people's opinions, because he doesn't. It's quite the opposite. But though he can't possibly agree with you, what you think matters to him."

"Dear child, it is not my pitiful thinking that your husband is interested in, pursued by—"

Olive said, "I've tried to be frank with you. And though I never could be a Catholic myself, if he wanted to, that I'd accept. As I would any church—Mohammedanism, the Jewish faith, if he wanted either of them. But for the reason you know—what you just said yourself—he can't be a Roman Catholic. Because we are married. Because we love each other. And that is the most important thing on earth to us both."

"On earth it is important."

"That's where we are," said Olive, "on earth. That's where we must live."

"In preparation for a better life."

To Olive the statement was unreal, a smug bit of theology.

She said, "I believe that what we should do is to make our life here as good and happy as we can. If there is anything afterward, it is out of our hands." Her thoughts struggled for utterance but she wanted to tell this man what they were. "I think it's wrong and rather abnormal to be contemptuous—or indifferent—to happiness and love."

She felt he was the enemy, as she had felt when he was in her home that night. He did not seem to resent her outburst.

He answered only, "The Catholic religion is not indifferent to love. It is based upon it."

"And suffering—"

"Because of love."

She flung herself back into her errand.

"I can't argue these things. I haven't studied them. But the point is, Father Kenedy, that Mark cannot ever belong to your Church. He's an outsider and must be and for some reason it troubles and confuses him. I came here today to appeal to you, to ask you not to see Mark, not to give him books on theology, not to bring him your problems. It's humiliating—I had to drive myself to do this—but I'd do anything for Mark. I've told him I thought he was letting you influence him too much. He doesn't believe that. He doesn't think you do. He's lost perspective. And he has work to do. A home. A family. I must keep him happy. I ask this as a favor—as a reasonable thing, since you see that he can't become a Catholic."

"It's a favor that is very easy to grant," said the priest. "The

Bishop has not yet made a public announcement, so I will ask you to regard this as a confidential matter for the time being. I am being transferred from this parish. My duties will be in a village at a considerable distance from here. The severance of any relation between your husband and myself soon will be complete."

Olive could not conceal the relief that swept through her, shone in her eyes.

"I needn't have come," she said at length. "I'm sorry."

"I am glad you came," said Father Kenedy.

"Perhaps I am too. I have the deepest respect for you, sir."

"My child," said the young priest, "I am glad you came, because it gives me the opportunity to disabuse your mind of some of these things which have disturbed you so greatly. First, let me assure you that the influence of no man—myself or anyone else—would be sufficient to convert your husband to the Catholic faith."

"But you do convert people—"

"No. A priest instructs a person who may be susceptible to conversion, in the tenets, the beliefs, and the duties of the Catholic faith. But I or another priest can go only so far. The ultimate conversion is possible only when God gives His grace to the convert."

"What is grace?"

"It is one of God's mysteries. It is the most powerful spiritual force. Against it—if it truly exists—and as long as it exists—human opinion, human love, struggle vainly."

"What do you mean? That this—this grace—might get into Mark?"

"Conceivably."

"But you said—we agreed—that he can't be a Catholic."

The priest was silent, and so answered.

"He would never leave me, Father Kenedy," said Olive, almost pityingly. "In your position as a priest you perhaps can't understand that. But no one—no church—nothing like this thing you mention, would come between Mark and myself."

She felt cold. She thought, I can see what he does to Mark. He's going away—that's the important thing.

"I must go. I've taken too much of your time."

The priest stood also, took her hand, and looked down at her.

"You are wise to understand his unhappiness," he said, and with his rare smile he added simply, "You are a good woman. You will help him."

26

THERE was a story in the evening papers several days later about certain changes which Bishop La Fresne had made in the administration of his diocese. This was routine news, for the duties and posts of the priests under his control were not infrequently changed at the discretion of the Bishop, but it was of interest to all the Catholics in the city and so had been printed on the front page of the second section of the paper. The change which affected Father Kenedy was in the middle of the column, and it was surprising that Pamela, carelessly scanning the newspaper after dinner, noticed it at all. But she had a quick eye for names that seemed important to her. She could always find her own almost instantly if it appeared in print, even if the list of subscribers or patrons was a long one.

"Brad," she said to her husband, "they're sending that priest away from here. I really am glad."

"Yes, dear," he said in a non-listening way, keeping his eyes on the last round of the fight on the television screen, and added, "What priest?"

"That Father Kenedy—the one they say is sort of a Rasputin."

"A Russian?"

"No—his name is Kenedy—I told you. But he's the one that was supposed to have a lot of influence on Mark. There was a story going around that he was trying to convert Mark. I spoke to Olive about it. She laughed it off, said there wasn't a word of truth in it."

"She ought to know."

"Just the same," said Pamela, "I got the idea that she was a little

[265]

worried. You know, it doesn't seem to me that Mark's been like himself for quite a while."

"He has a lot on his mind, Pam. He's not building that taconite plant on peanuts."

Pamela said, "One thing—do you know that Mark didn't give anything to the Planned Parenthood campaign this year? One of the girls said she hadn't had any response from Mark at all, couldn't even get to see him at his office. She asked me if I would talk to him."

"There are too many demands on everybody," said Bradley with sharpened interest, "you've got to draw the line somewhere."

Pamela was pursuing a different line of thought. She said, "That priest was the kind that tries to make converts. Everyone says so. They do that now. You know how the Catholics tried to get hold of Dick. I'm glad you put your foot down and told Dick that he couldn't make decisions like that until he's of age. You know— Catholics aren't at all the way they used to be."

"How do you mean?"

"Well, when we were growing up, there were Catholics of course. We had a second maid who always had a rosary in her apron pocket and it used to fascinate me, I remember. But we didn't know any Catholics—I don't mean that snobbishly, but they kept to themselves; they had their own friends and what not. Now it's quite different—they're much more in things—the provisional group of the Junior League has quite a few Catholics in it."

Bradley turned off the television for the fight was over. He said, "They won't bite you," and his voice came out loudly against the sudden silence.

"They may not bite. But think of Dick's saying he wanted to be a monk! He got that from those boys at school."

"If he gets any more fancy ideas he can get himself a job. He'll soon find how much he could earn in the monk business."

"He didn't talk about it at all when we visited him at school. I wanted to meet his Catholic friends; I'm completely broadminded. But he didn't bring them around. When he comes home, I'm going to have a little talk with Dick."

Pamela looked greatly like her mother as she planned that.

Gregory Searles also saw the news article. He read several other items, went back to look over the diocesan changes, and said to Lucy, "I see that Mark is going to lose his friend."

"What friend? Who's sick?"

"Nobody. But the Most Reverend Bishop La Fresne is sending Father James Kenedy into exile."

"Is he a friend of Mark's, for goodness sake?"

"That may be the wrong description. I think Mark knew him quite well. I'm sure he's been lending Mark theological books. Last time we were at their house, I picked up a very erudite one on the doctrines of the Catholic Church. It seemed a little out of character —or place—and I saw this Father Kenedy's name in it. I asked Olive if she was reading theology. She said no, that it was Mark. She handled the book with some distaste it seemed to me. Maybe not."

"He's that tall, dark priest, isn't he?" said Lucy, "I've seen him. Where is he going? Why do you say he is being sent into exile?"

"He had a good berth here certainly. He was one of the Bishop's aides."

"How do you know so much about him?"

"He was conspicuous. There was a Savonarola look in an Irish way about him that made him stand out against the local background. Anyway, he's being shunted off to this little dump in the western part of the state. It's obviously a demotion."

"He was good-looking," said Lucy.

"That may have been his undoing."

"You mean you think there was some scandal about him?"

"No, I don't think so," said Greg. "Not in the way you're thinking of. But it's interesting. Why did the Bishop want to get him out of the way? Particularly if he really was working on Mark."

"Working on Mark how?"

"Trying to convert him. He was lending him religious books for some reason. There's always a reason for a thing like that. And Mark would be a big fish for the Church to land."

"Oh, that's too absurd. Mark would never want to be a Roman Catholic."

"Want," said Gregory reflectively. "No—that's quite true. In the

[267]

literal sense. He probably wouldn't want it. It would offend his taste in many ways. It would humiliate him. You're right, he wouldn't want it."

"That's what I said."

"But there might be more to it. Even against his will—his taste—his frontal desires, Mark might be unable to help himself. You never know who may suddenly become a Catholic, my dear. It happens in unlikely places. In prison camps. In very aristocratic families. In Communist cells. It happens all the time."

"I don't think it happens to people like us."

"It would be improbable in your family. But not impossible."

"Well, don't sound critical. You stopped being a Catholic."

"I stopped being a practicing Catholic. I'm a lazy, lustful fellow as you know. But even your sins don't let you out of that Church completely. That's what we were taught. If I seem to be dying any time, Lucy, better call a priest."

"You're making fun—"

"No."

"And don't talk about dying. I can't bear it."

She flung her arms about him and he patted her and laughed rather absently. When she released him, he was still thinking it over.

"After all, you needn't worry about Mark. He's married to a divorced woman whom he adores. That would queer the pitch in any case."

Olive saw the announcement because she had been watching for it. She had not known whether it would be in the newspaper or not, and she had been afraid that something might happen to change the Bishop's intention to send Father Kenedy somewhere else. She wanted to be sure it was true before she told Mark that again she had a hope of pregnancy. She wanted Mark to herself for that news.

The name of Father Kenedy leapt at her from the printed page that evening. It was true. There it was. Where was that town? She held the paper while she found an atlas in the study, and saw that it was a very small place that must be three hundred miles away at the very least. He had told her the truth. What hard lives priests had, with no home, no permanence. But he wouldn't be here to worry Mark any more, to lend him books, argue with him. Mark would be himself again. Effective June first. But that was only two days from now. That was wonderful.

I don't wish him bad luck, thought Olive. He's a good man—he was even rather kind. But he did something to Mark. And to tell Mark that we had no right to be married! I wonder if Mark knows about this. I hope it won't disturb Mark. It's the best thing in the world for him.

She didn't mention it at once when Mark got home. He played with the children and there was the usual happy routine of the evening, while Olive held her secrets close. Watching to see if he picked up the second section of the paper. Tonight he did not. He read only the headlines, listened to a commentator on the air, and after she had taken the children upstairs and came down again, she found he was looking over some papers covered with figures. She picked up the newspaper herself, thought—I won't mention it.

"Anything in the paper? I only looked at the front page," said Mark.

She said, compelled, "I see that Father Kenedy is leaving the city."

Mark looked up quickly. "Kenedy? Where do you see that?"

"It's in the paper." She passed it to Mark, indicating the column. He read it with frowning astonishment.

"That's a hell of a note. Meadowville!"

"What's wrong with the place?"

"It's nothing but a whistle stop! And Father Kenedy is the one who is responsible for building the church at Baraga, as well as a lot of other things. This is outrageous."

"Then why does that Bishop do it?"

Mark said grimly, "I guess bishops don't have to have reasons. Or tell them." He abandoned the work he was doing, nervously began to smoke.

"Will it be a blow to Father Kenedy? Very disappointing?"

Mark said reflectively, after a minute, "He won't think in those terms, Olive."

"I suppose you'll miss him," said Olive, making it sound casual.

"Miss him? I didn't see much of him."

"You found him interesting though. Intellectually."

"He has a good mind. That's why this is so—a place like that—but it's the way they do things, of course. Do them deliberately. He liked what he was doing here. Maybe too much. Maybe that's the reason. They don't believe in ties. Not human ties—personal ambitions—they're taught to go without those things—"

"It seems so unnatural."

"Oh, believe me, they know what they're doing. They're master psychologists, don't fool yourself about that. Father Kenedy is dedicated. He won't allow himself to care what they do, where he goes—"

"I hope he won't," she said softly.

"It's only his relation to God that matters to him. It's stripped down to that. Everything else is expendable."

Olive made an excuse to leave the room. She didn't want to go on talking about this. Mark was taking the news in a queer way. He was disturbed, indignant as she had expected. But his excitement was strange.

When he followed her later, offering love, asking for it as if he needed it, she tried to make up any loss to him. But she did not tell him about her hope for their child. It might end in disappointment again and it was better, kinder to wait.

27

THIS was where Alan felt he belonged, the only place where he had a feeling of usefulness, of being personally needed. This was where he had a sense of being able to create, a chance to make something that would have his own stamp on it. Not in that suave apartment where he slept, almost always alone now, unless they both had a great deal to drink. Where he didn't breakfast because it was easier to stop in the cafeteria along the road for his coffee and eggs, and then he didn't wake Dot. Where he didn't have dinner at night unless Dot had invited guests and engaged temporary servants, because what was the use of her getting dinner for the two of them, and what was there to say to each other?

It was in the morning when he came in sight of the taconite plant that he had the feeling of getting home, when he saw the harbor shining in the sun, showing off the glittering trim on its waves, or looking moody and darkly threatening. In his first glance he could tell what had been done since yesterday, what needed doing at once, if there was any slovenliness or incompetence that needed to be checked up and corrected. It wasn't his business to do that yet but he made secret, silent decisions. He knew what he would do if he were running the show. He was rapidly becoming Becker's trusted assistant, his right hand on the job in spite of his youth.

The devotion which he could not give to the girl he loved had been transmuted into concentration on his work. The bitter, uncertain hours, the humiliation at having been a fool, the anger at Rose Mary for not putting him first, the jealousy, the sense of being trapped, the boredom, the lust in himself for which he had contempt, the passion that had to be satisfied, the recurrent cynical decision that it didn't make much difference—had woven a pattern. It made the Worthings believe that Alan and Dot were working things out rather well, and his associates on the job consider him a man who was on his way to the top in the mining business.

Alan was conscious of undeveloped power and ability in himself that hadn't been called upon. Sometimes it made him restless, sometimes slightly critical of Harry Tuttle's decisions, even of Mark's management. He would think he saw where a corner might be cut and money saved. He would figure that by increasing the volume of ore sent down the lakes from their new harbor, more profit could be made. He personally believed that it would be better to build their own ships instead of leasing ore carriers. Alan would speculate on the possibility of taconite lands having been overlooked on the southern side of Lake Superior. Or under existing villages on the Ranges. For villages could be moved if it was worth it. The blood of his exploring, gambling grandfather stirred in him, as well as the shrewd business instinct of his father, who had also learned to get along without a warm home life.

On this August morning excitement and pride were strong in Alan. The men from the East who had invested capital in this venture were here again, this time to celebrate the first shipment of taconite pellets from the Worthing-Ingalls plant. Last time they had only seen construction in progress. But today they would see a shining Diesel engine come down from the ore lands over the new tracks, hauling gondolas full of flint-like rock. They would see the steel balls grinding that rock so fine that it would go through a screen with ten thousand holes in a square inch. They could watch the souplike concentrate being filtered and cleaned and finally made into hard lumps. And then the long, slim, red ore boats which today lay in the new harbor, would sink a little as they took on the heavy load of pellets and moved swiftly, as if with invisible full sails, into the waterway of commerce.

Alan was not impressed by the presence of the rich men. He was excited because this was the beginning of the operation. The big shots would have a look to satisfy themselves and go back to the city for dinner, but the process would continue here. There would be faults in it, bugs to get out of it, though today no one would call attention to any bugs. There would be too many newspapermen and photographers swarming all over the location.

He reported in and found a message that Mr. Becker wanted to see him, so he went to the main office and found the superintendent looking unusually neat in a blue shirt and necktie.

Mr. Becker said, "Mark wants you to go along with the inspection party. In his car."

"Me? I have a lot of things to do."

"Get them done and hurry back here. Those are orders, boy."

"When will they be here?"

"About half-past ten."

Alan went through the rod-and-ball mill. He inspected the filters. Everything seemed to be in good shape. He found a tie in his locker, smoothed it out, put it on, and was back at the head office on time.

The cars were arriving. Mark was in the first one. He looked pleased when he saw Alan and called him over.

"I want you to come along with us. This is my brother, who has been one of the engineers on the job. Alan, I want you to meet Mr. Eliot. Mr. Eben Crane. And you know Mr. Tuttle."

They were using the old-fashioned, leather-lined limousine that the company had used for years to show visitors around the operations, referred to invariably in the Worthing family as the hearse. Mark was sitting in front with the chauffeur. Mr. Crane and Mr. Eliot spread over the back seat and Mr. Tuttle had perched himself on one of the jump seats. Alan took the other. It was the first time that Alan had seen Mark in this kind of company and before ten minutes had passed something struck him as offbeat. Mr. Tuttle was doing almost all of the talking and explaining as they went first to the railroad yards. Mark was leaving it to him. It seemed to Alan that Mark wasn't in good form. He couldn't be afraid of these birds from New York. He'd dealt with them before. But he wasn't putting himself out at all. It was almost as if his mind wasn't on the job in hand. And today was his big day.

"We planned to have lunch at twelve in the commissary—which you'll find much improved, I think—and then we'll show you the method—now in action—which takes the ore pellets to the boats," said Mr. Tuttle. "That's the program isn't it, Mark?"

"That's right."

"Is there anything else that you gentlemen would like to see before lunch? We have twenty minutes. Do you want to look at the power plant again? I think that was pretty well completed when you were here last time but—"

"I'd like to see your little village here again," said Mr. Crane. "How it looks when it isn't winter."

"Fine. Drive up through the village, Otto."

Alan did not want to see the village. He had not been in it since that day last year—the day when he and Rose Mary—My God, we even picked out the house, he thought—it was somewhere in here —there it was, she wanted a gray one—someone is living in it now, someone who had kids, for there was kid's junk on the porch—I let you down, Rose Mary—

[273]

"I remember the schoolhouse," said Mr. Eben Crane. "I remember that you had a problem about church services there, Mark—the Roman Catholics—did you dispose of that without any trouble?"

"It worked out all right," said Mark.

"You didn't permit it, of course?"

"There was nothing else to do. It was a temporary solution. But they're building a church. We sold them some land for it. Drive up the hill, Otto."

A church, thought Mark, looking at the roofed-over basement structure. Father Kenedy wanted the site so that the church would dignify the town. They'll never do it without him. But evidently they're having services there. The place looks as if it were in use.

"I beg your pardon, Mr. Crane?"

"You sold them the land for this building?"

"Yes."

Mr. Tuttle said, "It wasn't land we had any particular use for."

"How much did you sell them?" asked Crane.

"Between six and seven acres."

"Acres? Wasn't that more than they could possibly need for a church?"

"They thought they would want a school someday," answered Mark, "and a house for their priest to live in."

"I see," said Mr. Crane. "I suppose you made the same provision for non-Catholic places of worship. Where are they to be located?"

"I don't know," said Mark. "I haven't been asked to take care of that to date. They're talking about a community house for recreation. Maybe they'll use that."

Mr. Crane sat back frowning. He said, "I don't remember that this matter of selling property for a church came up before the directors—the general board."

"It didn't seem necessary," said Mark. "I discussed it with Mr. Tuttle and the lawyers of course."

Mr. Crane is getting sore, Alan said to himself. Mark could handle this better. Crane's right—the other churches ought to have the same break.

Tuttle said in his realistic, easy, placating way, "The way it was,

[274]

Mr. Crane, was that there has been a priest around here who was more or less aggressive. I admit he pressured us a bit, first for the use of the school, and then for the land for this church which certainly looks like a root house. I went along with Mark—we were employing, and still are, a considerable percentage of Roman Catholics. But from now on I don't think we'll have anything to worry about. This priest I mention isn't here any longer. He was pretty much of a pusher. I suppose the Bishop got on to it, and the Catholic Bishop is quite a diplomat."

Mark asked, "Is that why Father Kenedy was shipped out?"

"Oh, I don't know. Anyway, he's out of our hair."

"He had a good plan for this place," said Mark. "He wanted to build a church that would be something to look at as you came along the shore."

Mr. Crane said, with a harsh laugh, "You sound as if you wanted to turn the village over to the Pope, Mark."

And suddenly Mark was angry. Alan could see it. Crane had meant what he said as a joke—though it wasn't a very good joke. Mark couldn't seem to take it. To his astonishment Alan heard his brother say crisply, "I have no such intention. But Catholic people need a place to worship, Mr. Crane. Personally, I'd like to see it adequate."

"And how about those who aren't Catholics? What are you doing for the Lutherans? The Methodists?"

"When the others come along," said Mark, "when and if they do, we'll give them proper consideration, consider any requests. It's a free country. But one thing to remember is that it was the Catholic missionaries who discovered this shore, who got here first. They've got squatters' rights at least."

His voice was almost truculent. Howard Eliot kept Crane from pursuing the subject by saying, "Did you say we lunch at twelve?"

Mark told the chauffeur to take them to the lunchroom and went into silence. Alan tried to pinch-hit. He said, "From here you get the best view of the breakwater, Mr. Crane."

"Very impressive. What's your job, young man?"

Alan said, "I worked on the breakwater. Then on the coffer dam

[275]

that we had to put in before we could deepen the harbor."

"Alan is one of our most useful engineers," said Mr. Tuttle.

"Going to stay on?" asked Crane.

"If they keep me, sir."

"I guess you can count on that," said Tuttle. "Alan won't blow his own horn, Mr. Crane, but he's his grandfather all over again, a natural mining man. That right, Alan?"

"It's a lot of fun," said Alan.

Mr. Crane said, "I knew your grandfather slightly and your father very well. They were stable, sensible men. Their judgment could be trusted."

Alan was uncomfortable. He felt that Crane's praise was meant as a disparagement of Mark. And Mark certainly hadn't been tactful. Why had he talked back to the older man, baiting him with that missionary stuff, giving the impression that he was for the Catholics. It wasn't as if Mark had any use for them. Probably Crane was pretty bossy and Mark didn't like to be pushed around.

If Mr. Crane had heard what Mark said to me about not marrying a Catholic, he would know how Mark really stands, thought Alan. And he thought, maybe I shouldn't have listened to him. If I'd seen it through, she and I would be living up there in the village, in that little house. She wanted that house the minute she saw it.

28

IT was a momentous day for Olive Worthing also. She had known that Mark's time would be completely preoccupied from morning until late at night, and she had no responsibility for the stag dinner at the Town Club which would wind up the celebration of the opening of the taconite plant. Mark had suggested that women might also be invited to the dinner—"I'd like to have you there, darling"—but she had thought that over and advised against it. The visiting financiers were not bringing their wives with them and the local women whose husbands were connected with the project would not be congenial. Olive went over the guest list for the dinner with Mark and imagined Mrs. Becker, wife of Alan's boss, fiftyish and always showing her grandchildren's pictures for conversational purposes, being at the same table with Alan's wife, who would be wearing a Dior model and wanting another drink.

"No, it will be better if it's a stag affair," she said.

"I'll take your advice on it. But I'll miss you."

"I'll be thinking of you all day. This is your triumph, Mark. Promise to tell me all about it when you come home, repeat all the praises they sing."

"There'll be no chorus of those. They'll only be thinking of getting their money back. That's what's on their minds. What are you going to do today?"

"I've an appointment," she said, and suddenly felt breathless.

The appointment was with her doctor. And she looked at him with such yearning, frightened hope after the examination that he smiled as he rarely did.

"I think you've made it this time," he said. "There's no doubt that you're pregnant. You're elected all right. Of course, Mrs. Worthing, with your history, you will need to take very good care of yourself."

She left his office, holding the delicious secret close. She had time to plan how to present it to Mark so that it would be made most beautiful for him. He had no idea of this. In the early days of their marriage, he would have been watching the dates of the month as closely as she did, but for some time he had ignored any irregularity. She knew why. He did not want her to think that he was hoping or expecting something that probably would not happen. He did not want her to suffer over his disappointment as well as her own.

This was a wonderful evening, waiting for him. Olive told the children that they were going to have a special dinner. It was a party.

"Is it a birthday?"

"Not exactly a birthday. It's a beginning."

"I know—it's Mark's new railroad," cried Tim. "That begins to run today!"

"So we're all celebrating," said Olive, letting it go at that. They had lamb chops with colored frills on the bones and creamed potatoes and ice cream with maple sauce.

She had never put them to bed with more love.

"Do you want me to read you a story or a poem tonight?"

"A po—emm," said Jenny.

"A pome," said Tim, not to lose his vote.

Olive chose a book, searched the title page. One title struck her with delight.

"I'll read you a new one. It is called, 'The Making of Viola.' Now first the Father of Heaven says,

> Spin, daughter Mary, spin,
> Twirl your wheel with silver din,
> Spin, daughter Mary, spin,
> Spin a tress for Viola.

And then the angels say,

> Spin, Queen Mary, a
> Brown tress for Viola!

The Father of Heaven says,

> Weave, hands angelical,
> Weave a woof of flesh to pall,
> Weave, hands angelical,
> Flesh to pall our Viola.

And the angels say,

> Weave, singing brothers, a
> Velvet flesh for Viola!

The children were restless. Tim asked, "Who was Viola?"

"It's a poem about the way a little girl was made by God," said Olive, "but it's a little too old for you. I'll find you another one."

As she read the children a jingle about the king and the marmalade, the making of Viola rang in her mind. When they were asleep, she read it again, all of it—

[278]

Breathe, Lord Paraclete,
To a bubbled crystal meet
Breathe, Lord Paraclete
Crystal soul for Viola.

And the angels—

Breathe, Regal Spirit, a
Flashing soul for Viola!

I want Mark's child—our child—to have a flashing soul, thought Olive. A fearless soul in each of the children—that's what we must see that they have. Souls can be frightened in children—bewildered —dulled.

Mark came home shortly after eleven o'clock. His face lacked the excitement and satisfaction from accomplishment that Olive had expected it would wear tonight.

"Did everything go off on schedule?" she asked.

"Yes, we're actually producing and shipping taconite now."

"You should be pretty proud of yourself, Mark."

"Oh, I don't know. It was the technicians and the engineers that put it over, not me. As a matter of fact, Alan had more to do with the actual operation than I did."

"You headed it up. Held it together."

"Thanks, my darling. You always build me up when I need it."

Why did he need it? Why was he so unrelaxed? His mind was not on her. She could feel that. Although he had come home, he had not yet returned to her. She was in bed, where she had been reading and waiting, her pillows piled behind her. This, she had thought, would be the time and the place to tell him what the doctor had said. When he quieted down. He was certainly disturbed about something.

She asked, "How is Howard Eliot?"

"Fine. He sent you his very best, was sorry not to see you. Wants us to look him up in New York surely."

"And Mr. Crane was beaming, I suppose."

Ah, that was it. Mark said, "I don't know whether he was or not. And I don't much care. Hell, even if he should pull out, we can get along without him. Find the money somewhere and buy him out, if necessary."

"But why should he pull out? Things are just starting. What didn't satisfy him?"

"I don't satisfy him," said Mark. "He doesn't like me."

"Oh, Mark, you imagine that. He's getting old and not too tactful, but why shouldn't he like you?"

"He thinks I'm a priest-ridden fool," said Mark.

"But that's utterly silly—"

"He's had it in for me for quite a while," said Mark, "ever since I let Father Kenedy say Mass in the schoolhouse. From the start he wanted to make something of that. I ignored some questions in his letters. It wasn't his business. It was a local situation."

"Don't let it bother you. If he wanted to boss you, he'll have to learn better," she said, still lightly.

But Mark was not light. It did bother him. He said, "Crane began crabbing today because he hadn't been consulted when we let the Bishop buy a piece of land for a church. He didn't want Catholics in the schoolhouse—now he doesn't want them out of it. It adds up to an old bigot. Of course that's been the history of the Catholic church. It's always had to fight such people."

"With considerable success," said Olive. "You're tired out, Mark. Don't let that man get under your skin. It's not worth it."

"He said—this in front of everybody—that I was discriminating in favor of the Catholics."

"Maybe you were a little bit. On Father Kenedy's account."

"No, it wasn't on his account," said Mark impatiently. "If people believe in a religion they've a right to have a church, that's all."

"People believe in lots of religions."

"That's what he kept harping on. That if we helped one to get a church, we ought to set them all up."

"You'll take care of the others when you get to it. Didn't you tell him that?"

"Something like that. But I wish I'd stood right up to him." She waited and he said with sudden vehemence, "After all, Olive, how can there be more than one Church that's right?"

"Let's not try to settle that tonight, Mark."

"I'm not trying to settle it. I'm trying to get it clear in my own mind. If Catholic doctrine is the truth, there can't be another truth. Truth has to be single. It can't be all over the place."

"Who says it *is* the truth?"

He made no answer.

She asked laboriously—she did not want to ask it—"Mark are you trying to tell me that you believe it is the truth?"

He gave a heavy sigh. "I don't know. But that was the funny thing today. I felt a hypocrite. I felt that I should have stood up to Crane and told him that he could back all the churches he wanted to but that I'd stand back of the one I believed in."

"But you don't believe in it! Until a little while ago you thought that the Catholics were all wrong. Then that priest began to argue you into it—"

"It isn't the argument," said Mark slowly, "it isn't what you read, though you come to see the logic and the consistency even in things you find it hard to swallow. I can't explain it, Olive—it's not because of any advice or persuasion—that can take you just so far— but, like today, you suddenly find that something has taken hold—"

"That's what he said—"

As if he knew that they were thinking of the same person and was not surprised, Mark said, "Yes, he told me it might be like that with me—"

"But it's not like that with you!" Olive cried out. She flung back the bed clothes and wrapped the blue robe around her. She had to be on her feet to fight this. "Mark, you must get over this obsession —you must forget the things that priest said—they don't apply to you—they don't affect us!"

"I just want to think it through, Olive."

"But you're letting his ideas worry you, depress you—he tries to make you believe there's some sort of magic you can't resist—you have a better mind than he has—you don't have to take what he says—"

"They're not Father Kenedy's ideas."

"Well, wherever they came from, they're not good for you. You

[281]

have to throw them off and be your own self again. You told me that any connection with the Catholic Church is impossible for you, and because of their own ridiculous rules, their preposterous medieval ideas about divorce. They must do no end of harm to good people. Please, darling—oh please put it all out of your mind. Harping on it, brooding on it is changing you—it's spoiling things for you; look, how it spoiled this day which should have been a real triumph. Let's be happy again in our own way and think of the things that may be ahead, the lovely things—"

Mark said, "I'm not unhappy, darling."

She looked at him helplessly.

She said, "You miss Father Kenedy."

"No. But think of the strength of that organization," he answered obliquely.

"Strength?"

"The Bishop, who is a practical administrator, decides for some reason that he doesn't want Kenedy here. In any other organization Father Kenedy would probably put up a fight for his job. He wanted to build a fine church up on the shore. But he takes his demotion without a whimper—"

"He shouldn't. There's certainly a dictatorship in that Church."

"They call it acceptance of discipline."

"Call it what you like. It's still ugly."

"I don't think you're quite fair. Obedience isn't ugly—not if there's a good reason why the higher-ups insist on it. The Catholic reason is that they think we're on earth to save our souls—not our jobs—not even our personal happiness. They minimize the importance of those things. They'd rather have the Carroll girl be an unhappy old maid—"

"Don't talk about that girl! She started all this thing about religion."

"Olive, even when I was a kid I used to wonder what it was all about. And why. There never was anyone I could talk to about it. Mother was an exceptionally conscientious woman, but I never knew what she believed—do you know what I mean? I didn't know if she believed in anything—"

"Oh, she did!" cried Olive.

"Maybe—it didn't come though to me. And my father—he made a lot of money, had a good time in his way, I guess—but what tied it all up? When he died he went down like a buck that was shot."

"Mark, don't—"

"I'm sorry, dear. I shouldn't unload this on you tonight—it worries you, I know. Shall I go down and get us a drink?"

"No, thanks—I couldn't. Mark, what is it you want?"

"I don't know—just to see the thing clearly, I guess. Stop dodging the issue. And if there is a way of thinking, or living, or a truth that we've missed, I want to share it with you—"

"Mark, we share everything."

"Not as things are."

"You mean share the Catholic religion? No, I don't think I could ever do that—you see I don't like it, Mark. It doesn't appeal to me the way it seems to do to you. It's not for me. It never would be. And anyway it wouldn't accept us."

"I've been wondering about that."

"About what?"

"If maybe you couldn't get an annulment of your marriage."

"My marriage! Us—oh—you mean Tony?"

"Yes, there are quite a lot of things that can be what they call impediments to a Christian marriage, to the sacrament. Maybe you weren't really married to him at all."

She stared at Mark, remembering those questions the priest had asked her. Had Mark talked to Father Kenedy about this? She felt betrayed. Mark, sitting there, seemed like a stranger.

"I shouldn't have brought this up tonight," he said, "I'm sorry. I always spill everything to you, poor girl. We won't talk about it now. But it might be worth looking into. To see if you can't get an annulment that would wipe out the whole thing."

"But nothing could wipe it out. It did happen—I married Tony and I lived with him. I had two children of his. And now we've been divorced for years. That part of my life is dim—it's almost forgotten, and that's the way I want it to be. Why do you drag it up again? I have a divorce. What on earth would I need an annulment for? Why do you suggest such a thing?"

Mark's head was in his hands. He said in a baffled, miserable way, "Only because I love you so much. Because I want you really to be my wife—no one else's—"

For almost a moment Olive was utterly still. The almost involuntary disclosure Mark had made of the hold which the Catholic Church had upon him was like the shock of discovering infidelity. Mark's deepest loyalty, his greatest desire, was no longer for her. There was another claim on his mind and heart that made him feel a lack, become unsatisfied with their relationship. How long? When first? The terrible queries that follow knowledge of unfaithfulness choked her.

She said, slowly, "You don't feel that we are married?"

Mark heard the shock and saw her face. He quickly rose to come to her. "I don't mean that, of course—darling, don't say it that way —don't misunderstand—but if marriage is a sacrament, if they're right in believing that it can't be dissolved—"

She drew away. A shudder from his touch shook her. The thing that had been a living joy in her was shame. Humiliation, pride, and anger such as she had never felt before possessed her.

"If I'm not your wife, what are you doing here!"

"Olive, please—"

"Go out of my room—go away from here! Go to your priest and let him tell you that I'm your mistress! Ask him what you can do about it, how you can be a Roman Catholic—but don't bring his advice back to me! Go—I can't bear it—you—"

Her fury of words drove him from her, from the room. He heard the key turn violently.

When it was morning Olive forced herself into a kind of calmness because the children woke early, and they must not see the wreckage. She bathed and dressed. Also she began to build around herself the kind of shell which had protected her once from Tony Grant, when she had no illusions left but was still living with him. It was a ghostly thing to do but the way to do it came back to her, like a skill long unused.

Mark had fallen asleep on the sofa in the study. He looked gaunt, unkempt, neglected. She touched his shoulder and he woke with a start, staring at her, then remembering.

"My God, darling, what did I do to you—I didn't mean to hurt you like that—"

"You'd better go upstairs, Mark and clean up."

He stood up, held out rejected arms. "Won't you forgive me?"

"Better go up," she said again. She was wearing the expression which had been on her face when he first saw her. She wanted to be left alone.

Old tricks, ways to cover up what she felt and go on with the duties of the days, the things that had to be done, were in use again. Olive would not argue, she pretended before the children, she pretended even when they were not there. She evaded every effort of Mark's to come close, to try to restore what they had before.

"Olive, you must let me tell you," he would beg.

"There's nothing to tell me."

"But you misunderstood me—"

"No, I understood you. At last."

He had said that. He had felt, if only for that moment, that she was not his wife. So there must have been other moments. And there would be more like them. Of that Olive was certain, as she went about carrying Mark's child and wondering what to do about that. Now she did not want to tell him, nor want him to know that she was pregnant. Bitterness such as she had never felt would sweep over her, and she would say to herself that some day he probably would consider the child illegitimate. She thought, I won't have his child. I couldn't. I'll have an abortion.

And through the days his misery pursued her.

"Olive, I want to say just one more thing. There will be no more talk of religion between us."

"No," said Olive, "no more talk. I quite agree. It's no use."

But he will think about it, she told herself. He will think about it and keep it secret. As if it were another woman he wants and can not have because he is married to me. How mad—how horrible —to have a religion for a rival, a religion breaking up your marriage. Let him have the Catholic Church. He can't have both of us.

There were times when she pitied him. She would think, it's like an illness, he can't help himself. It's an obsession, a quirk in his psychology—perhaps a psychiatrist could help.

She suggested that once, impersonally.

"So you think I'm nuts?" asked Mark.

"Lots of people see psychiatrists with their problems."

"I don't think it's necessary in my case. Olive, you know that nothing in this world means as much to me as your happiness."

"You seem to live in a number of worlds," she said and went away to do something. She was keeping herself restlessly busy. Whenever it was possible, she and Mark were not alone. She kept the children with them. Or she accepted invitations which she would have politely eluded a few months ago. If on a week end they went to the lodge on the river there always were guests there. Olive could share a room with a man with neither intimacy nor quarrel. Mark was finding that out. She had never been gayer or more lovely to see than during that late midsummer, when she lived with panic because a child was growing within her.

Gregory Searles not only saw but felt that Olive had changed. He and Lucy had come down to share the river lodge with the Worthings for Saturday and Sunday. He liked being there because Olive always charmed him. But he wondered why she had refused to go on the river with Mark today. Mark had finally taken the children, Lucy had gone to visit an old friend who was visiting one of the camps nearby, and Gregory and Olive were where he had found her as he walked through the woods with his sketchbook, sitting on a bench set above the river in a circling grove of pine trees.

"Am I interrupting some good thinking?" he asked her.

"It's not good. Better interrupted. Sit down and tell me things."

"Pleasant here in your little cathedral of pines."

She looked up at them and the fatigue of emotion in her face was unmistakable.

"Yes," she said, "if a person could pray anywhere, it would be here."

"Some people can't conduct their own services," said Greg.

[286]

"I know—they aren't allowed to. Greg, you used to be a Roman Catholic, didn't you?"

"I was brought up in the Church. Believe it or not, I once was an altar boy."

"Why did you change?"

"I'm a weak guy," said Greg idly, "I guess it got a little hard for me to take. The Catholic Church demands a lot of things, you know."

"I know it does. Greg—what is it like to be a Catholic?"

"You expect me to answer that? That's a very tough question."

"You must know. You were one."

"It's different for every person. But it would make a great composite picture—you give me an idea there—what a background that would be, with every face clear and different. What's it like to be a Catholic? Well, it's to be the cardinal in his red robes with his every public action defined and traditional, and it's the little girl who isn't sure she can swallow the wafer when she makes her First Communion and is terrified, and it's the woman you see coming out of the confessional who's got something off her mind and will do it again next week. It's that priest who was just sent away from here, the missionary type—"

He deliberately paused but she said nothing. Gregory went on—

"It's the person who breaks all the rules against adultery but won't eat meat on Friday—the residual Catholic, that one—it's the nun who makes secret physical sacrifices that exhaust her, and a fat, rather greedy monk walking along a shaded walk in a Spanish monastery; it's the politician trying to get votes by talking about "our kind," the mystic who thinks she sees the Blessed Virgin smile at her, and the cripple at Lourdes who isn't helped but doesn't lose his faith. And the women who scrub churches on their calloused old knees for no pay. It's Joan of Arc and a poet like Gerard Manley Hopkins. It's all those people who don't want to get up on Sunday and go to Mass but they will get up and go—that's what it's like to be a Catholic."

"Why will they get up and go? Because they're afraid of the priest, or afraid they'll go to hell?"

"No, that's not why. Rarely anyway. The priest won't know

[287]

whether they go or not until they go to confession, and hell's remote. It's just because they believe, Olive—they believe that something in themselves can only be satisfied by adherence to the Catholic religion."

"You believed that once and got over it."

"I'm not a man of conviction," Gregory said.

"But you're happy. You have a good life!"

She was not thinking of his life and Gregory knew it. He was sorry he had said so much. The idea of the composite picture had carried him away. Now he laid his hand on her tense one, reassuringly.

"Of course I do," he told her.

In all of his life, which had always been lonely until he found Olive, Mark had never been so mercilessly alone. Olive was out of his reach, unresponsive to his glance or touch. When, before they were married, he had set himself to bridge the space which she put between them, he had always hoped, even when she was most resistant. Now it was different. He carried the fear that he had done permanent damage to their love. She might forgive him in time, but, unless he could make her believe that he had spoken out of the depths of his love for her in suggesting the possibility of an annulment of her marriage to Tony Grant, the wound would not heal.

She had taken as insult what he had meant as honor. That she did not understand and words would not make her believe it. For the mysteries which he had become interested in were incredible to her. I thought we might work something out, he would say to himself. If Olive could see how Catholics look at such things, he would find himself thinking, and realize the absurdity of his own thoughts. For he was not a Catholic. It was not for him.

That created the other void, the other loneliness. For more than a year, and Mark realized it now, he had been preoccupied by the challenge of the Catholic Church. His struggle with its beliefs had been secret, often interrupted but it had been absorbing. His desire to come to terms with Catholicism, whether enmity or love, had taken him to areas which he had never explored and where his mind found companionship and strength. He must give that up. It was going to spoil his life with Olive if he did not.

Deliberately he considered the faults, the crudities, the inconsistencies of Catholics and Catholicism. Seeing one morning the St. Christopher medal which the woman had given him on the plane, and which had been in a drawer in his bureau, he picked it up frowningly and thought, how many people probably have gone to violent deaths carrying a thing like this. It is ridiculous. Some smart merchant makes money out of manufacturing this junk.

He would see someone ordering fish and think cynically that the fish industry was built up by Friday abstinence from meat. It was one more diet that had caught on, probably because it was quite healthy, and in some countries where the Catholics had moved in, fish was all they had to eat.

He would think, as he compared samples of iron ore from Africa and South America, that it had taken billions of years to perfect these rock formations, and perhaps there had been no ocean between the two continents at one time. The Catholic Church was only a couple of thousand years old, and before it had been organized the world had been well populated by men and women who had other ideas and systems of religion. Desires and physiology predated all religions.

Was the idea of creation inconceivable? And if you accepted that and the infinitely slow perfecting of man in God's image—so it went with Mark through tortuous days. He had no peace, only the consciousness that somewhere there was sureness, somewhere truth. Not in the glib, digested answers of the catechism. Not in the rigidity of the laws of the Catholic Church. But that Church had some link with the supernatural which made life explainable—if there was anything supernatural. There must be. He felt it in his own misery.

An officious and bad-mannered priest who now seemed to have charge of the station at Baraga came to call on Mark at his office in the city. He annoyed Effie Dwight by his bland assumption that Mark would see him without an appointment. He also rubbed Mark the wrong way when he did get an interview. There was something about his attitude which took it for granted that Mark would give him what he wanted. He was trying to raise money to equip the chapel. The priest rattled off the needs for stations of the cross, kneeling-benches, confessionals, a baptismal font.

"Of course these articles need not be of the best quality—probably the parish here wouldn't appreciate them if they were."

Mark said, "It seems to me that your parishioners ought to be able to get these things for themselves."

"The collections are small," said the priest. "It's always uphill work in these little missions to get the people to do their duty. The Bishop can allow only a limited amount of money and service to each mission."

But he sent Father Kenedy away, thought Mark. I'd have been willing to help him out but not this priest. He's too cocky.

"We felt that since you employ so many of our Catholic people—"

"We employ people who belong to many religions," said Mark shortly. "We don't look into that. I don't believe that our company would want to make any donation at this time. Other churches are going to be built on the shore here and we can't do for one what we don't feel able to do for all of them."

"Perhaps you would care to make a personal contribution," said the priest. He sounded almost like a conspirator, actually lowering his voice, "I know how much you helped Father Kenedy."

"I'm not interested in doing that," answered Mark. "I'm very sorry but if you'll excuse me—"

The priest met Mr. Tuttle on the way out. Tuttle nodded abruptly and said to Mark as he closed the door, "Another one of those? They seem to be pretty much underfoot around here, Mark. Can be bad business."

"I don't get what you mean."

"You know that Eben Crane was sore as a boil because he thought the company was playing favorites with the Catholics up on the location."

"I can't help what Crane thought."

Tuttle stretched his legs uneasily. "He's not the kind of man who can separate his personal opinions from his business connections."

"That's obvious."

"I wouldn't give him anything to go on."

"What do you want me to do?"

"I'd keep these priests out of here, for one thing."

Mark looked at the blotter before him.

"I don't like to say this, Mark," said Tuttle. "I don't like to be the one. And what a man believes is his own business. But there's just one thing that spreads faster then news of adultery and that's a story of somebody's going in or out of the Catholic Church. I don't say it's fair or right, but people get suspicious that such a thing will affect a man's point of view, change his affiliations."

"I suppose it might," said Mark.

"You mean there's something to this talk?"

"I don't hear it," said Mark. "If it's any relief to you, I'm not going over to the Catholic Church. That doesn't mean I may not think it's right."

Tuttle stared at him.

It was the kind of gossip that infiltrated the city, although in neither business nor social groups was the matter one for general discussion. It was usually a conversational aside, deliberately unconfirmed. It was a story made up of fragments of happenings and impressions and leaks, such as—

Eben Crane, that New York financier, the one who had been backing the Worthing-Ingalls taconite project, isn't getting along too well with Mark Worthing . . . I don't know that he's going to pull out, I wouldn't say that, he's in pretty deep. . . . What's the trouble about? . . . I don't really know but I understand that it had something to do with the administration of funds . . . seems that Worthing sold the Catholic Bishop a big tract of company land up there on the north shore and his board of directors didn't like it at all. . . . No, Mark's not a Catholic; the family's Episcopal. . . . Yes, I heard that too . . . about that priest who was here in town for a while and was very chummy with Mark . . . they work fast, you know. . . .

Actually I don't know much about it except that Pamela Brooks

[291]

told someone that this Father what's-his-name, I forget . . . anyway it was a priest they got rid of for some reason . . . has hypnotic powers and the Worthing family was very much worried about his influence on Mark. . . . Young Dick, that's Pam's boy, was really queer last Christmas, wouldn't go to parties or anything, said he was going to be a monk, and it was on account of that same priest. Dick did go back to school but the boys his own age regard him as sort of a spook.

I've heard it said that the businessmen think Alan Worthing is the better of those two boys. More like his father. There's good blood there, of course. The old grandfather was the one who made the money in the first place. . . . Some little Catholic girl tried to get her hooks into Alan; he did take her around for a while . . . he wasn't willing to have his children brought up Catholics; he broke it off and married Dot Langhorne. . . . Say what you like about Dot, she gives wonderful parties . . . have you seen their apartment? It's out of this world. . . .

In private dining room C at the Chamber of Commerce, where some twenty influential men of the city were meeing to make plans for the annual drive for three million dollars for the United Charities, the gossip had done its work before Mr. Sinnott had called the meeting to order. Last June the intention of the men working on this drive had been to bring pressure on Mark Worthing to accept the chairmanship of the committee which allocated and sought major subscriptions. Mark had put over the drive for combined hospital funds. He was in line for this task, which was also an honor given to the most influential citizens. But Edgar Roff had talked quietly to Jones and Sinnott about that.

"I don't know about Mark's heading up the committee. There seems to be an impression that he's losing his grip."

"How do you mean?"

"I've heard that too."

"Well, I don't want to be quoted on this, but I know that Harry Tuttle is worried. He as much as said so to someone that I'm not at liberty to quote, but it's straight enough. Mark hasn't been tending to business I guess, not keeping his eye on the ball. What they say is that he's apt to go over to the Catholic Church at any time. Not that that isn't all right but it seems to show—you know what I mean—a certain instability."

"Funny thing—a man of his age—is something wrong with him physically? Cancer or heart?"

"I haven't heard anything like that."

"He always did impress me as sort of a dreamer."

"Yes, they say that the younger brother is the one who has the brains and drive in that family."

"You say Mark Worthing is joining the Catholic Church?"

"I don't know that for a fact—don't quote me on it. But you remember how he knuckled under to that priest on the hospital job. About the birth-control clinic. No need for it either—we'd have gotten the money, we went over the top."

"Maybe if he headed the special gifts committee he could help us get more money from the Catholics."

"I doubt it. That takes one of their own people. Mark's kind of a lone wolf."

Mark came into the meeting a little late. There were two vacant places left at the table, one by Joe Nolan and one by Isaac Elting. It was Elting who waved a hand and said, "Come over here, Mark." Joe Nolan looked up from his fish and went back to it again.

No one appeared to give Mark special attention. It was decided, without discussion, to ask Theodore Jones to take the chairmanship of the special committee. Complaining, but as they all knew also coveting the prestige, Jones accepted. Without caring, Mark knew that it should have been offered to him.

He was aware of it now when people looked slightly askance at him, when they were measuring his appearance or words against something they had heard. He could tell when a conversation was broken off because he had come into a group. He felt the new sharpness, like an edge of distrust, between himself and Harry Tuttle. Even Effie Dwight was different. She was no less efficient, no less quick to carry out his directions, but something had been siphoned out of their confidential relationship. The hero worship was gone.

[293]

Mark knew that. It was like a faint echo of what he had felt at home in these last months.

"Anything new, Effie?" he asked, when he went back to his office from the Chamber of Commerce that day.

She said, "Alan's here. In your office. He's waiting to see you."

"Alan?" Mark looked as surprised as his question. This was Friday and Alan should be on his job on the north shore. But there his brother was, and the office was full of the acrid smell of cigarettes, as if Alan had been smoking one after another. He got up from a chair rather nervously.

"Well, how are you, fellow?" asked Mark.

"Good enough."

"Anything wrong up on the job?"

"No, I just took a few hours off. Everything's moving along and Mr. Becker said it was all right with him."

"It's a good thing to do once in a while. You've had your nose pretty close to the grindstone for the last few months."

"I thought I'd stop by and see you. There was something I wanted to ask."

"Sure. What's on your mind? Need some money?"

"No. It's not about money." Alan seemed awkward, unlike himself, embarrassed. He found it hard to start. "It's a personal thing. I didn't take any stock in it, of course."

Now Mark knew what was on his brother's mind. He thought, this was bound to come. And he felt an irrelevant wonder at the fact that men seemed ashamed to approach this subject.

"I'll tell you anything I can."

Alan said, "I heard this story first from Dot. But she picks up all the gossip that's going around town, so I didn't pay any attention except to tell her it was crazy. Then Pam started beating the same drum. But it wasn't until this morning when somebody at the plant said something—it's actually got around to the men. There isn't any truth to this story that you've gone over to the Roman Catholic Church, is there?"

"No. I haven't done that," said Mark.

"Well, of course I knew that," said Alan, beating out a cigarette.

[294]

"I know how you feel about Catholics. I wanted to say so to Mr. Crane on that day we opened up the plant—you remember that we were driving around and he began to sand-paper you about letting the Catholics buy land for that shack they call a church.—"

"I remember—"

"He had you all wrong, the old buzzard," said Alan, "and I had plenty of reason to know it. But things kept coming back and sort of bothering me—Olive told me that Kenedy was bombarding you with religious books and that he'd even been to the house and of course he's fanatical—"

"I don't think so," said Mark.

"I do. That fellow won't give an inch. I had a talk with him, you know."

"That doesn't mean he's a fanatic. Maybe it's because he's right."

"You're kidding—"

"No, I mean what I say."

"But look, right here in this office, not a year ago, you told me what you think of Catholics. You told me to steer clear of them, that the Catholics couldn't think for themselves—you told me is so many words that you would never marry a Catholic girl because you'd have to share her life with a priest!"

"I know I said some things like that."

"You're not going back on them now are you?"

"I was pretty ignorant," said Mark. "I didn't know what I was talking about."

"My God," said Alan in a shocked monotone, "they have really got to you!"

"Nobody's got to me. I'm just trying to think straight. I've done a lot of reading since then, a lot of thinking. It comes out the same way every time. If there is a church that's right, it has to be the Roman Catholic Church. If you believe that Christ founded a church on earth—"

"Don't give that stuff to me," said Alan in a hard voice. "No, thanks. I'm not having any. You know you broke things up between me and Rose Mary, don't you?"

"You had to make up your own mind."

"Sure I did. But you did your best to poison it. Against Catholics and priests and the whole religion that you've become so fond of all of a sudden. I'd have taken a chance with Rose Mary if you hadn't talked me out of it. You know I loved her, don't you?"

"I've thought so. I'm sorry."

"I'm not asking for any pity," said Alan. "I can take what's coming to me. Rose Mary wouldn't touch me with a ten-foot pole now, even if Dot and I broke up. And we won't."

His silence, what he did not say, was as bitter as his words. Then he spoke again.

"But if I hadn't been such a weak fool I'd have married my girl in spite of anything anyone said. And what burns me up is that here you are going over to the institution that you thought was such a menace, going to join up with it—"

"I'm not going to join it."

"Why not? Why not go the whole hog?"

"I can't. Olive's had a divorce."

Alan took that in. Then he laughed as if he enjoyed the mockery. "Well, isn't that something? You mean they wouldn't take you because of that?"

"According to the Catholic Church Olive and I aren't married. Legally we are of course."

"Does she know that?"

"Yes, she knows all about it."

"Including your yen for the Catholic Church?"

Mark's face was gray and tired. His brother saw that but he went on mercilessly. "We're in the same boat, aren't we? I can't have Rose Mary if I should get divorced. You can't have Olive and the Catholic Church. According to the Church Olive must still be married to that rotter. And so by their count you aren't married at all. I suppose the priests would advise you to let Olive go, and marry some nice Catholic girl." Alan suddenly had a thought which changed his mockery to fury. "Maybe you have your eye on Rose Mary. She said you'd picked her up and driven her home. If—"

"For God's sake, Alan, get hold of yourself! I can't stand for this kind of talk! You know I'd never do anything to hurt Olive—that I worship her—"

Effie Dwight's voice came in over the intercommunication.

"Mr. Worthing, there is a call for you and they say it is urgent. Mrs. Worthing has been in an automobile accident—"

There was a doctor in the city who performed abortions. Olive had heard his name connected with them. He had been brought into court a couple of years before for such malpractice but nothing had been proved, and his name was still whispered as that of the doctor to go to if you wanted not to bear a child. He had been well educated and was skillful. Expensive, but you had to expect that, said his clients.

If I am going to do it, I must not wait, thought Olive. Not any longer. I must go soon. She called the doctor's office. He would be out of town until Friday, and Friday became a day which was three nights away, getting closer every minute, cruelly holding her to her resolve. On Friday afternoon then, at three o'clock.

She put the car in a parking lot a block away and walked to the building where the doctor had his office. It was in an old house which had been made into quiet-looking apartments. She was almost at the door when the action which she had been trying to blur in her mind came clear and definite. She knew she could not go through with it. I will not. I want it. I'll leave Mark—I can't go on living with him much longer as we are. I'll take all the children—this one too. I cannot kill it. I won't let anyone kill it.

She turned dizzily and went back to her car, thinking almost aloud, wondering where to go next, unlocking it, forgetting that she had not paid the parking attendant.

"I'm sorry. How much is it?"

"You weren't here long but it's thirty-five cents, I guess. Thanks. You'd better back out to the street. Just cramp your wheels to the right, then straighten her out. No, the right. Now straight back —hold it—there's a truck coming—"

She thought she put her foot on the brake. No—it was the accelerator and the car rushed backward. Olive heard the crash, felt the impact of the wheel, tried to guard it with her hands, lost consciousness.

Mark said, "Darling, you're going to be all right."

She was in a hospital bed. She stared at him, listless with drugs and asked, "Did I kill it after all?"

"You had an accident with the car."

"I had a miscarriage, didn't I?"

"Yes, but you're going to be fine. Olive, did you know you were pregnant?"

"Of course."

"Why didn't you tell me, darling?"

"But you said I was Tony's wife—"

"No—hush—"

"I was going to have an abortion. I couldn't—"

"Oh, my love—"

"That's what I started out to do this afternoon—"

"Don't talk now. You must rest."

"I wanted her so much. And I killed her. Because if I hadn't gone to that place today—"

"If I'd only known,—keeping this to yourself, carrying the worry—"

"I was going to tell you that night. After your banquet. That was the same day when I saw the doctor. But you were so unhappy when you came home. And you talked about religion—it had made you feel that we weren't really married—"

"I didn't mean that!"

"Yes, you meant it," said Olive wearily, "but I shouldn't have been so bitter. I was jealous of the Catholic Church. I wanted you all to myself."

"And you have me always."

"No," she said, closing her eyes, "but I love you. I have, all the time."

Next morning the doctor was very kind and very cheerful. He told Olive she was a very lucky woman. No fractures. There might be some delayed shock. But she'd soon be about again.

"But I won't have any more children, will I?"

He didn't lie. He said, "We'll talk about that later. Under the circumstances we had to be a little drastic. To prevent hemorrhage."

So she knew, and lay thinking about it while the room filled with flowers, and Mark came and went. Once he brought Tim and Jenny, and Olive made the visit an adventure for them and gave them the fruit that Pamela had sent and promised to be home again in a week. She lay thinking of the life which she and Mark had created and which they could not repeat. She watched Mark's stern, sensitive face, smiling when he found her looking at him but only then.

It was the morning of the fourth day and Olive was allowed now to sit by the window in her room and watch the distant lake. The nurse on duty had gone for a half-hour's coffee break and Olive was not sorry to be alone. There was so much to plan. When she heard the door open she did not turn her head.

"I don't want to disturb you, Mrs. Worthing. But could I ask you a few questions? For our hospital records?"

"Yes, of course." Olive looked at the girl. "Why, you're Rose Mary Carroll!"

"That's right."

"I thought you'd left the hospital."

"I was gone for a while."

Why did you come back, wondered Olive. But she couldn't ask that.

"At the time you came into the hospital there was considerable confusion, so we couldn't fill out the record completely. I thought I wouldn't bother your husband with it. He was so worried."

"That was nice of you."

"It's just a few details—"

Olive supplied them. Poor Alan, she thought, watching the beautiful face.

"I'm very glad you're making such a good recovery," said Rose Mary.

"Yes, I'll be all right very soon." Did this girl know what the miscarriage had meant? Was that somewhere in these records? How

[299]

much we know about each other, thought Olive. I know that Alan loved you—more than the girl he married—and that you begged Mark to help you, that he wouldn't—do you know that you've been on his conscience ever since, that you began something that I can't stop? You're having a good revenge, if you only knew it. Don't let her leave the room yet. I must talk to her.

"I know they must be very glad to have you back in the hospital, Rose Mary."

"And I was glad to get my job back. I didn't like it in Chicago. It never felt like home. Though I was with my aunt there."

"You're happier here?"

It was not a casual question. The girl hesitated and said slowly, "Yes. I shall be."

"I've always been sorry that you and Alan didn't marry," said Olive, "and I'm sorry that we did nothing to help either of you."

"Don't feel like that."

"We do. Both my husband and myself."

"It's probably for the best."

"I wish I could think so. But you would have been good for Alan."

Rose Mary gave Olive a grateful look. Then she shook her head, "Maybe not. Mixed marriages are seldom happy. When—when first you find you love somebody, you can hardly believe that. But later it's usually true."

"I don't see why it should be."

"Perhaps you would if you were a Catholic," said Rose Mary. "To live with someone and not share all that you believe is true, to have laws for one that mean nothing to the other—I wonder what kind of life it would be. And I doubt if Alan would have ever come over to the Church."

"And you couldn't give up your religion?"

"What would be left of me if I did?" The girl sighed, picked up her records, and left the room with a smile that was frosted with tears.

Olive thought, what will be left of Mark?

29

O<small>N A</small> Sunday morning a month later, Olive told Mark what she must do. She was well again. The trees outside the study windows were bright with autumn color and it seemed a day decorated for happiness. The children had gone outdoors to play and they were alone.

There was tenderness in her glance at Mark, but he had a feeling of frustration and impending climax. Since her accident and convalescence they had tried very hard. They had been delicate in every relation with each other. They had gone as far in intimacy as they could. But last night he had missed her laugh of happiness after love and what she always used to say, so softly, "I think this time—"

Now she said, "Mark, I have something to tell you. It's not going to be easy and I've waited because I wanted to be very sure. I am sure."

"You're ill? Something wrong?"

"Not that. Nothing physical. It's this, Mark dear. I'm going away."

"Going away? By yourself?"

"I'll have the children."

"Well—of course, if you want to—maybe a little change would do you good—where would you like to go?"

"I'm not talking about a little change, Mark. Please face it. You know what I mean, what I'm talking about. I'm not coming back."

"Of course you are. If you go. Don't say a thing like that."

"It was hard to say, but it's true."

"What's the matter—can't you forgive me?"

"Oh long since—if there was ever anything to forgive. I was hurt—it was worse because I was pregnant—but that's all over."

"It's been tough on you. I know that. But darling, it could be worse. You came through, that's the important thing. And you have two fine children—look, if you want to adopt a baby or a whole raft of kids, anything that would make you happy—"

"Mark, that's not it. But this isn't the life we had. We aren't happy. I've had happiness, so I know."

"We'll be happy again—"

"No. Mark, a long time ago, before we were married I told you that I had never been a real person. I lived among things that didn't belong to me. That's the way I feel now. I don't feel like your wife."

"Because we can't have a child?"

"Because I can't satisfy you. I can't give you what you want in your life. And it won't get better. It will get worse, more secretive, more polite, more fearful—it's that way now."

"Olive, you know I love you—"

"But you're no longer satisfied by love. You want something I can't give you by living with you. The strange thing is that the only way I can give it to you is by leaving you—"

"That would utterly ruin me."

"It would ruin a lot of things. But not you. You can become a Catholic if I go away and get a divorce."

"You're being fantastic. I don't want to become a Catholic."

"You don't want to admit it. But it's there. You're a man with a deep hidden desire, and it's not desire for me. You don't belong completely to me any more. Don't you think I know? You're a Catholic in your heart and mind now. You believe they're right."

"I don't know whether I do or not. But it doesn't affect us."

"Doesn't affect us—"

"How does it?" he asked incredulously.

She said, "I felt it—a kind of control over you. You think what they think. If you were a Catholic you would do what they said to do. Even about me. Mark, I don't think I want to be married to a Catholic. Even to you."

Mark remembered—I said that once to Alan.

And aloud, "Perhaps I've been mixed up. But it will straighten out. We'll be all right, Olive."

[302]

She shook her head. "That's what I don't want for us—just being all right. And you will never leave me—"

"Leave you—what are you talking about?"

"That's why I'm going to leave you, Mark."

"But I won't let you do that. You're talking nonsense!"

"I couldn't be more sure," she said sadly.

"Do you think I'd let you go?"

"You can't stop me. It will be hard—hard. But it can be done. I have to cut through the misunderstanding, the gossip—" she flung out her hands to show him—"the things we loved—but the sooner it's done the better. For you. For Tim and Jenny. For me, Mark. I can't stand this any longer."

"As bad as that, is it?"

"Worse than I can tell you."

He paced the floor and finally turned to say grimly, "If you feel that way, go away and think it over. But it mustn't be final. And remember that you're my wife, that I'm going to take care of you—"

"Your mother did that," said Olive. "I have her money, you know. Maybe it seems a strange way to use it, but I've thought—I remember little things about her, and I believe she would want this. It will give you what she never was able to give you and it will take care of Tim and Jenny"—she tried to laugh—"prevent juvenile delinquency!"

"You don't want your husband to take care of you?"

"You're not my husband in the eyes of the Catholic Church."

"I'm not a Catholic."

"You want to be one."

"I'm not at all sure of that."

"I am. You always were searching. I should have known it wasn't just for me. Then you found what you wanted. And resisted it. Pretended you didn't like it. I've seen men do that before when there was something—or some person—they couldn't have."

"I certainly don't want it without you."

"That's the price. The suffering they talk about. We can't have it together."

[303]

"We might—someday."

"No—" Olive sighed. "I told you just now that I couldn't be a Catholic. I wouldn't want Tim and Jenny to have to do what that religion tells them to. As you've liked it more, I've liked it less. Those churches in South America—the confessions of things that should be secret—no. One day in the hospital I talked to Rose Mary Carroll and I could feel the difference between us. Suppose you were a Catholic and I wasn't. Imagine the kind of life it would be. You wouldn't belong to me. And we'd be pulling the children in different directions."

"Olive, will it satisfy you if I never mention the Catholic Church again?" he asked harshly.

Her answer was as harsh. "No, it won't satisfy me if you damn your own soul!"

He stood staring at her as if she were a stranger. She turned from him, pushed up her hair in the familiar gesture and then looked at him with a quieted face.

She said, "I could have told you this last night, but I waited because morning is a truthful time. A time to make plans that you will go through with. Oh Mark, there were other ways to do this, but I wanted to face it with you. I might have pretended to go on a trip. Left a note on a pincushion, if I had a pincushion. I don't want it that way! I want to go bravely. Without whimpering. I think it will make me a real person again. And I want it to seem natural to the children, to take them away with their love for you in their hearts. I want you to wave us off with a smile!"

"So I came in," said Mark to Harry Tuttle, "to present my resignation. The annual meeting is next month and you'll want to make plans for reorganizing the company. I hope you'll have a good spot for Alan."

"Alan will be sitting pretty. He's made quite a name for himself already. But I think you're being too hasty, Mark. I've heard you've had some personal trouble—Pamela told me—"

"It's no secret that Olive has left me," said Mark.

[304]

"Even so, a man's private affairs needn't jeopardize his entire career," said Tuttle.

Mark said, "Crane will pull out if I stay on in any executive capacity."

"I think we might soften him up."

"Can you soften him up if he hears I've joined the Catholic Church?"

"I didn't know—of course people always talk—is that a fact, Mark?"

"It's a possibility. I've not been fully instructed."

"Instructed? Well, well. I suppose it's idle to say anything about it. I've never talked religion. But if you retire as executive, what are you going to do, Mark?"

"I'll get along. I have a little money. I'll be around," said Mark. "I've always wanted to do some studying. There are always a few queer ducks, Harry."

He held out his hand, and all Mr. Tuttle could muster up was a mutter that he was sorry and the thought that it was a damned shame.

Mark went to the office that was still his, although gossip had made his tenure shaky. Effie came in with the second morning mail and laid it on his desk. Her glance at him was troubled but hopeful. He saw a thick envelope with the name of a Philadelphia law firm in the corner. It was unopened. Effie must have guessed it was the divorce papers. And the envelope beneath had not been opened.

Effie knew Olive's handwriting well. Mark lifted it with a quickened heartbeat, a hope of rescue. She had decided not to go through with this. It must be that.

He read:

Dearest Mark, by this time you have been served with the legal papers. I told the lawyer to make it cruel and inhuman treatment. It's a conventional plea. But it's not conventional to me.

That's why I am writing to you. There is a little more to say— it may comfort you sometime to know how I have come to feel

[305]

about this in these days of being dead in life, for that is what they are like. The anger is gone—I get spells when I feel bitter and ill-treated but they pass. And last night and today I have been thinking of a curious thing.

When I got a divorce from Tony, I pleaded cruel and inhuman treatment too. It was true that he was cruel and he did not seem like a normal human being but like an animal, a beast without feeling even for his children. Now I plead in the same words. But not the same thing. For when I say that your treatment of me has been cruel and inhuman, the cruelty is really worse because I love you so much more. But inhuman means no beastliness. What you have done to us, what was beyond your control was because of the supernatural force in you. I cannot share it—I can't go along with it. But I can recognize that it is the immortal —and that I do believe—the immortal soul in you which makes you more than human, not less.

They all say, of course—Pamela, Lucy and the rest—that you have ruined our lives. They have written me that. I don't believe it. Certainly you ruined our living together. But even in this first hideous time of separation, with everything raw and hurting, I know that I have yielded to spiritual strength and been beaten only by immortal desire. It is defeat and yet I am proud—do you understand? And I hope that you will never let it be shame for you. With my great love, Olive.

30

Mark put the letter in his pocket as if it were a treasure. He told Effie, who tried in vain to read his expression, that he wouldn't be back today. Then he took his car out of the garage and braked it while he looked at a road map. Meadowville—over three hundred miles. It was late afternoon but he could make it by midnight.

There was a single tavern open when he got there and he asked the owner where the priest lived.

"Right next to the church, one block west—somebody sick?"

"Yes," said Mark, "somebody's sick."

It was a little shingled house, clinging to an ugly, shabby, wooden church. Seeing its ugliness even in the moonlight, Mark thought of Father Kenedy's dream for the church on the shore of the Great Lake. That was a long time ago. It was a long time since he had waved off Olive and Tim and Jenny—with a smile that had been covering agony.

There was a light in the front room of the priest's house. He knocked and Father Kenedy opened the door.

"Well, Mark," he said, seemingly without surprise.

"It's late," said Mark, "but I need to talk to you."

"Come in. I'm glad to see you."

The sitting room was small and shabby, but it was peaceful.

Mark said, "It was an outrage to send you off here."

"Oh no—it's quite an opportunity."

"This miserable little railroad town?"

"It's not a bad parish. Of course we have no school—as yet."

Mark found he could laugh. "But there will be?"

"If I stay long enough. How are things with you? And your family?"

"I have none. My wife has left me."

"Left you?"

"Yes, I finally drove her away. Or else the Catholic Church did."

"Do you want to tell me about it?"

"That's why I came. I'm a man in ruins, Father."

"God has such men under His special protection."

The priest listened. When Mark had finished, when he had blamed and accused himself and fumbled with explanations, Father Kenedy said, "She is a wise and generous woman. A rare woman. I shall pray for her."

Mark said, bitterly, "That won't help now."

"Yes, it will. She sees farther than you, Mark. The pain of separation which you are enduring is not easy to bear, and what lies ahead of misunderstanding and humiliation—"

"And loneliness—"

"And loneliness will be no easier. But she has smoothed your path—opened a door for you—"

"And how about her?"

"It is easier to do the right thing than to live with the wrong one," said the priest. "Mark, she has glimpsed the greatest values, the ageless values. She offers you comfort. God offers you comfort and He accepts your suffering—"

"Offer it up?" asked Mark cynically.

"You will learn how to do that. Mark, unhappy as you are now, you are happier than when I saw you first—"

"Why do you say that?"

They talked on and the hours vanished. It was dawn when the priest said, "Better find a bed, Mark. There's a hotel down the street."

"You don't know how this has helped me."

"Good."

"When can I come again?"

"It is better if you do not come again."

"I won't come this late."

"Don't come at all," said Father Kenedy. "This is the test, Mark. What you want is the Church and not a friend. You are seeking faith and that comes from God through any of his instruments. You must go to your own parish priest and ask him to give you instructions."

"My parish priest?"

Father Kenedy said, "You must be in Father Moore's parish—the old St. Anthony Church is the one. It's not a wealthy district except on your own street."

"I'd rather deal with you directly," said Mark.

"You're dealing with God, Mark. Good night—and God bless you."

This priest was old and brittle. The elasticity of argument had gone out of his mental joints, and he responded like a puppet when

[308]

something Mark said pulled this or that string of dogma. In as brief form as possible, Mark reviewed his situation, and he was quite sure that Father Moore had heard it before and that this was only corroboration.

He had the characteristics of many aged Irishmen, in manner and in egotism, and even his expressions of humility were unconscious tricks to draw attention to himself. Impressed by Mark's position, as a certain deference showed, he would swagger in his power.

"Now, Mr. Worthing, I must have certain information."

Was this the office of God? Where God did business with troubled sinners? This room with its line of overstuffed chairs, its limp curtains, its soapy look of having been cleaned up by some parish scrub woman and furnished with the pieces that some Catholic owner of a cheap furniture store couldn't sell—Olive, with what beauty you surrounded me; without you everything seems cheap and sordid.

The queries were even more depressing. The census. The date of your baptism? In an Episcopal church? You can ascertain the date? You have never been confirmed.

"Now as I understand, your wife—as we will identify her— and you are separated? Not living together in any sense or at any time?"

There was something obscene in this papery old man talking of sex.

"She is divorcing me."

"Her first husband is still alive?"

"Yes."

"I ask because it is well to make very sure of that." He rambled off into reminiscence of what he had done in a troublesome marriage case and told of how many letters he had written and to what strange quarters to establish the death of a married person, so that his wife could be reinstated in her relation to the sacraments.

"My situation is entirely different," said Mark.

"Of course this civil marriage of yours was never recognized by the Church. The divorce frees you legally. You were always

[309]

unmarried in the eyes of the Church."

Unmarried—Olive—I must be mad to do this—

"Now I will do all I can to help you."

The help of this man would be monstrously inadequate, almost insolent. He was utterly ignorant of the Protestant world. He was a silly dotard—is it too late for me to get out of this? To go to her?

"The Church welcomes its converts, those who come to her for refuge and for strength—"

I am a fool.

"I shall arrange for your instruction if you wish. I appreciate that in your case you have surmounted many obstacles to take this step, undergone much pain no doubt, much conflict of soul—"

The voice was different. The old priest seemed to be speaking on a different level. Not the census taker now, not the egotistic old Irishman. The man of God now.

"Have you sufficient faith to go on? Do you wish to be instructed?"

I can still call it off. I don't have to go on. I can say it was an impulse. Perhaps she will come back. Then? Do I believe this more than I love Olive? Do I believe in this Church?

He felt the stretch of his mind past himself, his desires, his needs. He felt his will as never before, sure and sustained.

"Yes, Father Moore," said Mark Worthing.

Set in Linotype Fairfield
Format by Marguerite Swanton
Manufactured by The Haddon Craftsmen, Inc.
Published by HARPER & BROTHERS, New York